D0292964

pure

REBBECCA RAY

pure

GROVE PRESS
New York

Originally published in Great Britain in 1998 by Penguin Books
Published simultaneously in Canada
Printed in the United States of America

Library of Congress Cataloging-in-Publication Data

Ray, Rebbecca.
    [Certain Age]
    Pure/Rebbecca Ray.
      p. cm.
    ISBN 0-8021-3700-8
    1. Teenage girls—Fiction. I. Title.

PS3568.A92175 C47 2000
813'.54—dc21   00-028012

Grove Press
841 Broadway
New York, NY 10003

03   10

For Nick. For Jules. For Tim.
Thank you

Acknowledgements

Christine Adams – for getting me started when a start was what I needed.

Cath Allan and all the Storehouse Writers – for being kind to me, for their encouragement, and for showing me that you don't need publishing to be a writer.

Sonia and George Archdale – for their hospitality and patience.

Dan and Bel Butler – for their constant help, for putting up with me in their house.

Peter Cox – for his interest and his honest opinions.

Chris and Nuala Dickman – for their massive generosity.

Jay Dickman – for stopping my head from swelling too much. Thanks to you, I can still just about get it through doors.

Juliet Ennis – for telling me to keep going when I thought there wasn't any point. For being my friend.

Sian Gwyn – for being a good teacher; I thought they were a myth. I wish I could have stayed to learn more.

Philip Joseph – for helping me when he didn't have to; for his advice, his support and for a very nice lunch.

Alec Newman – for teaching me and teaching me and teaching me. For being a wonderful uncle.

Paul Poole – for keeping my computer alive when euthanasia probably would have been the best option.

Hilda Ray – for her thoughtfulness, her kindness and her incredibly caring nature.

Stephen King – for being the only writer who inspired me to write myself.

I was about thirteen when I started letting the boys feel me up. There was a whole bunch of them, four or five, and at lunchtime we'd all meet up; smoking a spliff out on the pitch if it was sunny, round their table in the library if it wasn't. We'd all be sitting around, eating our lunches, and Joel or Craig or some other boy I didn't really like would start putting his hand up my shirt. Or my skirt, I had a really short skirt and fucking awful legs but I'd roll the waistband up on it to make it shorter anyway.

It was never some big major thing, they just did it while they were talking. I guess my tits weren't as interesting as talking about what makes the best roach material, but they kind of filled the gap between Rizla packets and tape covers.

I didn't talk much, just listened to them. Well, everyone listened really, you didn't have much of a choice. I guess they hadn't seen the sign on the wall that said SILENCE IS GOLDEN AND THIS LIBRARY IS FOR READING. But then, they didn't really have to pay attention to things like that because they were popular.

The tables in the library were arranged so that as many people as possible had to sit with their backs to each other, and they were fixed to the floor so no one could move them. The librarian's name was Mrs Midwinter, which sounds like something out of Dickens but isn't. Nobody believed she was a Mrs, either – she didn't have any wedding ring. She was a very tall woman and her clothes weren't quite tall enough for her body. She had a huge load of grey hair piled up on top of her head and really pink cheeks that looked like she'd been slapped both sides. She was the sort of person that always spoke in a whisper, even when she was shouting.

She was new to the school, a replacement for the old librarian, Miss Herbert, who'd had a nervous breakdown. I wasn't in the school then but I heard it happened when someone hacked into the computers so that every time anyone used them they locked out with one single message flashing on the screen. All eight printers going berserk, printing HERBY FUCKS HERSELF WITH A RULER UNDERNEATH THE DESK till they started chewing up the paper. Everyone said Mrs Midwinter was just temporary but I didn't think Miss Herbert would work with children again. I heard from our form tutor that she was a born-again Christian now, but people have funny ways of dealing with things. Maybe that was why they decided to hire Midwinter as a replacement. She looked like your granny on the surface, but I knew she'd trained with the marines.

Even Mrs Midwinter couldn't handle our table, though, because our table wasn't just five boys. Our table had Holly, and Holly could do what she wanted. Holly was perfect. Long, slim legs, big tits, big mouth, eyes; everything was big except her arse. Natural-blonde hair. She was the kind of person who warned everyone she was going to fart and gangs of blokes flocked round her, just to get a whiff. Sometimes, while everyone else was talking, she'd take out this little pocket mirror and lay it on the table, bend over it and spend an hour or so squeezing spots that weren't there. Her face'd go lumpy and swollen and all puffy when she squeezed, her eyes'd water. But red and lumpy looked good on Holly. I wished I could be red and lumpy like she was.

She hardly ever went out in town. I never did either, but I didn't have a good reason like Holly. Her sister was in university, and she went out to city clubs with her, I heard her talking about it sometimes. Clubs you had to have ID for, clubs you had to be twenty-one for, but all the clubs let Holly in for free. She didn't even have to let the bouncers feel her tits. Holly didn't have to let anyone feel her tits, but I wasn't like Holly. I never would be like Holly, so I had to find another way of getting along. I had to let them feel me up.

I didn't like doing it but I didn't really hate it either. It's one of those things you get used to, like bras that cut off the circulation in your nipples. It was necessary. I knew I'd never really be one of them, they'd all been friends since they were little so they could tell me to fuck off whenever they wanted. I never kidded myself, I knew that wasn't going to change. But I got to be sought after in a funny, dirty kind of way. I got the wolf whistles and the stares. Because I wanted them. And because I wasn't the kind of girl you had to like. I was the kind of girl you fucked.

3

Not that I did fuck them, any of them. Things never went that far. But still, they knew they could, if that was what they asked for, and I guess it added up to the same. It felt good in a way, though. I wanted to go to school every day, I wanted to hear their cat calls, I wanted to feel their hands. I guess I felt, for the very first time, like I'd been accepted.

I never thought I would be, you see. Things started off badly at High School and I never thought they'd get better. Things started badly from the very first lesson on my very first day. From the moment that I realized I needed a shit.

I was sitting in maths, mid period, they'd sat us alphabetically so we could all be friends. I went to the front of the room, trying to push my thighs together and still walk in a way that looked near normal. It didn't help. I could tell that they'd all noticed me by the way the room went silent. Everyone just sitting there and I could see on their faces the one thought going round: there goes a girl who needs a shit. The door sounded very loud when I closed it behind me.

The PTA had set up signs in every corridor pointing out the toilets. Only someone had crossed out Toilets on the one in the maths block. They'd written Shit Holes instead, and I guess I could see why.

The whole block had that damp lavatory smell and the concrete was stippled to hold the stains better. One of the cubicle doors was open and I could see toilet paper flowing out of the bowl and over the seat, clogged up, with a tampon on top like a cherry. All the paint was chipped off the doors and none of the locks worked, so that you had to piss with one leg up, holding the door closed, getting piss all over your leg. I headed for the cubicle on the corner, unzipped my fly and took a handful of paper to make a careful circle on the seat. I'd already let things roll by the time the voice said

'*Christ!* what a smell!'

I froze on the toilet seat, halfway to relief.

'Smells like a dog's!'

'It *is* a fucking dog's!'

Laughter. And I was only half through. I stared at the door in front of me. Someone had written LEILA FUCKS HORSES on it in Tippex.

'Smells like hippy shit.'

'Hippies smell like that anyway.'

It was still coming. I didn't believe in God, but I prayed then. I prayed it would be quiet. It wasn't.

'*Fuck!* There goes another one! Sounds like a veggie-burger just hit the fan!'

'A hippy burger, you mean.'

They said more than that. A lot more, but I don't remember much of it. I thought if I waited there in silence long enough they might start to believe they were talking to an empty lavatory. So I sat there, skirt around my midriff, trying to breathe as quietly as I could.

Being embarrassed, that was my mistake. If I'd walked out as soon as they'd started, if I'd made some joke about it, everything would have been Ok. But I was always the sort of person who tried to cover their farts and failed. So I froze.

And after about fifteen minutes, the voices stopped. I

thought I'd won; outwaited them. Either they thought they'd made a mistake, or they'd just got bored and left. I wiped. I flushed. I stood up and opened the door. And I came face to face with them.

'Have a nice shit, hippy?' She was blonde, but I didn't really see her face. I walked to the sinks, not looking at them but knowing they were looking at me, and I washed my hands.

'Hippies shouldn't be allowed to use the same bogs.'

'They stink 'em out for everyone else.'

'I thought you liked shitting in the bushes best?'

I dried my hands on one of those paper towels that are designed not to absorb moisture.

'Nice talking to you, hippy.'

'Fuck off back to your caravan.'

I dropped it in the waste basket as I walked away. And I didn't say a word.

Dad asked me about my first day just about as soon as he got home, and I'm not really sure why I lied to him. I was sitting in the kitchen watching Mum make the nut roast when he brought a bag of shopping in, bending through the door. I could tell by the way his breath went up and down that he was tired. Still, he spared a smile for me, sitting down at the kitchen table. Across the room, I heard Mum switch the radio on, and I didn't speak, biting my lip, waiting for him to ask.

'Christ,' he said, and pulled his tie out sideways, reaching for the shopping bag. The kitchen light made a little

6

warm spot on his bald patch. 'So,' he said. He looked across at me, pulled a beer can from the bag. 'How'd it go?'

'It was excellent,' I said.

'Really?' He gave a nod, slow and staring at the table. 'Good . . .'

'We did physics. They don't call it science, right – they call it physics. English, art . . .'

'Uh-huh. And how did that go?'

'What, the art? Cool. The teacher's really nice and she let us sit wherever we wanted. We started a self-portrait, right . . .'

'A self-portrait?' He looked up, cracked the can. 'You did those with me ages ago.'

'Yeah . . . but she says we're gonna learn how to do them with perspective.'

'We did that too. Last summer. Christ, you know these teachers spend half their time trying to catch up.' His eyes swapped back to the table. 'Oh well,' he said. 'You'll know how to do a good job, anyhow.' He breathed out and I saw him glance behind my shoulders. 'I bought some extra oil,' he said. 'I thought we'd probably need some if you're doing roast. You are doing roast, yeah?'

Mum nodded, starting from her place by the counter, but I didn't look at her for long.

'So can I see it then?' He took a swig. 'This self-portrait? If this teacher's as crap as she sounds then I'll still be able to help.'

'Help?' I looked up at him, and Mum's arm came down between us. I could see his face was raised to me, his

7

eyebrows kind of hopeful, and I was pretty relieved when Mum said

'This is Flora.' She tilted the bottle at him. 'It's 50p more expensive, Philip.'

I saw Dad's mouth open but I got there first. My laugh sounded too loud over the radio. 'Oh no! A whole *50p* more expensive? How *will* we afford it? *Fifty pence!*' I moved around her arm so he could see me shaking my head. 'Fifty pence . . .' I said, but Dad didn't answer.

'I could help you sketch it out tonight,' he said. 'Give her a shock next lesson.'

'I . . .' I looked down at the table, pressed my lips together. 'I'm not sure you're allowed help in High School. I mean, it's not that I don't want you to . . .'

'Oh.' I watched him put the can on the table. 'I see,' he said.

'It's just . . . I mean, it wouldn't be fair, would it? Me getting help and no one else.'

'Right,' Dad said. He shifted, leaning back quickly as his breath squeezed out. He didn't look at me. 'No, I can see why. You're in High School now . . . you don't want Dad looking over your shoulder at everything you do.'

'It's not that. It . . .' But I wasn't really sure what it was. I kept thinking of that blonde girl's face and the way her lip curled up when she looked at me.

'It's a big change after all,' Dad said. 'And I knew this would happen. It's a big move. You're going to make new friends. You'll change . . .' He looked at me. 'Just make sure you don't change in the wrong direction.'

Make new friends, I thought. Yeah, I'd certainly done a

8

good job today; maybe Veggieburger-Shitting Hippy was just a friendly kind of nickname. I bit my lip and looked at Dad but he'd already turned away. I felt my stomach sink.

'What are you doing?' His voice had got colder, watching Mum's elbow tilt as she poured oil into the roasting pan. 'Liz, that's cold oil for God's sake.'

She didn't look back at him. 'I'm going to put them in in a minute.'

I breathed out while he was looking away from me, rubbed my hand against the grain of the table. Thinking of the way his voice had sunk – *Oh I see* – sent a sharp thing through my chest. I wasn't even sure why I'd said no.

'In a minute?' Dad said, and his voice hadn't got any lighter. 'So, what: you're just going to let them lie there in cold oil? Those are parsnips aren't they? They'll get all greasy.'

'I wouldn't have done it if it was going to hurt them, Philip. I'm going to cook them.'

I looked up at the wall. There's a cork board up above our kitchen table where Mum used to hang a lot of our pictures, when we were only five or six. She doesn't hang so many pictures there these days, though. Which is weird really. We've got a lot better since then. Only because of Dad's help, though.

He doesn't help Michael so much as he helps me, but Michael's never appreciated his help, that's what Dad says.

And now I wasn't appreciating him either. I thought of all those hours he'd spent, teaching me about cross-hatching and structure. All that time, and after four hours in High School I was giving him the brush-off. Sitting at the table I pressed my ankles together, hard, so that they hurt a little bit. I bit my lip, but still that voice in my head was going round. *I thought hippies liked shitting in the bushes best?* And I wondered what that had to do with it.

Their voices bounced back and forward, like the ball on that old ping-pong computer game you still see around sometimes, and I picked at a hang-nail on the side of my thumb. I'd got a nice house. Not a semi-detached in town, but an old school my dad had spent a lot of money on getting converted. It's quite a way out of town, and in the morning you can hear the birds twittering to each other as well as the traffic from the main road. When Dad found it, it had no roof. He said it would be different, it would be wonderful, he said he knew because he had vision, and I guess he was right because it's got a roof now. It's not a tepee, or anything.

Dad's spent years trying to get our house just right for us, choosing all the stuff. He bought these great big sliding doors to go right across the front of it, but they're old and sometimes they get wet inside from all the condensation. Our cat licks the dribbles off when he's allowed inside. He lives on top of the washing machine in the porch, and he's got a little box there, full of old blankets and stuff. It smells, but Mum's always leaving the laundry on top of it anyway. You can tell when it's been left in the box, the clothes have got hairs all over them and patches of dried dribble. He doesn't mean to dribble, our cat, he can't help it because he's old. And all old cats dribble, I think. It doesn't make our house any different from anyone else's. There's an ironing board next to the washing machine in our porch, but no one ever irons on it. It's got cobwebs between the legs from never being moved, and sometimes the cat craps in the gap behind. He knows no one will find it for weeks. I wondered if that blonde girl'd got an ironing board, and where it was kept in her house.

'Christ.' Dad looked round at me. 'She always does this, you know?' I looked up, saw his slight smile settle as I nodded. Seeing that smile I felt something relax in my stomach, something that had tightened without me even noticing. I wished he'd smile like that more often. 'You fancy slimy parsnips for dinner?' He laughed. 'Mmmm. Cold and greasy. I bet you can't *wait*.'

I shrugged, measuring my smile exactly as I felt his pick up at the corners of my own mouth. 'Well, you know,' I said quietly. 'I've got used to them.'

Dad's eyes only rested on me a moment but it was a good moment. Long enough to take some more of that tightness away.

'You hear that?' he said. 'She doesn't want them covered in cold oil either, Liz.'

Their voices faded away again as Dad's eyes left me, and the thought of that blonde girl came back. It rose up, like indigestion when you eat too many chips. I wondered if cold greasy parsnips were a hippy thing too. I didn't know, that was the funny thing. I had no idea what made a hippy, what the little differences might be.

I tried to think through other people's houses, work out where that difference lay. Like the newspapers, maybe. Mum keeps those in the porch as well. Hundreds of them, mostly the *Guardian* and *Hello!* Lying on the floor, discarded like that always makes me think it should be called *Goodbye!* She keeps all the newspapers she reads and she reads loads. She says you never know when they might come in handy, but I do. I know exactly when they'll come in handy. When we find the craps behind the ironing board. She gets cross when people use them for that though.

They argue about the newspapers, Mum and Dad, because Mum doesn't care about our house or all the effort Dad's put into making it nice for us. He says the newspapers show that. He says people have to come through the porch to get to the house and they have to step over them. He says it gives the wrong impression, and I wondered vaguely what that impression might be. That this house was a hippy house, perhaps.

'Look, Philip. Are you *trying* to start an argument? You *trying* to piss me off?'

'Are you *trying* to make a horrible dinner?'

'If you don't like it, don't eat it, alright? I don't give a shit!'

'Well I can see you don't give a shit, woman! That's your problem!'

Dad wears suits most of the time, and I never saw a hippy wearing a suit. They look great on him too. He keeps all his clothes in his office, so they never go near the airing cupboard, he says, and I can kind of see why.

'Don't tell me how to cook a meal then! I *never* interfere with what you're doing! When was the last time you cooked a meal for the family? *When?*'

Mum calls it the airing cupboard, even though there's hardly any air in it. When I was very little and first understood that you were supposed to wear *pairs* of socks, Mum told me it was the Sock Monster's fault that I didn't have any. She said it lived in the airing cupboard and I believed her because it looked a bit like a monster's den. She said the Sock Monster ate socks but never pairs, that's why I had to wear one black, one blue. She said we were lucky to have a Sock Monster but I don't think Dad agreed.

By the time I lost my frog mittens, the ones with the strings that go through the back of your coat, I didn't believe in the Sock Monster anymore. Sock Monsters don't eat frog mittens with strings, otherwise they'd be Sock And Mitten Monsters, I thought. I found a spanner in the airing cupboard once, but it wasn't any big surprise. Dad's workshop was full of old clothes, so it seemed kind of logical.

'. . . *Just because you can shout louder, Philip!* Well, I can shout as much as you can!'

My friends' dads' workshops aren't anything like my dad's, but I don't see why that would make us hippies. Theirs are always small and usually part of the garage, and all the tools hang up on neat little pegs on the walls. Sometimes they're even labelled, and the nails and screws and those funny U-shaped pegs all have their own boxes – a place for everything and everything in its place. Work clothes hang up on pegs on the walls, aprons and gloves and stuff like that. Dad's workshop's different. It has pegs and shelves around the walls too but Dad never bothers with them, he just uses the floor.

'You're the one who's shouting, Liz. You're just fucking uptight tonight.'

There used to be a chair, somewhere inside the shed, that Mum asked him to reupholster for her sister's wedding present, but she got divorced before he could do it, and even though they're back together now, we haven't found it since.

None of that stuff ever changes, though. It's always been that way, like Dad helping me with my art. And watching Mum stand there, her face scrunched red against the background wall, I clenched my teeth together.

'I was in a great mood till you came in! And if I'm uptight

it's just because . . . because . . . *All I'm trying to do is cook you a meal! You can cook it your fucking self if you want!'*

'*Cook it yourself* . . . Thanks Liz. Thanks for a really nice dinner. I will cook it myself. And it won't taste like shit either.'

'FUCK YOU!'

'Yeah,' Dad nodded, but his smile was kind of sad. 'Fuck you too, love,' he said. 'It's so nice coming home.'

Dad kind of collapsed as Mum left the room. I watched him flop down on to the table, try to smile as he looked up at me.

'I'm sorry,' I said.

He shrugged, looked vaguely round the kitchen. 'Great welcome,' he said. I couldn't think of anything to answer though, anything to make it better. I looked at Dad's face and I wished he'd smile again. *Don't change in the wrong direction*, I thought. But I couldn't even work out which direction that was. Maybe it was best not to try.

'It'll sort itself out,' I said. 'Always does.'

'Yeah . . .' But his eyes didn't look any better, staring at me as he said 'I'm glad you had a good time anyway.'

'Mmm,' I said. A good time. I'd tried, I really had. Tried to have a good time, tried to say hello to people, all that stuff that you're supposed to do. I'd just failed. Funny really, I didn't even understand why. And, watching Dad's attempt at a smile slip further down his face, I drew a breath in, bit my lower lip. 'Well,' I said. 'Maybe . . . maybe if you still want to, you could help me with my picture. Yeah?'

*

15

Things got a lot better in school after a while, though. They got better when I worked out the way to act. Holly's way was just to be herself, she didn't need anything more. Mine was to let people touch me. It wasn't such a bad way really. And by the time I hit the Third Year things were pretty much Ok. Better than Ok: things were good. Because that was when I started noticing Robin. When he started noticing me.

Robin never touched me, that was the first thing I noticed about him, and it was strange because he could have done. He wasn't good-looking, but he had this aggressive kind of confidence that made up for it, and he was pretty high up in the group. A while before I got to know them all, Robin's mother had miscarried in her fifth month. Twins. Both dead. Everyone in school knew about it but Robin said he didn't give a fuck. He acted like it too. He was strong, I think, not physically but in some other way, and no one gave him any shit.

He was blond, smaller than Joel but bigger than Craig, and he didn't talk a lot like Craig did. His hair was so light that sometimes, looking at him from a certain angle, you couldn't even see his eyelashes. He had a slightly pug nose too. None of that mattered to me of course, I would have let him touch me. Only Robin never seemed very interested in me. Which was maybe why I was so surprised when I first caught him looking my way. It was June, I think, and we were out at the back of the pitch. It was the day that Holly announced she was pregnant.

Craig had got hold of a copy of *More!* and he was reading

out the problem page. Joel was there too but he was busy skinning up, so for the time being I just sat there, waiting for my turn.

'Listen to this, right.' Craig looked up from the paper, pages flipping and skipping in the wind. The sunlight made his hair look grey, an ugly kind of colour. '*Dear Kate . . . Please help me. My boyfriend and I have been sleeping together . . .*'

'SNORE!' Joel said, not looking up from his hands. He was having trouble holding the skins down in the breeze. He pinned them to the maths book on his lap and I watched him roach a corner from it, wondering when he'd be finished.

'Just wait, alright?' Craig grinned, looking back to the page. '*My boyfriend and I have been sleeping together for over a year and just recently I've begun to wet myself during orgasm . . .*'

'Fuck me!' Joel looked up from his hands. 'How fucking rough is that!'

'*My boyfriend says it doesn't matter . . .*'

'Yeah right,' Joel sniggered. 'I bet he does.'

'*But my confidence is suffering and now I can't have sex at all.* A Boyzone fan, 21.'

'Well that's her fucking problem right there.' Joel finished rolling, tapped it once against the flat of the book. His hair was dark, hanging down across his face towards his lap as he concentrated. 'She's a fucking Boyzone fan.'

'*Dear Boyzone fan,*' Craig said. '*The first thing you need to do is relax . . .*'

'WRONG!' Joel twisted the end, grinning as he looked

17

up. 'The first thing you need to do is . . .' But Craig was already nodding as they laughed it out together.

'*BUY A NAPPY!*'

Craig dumped the magazine behind him on the grass as Joel laid back on his elbows. He stuck the spliff in his mouth, leaned over, and flicked the lighter. I watched him cup one hand round it so it didn't get blown out. He frowned while he did it, I saw, kind of squinting as he looked for the flame. I heard the thud of a football somewhere quite a way behind us, and a scream, small and quiet on the wind, as someone shouted cunt.

I saw Holly when I looked up. She was steering her way through the goal posts and down the slope where we were sitting. The wind flicked her skirt up, like the holes in the football net. It made her legs look even longer.

There was a nudge in my side as she sat down, stretched herself out and leaned back in the grass. Craig was holding out a cigarette.

'Lambert and Butler are fucking rough,' I said.

'Oh *right*.' He took it back. 'And what do *you* smoke then?'

I didn't like the sarcasm in his voice. 'B&H,' I said.

'They're half an inch shorter.'

'Yeah.' I looked away. 'But it's all in the filter.'

Holly sniffed as she looked over at us but her eyes didn't stay on me for long.

'Guess what,' she said, and everyone turned. 'I missed a period.'

'*Really?*' I bit my lip, wishing it hadn't come out

sounding so interested. Still, I was kind of surprised any period of Holly's would dare not turn up.

'Yeah?' Joel grinned around the spliff. 'You pregnant then?'

She shrugged. 'I'm on the pill . . . but it's only 97 per cent reliable.'

'Does that mean you'll only have 3 per cent of a baby?' I said. It was meant to be a joke, but she barely looked at me, opening her bag. Inside was a box of hair dye – that pastel-blue colour that always means it's come from Boots. I wondered how a tint of mahogany-plum was going to help her period turn up.

'I got to do this,' she said. She took the box out, but instead of a shiny, manageable, nourished head, it had a picture of a pregnant stomach. *Pregnancy Test*, it said, and *Put your mind at rest*. I wondered how it was going to put her mind at rest if she ended up looking like the stomach on the front. 'It cost a fiver: tight or what. You're s'posed to buy two,' she said. 'But that'd be a tenner. I bought a little pill instead.'

'Put your mind at rest,' Joel said, and she laughed.

I had to wonder why she was bothered about money at all, though. She worked as a waitress in a wholefood café called The Herb Garden. She got paid £4 an hour to get stoned and serve hot crusty rolls to the coolest people in town. It didn't sound like a bad job to me.

'What do you do with it?' Joel said.

'Piss on it.'

She looked down at it, considering, and I watched her push a strand of hair back from where the wind had put it. She had long nails, and the sunlight made them look cleaner than they were. Skinning-up nails, she called them.

'And?' he said.

'And if it turns blue you start looking for a good-sized coat hanger.'

I didn't think she had anything to worry about, though, there was no way Holly could be pregnant. I'd read that you had to see a counsellor when you had an abortion, one of two categories. Either a fifty-year-old guy with half-moon spectacles and a frown that's too big for his face, or a woman of the same age with unshaved legs, shin-length skirts and too many smiles. I couldn't see Holly talking to anyone like that.

But then, I couldn't really see Holly talking to anyone at all. Except maybe in my fantasies, when she'd come running up to me and say *This terrible thing has happened! Oh God! I'm so unhappy! I have to talk to someone and you're the only one I trust* . . . And somehow I couldn't see that happening anytime soon.

Joel stretched. The sun coming from behind him made his cheeks look dusty, I could see the tiny hairs. As he took another drag, I felt his hand flop down on to my thigh.

And it was just as I looked up, past Joel's bitten finger-nails and on to Holly's face, that I spotted Robin. He was staring at me. At us, I guess, because his eyes were over Joel's hand. His mouth was turned down around the corners and I could see his face was flinching up.

Disgusted, that was how he looked. And in the space between the conversation, he looked up at my face as well.

Disgusted, as those fingers worked their way up and under the hem. I watched Joel breathe out and the breeze whipped the smoke away, back and then gone. It looked very thick against the sky, and I wondered why he'd be disgusted with me. He could have touched me too.

Joel's thumb brushed up against my pants, fake silk, and for a little while I closed my eyes.

Disgusted, I thought. It was a nice-sounding word.

I thought about Robin that evening, watching Dad fill out some form or other. The sound of the Hoover was muffled from Michael's bedroom, and I could hear the cat was scratching to get in. I hummed, trying to rest my elbows on the table in a way that looked like Dad's. A cigarette stuck up from his left hand, holding the paper flat as he scribbled. Dad's got big knuckles, they wrinkle in spirals and he holds the cigarette between them. I've always kind of liked his hands. I watched the smoke dangle, up by his eye, and I watched him squint to keep it out.

Dad doesn't like doing forms, they make him cross because he's got better things to do with his time. I think they make him sad as well though. Usually they're all about money and filling them out reminds him that we haven't got enough, even though he works all the time. He says he feels bad because he can't afford to buy us all the things we want. I try to tell him I don't want anything and I never ask for pocket money, but it doesn't seem to make any difference. He says we're very lucky, there are loads of people much worse off than us. And he's right of course, but I know it doesn't stop him feeling bad about it. I know, because he tells me all the time.

Sitting at the kitchen table though, he wasn't saying much at all. Every now and then he'd look up at my face and I made sure I was smiling each time. Looking at him there though, still working even though it was the evening time, the smile didn't feel very real. In my stomach, I felt guilty.

He'd hate them, you see, Holly and Joel and everyone. He'd hate them all, but Robin in particular, I knew it. He'd hate the way Robin's mouth went down around the corners when he smiled. He'd hate the letters on his bag, FUCK THE LAW, SMOKE THE DRAW, stencilled in Biro. He'd hate how Robin never answered yes, just gave a little *uh*.

I saw him cough a little, flatten down the paper, and I readied my smile just in case he looked up. Hate them, I thought, and I wondered why those words would make me feel so strange.

'You Ok?' he said. He looked up at my face, already settled in a grin.

'Great,' I said.

I watched him nod as he reached to flick the ash off. And from the other room, I heard the sound of Michael's footsteps come towards the door.

Michael's two years younger than me, but he doesn't really act it. His room's just about the only tidy place in the house. I think it looks like a hospital, what with all his toys stacked in boxes, labels on the front. I've told him it's the first step to insanity, soon he'll be washing his hands with the kettle, but Michael doesn't really listen to me. He's got a piggy bank in his room where he keeps all his pocket money, even the pennies. Every month, he stacks the coins up in order and takes them down to the bank. He's even got a stash of those sealed plastic bags.

Michael's going to be a technical genius. Dad says he's known since Michael was little, but really it started when he failed his English SATs. I remember coming home one night, when Dad had just read the report, and they were sitting at the kitchen table, both of them bent over some part out of the car. Or maybe the Kenwood mixer.

There were screwdrivers and bolts and all that other stuff that holds things together strewn out across the table. I remember thinking Mum wouldn't be using her mixer that night. Either that or we'd be walking to the bus next morning.

'So you see . . .' Dad had said. 'This part . . . pushes down on this part and turns the . . .'

'Mmm . . . *Dad?* I've finished the fourth level on *Sonic The Hedgehog.*'

'But it turns it *counter*-clockwise. Can you see that?'

'Yeah . . . *Dad?* It's got this really cool end-of-level baddy right? With this *huge* gun!'

I remember thinking even then that they'd do better reading him the *Financial Times*.

Dad looked up as Michael came in through the door, but he didn't look for long. I watched him take a puff on the cigarette. I watched it reflect back off the paper as he breathed it out.

'So,' he said, still writing. 'Looking forward to Friday?'

'Friday?'

'I thought it was Non-uniform Day.' He leaned back slowly, pushed the form away.

'Oh that,' I said. Michael walked across to the cupboard. I watched him take a loaf of Kingsmill out. 'It's no big deal.'

'What're you going to wear then?'

'Haven't thought about it much,' I said, but I guess that was a lie. I'd been through just about every outfit my wardrobe would cough up. None of them looked normal.

'Probably just jeans,' I said.

'Jeans? Is that what everyone wears?'

'Pretty much,' I said, and I heard a snigger from behind. 'What?' I looked round.

'Nothing.' Michael reached for the margarine. 'Just that you've got no imagination.'

'Right,' I turned away. 'So what are *you* going to wear? I saved you some Kleenex boxes . . .' I don't think he's a technical genius anyway. I think he's just crap at English.

'God,' Dad said. 'People in school are such arse-holes aren't they.' I didn't answer him, though, it didn't sound like a question. 'Can't even be an individual anymore.'

'No . . .'

'Anyway.' He shifted in his seat. 'I guess it's up to you what you wear.' He caught my eyes, halfway to reaching for his Biro again. 'Just a shame you don't want to break out from them anymore . . .' he said. And looking across at me, he did seem kind of sad.

I thought about Robin all through dinner, Robin and Non-uniform Day. I wondered what he'd like to see me wearing, or if he'd even care, and I ran back through my list of clothes. Short skirts and a jumper, long skirts and a little top. I tried to remember everything he'd said, something that might give me a clue. I couldn't think of anything, not straight off, but it was funny. I kind of liked the idea of dressing just for him.

I thought about it while we ate and after, with Mum stacking the dishes away. I thought about it and I smiled. Right up until the phone rang.

I was flicking through the *Radio Times* when I saw *Ren and Stimpy* was on. *Ren and Stimpy*, Robin's favourite television programme, I knew because I'd heard him do the voices, and I wondered how I'd look next day, just wandering across the pitch. *Hey, anyone see* Ren and Stimpy *last night?*

'Dad . . .?' I looked up at him, past Michael on the sofa, and I heard the clink of dishes as Mum shut a cupboard door. 'Fancy watching *Ren and Stimpy* tonight?'

'*Ren and* what?' He picked his beer can up, but he hadn't said no yet.

'*Ren and Stimpy*. It's this really cool cartoon. A bit like *Tom and Jerry*, only . . .' Only I didn't know a single thing about it. 'Only cooler. Like a cult,' I said. Dad liked cults, he'd told me, and I watched his head pick up. 'Everyone watches it in school.'

'Oh . . .' he said. 'Well, I was going to ask if you fancied watching a family movie.'

Michael sat up. 'I'll watch a movie. What about *Predator*?'

he said, but Dad only glanced around, even though he loves all those explosions and stuff. It's strange though, every time we put on an Arnie movie, Mum suddenly gets an insatiable urge to clean the fish tank. And we don't even have a fish tank.

Dad pushed a finger round the rim of his beer.

'I mean, I can see you want to watch it if it's . . . if it's the in thing or whatever. Like wearing the same clothes as everyone else.' He paused. 'I'm just a bit knackered. You know, I have been out at work all day. I was hoping we could all watch a movie together.'

'*Terminator?*' Michael said as Mum walked back across the room.

'You don't mind, do you?' Dad looked over at me. 'I thought it'd be nice . . .'

'I . . .' Dad watched me, a funny kind of look on his face, and I thought about him bending over that form. I thought about Holly too, though. Holly and Robin and how they'd dissect the episode tomorrow. I'd sit in the corner as usual. I'd sit there in silence again. 'Couldn't we watch a film afterwards? It's only half an hour long.'

'Christ,' he said. 'Is it really that important? I've been waiting all day to finish work, get all that fucking paperwork out of the way, so we could all sit down and watch a family film. Does that really sound so boring?'

He stared at me, with Michael staring too, and smirking.

'You can't always have it your own way,' Michael said. 'We want to watch a family movie, you're outvoted.'

'Hang on.' Mum was sitting down, picking up the newspaper. 'Outvoted on what?' Mum likes *Pride and*

Prejudice and *Emma* and stuff like that. Dad says if he wanted to watch a bunch of uptight English people in stupid clothes then he'd put on the Queen's speech every Christmas. I have to say, usually I'd agree. Mum gives good reasons and that, for not liking explosions, I mean. She says there's no plot or character development. But I think the real reason she hates them isn't because of the lack of sub-textual conflict, it's because of the lack of A-line taffeta ball gowns. No taffeta ball gowns in *Predator*. Just a lot of dirty vests and people saying *Make my day, motherfucker!*

'Me and Dad want to watch a *family* movie.' Michael held a hand out towards the TV. I thought he looked a bit like an estate agent. 'But *she* wants to watch some stupid cartoon that no one's ever *seen* before. So she's outvoted.'

'Well . . .' Mum looked round at me. 'Maybe I'd like to watch this cartoon too.'

'What?' Dad turned away from me. 'You don't even know what it *is*. You don't want to watch it.'

'I . . .' I opened my mouth to tell him that it didn't matter but he wasn't looking at me. I was kind of relieved.

'Well maybe I *do*, Philip. Maybe we don't want to watch . . . *Slash and Mutilate II*.'

'Well maybe . . .' Michael's voice was getting louder as he glanced across at Dad, 'no one cares what you think. *We're* going to watch a family movie.' Dad nodded.

'Oh,' Mum stared at him. 'So I don't get a say at all then, is that it?'

'We have just discussed it, Liz. Please don't start sticking your bloody oar in.'

'Is that right?' Mum was nodding. The kind of nod that says she doesn't agree at all.

They never agree on much, though. Not that other parents agree more than they do, it's just that mine like to air their grievances on a regular basis. Dad says it's healthier that way. I think so too.

'*Is that right?*' Michael made a face like Mum's. He was pretty good at voices too, but then I guess he learned it from a pro. I watched Mum open her mouth, dumb, like a fish in a glass bowl. And that was when the phone rang.

I was kind of glad, walking into the kitchen. Even if it is healthier to air your grievances, sometimes it gets kind of noisy. It makes Dad sad as well. I know it does, even though he doesn't say so. Dad's like that, though, he says he's not the sort of person to burden others with his feelings.

Picking up the receiver, half listening to things wind down next door I played with the light-pull in one hand. I'd look good, I thought, just standing there and toying with it. I'd look good if anyone was watching.

'Hello?' the voice said.

I almost didn't recognize it.

I remember, when I was eleven, I used to pretend my best friend was raping me. We did it on the bottom bunk and I used to have to push the Care Bears out of the way. Dawn had four Care Bears, and I was always kind of jealous of that. She had lots of stuff I was jealous of; her stepdad bought it so that he didn't have to be nice to her. He was nice to me, though, which made me feel a bit bad. He was always asking her why she couldn't be more like me, which I thought was stupid because she was obviously trying. I can remember wishing that I had a stepdad who didn't like me too. Not that I wanted anyone but my own dad, I never would have wished for that, just that it would have been nice to have all her stuff.

Dawn was always ill. She had really bad asthma and kept a contraption at home with a face mask for when she had fits. She'd been born with a hole in the heart, which I thought sounded kind of romantic. The scar down her chest wasn't romantic, though, it looked a bit like Frankenstein. She was allergic to every animal I'd even bothered to ask about, but her mum didn't seem to mind. She kept two dogs and four cats and Dawn spent her whole life walking round the edges of rooms to avoid them.

Her room was really small and it had a fish tank at one end because she wasn't allergic to fish. Not that I ever saw any fish, just a plastic treasure chest and lots of pond weed. I thought the fish had died a long time ago, a bit like her real dad, but I never told Dawn that. She had bunk beds there, even though she didn't have any brothers or sisters. There were butterflies on the duvet covers, and her room was always tidy because her mum did it for her. I had a weird idea about Dawn's mum and her bedroom. I didn't believe her Mum picked up anything at all, I saw her a bit like Mary Poppins, where she'd just stand by the fish tank and magic things into drawers. Probably singing while she did it. I don't know why I thought that; Dawn's mum didn't look a bit like Mary Poppins, and she had a really croaky voice. She smoked a lot of cheap cigarettes.

When we weren't talking about her asthma or her allergies, Dawn and me would go up to her room and play The Game. It didn't have a name because we never talked about it, so I just thought of it as The Game. Dawn would stand outside for a couple of minutes and I'd sit on my own, staring at the fish tank. I'd pretend I was sitting on a park bench somewhere and looking at a lake. A lake with no fish. And then, after a while, Dawn would open the door really quietly. I could hear it anyway but that wasn't the point. She'd creep up and grab me and say something that never seemed to fit. I remember wishing that she wouldn't say anything at all. That way I wouldn't have to hear her voice.

'There's no point in screaming. There's no one here so just shut up!'

I'd scream anyway because that was part of the rules, but I'd always do it quietly. Dawn's mum liked to nap in the afternoon and she got pretty grumpy if anyone woke her.

'What do you want?' I'd say. 'Leave me alone!' And she'd drag me over to the bed, only she never had to drag very hard. I was heavier than her and if I'd tried to stay put she probably would have had an asthma attack. She'd fling me down on the bed and put a hand over my mouth. I remember she had very dry skin on her hands, wrinkled like an old person's, and I had to press my lips in while she got on top so I wouldn't have to feel it. She'd bounce up and down then, and I'd say

'Stop! Please don't! Stop!' But of course I didn't want her to.

We'd bang our hips together for ages and it felt nice even though it hurt. It felt good and I didn't want to stop. We never touched each other. Well, I never did very much at all, I just liked to lie there. I liked to be underneath.

And there was nothing friendly about it, or pretty or nice. It didn't even feel naughty. It just felt like something that needed to be done.

We used to pretend we were twins, me and Dawn, even though we looked nothing like each other, and I was kind of glad about it. I thought she was pretty funny-looking, even then. Tall and gawky and her hair was always pretty greasy. We put each other's make-up on. Well, I put hers on, I didn't want her touching mine. We had baths together, and she was a really early developer. She had tons of hair, in her armpits, on her legs, and I remember wondering if all that hair was as greasy as the stuff on her head. She'd started her periods too, even though we were still at Primary.

'Everyone laughs,' she said. 'They can all see the log . . .' She stared sadly at the fish tank. Like that was romantic or something.

'The log?' I thought it sounded pretty barbaric, all that rough bark.

'The sanitary towel! Don't tell me you haven't seen them laughing,' she said. So I didn't.

I scuffed my shoes against pink carpet, sitting on the bed. 'Why don't you wear tampons?'

'I'm too heavy – my flow. I'm not lucky like some people, they don't stop the blood.'

'Is there a lot of blood, then?' I hadn't started my periods, and Mum had never given me The Talk. Instead she put *The Body Book* in my Christmas stocking one year. I was pretty disappointed actually, I'd been hoping for a Gameboy. 'Like, really loads?'

'Enough to turn a bath red.'

'Really?' From then on, I decided, she'd be getting in the bath after me.

'And black bits too.' She looked down at her nails like there might still be some there. 'Like clots. Clots of blood or something.' She shook her head, really long and slow. 'Miss said last year I could be a really good swimmer, Olympic standard, she said. Can hardly swim now, can I? Not when they can all see it in my costume!'

'No,' I said, but I didn't really know what she was worried about. No one ever looked at her costume in swimming. The acne on her back was loads more interesting.

'I could have been really good at something . . .' she said. I didn't bother to disagree.

Sometimes I found bruises on my pelvis after I'd been to Dawn's house. Little purple yellow things that spread over the bony bits. I used to press them to see what colour they turned under pressure. I don't think I ever showed Dawn the bruises, I don't think I wanted her to see. But I never minded them. When I got home I'd take my trousers off and search around to find one. I remember thinking that they looked kind of pretty.

Dad always asked me how it'd gone when I'd been to stay at Dawn's. I think he liked the fact that we were friends because he worked in the same place as Dawn's stepdad. Dad just called him Jack, though. They knew each other pretty well, he said, because Cartwright's was a 'small, friendly kind of company', and I guess that meant that the daughters had to be small and friendly as well. Dad worked as the Personnel Manager there, but Dawn's stepdad was just Manager, and I always wondered what there was left to Manage after Dad had done the Personnel. The cardboard boxes maybe; Cartwright's made a lot of cardboard boxes. We always had plenty at home.

'Did you have fun?' he'd say, and I always answered yes. Even if Dawn had been really depressed that day, it was nice of him to care. 'It's great that you and her get on so well.'

'Yeah . . . Did you know Dawn's stepdad bought her a stereo? He buys her loads.'

'Well, Dawn's going through a few problems at the moment. Jack's just trying to cheer her up. And it's good that she's got a friend like you, right?' He looked at me.

'Sure . . . It's got two decks and everything.' Dad didn't answer. 'Not that it makes her happy,' I said. 'Because people who have everything all the time don't appreciate it, do they?'

'No.' Dad smiled.

'Because it isn't special anymore, right?'

'Right. What's special is having a friendship like you and Dawn's. Where you both support each other, help each other . . . That's what's important.'

'Mmm,' I said, but I couldn't really remember Dawn helping me. She did up the back of my dress once, when I couldn't reach. 'Yes,' I said, and I smiled back. 'That's definitely what's important.'

But I guess it wasn't that important, not to Dawn's stepdad anyway. Because it was only a year or so after that he decided to send her away. She went to a boarding school instead of proper High School, the kind you had to pay for. And it was funny, I'd never really thought about it before, but I wasn't that sorry to see her go.

'Hello,' she said.

It was her breath that reminded me. The way it fell down at the end, ready to hitch.

'It's me,' she said. 'You know? Dawn? . . . I didn't think you'd remember my voice.'

'It hasn't been that long.' I dropped the light-pull, let my arm hang down loose by my side. 'You know,' I said, but my laugh sounded stupid. 'Course I remember your voice.' I waited for a second, trying to think of what came next. 'How are you?'

'Alright,' she said, but she didn't sound alright.

'How's school?'

'Boring.'

I expected her to say something else. She didn't bother though. 'How're the flute lessons?'

'I haven't got any better.'

'Oh,' I said. I wondered vaguely if I was supposed to disagree. I wondered why she'd rung. 'Well what grade are you on?'

'Two.'

'Oh,' I said again. She really hadn't got any better. 'Well it's nice to talk to you.'

There was a pause before she said 'I've got some news. If you're still interested . . .' I wasn't quite sure what she meant by that. I didn't stop to ask. 'I'm moving.'

'Moving,' I said. The word came out sounding dead, like it'd had all the meaning drained out of it. 'Moving house?' But I already knew that wasn't it, and down below my stomach I felt something a bit like a period cramp. It made me think of conversations in her room. Black bits, I thought, and I hadn't even known then what a period smelled like.

'Moving schools,' she said. 'They're just . . . not really my sort of people here. Not that we can't afford it.'

'No,' I said. 'No, course not.' But I wasn't really listening. I was thinking about Holly with her preg results coming up, about Robin and that look in his eyes. I was thinking about Joel and Craig and all the others. About the expressions on their faces when they'd see her. Leaning back against the cork board, I heard the paper rustle behind my back. And I closed my eyes. 'Moving to my High School,' I said.

'I know you probably don't want me back . . . probably embarrassed about me in front of all your new friends . . .' I listened to her pause, could almost hear the question mark.

'No I'm not.' My stomach rolled again.

'You're not? I thought . . . maybe you wouldn't want to be best friends anymore. I mean, I know you've got new friends . . .'

'No,' I said, and it came out quiet in the empty kitchen. I looked out, across the draining board, stacked dishes and the mess across the counter. 'That's . . . that's nice,' I said.

'Really?'

'Well . . . yeah.'

'So you do want to see me again?'

'Of course,' I said, I didn't really have much choice.

'You know,' Dawn said quietly, 'you're still my best friend.' I was glad when she didn't leave any space for an answer. I'm not sure I could have thought of one. Best friends. It sounded like something out of Nancy Drew. Standing still by the phone, I listened to her breath trail away, off into some kind of sigh. 'I can't wait to see you,' she said slowly. 'It'll be just like before.'

I leaned against the kitchen wall after Dawn hung up. I pulled at my bottom lip. In the living room, things had gone quiet. I heard Dad pop a beer can so all the rowing must have died down. Still, I didn't walk out for a moment. I listened to the boiler finish its cycle and I felt my stomach tip. I had a horrible feeling she was right.

I didn't tell Dad about Dawn that night, even though I knew he'd want to hear. I couldn't quite bring myself to talk about it. Talking about it would make it real, and I just couldn't face that yet. I figured I still had one more

day before she got there. She was arriving on Friday –
Non-uniform Day – to make it worse, and I tried not to
think what she'd wear. One last day, I thought, and I'd
make sure it was a good one.

As it happened, though, I didn't have to make it anything.
It was a good day anyway, for two different reasons. Most
important, it was the first day that Holly really spoke to
me. Even though I'd been hanging around for quite a
while, she'd never really said much, maybe made a joke at
me once or twice. That day was different, and I knew it
straight away. We had double biology first lesson on a
Thursday. And Holly came to sit next to me.

'Hi.' She was grinning, and I wondered if that was a
good thing.

I opened my mouth. 'Uh?' Was that meant to be a
word? I had a horrible feeling I might be dribbling.

'Wanna see my results?'

'What results? We don't get them till tomorrow . . .'

'Not biology, mongy. My *test* results . . .' She stuck her
tongue in her chin and made a spazzy sound. I have to
admit, though, it was probably pretty accurate. I saw her
reach into a pocket, pull something out, and she waved it
in front of my face. 'Wanna sniff?'

'Oh, *fuck* . . .' I got snagged on the words. 'How'd it
go?'

She moved it to her mouth, stuck her tongue out as if
to lick it. 'Mmmm! Mm-hmm!'

'Come on,' I said, and finally she held it out so I could
see.

'Well?' She looked at me. 'D'you reckon that's blue?'

'It could be green . . .' I said.

'Doesn't go green. Blue or clear.' She looked down at it, turning it slowly over end.

'Well, it's not clear,' I said.

'I can see *that* . . . I'm not a fuckin mong . . .' But she didn't look up, still concentrating.

'D'you think it was . . .' What was his name? 'You know . . .' But she only shrugged. So *cool*: fuck knows who the dad is, I've slept with so many people. I've slept *around*.

'Anyway!' She dumped it on the desk, didn't even look to see where it landed. 'I've got some way more interesting news! You're not gonna fuckin *believe* this right? I was talking to Robin last night, like I went over to his house for a bif and he was like asking me all this stuff about you and shit. I tell you he's way into you. Like big time. Totally. And I reckon you'd be so good together. So are you gonna go out with him?'

She looked down at me, nodding. I saw her pause for a breath, but all I could say was

'What?'

'You and Robin. I'm gonna get you two together right? It's gonna be totally wicked!'

'Robin?'

'You and Robin.' Her eyes wouldn't leave me alone. '*Yeah* . . . ?'

'I . . .'

'Wicked!' she said. 'Excellent!' she said. And the only thing I could think of was 'Oh.'

*

38

But I was happy, walking out on to the pitch with her that lunchtime. Really walking *with* her, like we were just the best of all possible buddies. I was so happy that for a while I almost forgot about Dawn. It was a pretty perfect day, kind of blue with those quick clouds shooting through between the goal posts. Holly's hair got in her eyes and I watched how she pushed it back, one quick little flick. I'd practise that tonight.

The grass turned to dried-out mud around the net, Nike footprints crossing over each other. And ten yards behind that I saw him. Robin lay with his chin on his hands and his elbows on the grass. I watched his expression get weirder and weirder as we walked towards him, I wondered if mine was doing the same. I could see a grass stain had made its way up his shirt, and his hair, pale blond, was in his eyes. I didn't say anything as we walked up to his side. His face was level with my ankles.

'Hello,' I said.

'Hi,' he said.

And that was how it started.

The bus drive home was pretty quiet that night and, holding my folder on my lap, I thought about everything that'd happened. There's only girls on our school bus these days. It used to have both on it, loads of people from all the different years. Going home was still quite a laugh then. I watched them all play Truth or Dare, snogging and trying not to feel travel sick. No one used to do their homework on the bus then. They split us up on the day that our driver complained. He'd run a red light when one of the ripped-off seat covers had flown through the air and landed over his head. He hadn't been able to hear the passers-by screaming at him over the sound of girls singing 'I'm Sandra Dee' in the back seat. I guess he thought it was dangerous.

Sitting halfway down the aisle, my mouth was smiling on its own. Robin's girlfriend. The words went round in my head, and I thought about people looking at me, pointing me out. *That's Robin's girlfriend.* I had a title, an important one, and Holly had sat by me through a whole double lesson.

I watched the traffic go by on the other side of the road, glossed over with my own reflection. I would be Robin's from now on. It sounded so much better than just being anyone's.

Dad grinned at me as I came through the door. I suppose there's less personnel to manage on a Thursday because he's always home early. I grinned back at him. Dad doesn't get happy a lot of the time, it was nice we could be happy together.

'D'you have a good day?' he said. He was standing in the living room, his jacket off, like he'd been waiting for me to get back.

'Brilliant,' I said.

'Brilliant, eh?' He nodded, swapped his hands around from back to front. 'I bought you a magazine on the way home, by the way. It's . . . uh . . . *Just 17*, I think. That Ok?'

'Great!' I smiled, reaching out for it. Holly never read *Just 17*. She said only spazzy First Years read it. Holly was into *Mixmag*, but I'd only ever seen the cover. 'Thanks.'

I flicked through the pages quickly. Lots of pictures of women in fake leopard skin and platforms reaching orgasm in ten easy steps. *Just 17*, I thought. Should be called *Just 12*. 'So . . .' I looked up at him. 'Did you have a good day too?'

'Uh-huh, uh-huh. I heard the great news, by the way.'

'News?' I hung the magazine down by my side. He looked funny standing there, I thought. Like he didn't quite know where to put his hands. 'What great news?' I said.

'Well about Dawn. Jack said today . . .' He paused for another grin. 'I'm really glad.'

'Oh,' I said. 'Dawn.' I nodded, walking out from the doorway, and I dumped my folder on the floor. 'Yeah, nice isn't it. She won't be stuck somewhere she doesn't like anymore . . .'

'Well . . . yeah,' I heard him say behind me. 'It's more than that though, isn't it? Means you two can be back together again. I bet you've got *loads* to catch up on.' He was right as well. I still hadn't heard the full details of just how bad a boarding school could be. 'She's really looking forward to it,' Dad said. 'Seeing you again and everything.'

'Is she?' I turned round. 'Did her . . . did Jack say that?'

'Well he told me how unhappy she'd been. You know, without a really close friend.'

'Oh.' I couldn't think of much else, but I did smile as he put a hand on my shoulder.

'You must want to see her again *too*,' he said.

41

'Yeah . . . yeah I do.' It was difficult to talk like that, seeing him so happy. 'Course.'

'Well then.' He patted his hand down on blue cotton, that ugly kind of grey-blue that they'd picked out special for our uniform. 'And anyway,' he said, 'it'll be nice actually *knowing* some of your friends again. I mean, I know you don't want to bring them home anymore but . . . feels like I've kind of lost touch with what you're doing.'

'They . . . they're just not that interesting. I mean, they're only school friends.'

'There must be something interesting about them . . . I hardly know what you're doing these days.' He looked away, out of the french windows, with his hand still resting there. The sun made them look dusty, I thought. Like they needed a good wash. 'Anyway,' he said. 'I'm . . . I'm glad she's coming back.'

'Well . . . me too.' I glanced down, out of sight. 'I have to do some biology,' I said.

'Biology. Oh . . .' I watched him nod as his hand dropped away. 'Ok . . .'

'Thanks for *Just 17*,' I said. But he only shrugged, walking back towards the kitchen.

I don't like being on my own usually. It makes me feel kind of bad, hearing Dad and everyone downstairs. I always end up thinking about arguments or stuff at school, stuff that makes me feel shit. Usually, it's just easier to be with the family. But, dumping *Just 17* down on the clothes by my bed, I didn't feel so bad. I had an outfit to pick, and a reason for picking it. I tried not to think about Dad on his own in the kitchen.

I put the radio on, a little one that I'd borrowed off Mum, picking out my pants. They were the easiest because I didn't have a lot to choose from. And stepping over a teddy bear, standing on my own in my bedroom, I didn't listen to the voices in the background. I guess it was just nice to have them there.

Black jeans. Black fake-silk pants. A red bodysuit just thin enough to show my nipples. Robin wasn't in my form for registration, but I knew I'd see him pretty soon, and hoisting my bag up over my shoulder, I kept my head high, walking into the classroom. There was lots of colour there without the uniforms, I thought. Lots of patterns and clashing and not many faces. Even though I knew who they all were. I listened to the bell and I flicked my hair. Just like Holly sometimes did.

It'd been cold that morning. The room didn't feel like it'd been heated, and I tried not to shiver, sitting down at my desk. It'd make my nipples hard, at least. I heard the sound of talking die away as our form tutor stepped through the door. And it was only then, in the quiet left behind, that I heard a voice next to me say

'Don't say hello then.'

It was worse than I could have imagined really, and I'd tried not to imagine anything. She was wearing a black T-shirt, very baggy, so she looked like a boy. Which was funny really because the guy on the T-shirt looked like a girl. He had long blond hair and scarlet patent-leather jeans that matched his lipgloss. He was leaning backwards with a microphone and I wondered if he had some kind of spine disorder, the way he was bent like that. The words above his head said Skid Row, printed in a cheery cherry colour, like the last bloody death scrawl of a butchery victim.

'Hi Dawn,' I said, trying to smile.

Her spots had got worse. I could see that straight off, even though she'd tried to paint them over with some cheap foundation. It looked very bright, an unreal kind of beige against the background wall. It made her eyes look too small, too red, like they'd been swamped in make-up fumes since six o'clock this morning. Half a tube of base on there, and still it had managed to go shiny round her nose. I could almost see my reflection, dotted over with her blackheads.

'Sorry,' she said. 'Were you trying to pretend you didn't know me?'

'Course not. I didn't see you.' I picked up the corners of my mouth. 'Still half asleep,' I said.

Yawn. Stretch. Yawn.

'Dawn . . .' I shook my head. 'You look . . . you haven't changed at all.'

'Sorry.' She looked off, waiting, and I saw she already had a pen out. 'I can't help the way I look.'

'I know you can't, I didn't mean that. You look . . . nice.' The tutor called a name.

'You've changed.' It sounded like an insult and I wondered if she'd meant it like that.

'Well,' I said, but that wasn't much of an answer. 'Yeah.'

'I can see your . . .' She looked down, pointed a finger at my chest. 'Everyone can.'

'So how are you? What do you think of the place? Did you find the classroom Ok?'

'No, I got lost.' I couldn't tell if she was being sarcastic. 'I'm not thick,' she said.

'I know you're not.' I breathed out. 'Look, I'm sorry I didn't see you there.' I watched her shrug. 'I *am*,' I said again. 'I wasn't ignoring you or anything . . . It's nice to see you.'

'Really?' She brought her eyes back up to me and seeing them again, I bit my lip. They weren't red because of make-up. I guess that was a stupid thing to think. I saw the way they puffed under the foundation. They were red because she'd been crying.

'Really,' I said, and I looked at her straight. 'Let's . . . let's start again Ok?'

'Ok,' she said. She smiled a little bit. Problem was, I'd only meant the conversation.

I talked to Dawn a lot that morning. I didn't really have a choice, they'd put her in all my classes. It was Ok, though. Robin wasn't in my class for French or physics or English, he was a couple of sets down so he didn't see us together. Holly didn't either, she'd taken different options from me, and for the first time I was glad about it.

So everything went alright for a while. She told me about boarding school and how horrible it had been.

'They're just snobs. All they care about is how much money you've got in the bank.'

'Mm,' I said. My statements have read a steady 72p since I was six. Michael probably would have fitted in, though. I uncrossed my legs, feeling the sun through black denim.

'I could have been horrible back,' she said. 'But I'm not like that . . . I'm not nasty.'

'No,' I said.

'And anyway, I wouldn't want to sink to their level.'

'Yeah . . .' I said. But I didn't really like thinking about that sort of stuff. Not anymore.

I guess there were good sides to Dawn being back, though. I got a lot of work done. And I didn't mind nodding while she talked. I didn't even mind that talcum-powder smell she seemed to carry round with her. Even though it tickled my nose. It made me think of her fish tank, her mum and those cheap cigarettes, it made me think of a lot of stuff that I hadn't remembered for ages. The creak that her bed had made, and I bent down to do another sum.

It was better than I'd thought it would be, anyway. Better, I guess, until biology came.

Holly spotted her straight away, just like I'd known she would. I watched a wince spread out across her face, walking up towards me. It was capped off with a smile, I saw, and that old earth-opening-up phrase ran round inside my head.

'Ah . . .' she said, but she didn't go to sit somewhere else. 'You've got a new *friend*.'

'This is Dawn.' I didn't look up from the cover of my exercise book. 'This is Holly.'

The cotton of my bodysuit was sagging forward, bent over like I was. It was a stupid choice anyway, I thought. Stupid to believe it might have looked alright. Holly was wearing jeans as well, but they weren't the same as mine. They were blue, proper Levi's, and the vest she wore on top didn't show her nipples. I guess it didn't need to.

'Dawn . . .' Holly said. She looked up at the ceiling, like she was enjoying the way it just rolled off her tongue. Dawn was grinning, but then she didn't know just what was going on. I thought she looked a little like a dog. Like the way it pants when it goes on heat. 'That's a nice name.' Her smile slid up one side. 'Like the morning dew . . . like a beautiful sunrise . . .' she said, and looked back down to where we sat. 'Nice acne too.'

Dawn's smile slipped a little bit, but Holly had already looked away.

'Seen Robin yet?' she said. 'He's gagging for it, I reckon. Said you didn't even snog.'

'Bell'd almost gone. We didn't have a lot of time.' I tried to make my grin kind of letchy. Not just pathetic, like the way it felt. 'I'm sure we'll make up for it,' I said.

'Nice what?' Dawn said.

I couldn't quite bring myself to look round.

Holly let her bag slip down to the floor. I watched her pull her pencil case out. Not a zippy one like mine, like everybody else's. Holly had a tin and she didn't even need to look after it. It had a lot of names on in Tippex, a lot of funny insults and cartoons of dicks. My name was there too, I saw, even if it did start the sentence ... LIKES IT UP THE SHITTER.

'Have you been to see the doctor yet?' I said.

'The doctor? You're the one that needs cosmetic surgery.'

'About the test, I mean.'

'Oh that. Na, I did another test. Came out clear. Are you gonna fuck him?' she said.

'What d'you mean *nice*...?' Dawn's voice whined round, like a Hoover shutting down.

'Fucking him,' Holly said. 'That's so rough. I know he's my friend and everything, but he *has* got a bit of an Oxy problem.' She laughed. 'Whiteheads all down his back.' She shrugged. 'Your taste,' she said. And I couldn't think of any answer. My legs hung, short and stubby underneath the desk. I could feel the way the stool made my thighs spread into cellulite. You take what you can get, I guess. I opened up my book.

Holly glanced at Dawn one last time. It looked like she was making sure.

'*Nice* T-shirt,' she said.

And I sort of couldn't help but laugh.

Dawn went to meet her new flute teacher at lunchtime, and I tried to hide my sigh. I was meeting Robin by the football posts, acne or no, and the thought of taking her along had made my stomach go all hard.

I watched her walk off as the bell rang. Her hair hung

down, looking flatter by the minute, and her boots scuffed the concrete every step. The sun had come out full and it must have been seventy degrees. She was wearing tight black jeans as well, throttling her down to the ankles. I wondered vaguely if she was in mourning, starting off across the pitch.

I found Robin down by the river, past the end of the goals where he'd said we'd meet. Down the slope and through the brambles, and I'd got mud on my boots by the time I got there. He was smoking a spliff, I saw, but he didn't look as nervous as me.

'Hi,' I said. I couldn't think of anything else.

'Hi.' He didn't look up, though, as I sat on the grass by his side. It was still pretty wet from the dew. 'You're late,' he said.

'Sorry, I had to . . . talk to someone.' I moved my bum, tried to get comfy. 'You Ok?'

He only shrugged though, still watching the water as it moved. It was brown, kind of cloudy as it bubbled over the stones. There's an ICI factory just a few miles upstream from the school and sometimes, on a really good day, you can see the oil that their chemicals leave in the stream. The boys used to jump in it when I was still a First Year, splashing and shouting and stuff, and it was kind of fun to watch them. That all stopped a while back, though, when their skin started flaking off for no reason. I guess the teachers thought it might not be a good idea.

Robin glanced back a moment, tapping the ash off his spliff.

'I can see your tits in that,' he said. 'D'you do it on purpose or what?'

'I . . .' I looked down at my front. Maybe I should have listened to Dawn. 'No,' I said. 'I didn't realize . . .'

'Got lipstick on as well.' He shifted his shoulders, breathed out as he turned round.

'Well . . . yeah.' I tried a grin. 'Makes me look a bit better.'

'It makes you look like a slut.'

Thanks, I thought, but I didn't say anything to him.

'Here.' He looked at me properly for the first time, handing me a handkerchief from his pocket. I'd sort of expected a piece of snotty kitchen roll. It was expensive, though, proper cotton with his name stitched across it.

'Nice hanky.'

'You taking the piss?'

'Course not.' I wondered if I should say something else, but he looked away. I waited for him to look back before I wiped it off. There was a funny look in his eyes when he turned back to me to watch. It was a nice look, but kind of angry at the same time. His mouth looked like it was trying to smile, going down around the edges. I wiped the cotton across my mouth. I wiped it hard and it rubbed a little bit, but that was sort of nice as well. Intense. That was the look: intense.

'You've missed a bit,' he said.

'Where?'

He picked his finger up, really slow, and moved it towards my face. His hand was steady, but his finger wobbled just a tiny bit. There was dirt down the crack at the side of his nail. Bitten nails. He didn't jab or poke. Nothing fast, nothing violent. But he put his finger against the corner of my mouth and he pressed. Hard. I felt the nail bite in a little bit, even though it was short.

'There,' he said.

Still looking in my eyes, I felt his other hand slide on to my stomach. It stretched a little bit, moving towards my boobs. And that was when he leaned over and he snogged me.

It wasn't a nice, romantic kiss like you're supposed to have in the open air. It was wet, full of spit, and I could feel his teeth clicking against mine. His hair got up my nose, and he tasted of cigarettes and breath mints. He squeezed my tit so it hurt but I didn't say anything. I couldn't really, with his tongue in my mouth. A big tongue, I thought. Bigger than anyone I'd snogged before. He squeezed, and it was nothing like the first day Joel had touched me. He didn't feel afraid. Feeling him squeeze like that, I thought about the things he'd said. A see-through top, and I did it on purpose so they could all see my tits. He was right, I guess. Right, as he squeezed harder, and I wondered if his dick was big enough to match his tongue. I wondered if I'd even know, not having anything to compare it to.

We snogged for ages. I was bored after seconds. Not that I wanted to go any further. It made me wonder why I did any of this stuff anyway. My tongue was starting to ache and I could feel my hair matting up at the back, where it was rubbing on the ground. I thought about what Holly had said, whiteheads all down his back, and he breathed. Hard breath, like he'd just been for a jog.

No, I didn't really want to go any further. But I didn't stop him when he put his hand down my trousers, I was just glad I'd picked out the right pants. The same pants that Joel had liked so much, I thought, and Craig as well. I wondered if he knew that.

Then he stuck his fingers in them. And I stopped wondering.

I did have pubes. Not loads but enough, I thought, enough not to feel stupid. He rolled over on top of me and he wasn't as heavy as I expected. But my hand got trapped underneath, and I wondered if I should say something. He was thin and the bones of his pelvis rubbed against mine and hurt me. Then, with the hand he'd been bruising my boob with, he grabbed my own hand. It felt much smaller than his, and the way he grabbed made the bones in my fingers rub against each other. He put it down the front of his jeans. And it was funny, I suppose. He wasn't so quiet when he got rolling.

He had loads of pubes, but he wasn't any older than me. I don't know, maybe boys are just hairier than girls. My one hand was bent at a weird angle in his waistband, the other was going numb underneath my arse. I thought about whether I'd be able to pull it out without him noticing. I wanted to ask him to undo his fly but the way he'd pulled my hand like that made me think he might get cross. So I put up with it. I felt around.

It was big. Bigger than I'd expected and harder as well. Penises don't have bones in them. I knew that from biology, but it really felt that way. I squeezed and he grunted into my mouth. It made my teeth vibrate. So I'd squeezed then. I wondered what to do next. Squeeze again was all I could think of, though. It seemed to work.

I felt his hand search around for a while, pinching my pubes into the fold of my jeans.

He stopped feeling pretty quick, though, and I guess he found what he was looking for. Because that was when he put a finger inside me. It hurt. It hurt a lot more than I'd thought it would, not that I'd spent hours considering it or anything. It also reminded me really strongly of something I couldn't quite put my finger on. I squeezed his dick for the third time, trying to remember what that feeling was. It felt too big, like it shouldn't really go there, and I measured the difference between the size of his finger and the thing I was holding in my hand. I tried not to think about it.

Then he said something in my ear and I couldn't quite make it out. I didn't want to ask him what it'd been, it seemed out of place, but I couldn't think of any other way.

'What?' It sounded too loud with only his heavy breathing filling the last few minutes.

'Wank it,' he said, and I had time to wonder what he meant before he put his finger even further in and I remembered what it felt like. What it felt *exactly* like. Inserting a tampon. It seemed obvious once I'd thought of it. Only tampons don't have sharp nails, and they have proper plastic applicators so they go in easily. I grunted, and I suppose he must have thought it was pleasure because he did it again, harder.

'Wank it!' he said for the third time, and I tried to conjure up the image of the gesture people made, I made, with my hand when they said wanker. I moved my hand up and down. Then he bit down on my lip, so hard that I thought it would bleed, and I was tempted to stop moving my hand, just in case he did it again.

He moved his finger in and out and in and out, till it felt like he was trying to rub two sticks together and start a fire. And he grunted and groaned and said other things I couldn't make out. This time I didn't bother to ask what they were.

I don't think he came. I didn't feel anything like that. But eventually he rolled off me and he took his finger out. I closed my eyes, head back against the bank. I was glad.

I didn't walk back with him when the bell went. I heard his footsteps trail away and he didn't say goodbye. And, still lying there, I remember wondering if he'd tell Joel or Craig or even Holly. I remember being kind of glad that I didn't have anyone to tell.

Dawn was waiting for me in afternoon registration, and I could tell just by the look on her face that she'd slipped back down into depression. She didn't smile at me as I made my way through the desks.

'How's it going?' I said.

She shrugged.

'Well . . . How was the flute lesson?'

'It ended half an hour ago. I tried looking for you but you were obviously . . . busy.'

She pushed her pencil case back and forward across the table as I sat down. I touched my hair, trying to push it back into place, and I wondered why it felt like there was a sign on my forehead. Flushed and crooked: *I've just been wanking off my boyfriend.*

'I'm sorry,' I said.

'It's Ok. I don't know why I thought it'd be any different here than boarding school.'

'What?' I couldn't quite get my head round the conversation. I tried to blink it clear.

'You're busy with *Holly* and *Robin*. I'll just end up on my own again. I should've known it wasn't going to work out for me. Nothing else ever does . . .'

'I . . . I thought you had your flute lesson.'

'You don't care about my flute lesson! You don't care about anything except your new friends! Just letting her laugh at me! You promised we were going to start again!'

'And . . . and we are.'

'Then prove it!'

Her lip was wobbling, halfway to a sob, and I could see her foundation had wiped off in a streak across her forehead. Looking at her like that made me think of Dad, his hand on my shoulder while he'd talked. How unhappy she'd been without a proper close friend, how he didn't even know any of my friends anymore. Her nose cast a shadow, heavy on one cheek, and I wondered if it could all be true. I wondered, still feeling my pants pushed up into a knot, pushed up where Robin'd put them.

'*I'm sorry.*' But she only looked at me, the reflection of a window crossed white inside her eyes. She had dark eyes, pretty when you looked at them close. 'I'm sorry.' She had eyes just like Dad's.

So, for the next couple of weeks, it was splitting my time down the middle. When it was just me and Robin, I split the lunchtime half and half; first half with him, second with Dawn. And she'd ask me sometimes what I did with him, why I wanted to spend time with him at all. I gave a lot of different answers to her, that he was kind or funny or whatever, but none of them were really true. I guess the real answer was I didn't know. I'd never stopped to think.

I didn't like Robin, but I had a lot of respect for him, and that sort of made up for it. It didn't matter that he had spots, or that he was ugly, he had this aggressive confidence that made you forget. He was nasty, and even though he fancied me, he hated me as well. He made that obvious from the start. I sort of liked him hating me though. I knew exactly where I stood: right at his feet. I remember watching a nature documentary once, about these animals called ring-tailed lemurs. The pack was matriarchal, but when the mating season came around, the guys were pretty much free to do what they wanted. What they wanted to do was fuck. They'd meet each other, but they didn't bite or scratch or hurt. They screamed, they wagged their tails around over their heads, and after a minute or so, the weaker party would just give in. Roll over on its back, its stomach in the air. Robin reminded me of that, like I'd come face to face with something stronger than me. And I rolled over. I served, and I did it as well as I possibly could.

I knew who I was when I was with Robin. I was his girlfriend, and it was satisfying, like doing a good essay. Only Robin never marked my mistakes in red ink so I never knew what I'd done wrong. He was like Dad in that way.

He told me I was fat and I should eat less. I agreed, and I didn't need him to tell me. He didn't let me wear make-up either. I felt naked, not wearing it, and maybe that was why. Every morning we'd skip Assembly together and he'd take me to the toilets so I could wash it off in front of him. He liked to watch me doing it. Sometimes, at break time, I'd go back and put it on again. Not because I really thought it made me look better, blusher and mascara and lipstick, not even because I thought he wouldn't notice. I knew he'd notice. I wanted him to. I liked the expression on his face when he watched me wash it off.

He taught me how to inhale, how to skin up. He taught me lots of things and I preferred dope to booze. It didn't make the room spin and it didn't make me throw up. And when I woke up the next morning, it didn't feel like someone had spent the night beating me over the head with a stick of hot candy floss. Also, it stopped me thinking. Everything would be repeated over and over in my head until it became gibberish and that was fine with me because I never had much interesting to think about anyway.

We'd sit out on our own by the river at lunchtime. I'd ask him to skin up and he wouldn't. Not at first anyway.

He'd make me suck his dick or let him touch me. He never got a proper hard-on, though. He never came either. I don't think he wanted to: he might look stupid, or say something stupid, he might give too much away. But afterwards he'd always skin up, or he'd watch while he made me do it. I was crap at it.

The days I liked best, though, were the ones he let me spend with everyone. Even if Dawn had to come with on those days because I couldn't split them down the middle. I wanted to be with Holly and Joel and Craig. They had a lot of laughs at lunchtime and I wanted to laugh with them. We shared spliffs while they put Dawn on watch duty so they didn't have to look at her face. She sat and ate her packed lunch and didn't say a word. But then she wasn't there to make friends. She was there to keep an eye on me.

We'd all be laughing and joking, and sometimes they'd even crack gags about her, and that was hard. I couldn't laugh, because she was sitting there. I couldn't not laugh, because I was *their* friend now. I developed this half-smile just for those special occasions. Smiling with half of my face. The half that she couldn't see.

I could have made it easy for her. I don't know, I could have made it look like I really did care more about her than anyone else. But that would have meant no Robin, and no Robin meant no Holly. No new friends. I didn't want to lose them. I couldn't lose them, not after being so happy. I didn't want to be myself again.

I didn't mind touching Robin. I could make him happy, make him pleased, even though he never came. Sometimes

I wondered if he saved it all up and got home and wanked, where no one could see the funny expression he might get on his face.

I would have let him fuck me, I even went to the family planning on my own to get some morning-after pills in case he did. I liked to do things for him. I liked to suck his dick, kneeling in front of him. I liked the position of my body when I did it. I liked the way he looked down at me from way, way up. I liked the way it hurt my knees.

But I hated him touching me. Letting him do it made me feel sick. I hated the feel of his hands. I hated the look in his eyes. I hated my body, and I think he knew it. Sometimes he told me to lie still, and he'd just look at me and not do anything. Sometimes he tried to make me come. I think he wanted to be the only person who could do it. He touched me and I lay there like a rock, feeling sick, trying to think of anything except what he was doing. Humming to myself so I couldn't hear his noises, I'd wait for the moment I could suck his dick. The moment when he'd let me alone.

And it was weird. Letting Joel and all those other boys feel me up hadn't been disgusting. I hadn't really cared. I only knew that it helped, and they liked me, and that suddenly I had friends. But Robin wanted to make me feel good when he did it, I guess that was the difference. And I didn't want to feel good. I didn't want to like it. The idea of liking it seemed kind of gross.

Still, it was Ok for a while. I could pretty much put up with it. And I suppose Dawn was always useful like that too. If things started getting bad I had a good excuse to go. The sad thing was, I think she knew it. Even if she couldn't quite put it into words, she didn't like to think about sex. But sometimes when I'd meet her, halfway through the lunchtime, she'd watch me tuck my shirt back in and her face would shut up tight.

'You only come to see me when you're bored of him,' she'd say.

'That's not true.' Pulling my pants out of the crack, trying not to remember his hands.

'I wish . . . I wish I was as interesting as him.' She'd look up at me then, but I could never quite make sense of the expression on her face.

Dawn was better than an excuse, she was a reason. Which was maybe why things stayed Ok until the day that she had flu. It was well into the summer, a couple of weeks before the holiday, and I remember it pretty well because Dawn never missed school. I guess if she'd taken days off for being ill she'd still be learning the alphabet by now.

It went to her chest, though. That was the difference, and she'd said the day before that things were getting bad. Dawn never talked about her asthma much, which was funny because she moaned about so much other stuff. She never used her inhaler in class either, she'd go out to the loo to do it, and everyone thought she had permanent diarrhoea. But the day before she called in sick I could still see something was wrong.

She had the flute's hard case under her arm, walking towards me from the music block.

'How's things?' She shrugged, staring up through her hair. 'How was the lesson?'

Her eyes didn't move. 'You don't remember anything,' she said.

'What d'you mean? Remember what?'

'Oh, nothing important. Or not for *you* anyway. Nothing *big*. Don't *worry* about it.'

'What is it? I'm sorry . . . You know my memory.' I tried for a laugh and failed.

'It was my exam today,' she said. She looked down at the ground, and I could see somebody's half-eaten sausage roll there, squished into the concrete. 'My flute exam.'

'Flute . . .? Oh shit, Dawn. I'm sorry. I should have written it down . . . How'd it go?'

'How do you *think* it went? I can't do it. It's as simple as that . . . I'm just not good enough, I . . .' But she turned away then, coughing with a shallow kind of breath. She looked like our cat, I thought. Our cat when he got furballs. 'Nevermind.' Her hair shook in ripples, shrugging as she coughed.

'Are you Ok?' I watched her wave a hand at me. 'Should . . . should I pat your back?' She straightened up though, not catching my eye. I wondered if her mascara had run.

'I have to go to the toilet,' she said. Her face was flushed under the foundation.

'Should I come with or something . . .?'

'No!' She coughed again, and she didn't look so tall, I thought, bent over in that way. 'I'll be fine,' she said, backing away from me, her shoulders still jumping in a twitch.

And I felt a little stupid just standing there. Just watching her walk off.

*

The day after that was a Friday, the day that she didn't come in. And I thought about it all that morning, no excuse, no reason. We'd spend the whole lunchtime together. I was nervous, I guess. But I was kind of excited as well. Like the way you get excited when you're little and you know you're going to the seaside. I spent the morning with Holly, just listening and laughing. Tapping my fingers on the desk. And I waited for lunchtime to come.

He took me down to the river, the same place as usual but I think we both knew it was different. We didn't really talk, and he didn't skin up as soon as we got there. I lay on the grass there, waiting for whatever would happen, with the nettles and the brambles and the river drying into mud.

He had his hand in my pants when it happened. I could feel my toes biting into the end of my shoes with nerves. I was chewing the skin off my lip, moving my hand up and down, which I'd got pretty practised at, and wishing for the bell to ring. A fire alarm would do nicely, I thought, and he leaned over and said something in my ear.

'I'm going to make you come.'

I could feel the little droplets of spit hit the inside of my ear when he said it. My stomach rolled over and I wondered if I was going to vomit. I hoped so. It might give me an excuse to go back to the school. Still, that feeling wasn't quite as bad as when he started to move away. He got up on his knees, pug nose just poking through his hair, and he backed down the bank. Till he was level with my knees. I think that was when I realized. He was going to put his mouth there.

The thought of it made me want to puke, made me want to curl up in a ball and hide somewhere. It was the most horrible thing I'd ever thought of. Disgusting. I wanted to run away. I wanted to beg him not to do it, please not to do it. But I didn't say a word when he pulled down my pants.

I remember he only got them halfway down my thighs. I remember they cut into me, lying there on the grass. And that was good, because it gave me something else to think about. I remember wishing I was dead, and then thinking that was stupid; I could get through it. It was such a little thing.

It felt like washing in the bath, and I closed my eyes and concentrated on that. On imagining Robin away. On being on my own. Washing in the bath, I thought. Washing in the bath. Washing in the bath washing in the bath washing. Until the words weren't mine anymore. Meaningless, ugly syllables and I could almost smell shampoo.

I opened my eyes when he stopped, so glad. I watched the top of his head stop still. And when he looked up he had blood around his mouth.

'There's blood under my nails,' he said quietly. 'Is there blood round my mouth?'

'No,' I said, 'but . . . let's go and have lunch anyway. I need to go to the loo.'

He knew I was lying. He always knew. And he wiped his sleeve across his mouth. I lay there and I stared at him and I wondered why I was so scared. The sleeve came away purple. Red on blue cotton. He looked at me for a moment longer. I wished he would say something.

Something funny, like he did sometimes, to let me know everything was Ok. But he didn't say anything funny. He hit me instead.

It wasn't a hard hit. I think even while he was doing it he knew that he shouldn't be and held back. It was an open slap instead of a punch, like he sometimes punched the blokes he was fighting with. I was surprised. But I wasn't surprised because he hit me. I was surprised because I liked it.

I just stared at him, and I could feel this lovely redness spreading across my cheek. I lay there, a thirteen-year-old girl on her lunch break, lying in the open sun with the elastic of her knickers cutting into her thighs. I lay there, and I smiled.

He got up then. He got up, zipped up his fly, and walked away. I watched him top the rise and disappear on to the football pitch. I was still smiling when I pulled my knickers up. Still thinking about the redness, about the way it felt. Hot, sliding across my cheek. I thought about the way my flesh crushed against my teeth, the expression on his face. I thought and I felt. And I knew that this was what they called sexual excitement.

Dawn was Ok again by Monday, or back in school at least. I saw her out ahead of us as I walked over to the D&T block with Holly. She had her knee-length skirt on instead of trousers and it looked out of place with all the other girls in belts. Her calves came out, long and blotchy, from under a nylon hem. It was funny, I thought, how they managed to look stumpy even though she was so tall.

'She's got such *nice* taste in clothes,' Holly said. 'I just love polyester.' She giggled.

But then she didn't really get it. Dawn would have looked just as bad in Holly's clothes. Even French Connection can't hide insecurity like that. Sometimes though, looking at her from a distance, I almost thought she could be changed. The right make-up or something like that.

I pulled my bag up higher on my shoulder, glanced out towards the English block. The windows looked blank, just blue-grey like the uniform, and I could see the paint was peeling round their frames.

'I better go and say hello.'

Holly looked at me. 'Yeah right . . . or *Dawny might get upset*. So sweet, you two . . .'

I didn't answer her though. Biting my lip, there wasn't much I could say. I guess it just had to be done. Speeding up my walk, I caught up through the lines. I saw Joel out of the corner of my eye, carrying his folder. He's really into D&T, even if he thinks school is shit, and I gave him my best sexy smile. Which was why it seemed so odd, I think, that he only laughed down at Craig, walking by his side.

'How are you then?' I said. 'Are you feeling better?'

'Huh?' Dawn looked round. She had a very long face, Dawn, only all the length seemed to be in her nose. 'There wasn't anything wrong with me,' she said quickly. 'I don't know, it's Mum. She thinks I need to stay in bed or something when I'm ill. I'm *Ok* . . .'

I nodded. 'Well . . . good.'

'You didn't ring,' she said, taking the steps up to the door. She held it open for me.

'No I . . .'

'It doesn't matter.' She stopped, looking flat at the classroom. 'I know why,' she said. And I didn't bother to correct her.

I sat with Holly on a desk for two that lesson, with Dawn tucked in on the end. We were doing isometric projection but I hadn't really started mine yet. I've never been very good at D&T. I don't even understand cogs.

'Listen.' Holly bent forward suddenly, but I only looked up in time to see her slide back in the chair again. 'No nevermind.' She laughed. She had such a pretty laugh. When I laughed all you could see was the gap in my front teeth. 'Forget it,' she said.

'She can't forget it now you've *said* it,' Dawn said. Holly didn't bother to look over.

'Look I've just got to ask you this one thing,' she said. 'Fuck it's *so* rough. I *have* to know if it's true.' She looked at me, waiting, and I thought again of Joel's laugh.

'What?' I had to lean forward too then. I didn't want to be the one left out.

'Is it . . . Oh Christ! . . . Right.' She straightened her face. 'Is it true about the gob job?'

I felt my stomach roll.

'What?' I tried to keep my face in the same position as it had been before those two small words. Gob job, I thought. I put a hand up to my cheek. 'What d'you mean?'

'Robin said . . .' She bent over double. Collapsing, like it was too heavy to come out of her mouth. 'He said he gave you a gob job and . . .' She made a retching noise. 'And got *period blood round his mouth!*' Beside me I could almost feel Dawn stiffen up. I heard her breath, though, sucked in like a fish. I wondered why *she* was worrying.

'Period blood! Fuck *OFF!*' I tried her retching noise out. It came out pretty well too.

'Robin said that?' Dawn's head seemed even longer and her face was very still.

'So it's a lie?' Holly looked at me a moment before she burst out laughing. '*Rough!*'

'*Course* it's a fucking lie! God what an arsehole!' My stomach kept on going, rolling round and over as Joel's laugh spun out again. 'I can't believe he'd say that! *Fuckwit!*'

'Better sort him out . . .' Her laughter trailed off, leaving a smirk. 'He told everyone.'

'Really?' I looked at her, but still there was a smile. 'What a *cunt!*' I said. And finally she dropped her eyes. I breathed out. Everything seemed a little easier when Holly wasn't watching. And leaning back in my seat, I caught sight of Dawn's face. It was twisted up, all anger and embarrassment.

'I don't like him,' she said quietly. I wasn't hugely surprised.

Holly was right too, I did have to sort him out. She wouldn't have stood for it so I couldn't stand for it. QED. And I tried not to think about what he'd say, tapping Dawn on the shoulder as the bell rang for lunch.

'Um . . . Dawn, I need to ask a . . . a sort of favour.'

'You know you can always ask me for anything. That's what friends are for.'

'Yeah . . . and that's good. But I need to spend this lunch with Robin. I have to talk this through with him.'

'You can't have him talking about you like that. If he loved you, he wouldn't talk about you behind your back.'

'*Loved me?*' Yeah right. I could almost see them talking about it, Robin and Joel and Craig. All of them sitting forward, passing the spliff round. I could see the expressions on their faces, half disgust, half laughter. *And then I looked up at my nails* . . . Hippy blood, I thought, and I clenched my nails in tight. 'I've got to sort it out, anyway . . .'

'Sort him out, you mean. He treats you like dirt, you know. And I hate to see you hurt. It's only because I care about you. Because I care about what happens to you.'

'I know you do . . . but . . . you understand I mean all lunchtime. This isn't going to be over in five minutes, and I can understand you being pissed off, I mean: he treats me like this and what do I do? Spend more time with him, right? And what do you get – dumped. I can see how it'd look like that to you, I really can. But you have to under-stand that I . . . I *really* don't want to do this. I . . . I just have to and . . .'

'It's *Ok.*'

'What?'

'It's Ok. Don't worry about it. Take as long as you want. I know how these boyfriend/girlfriend things take . . . you know, time.'

'You do?'

'Course I do. I'll see you at registration. You can tell me how he took it.' And she walked off, waving. She was smiling a huge smile, but it wasn't pretty. A generous kind of smile, I don't know. I just watched her go. I didn't want to change her mind. And I didn't have the time to ask how he'd take what.

I found Robin down in the same place as usual. He was trying to get a lighter going in the breeze, holding a little wedge of hash in one hand. I saw him glance round at me, hearing my footsteps. I saw him look at his watch and I tried to think if I'd made some kind of promise that I couldn't now remember.

'Where the fuck have you been?'

'I had to see Dawn.' I watched him, trying to see if he knew what I was going to say.

'Why?'

'Cos she needed to talk to me.' I didn't sit down. 'She's got no one else to talk to.'

'That's her own fault for being such a rough bitch.'

'Don't put her down like that.' I tried to take a breath but everything felt clogged.

'Why not? You do.' I couldn't think of anything to say to that. I wondered if I should dive right in or talk a little around the subject first. I wondered if I really had a choice.

'How are you anyway?' I walked down the bank to stand next to him, watching him wave the lighter underneath his hand. He didn't look at me, but that was Ok. I guess we were both concentrating really.

'Excellent,' he said, dropping the lighter. 'Mum and Dan had a fight last night.'

'That's good is it? Your mum and dad having a fight?' I wondered if I was being sarcastic.

'He's not my fuckin dad. *Dan*, I said.'

'Oh.' I swallowed, bent my fingers round each other, looking for something to watch.

'He's a fuckin prick. You never know . . .' he said. 'Maybe they'll keep fighting.'

'You don't like him,' I said, then wished I hadn't.

'No,' he said coldly, not looking at me. 'I don't like him.'

'But your mum likes him.'

'She's got shit taste.' He paused for a minute, pinching out another clump of tobacco and spreading it over the papers. 'She's thick anyway,' he said, as though that proved it.

'She can't be *that* thick.'

'Why not?'

'Well . . . she's a primary school teacher.'

'So she's a thick teacher. She can't do a fuckin thing. That's *why* she's a teacher.'

I thought of Dad then. Those who can't do, and I wondered if I should say something else.

'Why don't you like your dad?'

'He's not my fuckin dad! He's a prick . . . My dad wasn't a prick.'

I nodded, keeping quiet for a minute while he settled down. 'Where is he now?' I said.

'Fuck knows. He was right though. Getting the fuck out of there, with her bitching at him all the time. I'm glad her fuckin kids died. I don't want his kids in my house . . .'

'Was she sad?' It was strange, even talking about her she didn't feel real.

He shrugged. 'I don't give a shit. It's her fault if she's

sad. She shouldn't have shacked up with him.' I waited but he didn't speak again. I guess there wasn't much left to say.

'Holly told me something today,' I said. He didn't look at me, though, staring down as he held a flame to the end of his spliff. 'Holly said you told everyone . . . that . . . that . . . you told them all about what happened.' God, that sounded pathetic.

'What you talking about?'

'She said you told everyone about . . . about giving me a . . . giving me oral sex.'

Oral sex. The words sounded like they'd been invented stupid, specially to embarrass anyone that had to say them.

'She's lying,' he said. His hair looked very bright, with the sun shining in from behind.

'No she isn't. She . . . she knew. How would she know if you didn't tell her?'

'I don't know.' He tapped the ash off, looked over at me. 'Maybe you told her.'

It was funny, he seemed so calm sitting there like that. Just smoking a spliff, just watching the river go by. And it was hard to join that picture up to the feeling of his hand coming down on my cheek.

'But I didn't tell her,' I said quietly. It came out so soft that I wasn't sure he'd hear it. Over the stream, shouts and laughter in the distance behind us, he didn't answer me. He turned round instead. Balancing his forearm on one bended knee, he looked at me. And I saw the spliff wobble, in between his fingers, when he shrugged.

*

I don't know what I felt, walking back to registration at two. Only that I wasn't nervous anymore, or scared. It wasn't a bad thing, I guess, just to let it lie. I thought it was a kind of grown-up thing really. And at least we hadn't fought.

No, collapsing in a chair by the window, I wasn't sure how I felt at all.

Thinking about it though, it didn't really matter.

I didn't like Dawn's smile, wandering through to sit next to me. She looked like a clucky hen, and her head was too far up. It made me wonder what was wrong.

'So how'd it go?' She grinned, folded down into the seat.

'How'd what go?'

I watched her blink. 'Well, he didn't scream or cry or anything?' She looked past me, at the concrete through the window. 'Shows he never loved you in the first place.'

'What are you talking about?' I tried for cross, or even confused. I didn't really get there though. I didn't really care.

'Well . . . well you did dump him didn't you? Tell him where to get off?'

'Dump him?' I said. 'Course I didn't dump him.'

And that was when her face fell off.

'But . . . but after all the things he said . . . after the *horrible* way he treated you!'

'He hasn't been horrible to me, Dawn.' I looked away from her. God, I felt tired. 'Just leave it Ok?'

'Leave it.' Her voice was flat. Staring down at the stippled grey plastic of the desk, it made me think of board games with her. Monopoly when she was losing, and I gave a little sigh. 'Leave it. That's all you can say to me. After trying to *help* you . . . after trying to make you see what a . . . what an *arsehole* he is!'

I didn't answer her, even though she left a pause. It didn't feel worth the effort.

'Well I see,' she said, but I wondered if she did. I wondered if she really saw anything at all. 'You don't know what's best for you. That's all,' she said.

And she was quiet for a moment before she spoke again.

'Just a good thing that I do.'

I can remember when I first met Dawn, even though I was pretty young. She was much more shy then, and her nose wasn't quite as long. I remember it well because she wasn't like the other kids at Primary. I knew that straight off, when the headteacher took her up in front of the Assembly.

'This is Dawn,' she said loudly, with Dawn staring down at her tights. Her hair was lighter then, I think, and it didn't drag her scalp down quite as much. 'Dawn's a very special girl,' Miss Higgins said, with one hand on her shoulder. 'Because Dawn is the tallest girl in the *whole school*. Isn't that nice?'

No one really thought it was nice though. That was obvious by the way that no one went to be her partner in Dance and Movement. I guess if we were all pretending to be flowers, no one wanted to be partners with a climbing shrub.

Dawn had big feet. Everyone stared at her when she

took her shoes and socks off. She wasn't an eight or nine, you see, she'd already gone into grown-up sizes. Dawn was a Size One. I remember it so well because it reminded me of Michael. He wasn't even in Infants yet but he had big feet too. Mum said that meant he'd be tall when he was older, but Dad had only laughed. He said he didn't think Michael would be tall at all. Dad thought he'd be a normal size, he'd just have surf boards for feet.

I told Dad about Dawn as soon as I got home that day. Her dad was still alive then, I think, and I'm not sure Dad had even heard of Jack. He was still interested though, as soon as I told him. Dad was always interested in my news from school.

He nodded as I told him what she looked like. He even told Mum to switch the radio off while I was talking. And when I finished, he leaned across the table towards me. I remember that because I had to stop my legs from swinging in case I kicked him by mistake. I didn't mind stopping, though stuff like this was just way more important.

'Tomorrow you go into Dance and Movement and you ask if *you* can be her partner.'

'That's what I thought!' I said. But I guess it really hadn't been.

'You don't have to be like all those other arseholes,' he said. 'We're different, right? *We* don't pick on the underdog.' And I remember that he smiled at me, leaning back into his chair. 'Now come on,' he said, grinning. 'Let's go watch TV.'

*

Dad wasn't grinning when he got in that evening, though, the evening after I'd talked to Robin. I wasn't surprised when he came to sit next to me at the kitchen table. I was doing my maths homework, and in the other room Mum was reading the *Guardian*. He'd done a big paper chuck-out the day before and she was having trouble getting through all the ones she'd bought since. I didn't know where Michael was. I didn't really care.

Dad lowered himself into the seat. His tie was slightly undone, along with his top button, and I could see the way his neck skin folded over his collar in tiny little wrinkles, staring at the table. No, I wasn't surprised. I guess I'd known already that something was up. I could tell by the way his face hung down, by the way he kept turning it towards me.

He sighed instead of saying hello. It had the same effect, though, and I put down my pen. I watched it roll into the spine of the text book and sit there casting a shadow. From the other room, I heard Mum turn the page.

I was nervous, and my stomach did feel heavy inside the elastic of my tights. There was something else as well though, watching him prepare himself, trying to think of what he'd have to say. It made me think of Holly and her dad giving her a Talk. I pushed my hair back behind my shoulders, waiting. I guess we're just both too rebellious.

'I . . . I got a phone call today,' Dad said. His tone of voice made me think of the PTA, school secretaries. *I'm disappointed to report that your daughter* . . . And I crossed my legs beneath the table. I'd tell Holly, I thought. First thing tomorrow I'd tell her.

'Off Dawn,' Dad said. And I stopped thinking about Holly.

'Dawn? *My* Dawn?'

Dad shifted his bum like he couldn't get comfortable. 'Your Dawn . . .' he said. 'Yes.'

'Why?' It came out too loud, and through the kitchen wall I heard Mum cough. Loud, I thought, and guilty, and I wished I hadn't said it. I wasn't guilty of anything. He didn't answer me at first, taking it all slowly. 'She caught me in my lunch break.'

'Sorry,' I said. I wasn't really sure what I was sorry for though, and he just shrugged.

'We didn't talk for long.' Talk, I thought. Not chat, *talk*, and I remembered Dawn's expression in registration. You don't know what's best for you, she'd said. And I don't know, maybe she was even right. 'She said I ought to . . . to talk to you,' he said.

'Talk to me . . .' I tried to make it sound light, but Dad's face dragged it down. 'Ok,' I said. Thinking about it, there wasn't really much else I could do.

'She told me about this boy you've been . . . been hanging around with.'

I didn't say anything, just nodded slowly, trying to get my brain to work. Boy. I didn't like that word. I wondered if that was how Dawn had described him, a boy. Like she had the right to look down. Robin wasn't just a boy. I didn't want Dad thinking that.

'Well is it true?' he said.

'Well . . . well yeah.' I recrossed my legs, sitting opposite him. I tried to lift my head a little bit. 'His name's Robin,'

I said, and then I wondered why. It wasn't even a very good name, not like Jack or Philip. 'He's nice . . .'

'That's not what Dawn said.'

He frowned like he wasn't quite sure how to go on. Not what Dawn said. Somehow I wasn't surprised. Dawn buckled when you said a swear word. Dawn hated cigarettes, and she had never even snogged anyone. Dawn, I thought, just didn't understand.

And sitting at the table there, seeing Dad's face so constipated over what to say, I wondered how I looked to him. After all, it wasn't such a big deal. I had a boyfriend. I was almost fourteen. I wondered if I looked pretty, my hands resting on the wood. I wondered if I looked grownup.

'Said you've been smoking.' He said it low: just thought I ought to mention it. 'I'm probably not a very good influence on you. But you know, just cos I do stupid things doesn't mean you should follow my lead.'

He looked at me but I didn't say anything. I wasn't following his lead, I thought. I just *was* a smoker. Like Holly and Robin and nothing like Dawn. That, I thought, was me.

'She said he was, I don't know, not a very good influence on you. Said he did drugs.'

I looked away, wondering how he would handle it. I knew he'd smoked dope. He said back in the sixties it was just the done thing. I wondered if it was the done thing now.

'I don't know if he does drugs.' Small lie. White lie. 'I've only seen him in school.'

'Thing is . . .' he said. 'She sounded worried about you. Why would she be worried?'

'She worries about everything.' Not a lie, not a lie at all. 'That's just how she does things. She's always worried.' I smiled my best grown-up smile and it felt good on my face. 'It's no big deal . . . He's more of a friend than anything,' I said.

I looked up at him then. I don't know why, it was a stupid thing to do. But I stared into his face. And I knew my look said something different.

'I . . .' Dad didn't finish the sentence, though. Maybe it never had an end. He turned away from me, reaching into his pocket for a packet of cigarettes. His lips were pressed together. A funny kind of feeling was running through my stomach. Not nerves now, too tight and quick for that. It was excitement. And I wondered why that was. Still, I couldn't quite look at him. Looking at him now, at the hurt across his face, would make that feeling go away. I didn't want it to go away. Things felt safer, having it between us, and I stared up at the cork board instead.

He pinched a cigarette out, almost dropped it. I read some list still pinned on the board from a while ago, hanging just below Michael's drawing of Spiderman. Or it could have been a pot-plant. Bread, the list said. Milk. Marathon Bar. Quite a while ago, I thought.

'You . . . you want an ashtray for that?'

'Oh. Yeah.' He didn't speak again as I got up, going to the cupboard. It felt better to be doing something. It felt better to be busy, moving the way I did in school. I wondered if he could see that, see the Robin in me as I bent down.

'You . . . you'd like him, I think.' Big lie. Nevermind. I moved a pot of hair gel, left over from when Michael was eight and he got obsessed with the Mafia look. Behind that was a screwdriver with the handle broken off. An old toothbrush covered in boot polish. It looked like my bedroom floor, that cupboard. I found the ashtray behind an old *Observer*. It was brown and lumpy, the ashtray I mean, not the paper. 'Home-made' Dad would have called it. I thought 'shit' was probably closer. And I smiled, shutting the door. Robin would have thought so too. I tried to hold that thought.

'Cheers.' But Dad stopped then, seeing it properly. 'Oh,' he said. 'Look at that.'

'What?' It was just a load of clay, but the look on his face made my excitement dry out. I tried looking at the cork board again. It didn't seem to help this time.

'I s'pose you don't remember do you? You made it . . . when you were six or seven.'

'Not really,' I said. But that explained why it was blob-shaped with a big hole in one side. I wished he'd stop looking at it, get back to the important stuff.

'That's s'posed to be a face on the front.' He smiled. 'Said you modelled it on me.'

'Yeah,' I said. 'But I wouldn't worry about it. Kids have a funny idea of proportion.'

He didn't laugh, though, and all of a sudden I wanted to take the ashtray away again. Make things like he'd never seen it. Holly would never have made an ashtray for her dad. Robin didn't even like his. It was a stupid thing to do. A fucking stupid thing.

'You gave it to me for Christmas,' he said.

When he looked up at me, his eyes were too shiny under the 60-watt bulb. It made me want to apologize, say everything was fine. I tried to find that little ripple of excitement again, that way I stood in school. Just chatting with my friends, just sucking off my boyfriend. It was no good, though. It was gone. And all I could do was sit down.

'You don't want to ask him round, I s'pose.'

'What?'

'Don't want to bring your boyfriend home . . . meet the old folks, right?'

'I . . . I never said that.'

'It's Ok if you're embarrassed of us. I can understand that. Old fogies and that . . .'

'You're not old fogies! I don't think that. And . . . and I wouldn't be embarrassed.'

'You don't have to pretend. I know, you know, families; they just *are* embarrassing.'

'You're *not* embarrassing. Honest you're not. I'd . . . I'd like him to meet you.'

'Really?' He looked down at the ashtray again. I'd given it to him for Christmas, just to say I loved him. A little present, just to let him know. I wondered if he knew now, if it still showed. Because I did still love him most, I guess, no matter how much I looked away. 'Ok,' he said quietly. 'But . . . as long as it's your choice.' And somehow, even knowing that he loved me, I couldn't quite help thinking I'd been conned.

I wasn't really angry at Dawn for telling him. It was true what she said, she just cared about me. Thinking about it over the next few days, the idea of Robin coming round felt strange. It wasn't just Dad who'd hate Robin, Robin'd hate him back too. I knew because Robin was always talking about hating authority. That was why he smoked dope. I wondered what they'd say to each other, and the idea made me sick with nerves. Most of the time.

Because every so often I'd get a dash of what I'd felt before. Excitement running through my stomach. I didn't really want it to be there, it made me feel guilty. A chain of things, going round in circles. I couldn't stop it though, that was the thing. Because I kind of liked it too.

No, I wasn't angry at her. Maybe what she'd done would turn out for the best. Dad and Robin. Meeting. The thought made my fingers shake. Her phone call had made me think of something else though. Something I'd never considered before. I guess I'd thought it was out of the question, but working my way round to asking Robin over, it popped up more and more inside my head.

I could find a boyfriend for her.

Actually, I thought she had quite a lot in common with Robin. Definitely more than I had in common with *either* of them. I wondered if the best solution wouldn't be just to dump Robin and make him go out with Dawn. They liked the same music, they both watched MTV. Neither of them washed their hair. The only problem was that they hated each other. But then, Holly told me once that when two people can't stand each other it often means they fancy each other. I was pretty sure that was bullshit. I hated Willem Reed, the fat boy who sat at the back of the class and only talked to teachers because he didn't have any friends. He had acne and stank of piss, and he seemed to think he was cleverer than everybody else just because his dad was a civil servant. I did *not* fancy Willem Reed.

Funnily enough, Willem died six months after he moved to another school in the Fourth Year. He was run over by a Walkers Crisps delivery truck as it headed up to Gateways. It seemed a bit ironic really, being as he was the one who bought all the Walkers Crisps they had in Gateways. And I wondered vaguely if you could class that under euthanasia.

Everyone in my class, his old class, bought flowers and went to the funeral. I thought they were stupid, because they'd all hated him just as much as I had, and being dead didn't make him a nicer person. It probably made him more bearable, but it certainly didn't make him any *nicer*.

I didn't go to the funeral, but I heard it was lovely.

The second person I thought of for Dawn was Craig. He wasn't good-looking, he'd never gone out with a girl, and he listened to his Walkman constantly, so he wouldn't be able to hear a word she said. I thought he was perfect. Dawn, on the other hand, thought the guy out of Skid Row was perfect. I tried to work my way around it but somehow I couldn't see Craig in lipgloss. He was the lead singer and his name was Sebastian Bach, the guy who'd been on her T-shirt that first day in school. She loved him,

I think, even though she didn't really want to meet him. She didn't need to, she was happy crying over him in the dark. I tried to tell her not to set her sights too high, there weren't many people in school who wore patent-leather jeans. I don't think she really understood though.

'I could never go out with someone else. I don't *like* anyone else.' She was whispering, looking pretty embarrassed as we sat in the library. I was eating, Dawn wasn't. So I guess she'd seen the sign. I watched her glance around, make sure no one was looking. 'I could never go out with anyone I didn't . . . like.'

'Yeah, but Dawn . . . if you take that attitude you'll never find a boyfriend.'

'I don't care,' she said. 'It's you that wants me to get a boyfriend.'

'I don't "want you to get a boyfriend". I just thought it might be nice.'

'Yeah, so you wouldn't have to spend as much time with me,' she said. She didn't seem to be putting her heart into it though. Like she was thinking about something else. 'What's so great about boyfriends anyway?'

'Well . . . to like, make you feel good and stuff. Tell you that you look nice.'

'I've got you to do that,' she said.

And she was right. I did tell her, all the time. But I was lying, and I think she knew it.

'Anyway, I don't need a boyfriend. I don't have to have one, do I?'

'No, but . . .'

'Just because I'll be fifteen soon doesn't mean I've got to have french-kissed a *boy*.'

'No,' I said. 'No, course not. I mean, I'll be fourteen in *two weeks* and there's loads of stuff I've never done.' I watched Dawn run her finger down the spine of her book. It was old and reread with a picture of a woman in armour with a sword on the front. The words said 'Darkness & Light' but it looked more like 'Tits & Arse' to me.

'Like what?' she said finally. 'What haven't you done?'

'Well . . .' I thought for a moment. 'I've never been hang-gliding.'

In the end, though, I convinced her. I said we'd go out to the end of term disco next Saturday. No pressure, just see what happened. I was pretty sure that I could get her someone though. Alcohol does funny things to people's eyesight.

She'd have to wash her hair. I'd make *sure* she washed it, and with my shampoo too. Not the olive oil she used. I'd make her practise walking with a straight back and I'd pick out a short skirt for her to wear. She had the legs for it after all. Make-up – *I'd* do it. Booze. All in all, I thought, I could make it a success.

I told her it would be fun, a girls' night out on the town sort of thing. I think she liked that idea too, even though she didn't say it.

'I can't dance.'

'You don't have to dance.'

'I've got nothing to wear.'

'I'll lend you something.'

84

'It won't fit. You've got bigger . . . bigger breasts than me. Nothing you've got'll fit.'

'Then we'll find something in your wardrobe.'

We would too, I thought. I'd get a lift over in the evening and none of those things would be a problem. The problem was the timing. Saturday was the day that Dad said Robin should come over.

I had to wonder if he'd still be in the mood to drive me, after Robin had been round.

I asked Robin what he thought too. I guess I just wanted to make sure it was the right thing to do. I asked him if Craig had said anything about her, what he thought our chances might be.

'Shit,' he said. 'He wouldn't fuck her if she was the last rough mongy dog in school.'

I hadn't asked him to be honest though.

We hadn't talked much about the gob job since the whole thing had blown over. It just didn't seem like the kind of thing you could bring up in the middle of small talk. Not that I wanted to say anything about it, I was kind of glad I didn't have to think about it anymore. Just that it didn't seem like the whole thing could be over yet, been and gone so quickly. It felt like there should have been more to be said. We'd stopped doing so much snogging since then too, and he'd stopped trying to make me come. In fact, he'd pretty much stopped touching me completely. So I guess there was one good thing to come out of the whole business.

The funny thing was, sometimes I'd think about it while

I gobbed him off. Not the blood or anything, but about what happened afterwards. Sometimes, trying to not get bored, I'd think about the expression on his face just before he'd hit me. The way the blood swelled up. And on those times, working away in silence, I almost changed my mind about it. I almost wished he'd touch me after all.

He hadn't hit me again, though. Not all the while since, and after that day when Holly'd told me she knew, he'd pretty much stopped talking to me too. I guess I knew the reason. Thinking about it, it wasn't hard to work out. He didn't have to talk to me anymore. And I guess I'd been the one to prove it.

He talked to me that day, though. The day I asked him about Craig and Dawn. He sort of had to talk really. I asked him a question that he couldn't leave alone.

'Wants to meet me?' He laughed.

'On Saturday,' I said. 'Like, Saturday morning.'

'Why the fuck would your old man want to meet me?'

I shrugged, trying to make it look like I didn't care. 'He thinks you might be a bad influence,' I said, and then we laughed together. I heard mine trail off much too quickly, though, and it only left a silence. 'So will you come?' I said.

'Yep. Right in your mouth.'

I laughed, but it wasn't true. He'd never come in my mouth. He'd never come at all.

'No: really.'

Robin lifted his shoulders, not bothering to make a shrug. 'Might be a laugh,' he said.

'Yeah . . . yeah.' But I couldn't think of anything to say after that. I guess I was just shocked that he'd agreed. I watched the smirk on his face, it made him look lopsided in a cool kind of way. And we didn't speak then, for a while.

I thought about Dawn, my birthday coming up and a night out on the town. I thought about a lot of things, not wanting to disturb him, but none of them were as exciting as the thought of him coming round. Strange really, when I couldn't even work out why.

'It's my birthday soon,' I said.

'So?'

'I don't know . . . nothing.'

Talking about birthday presents was taboo in my house, like watching *Strike It Lucky* or agreeing with a Tory party policy. Everyone knew they were coming, and we'd spend hours talking about the parties, but mentioning presents got you ten minutes of Dad's heavy breathing. And the week before a birthday came along was a secretive, glancing-out-of-the-corner-of-your-eye kind of week.

Presents were surprises. It would have been the eleventh commandment, but Dad didn't believe in the other ten, so really it was just the first. We weren't allowed to give normal presents either. That was the second commandment. No shaving brushes, no deodorant, no umbrellas. *Definitely* no socks. And the only exception to the rule were felt-tip pens. I got 100 felt-tip pens every birthday and, three months later, Michael got the same. It didn't seem to matter that five minutes with your hand down the back of the sofa could provide three complete sets for free. Or maybe that was where they came from. Maybe I only ever had one set of felt-tip pens. They just got repackaged every year.

'We get surprises for our birthday presents,' I said. 'Me and my brother, I mean . . .'

Robin only looked at me. I guess he was right as well. It was a stupid thing to say.

'Don't . . . don't you think that's babyish?' I said.

'What?'

'Getting, you know, surprises on your birthday.'

Robin shrugged though, turned away from me.

'Do you get surprises on yours?' I said.

'Jesus! What the fuck is it with birthdays?'

'Nothing,' I said. 'Sorry: nothing.'

And it was nothing really. I wondered why I'd mentioned it.

Robin's mum offered to drop him off that next Saturday. So did his stepdad, whatever kind of prick he might have been. Robin said he'd cycle over, take the bus or get a taxi. I knew none of those things would happen though. Dad wanted to pick him up.

I asked Mum if he could just come round for dinner – if we could get a take-away or something, then at least we'd have something to do with our hands. She didn't get it though. 'He's not coming round here to *eat*, is he?' She shook her head with a smile.

'Well,' I said. 'He would be if we had dinner.'

'He can eat at *home*. He's not coming here to eat.'

'What *is* he coming for then?'

'Well, he's coming here for us to meet him.' She said it like it was obvious, what else could he be coming for? I thought she was wrong though, even though she sounded sure. He wasn't coming so that *they* could see him. He was coming so that Dad could.

Half past eleven, we were meant to pick him up. It wasn't an unreasonable time, Dad had thought of it himself. Which was why I couldn't work out why he was still in his dressing gown five minutes before we should go.

'Put the kettle on, will you?'

'It's almost eleven o'clock.'

'So?'

'Well . . . you know . . . it takes twenty minutes to get there.'

'So we'll be a bit late. What's he going to do? Refuse to come?'

'Yeah . . . but it'd be nice to be on time.'

'I'm driving. I'll go when I want. Put the kettle on please.' So I did. There wasn't much I could do about it really, but I was kind of relieved when Mum came into the living room with the Hoover.

'Oh,' I said. 'You tidying up?'

'Well, make a good impression and all that. You look nice.'

'Thanks.' I didn't though, which was probably why she said it. Her hair was tied in a ponytail and she had a polo-neck on. I was glad. I thought she looked pretty normal. She walked round, coughing and picking up newspapers and cushions and all the other stuff that was lying on the floor. I sat on the sofa and she tidied round me. I tapped my fingers on the arm. It was five past.

'Is Dad still in the bathroom?'

'Huh? Yeah, must be. Shaving probably.'

'Oh.' I hadn't noticed any stubble when he'd gone in. He came out of the bathroom at quarter past. We were five minutes late already. He was wearing jeans and a T-shirt with a picture of Tony Hancock on it, in his hat. I tried not to wince. 'Not wearing a suit, then?' I said, trying to laugh like it was a joke.

'Why would I wear a suit? It's Saturday.'

'Yes,' I said, and looked at the clock again.

'Stop hassling me!'

'I didn't say anything!'

'We'll get there when we get there.' I nodded, but I thought that was pretty obvious. I was glad when I saw him put his sunglasses on though. They were a thin shape, like flies' eyes, and they made him look a bit less harmless. He brushed his hair back behind his ears. 'Are you tidying up, Liz?'

'Just doing a bit,' she said, looking up from the grate around the fire. 'Make the place look a bit more presentable.'

'Don't do that,' he said, leaning back against the doorway with the car keys in his hand. I could see Mum's face in his sunglasses. She looked pale in the reflection. Bent down, and sort of out of shape.

'Why not?'

'Why should you? He's not the fucking prime minister.

He's just a bloke for fuck's sake. You don't have to tidy up for him.'

'Oh thanks, Philip. First you're always saying I should tidy up my papers . . .'

'Well not today, eh? If she wants it tidy she can do it herself.'

'I'll do it,' I said, but I had a feeling I was a bit late. 'If you'll wait twenty minutes . . .'

He looked at me. 'Wait for what? If it takes so long to get there then I've got to go.'

'Go?' I looked at him.

'For God's sake.' Dad turned away from me, shaking his head. 'You've met him already. If you don't mind, I'd like to go on my own.' Whether I minded or not, that's what he meant to do and his brow wrinkled in three straight lines. Like stripes above the sunglasses.

'*Why?*'

Now I was scared.

'Why not?'

'Well, you won't have anything to talk about! Please! I want to come!'

'Just leave it, alright.' I looked at him, mouth hanging wide open. 'See you later,' he said, and shut the door before I could say anything else. I stared at Mum, waiting for her to do something. Even though I didn't really think she could help.

'Oh well,' she said. 'Do you want some tea?'

Dad married Mum when she was twenty but I'm not really sure how they met. I guess it could have been at school or college or something like that. And as Mum came through with a mug in each hand, a strand of hair falling across her face, concentrating, I wondered how different Dad had looked then. I wondered if he'd looked like Robin.

'There you go.' She set one down on the table next to me. 'Nervous?' she said, settling into the sofa, tucking her hair back behind her ear.

'Nervous?' I laughed. 'There's not anything to be nervous about.' But I was really, even if I didn't want to tell Mum that. I half thought that Dad wouldn't come back with Robin, he'd just be alone in the car. I had funny visions of Robin getting in and refusing to say anything. Or he'd say 'All dads are pricks' and Dad would just stop the car there and then. Or Robin would refuse to get in at all in case someone saw him there, with a man wearing a Tony Hancock T-shirt. I didn't want that to happen, even if I wasn't quite sure why. The whole thing would've been pretty pointless, I thought, if Robin never even got here. If Dad didn't see us together.

'No,' I said again.

'Well . . .' She nodded, but she didn't look like she had a lot more to say. 'Good.'

We sat in the quiet for a little while, listening to each other slurp the top off our tea as Mum stared out of the windows. Funny, I couldn't really think of much to say either.

'So . . . is he in many of your classes then?'

'Not really.'

'Well anyway . . .' She clapped her hands down on her slacks. 'I'm sure we'll all get on.'

'Mm,' I said, but I wasn't really interested. I picked up my tea again, with Mum nodding away into nothing. It felt like the countdown to autodestruct they have on *Star Trek*. Only oo hours, 33 minutes and 16 seconds to go. I felt every one of them and it made me wonder just who I was nervous for. For Mum and Dad? Or Robin? Or maybe just for me? It made me wonder where all my excitement had gone, now everything was close.

'So . . .' Mum glanced over her shoulder. '*Michael?*'

'What?' His head came round, through the open door.

'Your sister's got a friend coming round.' She smiled. 'Be nice if we were all here to meet him.' He raised one eyebrow. I wished I could do that – totally unimpressed. People said it was genetic, but people were liars.

'I don't *want* to meet him,' he said.

'For God's sake, Michael.' She dragged at the collar of her polo-neck, looking away. But she sounded like she'd been expecting it. 'All you have to do is show your face. Make a good impression.'

'His face doesn't make a good impression,' I said.

'I'm staying in here.' And he smiled too. 'I don't want to be around when the fighting starts.' I watched him. It was the perfect opportunity really. Ever since he was six and I put that dead, cat-disembowelled vole in his sleeping bag, he'd been waiting for this. But that was Ok. That was just fine. Because *I* was going for the maturity angle.

'It doesn't matter, he's obviously *busy*. Got an important lobotomy to have done?'

'Yeah?' he said, but I didn't think it was a particularly snappy comeback. 'Bet Dad hates him.'

'Ever thought of getting yourself committed? They've got these really nice jackets there. Might just find they're a bit long in the arm . . .'

Mum was bent over, elbows on her knees. She looked a bit like people do when they get nausea, with a washing-up bowl between their feet.

'Please don't,' she said quietly. But I don't think she expected us to hear.

I drank six cups of tea in the forty-five minutes it took them, and I went to the toilet five times. I was in there when I heard the car in fact, tyres squelching as it drove past and parked. We had a Rover, so nothing to be embarrassed about there. A Rover was normal, I thought. I waited out in the hall as I heard the front door open, and I listened to the cistern flush away behind me. I tapped my fingers on my jeans. And standing there, smoothing the denim down even though it wasn't lumpy, I wondered for the first time what I wanted out of this.

I wondered why I'd let it happen.

'Cool car.' Robin's voice came through into the hallway. I breathed a long breath but it didn't seem to go all the way down.

'You like it?' I heard the shuffling of feet. 'Oh, Robin – this is Liz.'

'Nice to meet you.' His voice, I thought, but it didn't sound right, and I couldn't match it to the picture in my head. Standing in my own house, it didn't fit with the face I remembered. Doesn't matter, I thought. Doesn't matter, nevermind, like a little circle as Dad's voice came through again. 'Does nought to sixty in eight and a half seconds.'

'Eight and a half? That's like, good is it?'

'That's *like* top of the range.'

I smoothed my hair again. I heard the sofa creak as Dad sat down. Not once had I heard Robin mention cars. He rode a bike, but I hardly thought that qualified him for a detailed discussion of the pros and cons of modern hatchbacks. Obviously I was wrong. Obviously he watched *Top Gear.*

Doesn't matter, I thought. But it was the way he'd said it, like something in his voice was trying. Maybe that was why it didn't fit. Nevermind. I pulled at my jeans, my skinny rib, thinking of the way that Sandy looked in *Grease.* Just after she'd had her hair permed and learned how to inhale, the way she smoothed down the curls on her neck. The way she stood with one leg cocked out in those patent-leather trousers, tilted one high heel. I wasn't wearing high heels, but that was just a minor detail. I strained my back, sucked my gut in, tits out, I pooched my lower lip. And then I stepped into the living room.

'Hi Robin.'

'Are you interested in cars?' Dad said. He settled himself back, one hand dangling off the long arm of the sofa. His sunglasses hung from his fingers.

'Sort of.' Robin's back went straight up from the seat. He'd washed his hair as well, I saw. It was tucked in flicks behind his ears.

*

95

'*Hi*, Robin.'

'Interested in mechanics?'

'Yeah . . . I guess.'

'I've always thought it's something they don't teach enough of, practical engineering. Spend too much time filling people's heads up with bloody algebra, right?'

'Yeah . . .' Robin's laugh came, plucked out like the wrong violin string. 'Algebra is like . . . a bit shit.'

' . . . *Robin?*' Yes, my leg was out, chest up. Gut. Arse. Heel. What the fuck was up?

'Oh.' He turned a little bit towards me, half a swivel with his shoulder, and it looked like he needed greasing. 'Hi,' he said.

'So exactly what are you interested in, Robin?' Dad reached for a cigarette. So casual. 'If it's not algebra or mechanics.' Out it came, sliding right between his fingers.

'Uh . . .' That stupid laugh fell out again. 'Dunno really.' His eyes looked too pale in the light from the french windows. It made his spots stand out against white skin. I looked around the three of them, Mum and Dad and Robin. This wasn't how I'd imagined it. And after a moment I sat down.

'Fucking the law?' Dad said.

His index finger was stretched out towards the bag by Robin's feet. It was crumpled on the floorboards but you could still read the words. I felt that runner of excitement, smaller now but still there, make its way up to my chest. Robin didn't speak, though. Staring at Dad, he didn't speak at all. And I watched Dad's head roll back, gazing at the ceiling for a moment.

'Ah . . . The law is an ass.'

He sounded like he might be quoting something but I wasn't sure what it was. Robin looked like he knew though. Obviously he had a secret love of witticisms too. Dad turned the cigarette between his fingers, bringing his head back down. 'And it's certainly a fucking ass at the moment,' he said. 'Tories've seen to that. *Thatcher* saw to that.'

'I . . . like, I wrote that a long time ago,' Robin said. He didn't add that he'd been filling in the faded spots last week. 'Just haven't like . . . got a new bag yet.'

Dad didn't sound like he'd heard. Either that or he didn't care. I guess he'd found a favourite subject though. 'You know, her first bloody action – the *first* thing she ever did as soon as she got any power – was take away kids' free milk. Start as you mean to go on, right? And now she's a baroness. A fucking *baroness*, I mean *Jesus!* She's systematically destroyed this country, health, economy. It's dog eat dog, it's every man for himself. And why? Because that's how she wanted it! Right from the start, fighting amongst ourselves for the few decent wages left. There is no society, right? There's only the individual.'

'Right . . .' Robin said. His lips looked too thick, like they were muffling his words. 'I really like milk too.'

Dad just shook his head, staring at the floorboards, and I heard the leather on the sofa creak as Mum shifted to get comfy.

'Pity we can't all sit outside . . .' she said. 'What with all this lovely weather.'

'Why can't we?' Dad said, and Robin looked up.

'Well . . .' She shrugged a little bit, and I saw her jumper crease up in the armpits. 'The ozone's worst in August.'

From Michael's bedroom, very quiet, came the sound of *Sonic The Hedgehog* booting up. Robin rubbed his feet in small straight lines along the floor. I'd never seen him do that before. I wasn't really sure I liked it.

'Ozone . . .' Dad raised his eyebrows up in a cartoon arc. 'Want to sit outside, Robin?'

He looked from Dad to Mum and back again. His jeans looked too baggy, I thought, flattened out over his knees. And between his turn-ups and boots, I saw, his socks were pulled up tight.

'They say the hole's fifteen miles across now,' she was saying. 'And because it's not so hot this year, it's easier to get burnt. Feels cooler because of the breeze. Only that doesn't make any difference to the . . . oh the . . . UV rays,' she said. 'Have you got any block?'

'For God's sake, Liz. We don't need any *block*.'

'Skin cancer rates rose, I don't know, 30 per cent or something stupid in the last five years.'

'Probably the stress of people getting nagged about putting on block,' Dad said. Me and Robin laughed. Mum didn't laugh, though, she only raised her eyebrows. She wasn't quite as good at it as Dad.

'You won't think it's so funny when you get . . .'

'Look,' Dad said, and Mum stopped talking. 'We don't need any sun cream, alright?'

I watched her open her mouth to say something else, but Dad was still staring at her. Robin hadn't seemed to notice, but then Robin didn't seem to be noticing much at all today. Maybe he was waiting to hear what Dad'd say next.

I watched Mum press her lips together. And, after a moment, I watched her look away.

'So . . .' Dad's face swept me then Robin. 'Shall we go outside?'

He didn't wait for any answers though, he just got up, the cigarette still stuck between his knuckles. He reached in his jeans pocket for a lighter. Finally, I thought, and I waited for Robin to get one out too. I bent forward a little bit as Dad cupped the flame. He'd take it out, I thought, and then I'd ask for one too. Even if it was just a roll-up, that wouldn't matter. Same difference, I thought. Same difference, and I bit my lip.

Robin didn't move, though. He didn't move a muscle.

'Ahh . . .'

Dad looked out through the window, took a long drag and blew it out at the ceiling. It had a yellow look to it, streaming out through the light from the glass. Still, Robin didn't move.

'You . . . you can smoke,' I said. 'Like, no one minds or anything.'

Robin looked up to me. He seemed thinner, sitting in an armchair in my living room, like it wasn't really him at all. He looked pasted on, I thought, the way they do in films. Like in *Chitty Chitty Bang Bang*, where the car flies through the air but it just looks cheaply done, and everyone knows it's a fake.

Everyone knows, because cars don't fly through the air. 'I've given up,' he said quietly.

And with the heel of one foot, he pushed his bag behind the chair.

I went with them when Dad took Robin home, sitting in the back seat, listening to them talk. I didn't say much. I was meeting up with him again, though, outside the community centre, so I guess I didn't really need to. I felt empty, with the car humming quietly underneath my feet, and I couldn't hear their conversation properly. I felt the same way you do when you eat eight bags of crisps because you're hungry and then realize you still want dinner. The same way I felt about the gob job, I guess. Like it shouldn't've been over yet.

Dad took me straight to Dawn's after dropping Robin off, and for a while we didn't talk at all. He wasn't breathing heavy, though, and he tapped the drums to some old song going round his head in a light patter on the steering wheel.

'You seeing him tonight then?' Dad smiled, glancing round from the road. 'Meeting up or something?'

I just shrugged though.

'Dunno,' I said quietly, and I looked back to the window.

Dawn had cold feet already when I got there, going on about how she'd look a fool and everyone'd laugh at her. It took a while to talk her round again, but then I guess I wasn't really trying hard. I curled her hair for her, put it up, and I did her make-up carefully. And she did look better. A bit. It took me a long time to get her into a miniskirt though.

'It'll just make me look taller. I don't want to look taller.'

'But you've got great legs. If I had legs like yours, I'd wear a miniskirt.'

I was lying really, though. If I had legs like Dawn's I'd probably watch *Boxing Helena* for fun.

I looked at the clock on the wall. It was six-fifteen, I was meeting Robin at nine. That gave me three hours to get her dressed, out of the house, drunk and hooked up with someone. I was having second thoughts myself.

We got out of the house by seven, Dawn's stepdad saying goodbye to us as we left.

'You're not going to wear *that* are you?'

'What's wrong with it?'

'You look like a tart. An ugly tart. See you later.'

She looked at me, at herself, then at me again.

'You'd trust *his* taste?' I said. She bit her lip and I pushed her out before she could say anything else. We stopped at The Wine Cellar, past Audiovision and just before Boots. I bought a six-pack of alcoholic lemonade and made her drink two of them on the trot. I watched her gag as she finished the second.

'See? It's nice really, isn't it?'

'No.'

'You look great. Really great.' She looked over-made-up. Too much blusher and cover-up, with the acne just peeping through. Her hair was going flat. I figured it didn't matter. It'd be dark soon.

She was halfway through her third bottle when I started

to notice the change. Her back was upright, her head was high. She was walking tall, if not quite straight. I started looking for Craig.

We got to the dance at eight-thirty and Joel was already there. He had some girl I didn't know plastered across his face. Craig was there too – so far so good. Except he wasn't wearing his Walkman – he'd hear everything she said, and I winced when I saw that. He was looking at her legs though. And he wasn't laughing.

It was too quiet, standing out there on the grass, and the spaces in between each noise all sounded much too big. The bass drum and the snare floated off too quickly, and it wasn't dark enough to hide the flower beds, or the car park across the road.

Dawn straightened her skirt but she didn't look like she was trying to pull it down.

'Hi Craig,' she said. I almost fell over.

'Hi,' he said back. This, I thought, could be a very good night.

Joel and his blonde were leaning back against the handrail. They set it up a while ago, the council I imagine, edging off the paving slabs that lead up to the door. The old women use it to rest their handbags on, queuing up for Bingo.

Dawn reached for another lemonade as I leaned against the wall. I almost stopped her – too much of a good thing. But she seemed to know what she was doing. I let the pebbledash dig into my shoulder blades and I wondered what Holly was doing.

'How's things?' Dawn said, looking right at Craig.

'Good enough,' he said. 'How's you?' He offered her a cigarette and she reached out and took it.

'You don't . . .' I said. But obviously she did. Tonight anyway. I watched as the girl, whoever she was, peeled herself off Joel.

'*Hi!*' she said, and flung her arms round me. 'I haven't seen you for *ages!* How *are* you?'

'Great,' I said, watching Joel wipe the lipstick off his mouth.

It reminded me a little of blood, and I wondered why the thought annoyed me. Inside, I heard them switch Madonna for The Prodigy.

Dawn had taken a step towards Craig, I noticed. She was about three inches taller than him, but Craig didn't seem to mind. She was puffing away at her cigarette. I thought she looked stupid – she wasn't holding it properly. And I could see her pantyline through her skirt. I thought of mentioning it, but then the girl was hugging me again.

'I like your hair,' Craig said.

'I like your . . . um . . .' Dawn replied. Me too, I thought. 'T-shirt,' she said. The blonde got off me, flicking her hair back from her shoulders. She sighed, gazing up past the roof gutter, and I wondered if she thought that looked romantic. 'So,' Dawn started again. 'What's going on in Craig-World?'

'Oh . . . um . . .'

She slung her cigarette butt on to the ground and it bounced on to Craig's trainer. I saw she'd almost finished her fourth bottle now.

'Whoops!' she said. He didn't say anything, but his smile was gone. His trainers were Nike Air and they'd cost him £90. I knew because he'd told me. He'd told everyone. 'You know . . . you know who you look like, Craig?'

'What?' He was still staring down at his Nikes.

'You know who you look like? Butthead! You know: out of *Beavis and Butthead?*'

'Sorry?' he said.

'Heh heh heh! Hey, Butthead! Let's liquidize some frogs. Heh heh heh! Cool!'

Then she started head-banging. 'Da-da-*DAAH!* Da-da-*DAAH!* Da-da-*DUM-DUM!*' Her hair flopped from side to side, just about held in by the clips. 'Heh heh. Cool!' The front of her blouse drooped and stretched as she banged up and down. I looked away.

'Uh, well . . . yeah,' Dawn said. 'Beavis and Butthead.' She looked down into her empty bottle. 'Any more lemonade?'

'No,' I said, and I think she got the message.

Craig's hair was standing up in little brownish tufts. It looked like he'd slept on it, I thought, but I guess he'd gelled it that way on purpose.

'Dawn plays flute, you know,' I said. 'Didn't you used to play that, Craig?'

'No.'

'No? Oh . . . funny that . . . I thought you did.'

'Yeah,' Dawn said. 'It exercises your lips, you know. I've got very flexible lips.'

'I'm sure you *have*,' the girl said, and giggled.

'No. Honestly.' Dawn carried on. 'I do exercises. Look.'
She flexed her lips about.

'If you ask me,' I said, even though none of them had,
'that flute teacher's a perv.'

'He's got fuckin awful hair as well,' whoever-she-was
said.

'I mean, he's gotta be fifty and he's still like, letching
over all the girls.'

'All sort of combed over the top,' she said. 'Like he
thinks it'll cover his bald patch.'

'He could have the longest hair in the fuckin world,' I
said. 'He'd still be a perv.'

I thought that'd shut her up. It didn't seem to, though.

'He's got plenty of nose hair though. He should graft
it to his scalp. He's got enough to make it shoulder length.'

'That'd look bizarre. Nose hair's all crinkly,' Dawn said.

'Ugh! You've got crinkly nose hair?'

'Well, isn't yours crinkly?' Dawn said.

'I,' the girl said quietly, 'don't have any nose hair.'

'Oh bollocks.' I watched Dawn turn to look at me.
'Everybody's got nose hair.'

'Not me,' said the girl. 'I'm more evolved. More
hair you've got, less evolved you are.'

'Duncan Goodhew must be pretty fuckin evolved then.'
Joel said. No one answered.

I put the sole of my shoe against the wall, the way you
see prostitutes stand in films.

'How come all the characters on *Star Trek* have hair
then?' Craig said. 'They're meant to be, like, 400 years in
the future. Even the Vulcans have got hair.'

'*Star Trek*'s just a TV programme!' I wondered who she was to question, no one even knew her name. 'It's not *real*,' Miss Blonde said.

I wondered if Robin would be out by now. I tried to think what he'd look like, what clothes he'd have on. It was funny though, there weren't any feelings joined on to those thoughts, and my brain kept slipping back to what he'd said. I really like milk too. Like *that* was important.

'I know it's not *real*,' Craig was saying. 'But it's like, *based* on reality, isn't it?'

'Aren't the Klingons bald?' Dawn said.

Craig rolled his eyes. 'No, they're not *bald*. They've just got big foreheads.'

'Oh what, like foreheads that go back to their necks?'

'Anyway,' Craig said. 'Klingons are the *least* evolved. That's why they're always fighting.' I had to admit, he had a pretty good breadth of knowledge. Still I was bored.

'If they're so unevolved,' Joel said, 'how come Warf's a lieutenant?'

'He's not a lieutenant.' Craig flopped his hand out. Like a limp-finger gesture illustrated not being a lieutenant perfectly. 'He's Chief of Security.'

'Whatever . . .' Joel said. I looked past his shoulder into the distance. The roofs of all the cars reflected bluish from the sky. There was a block of public toilets there, grey pebbledash instead of white, and past that was the High Street. I couldn't see any of the shops, though, they were hidden by the loos. Thinking about it, I didn't really care. And I reached down for another lemonade.

'*Star Trek*'s shite anyway,' the blonde girl said. Everybody nodded.

Robin was drunk.

He didn't come to the community centre at all, and after a while I had to go and look for him. I found him halfway out of town, on the road that leads out from the High Street and eventually gets to the seaside. It'd got to almost twilight by then and the street lamps were coming on either side of the road. He was standing in the middle of the road and I thought it was a pretty good thing that there wasn't much traffic about. He didn't look like he'd have noticed if there was.

He wasn't just tipsy or merry. Robin was rolling around drunk, and it kind of put Dawn into perspective. I almost felt like a prude – the only person who wasn't going to spend the last of the evening vomiting up their cash.

'Where the fuck've you been?' he said, and lurched over the dotted line towards me. I stood on the curb and I didn't move, thinking of the Green Cross Code. 'Fuckin nine o'clock, I said! Call this fuckin nine o'clock?' He lifted his arm up like he was going to stare at his watch. I didn't bother to tell him that he hadn't rolled his sleeve up.

'Am I that late?' I said.

'Uh.'

He dropped his hand and I watched a smile surface on his face, like scum rising to the top of a pool, I thought.

'Alright then,' he said.

He stepped closer, and I had a horrible feeling he was

going to hug me. I moved out of the way. And as he fell past, I caught the smell of beer and sweat. Something was clotted in his hair, I saw, and there was a stain down his white top. He tripped and almost hit the tarmac, but still I didn't go to help him.

He didn't quite fall though. He started laughing instead, all bubbly and high-pitched. He was laughing at himself. He kept wandering off, his feet making wide arcs round each other, and I remembered when we'd been in school one time, Robin'd had his fly undone, and Craig had laughed at him then. Not a big laugh, not even nasty, but Robin'd hit him anyway. A proper hit, right across his jaw, and Craig'd had a big purple streak there for almost two weeks. It went a sick yellow before it disappeared, but he never laughed at Robin again. No one did. And Robin *never* laughed at himself. He was a serious kind of guy. Looking at him now, though, made me remember Dad. *What exactly are you interested in,* with that stupid laugh that'd followed.

'Y'look nice,' he said. He wasn't looking at me, though. He was looking down at his own legs with a stupid expression on, like he didn't understand why they weren't doing what he told them. I could have told him why, but I didn't really want to speak.

'Robin you're . . . you're drunk,' I said. 'Maybe you should go home or something.'

'Tell me to fuckin go home! Can get drunk if fuckin want!' He spun round, and I heard his heel squeak on the tarmac. I wondered if anyone had seen him. I hoped not. I hoped no one was near. And it was strange really. I remember thinking, when we first started going out, that it'd be nice to hear people call me Robin's girlfriend.

'What . . . what've you eaten?' I said. 'Maybe you should eat something, yeah?'

He frowned, like he was thinking hard. Then he shrugged. I saw that one shoulder went higher than the other.

'Let's get some food.'

I didn't really want to go anywhere with him, and I definitely didn't want to watch him dribble food down himself, but I thought it might sober him up. Maybe he'd be more like usual.

Maybe he'd stop reminding me of things I didn't want to think of.

He had to lean on me as we walked to the hot dog stand. It'd set up camp in the parking lot across from the community centre but most of the people had gone in by now. The bass drum sounded louder, I thought, not muffled by the light, and I tried to get Robin to stand straight.

His head fell to one side, like his neck wasn't working anymore, and I tried to shift him higher against my shoulder. Walking through the cars though, a funny kind of thought crossed my mind. It wasn't the sort of thought I was used to having round Robin. And when it came I felt a little cramp.

I wondered what it would be like to let go of him.

I led him to the stall and took his money out of his pocket for him. The guy behind the counter had rough stubble and grease on his hands. His fingernails were dirty too. I wondered what that black stuff in his nails could be, where it had come from. It must have travelled a long way, I thought. It must have seen a lot of places, done a lot of things, and all just to end up in Robin's hot dog. He looked at us both like he'd seen it all before. He probably had.

'What d'you want then?'

'Beer! I wanna . . .' Robin fell sideways. I thought again about letting him go. I figured the guy with the dirty fingernails wouldn't care. But Robin caught himself and stood up again. Not straight, but kind of diagonal. '. . . beer,' he finished, like there hadn't been any gap.

'Only do soft drinks,' the guys said. 'Soft drinks, hot dogs, crisps, chips, Mars Bars, hamburgers, beefburgers.' I wondered if his beefburgers even knew what a cow was. Maybe once, a very long time ago, they'd seen one. 'You want onions?'

I looked at the hot plate where the onion rings were lying. They weren't really frying, more sort of stewing. They were yellow with black bits where they'd stuck too long to the dirty plate. They smelled disgusting. I watched Robin's eyes narrow. He looked suspicious, but I thought he was probably just trying to focus.

'He wants onions,' I said, and Robin didn't disagree.

'Just onions?' the guy said, looking at me.

'No. He wants a roll, sausage, ketchup, mustard. And onions.' I looked at him squarely. He nodded and started picking things up. With his bare hands, I saw, but I didn't care. None of that stuff was going anywhere near my mouth. I saw he had a ponytail as he turned round to get the bun. One of the long stringy kind – the ponytail, not the bun. It was lank and stuck to the back of his coat. It didn't have enough hair to keep the band on, it was slowly slipping off. I wondered which customer would end up with it in their hamburger.

He handed the hot dog to me in a sheet of grease paper and I took it, careful not to touch his hand. I looked at the coins in my other hand, about six or seven quid there in all. Six or seven quid that Robin was going to spend on more beer. I looked at him, but he was staring at the ground. And I looked at the guy with the ponytail.

'That's right, I think.' I handed the whole lot over, and with it lying in his palm he didn't even pause.

'Yep. That's right.' And put it in his pocket. I handed the hot dog to Robin, making sure none of the sauce got on me. He stared down at it like he didn't quite know what it was. Maybe he didn't.

'It's a hot dog, Robin,' I said. 'You should eat it.' He looked at me doubtfully. I guess he had the right to – under the correct, trade description definition, I wasn't really sure it was a hot dog. I wondered why I felt so sick. 'Please eat it,' I said. My voice sounded funny, I thought. Different, but I couldn't quite work out how.

He did eat it, though, and he did spill it down himself. I turned away because I didn't want to see, and when I turned back, he'd finished. Half an onion ring was caught on the collar of his top. I would have brushed it away except I didn't want to touch him. I waited to see if he was going to try and hug me again, or kiss me or something. I needn't have worried, though. All of a sudden Robin was pretty much preoccupied.

'Shit,' he said.

Very dead-pan, and it would have been funny if he hadn't stumbled away a moment later and vomited on to the concrete.

There was a lot more vomit than I would have believed if it had been in a film or something. But I had to believe it; it was splashing out not three feet away from me. Most of it was liquid, a funny yellow colour underneath the street lights, and I could see lumps of undigested sausage and bread in there too. It looked a bit like whole orange juice, I thought, the cartons that come with the peel and pesticide included. There must have been two pints of the stuff.

He looked up at me, after staring at the puddle between his feet, and he grinned. He grinned like he'd just cracked a really good joke. It reminded me of Dawn.

Then he threw up again.

He held one forefinger up to me just before he did it, like to say *Hang on just one sec, got to take this call* . . . I heard the guy behind the counter gasp, and I thought that it must be a pretty big deal – the kind of hot dogs he was serving, he must have seen a fair few people puke.

There were stringy bits in it too this time and I thought they must have been the onion. The one stuck to his collar had been lucky after all.

The sick splattered over his trainers and on to his jeans. It formed a little river and ran off on its own. I thought it probably had the right idea.

He leaned against the wall when he'd finished, still grinning that stupid grin like he thought he'd done something clever. Canted to one side and I could see the top of his boxer shorts above his waistband.

'Come here,' he said, only it came out *cummeeer.*

He reached out towards me, wobbling around, but he managed to keep upright, and he put a hand on my shoulder.

Sincere. Earnest. He looked me dead in the nose.

'I love you,' he said.

And I froze.

Robin's face looked very heavy, three inches from my own. It looked like the chin outweighed the rest of it, and it dragged his blue eyes down as well. The street lights made his skin too sallow, and his hair was green instead of blond. The edge of one strand had stuck to the spit in the corner of his mouth. It hung there, I saw. Spit over gravity.

His hands pressed down on my collar bone, first one side heavy then the other as he tried to keep upright. I wasn't really thinking of him, though. The snare had speeded up behind me, with the sound of someone fighting too. But I wasn't thinking of that either. Robin smelled of cigarette smoke.

Up close there was no mistaking it, through the sick and the cider and sweat, it was there. It drifted up my nostrils. *I've given up,* I thought, and my tongue stuck to the roof of my mouth.

I stepped away from him.

Just like that, it was gone. Anything I'd ever felt for him. All that fear, all that respect and all my need to please. It was all gone. And it was gone so suddenly that for a moment I just stood there, wondering what had happened to me. It felt like someone had just turned off a switch. I didn't fall out of love, not even out of lust. But something that had been there was gone.

And I didn't ever want to touch him again.

'I don't want to go out with you anymore,' I said.

It came out easy. Much easier, I thought, than telling Dawn I couldn't see her at lunchtime.

'I said: *I love you.*' He said it slow, like he was talking to a French exchange student.

'And I said: I don't want to go out with you anymore.'

It was funny. I didn't feel relieved, or sad. Not even guilty. I felt nothing. But somehow not feeling felt good.

'But I love you!'

He couldn't seem to get it through his head. Which was weird, I thought, because I had it off pat already.

'*Why?*' he said, and fell further to the left. I tilted my head so I could look at him straight. And I searched for something to say. Something that would really make him understand. Something final, totally original and brilliantly witty. Something that would encapsulate our entire relationship in one concise and easily pronounceable line. And then I thought of *The War of the Roses.*

'Because when I watch you *eat* . . . when I see you *sleep* . . . when I even *look* at you these days, I just want to smash your face in.'

Fuck Olivia Newton-John. Enter Kathleen Turner.

I remember, when I was pretty young, Dad used to set up huge parties for my birthday. They were a really big deal and we spent weeks planning them together. He'd hire out some big hall, even though he said it was really expensive, and he'd draw on big banners to go across the walls. He liked fancy-dress parties the best and he'd spend hours sometimes, making me costumes for them.

We had a monsters' party once and he fixed me up this cool Frankenstein bolt to go through my neck. I spent the whole week before the party practising my zombie walk for him too. We also had a baddies' party, and I remember Dawn got upset because no one recognized hers. I went as Spatz Columbo, who had to be the coolest baddy of the lot. I didn't really know who Spatz Columbo was, but Dad said he was out of *Some Like It Hot*, and that was one of Dad's favourite films, so I guessed he had to be pretty cool. He made me spats to go over my party shoes and I combed my hair with Michael's gel. Michael came as my henchman, I remember, wearing one of my school ties.

There were always loads of decorations at my parties, loads of presents and jelly and ice cream that Dawn couldn't eat because of her sinuses. We did Pin the Tail on the Donkey – Dad would have made the board himself – Blind Man's Bluff, musical statues and Murder in the Dark. They were really cool, my birthday parties, really wonderful. And it was all because of Dad.

I don't really have birthday parties anymore. And I don't really want them or anything, I know fourteen's too old for it. But I remember how happy he used to be, getting everything ready for them. Sometimes, sewing some bit on to my costume or writing out a banner, he'd smile across the room at me. He never seems to be quite that happy these days, which makes me wonder if it's my fault.

Helping Dawn back to her house that night, I thought about what Robin had said. Her clothes were all fucked up and she was singing some song by Metallica. Her hair had come all loose. I don't know, maybe Robin had been right. If fourteen's too old for birthday parties, maybe it's too old for surprises too.

I took Dawn in the back way in case her parents had been waiting up. It felt late, I thought, but it wasn't even midnight as I opened her bedroom door. She was making shushing noises as loudly as she could, holding one finger up in front of her lips. And in the light from the hallway behind us, I could make out every drop of spit.

'You're great,' she said, falling back on to the bottom bunk.

'Yeah,' I said. Just like Kellogg's Frosties, as I took the first step on the ladder.

'I don't . . . I don't know what I'd do without you.' I didn't say anything, trying to cram myself into the space between the top-bunk mattress and the ceiling. I wondered how she slept up there. The Glo-Bugs on her window sill cast plastic-green shadows around, and I could just see Sebastian Bach pinned up on the ceiling. Three inches from my face, he pouted at me, showing off his lipgloss. I wondered vaguely what he wanted.

'I'd be on my own without you,' she said. 'I'd be like . . . ugh.' I heard her roll over on one side. 'I don't want a bloody boyfriend anyway,' she said. 'I hate bloody boy-friends.' Me too, I thought, but I didn't answer her.

And for a time, while there was silence, I thought she'd gone to sleep.

Robin hadn't been bad to me, though. I was pretty sure about that whatever Dawn had said. I thought he'd been pretty good really, what with all the mistakes that I'd made. I thought that that must count for something. She'd said he hadn't cared about me, not properly, not with the way he treated me. I guess that much was true. I'd never expected him to care about me, though.

Thinking about it, it all felt a little strange. I couldn't remember just what I had expected out of going out with Robin. Or if I'd expected anything at all. Looking back over the last two months, I couldn't find many reasons there.

'Don't go away again.'

Dawn's voice was quiet and awake. There wasn't any pause there.

'I don't like being on my own,' she said.

I should have answered her, I guess. But lying on the bunk above her, I only held my breath. I watched her Glo-Bugs fade as their light ran out and I was surprised again by just how little I felt.

The beginning of that summer holiday didn't feel much different to last year's or the year before's, not even after everything that'd happened. Funny how summer holidays have a knack for doing that. I spent the first day with Dawn, trying to help her get over her hangover, and I wondered a couple of times if Robin might be trying to call me at home. I was kind of glad I didn't have to talk to him, but still the idea sounded good. Forsaken boyfriend tries to tame wild soul of his loved one. It sounded pretty romantic. But then I guess anything would have sounded romantic in comparison to making Dawn a Lemsip.

'It's the flu,' she said. She was still in her dressing gown even though it was getting on for eleven. One of the pink fluffy kind that only looks good on small children in movies. It just about came down to her shins. Last night's make-up had refused to go away, I saw, and her face looked like a negative, double-exposed. 'I should have my temperature taken,' she said. She rested her head on the table.

I didn't answer. Instead I tipped the kettle, smelling that cough-sweet smell that always makes me think of gastric illnesses. Carrying the mug over to the table, I sat down across from her. Clouds had built up outside and I could see them waiting outside the kitchen window. I wondered when her parents would be back from shopping. 'So . . .?' I said.

'So what?' She turned her head away, resting her cheek on one forearm. Her hair still smelled of hairspray and someone else's cigarette smoke and between the dark brown roots, I could see a little of her scalp shine through.

'So what happened?'

'What do you think happened? They left. They only talked to me cos you were there.'

'They left?' I tried to make it a question but I wasn't really surprised. 'All of them?'

'Yes all of them! And I just hung around and waited till you'd finished . . . whatever you do with Robin. I hung around on my own and I waited for you. Ok?' She sounded like she was waiting, but watching the steam rise out of her mug, I could only think of

'Oh.'

'It's not like I would've got off with any of them anyway.' Her eyes were level with the mug handle. 'I'm just too choosy I suppose . . .'

'I'm sorry,' I said. Looking away, though, I wasn't really sure. I'd done what she wanted. I was single. 'Well, you won't have to hang around anymore, anyway,' I said. 'Me and Robin split up last night.'

Her head came up slowly from the table. She almost looked suspicious. 'Really?'

'Yes.'

'For good? Like, you're not going to get back together with him or anything?'

'Nope.'

'Not . . . not even if he asked? You wouldn't get back together with him then?'

'No,' I said. I watched her eyes loosen up, she wanted to believe me. I didn't think Robin would call and ask me back out, though. He just wasn't that sort of guy. And anyway, it wasn't as if we'd really liked each other or anything. Dawn's smile spread out slowly, and it showed the line of lipstick a little way down from her mouth, where she hadn't washed it off.

'I knew you'd dump him,' she said.

'It wasn't like that. We . . .' I looked away from her again, her smile made me a bit annoyed. She was shrugging already, though, too happy to wait for what we'd done.

'I knew he was never right for you! I told you. See? Now we can spend the holidays together! It'll be great! I mean, you won't have to put up with . . . with all his demands anymore.' Demands. I wondered what she'd meant by that. Robin'd never really demanded anything, he hadn't needed to. 'Did he cry?'

'Not really. We just . . . It was a mutual thing.'

'I told you he wasn't right. Didn't I say he wasn't right for you? This is *so* great.'

Dawn rapped her fingers on the table, grinning. Maybe she was thinking of all the stuff we'd do together now. And it was nice to make her happy, I suppose, nice to see her smile. It wasn't as good as making Robin happy, but then I didn't think anything could be as good as that, as difficult and satisfying and as easy to make mistakes at. I didn't think anything could even come close. Funny, how you learn.

I wasn't intending to tell Dad. I left Dawn's at two-thirty, got back at almost three, and I saw Michael had brought his Sega Megadrive into the living room. His face was pinched, leaning towards the TV, and he wasn't talking to Mum at the table behind him.

'Hi.' I wiped my feet as she looked up from her jigsaw. She'd got really good at jigsaws recently even though Dad said they were pointless. She only did four-figure ones.

'Have a good time?' She looked between me and the splash of pieces on the table.

'Ok,' I said.

'Great. Well, it's the holidays now. You can relax a bit, eh?'

'Yep.' I hung my coat up on the peg but I couldn't walk away with her mid sentence. I never really know what to say to Mum, even though I'm a girl and girls' best friends are supposed to be their mothers. I've done all the daughter stuff with her, all the puberty stuff and that, but it's never really made any difference. She bought me tampons before I'd even started, but she never told me what they were for. She took me out to buy my first crop top, I remember, when I was pretty young. She seemed really weird about it, so I tried to help her out by explaining it was absolutely normal at my age. She thought I was trying to be smart. And she took the easy option in the end, she only paid for items that had SPORTS written on the front in large letters. I guess she thought no one could creep up and pluck my cherry if I was busy with goal attack.

On the TV, brown and milky from the sunlight, I saw Sonic leap a nasty-looking wasp. Mum turned a piece of jigsaw over in her hand. Looking at her, I thought again of Dawn's reaction and I wondered how I'd fill six weeks. 'How's the jigsaw going?'

'Great,' she said. 'Great.' But I didn't bother to ask her what picture she was doing. The Sahara at night or something, and her nod went from quick to dead in one second. There was a pause before she picked up another jigsaw piece. She only glanced at it, though, before she put it down again. Sonic screamed an electronic death cry, and bounced off the edge of the screen. 'Well.' Her hands fell flat into her lap and she pushed her eyes away from me. 'Philip's been waiting for you, anyway,' she said.

'Right.' I stepped away. And I didn't watch her fade back to her jigsaw, walking out.

Dad was dressed in the same clothes as he'd been yesterday, same ones as Robin had seen. He didn't look much different expression-wise either, turning as I shut the door. I smiled.

'Seen Mum's jigsaw? She's done loads.' I don't really know what made me mention it, I knew what his reaction would be. Sometimes though, trying to talk to her, it makes me annoyed that I can't think of anything to say. It makes me wonder why she always asks the same questions.

'Sorry, but Liz can stick her fucking jigsaw up her arse.' His expression didn't change though, he didn't even look annoyed. 'All day long she's been fucking bitching at me.'

'Oh,' I said. I wondered if that was why she'd been so weird.

'But anyway.' His smile resurfaced. 'Did you have a good time?'

'It was Ok . . . The disco was boring.' I looked across the room, pushing back my hair.

'Really?' He wasn't doing anything, I saw. I looked down at the table where he was sitting, but there wasn't any paper. I saw a pair of pliers and a book on papier mâché. Four dirty glasses and three mugs half-full of cold tea. An ashtray. And just below last week's *Hello!* I saw the hairbrush that Mum'd been looking for since Friday. Nothing for Dad to do, though. 'Well, can't win 'em all,' he said. 'Make up for it next week.'

'Next week?'

'Your *birthday*. We could go to the beach or something.'

'Oh,' I said. I felt my stomach sink a little.

'Well.' He shrugged, his shirt runkling up as he glanced away. 'Don't have to go,' he said. But it wasn't the beach that'd set off that heavy little drop. I like the beach, I have since I was little. I like the funny towns you find on the coast. All the houses are painted pink like they were designed by Mattel, and the streets look like they should have My Little Ponies trotting down them, not smelly old donkeys called Albert attached to smelly old men who are always called Albert too. I haven't had a donkey ride since I heard you were more likely to die on one than in a plane. Considering all the plane crashes you see on TV, I was surprised anyone would risk a donkey.

Still, it wasn't donkeys or stupid-coloured houses that'd made my stomach sink.

'Just thought it would be nice, that's all,' Dad said. 'The pier and that. Nevermind.'

Dad's always liked piers. He says he likes the way you can see between the wood struts and into the sea. I've never been too keen on it myself; you can also see the way the floor buckles underneath the slot machines. I didn't say anything, though. His smile made me feel a bit guilty, knowing what I had to say. And I wondered if it was really worth it.

'No,' I said. 'No, I wasn't thinking about that.' I found a smile but it didn't last very long. The feeling of it on my face reminded me of those complimentary soaps that you get in B&Bs sometimes, if you must wash, please don't use more than two wipes. It was a nasty feeling, and I hoped he hadn't seen it. 'Be great . . . Really. I'd love to go.'

'Only if you want to,' he said. 'I'm hardly forcing you or anything.'

'I know that . . . I *want* to,' I said. But I licked my lips, staring at the floor before I spoke again. 'Dad? I was going to ask you something about my birthday actually.'

'Yeah?' But he didn't sound too bothered now, and I wished Mum wouldn't put him in these moods. It made everything loads harder. I wondered if now was the right time.

'I . . . I was just thinking about my birthday present.'

'I don't want to talk about your present.' He said it like it was the most obvious thing in the world. Maybe it was. 'Hardly be a surprise if we sit around chatting about it.'

'Well that's sort of what I wanted to talk about.' I took a breath. Looking at him now though, I wished I hadn't brought it up. 'It was just something Robin said,' I finished.

'Robin.' He looked up, but I guess I was too busy to hear his tone of voice change.

'Robin said he chooses his own birthday presents. Like . . . like last year he had a TV.'

It came out rushed, like an apology by someone with too little practice. Dad was quiet.

'A TV.' He nodded at the table. 'So he can sit up in his room all night. Great family.'

I swallowed.

'Look,' he said, 'We may not have the money to get you a TV, but quite honestly I think you do alright. You saw

124

Robin's house. Nice little terrace on the council estate? It's not like his parents are rolling in it. If they want to spend their money on stupid extravagant presents instead of sorting out a good standard of living for their children, it's up to them. Stupid as it may seem, I thought you'd prefer things this way round.'

'I . . . I do.' It was difficult to remember your reasons sometimes, listening to him talk.

'Well then,' he said. 'I don't see what you're complaining about.'

'I . . . I wasn't complaining. I'm sorry. It's not like I want anything big. It's . . . it's just the way he talked about it. I don't know. It sounded . . . sounded a bit more grown-up.'

'Grown-up.'

'I mean, I'm not saying that's what *I* think. Just . . . just that that's what he thinks.'

'What *he* thinks? Why would you care what he thinks? Thought you two just split up.'

'What?'

The sentence I'd been working on slipped away.

I stared at him.

Dawn's face came back to me, then. Sitting at her table, with mouth smiling round her sentences as she told me how great it would be. Two-thirty when I'd left, I thought. Three o'clock when I'd arrived. And I wondered how long I'd been gone before she'd picked up the phone.

'Well if you split up, why would you give a shit what *he* thinks? You shouldn't care.'

I opened my mouth but nothing seemed ready to come out yet. I shouldn't care. He'd told me that when I wore my favourite dress to my first High School Non-uniform Day. In the First Year that'd been, and I'd been more entertaining than the lunchtime disco. Not that it was hard. I hadn't worn that dress since then. It'd stopped reminding me of princesses; stupid fat ugly twelve-year-olds had seemed to come more easily to mind. I'd probably outgrown it now.

'I . . . I don't,' I said quietly. 'I don't care what he thinks.' It was true.

Dad looked up, letting my sentence sink in.

'Well,' he said quietly. His face swivelled away from me. 'He's probably right.'

I didn't answer him though. In his profile I could see the greyish patches of regrowing stubble, the shadow that his collar cast across his throat. I could see the skin was tight, stretched over the lumps of his Adam's apple.

And in the other room, I heard a tiny patter as some jigsaw hit the floor.

'It probably . . . it probably is pretty childish.' He laughed, but the skin on his throat reined his laughter in as well. 'I don't know . . . when you get to my age there isn't a *whole* lot of stuff that's much fun anymore.' He said it like he was cracking some joke. I wished that I could close my eyes. 'I mean, you know . . . the job and the bills and everything.' He jerked a thumb out in the direction of the living room. 'Then I've got her nagging at me the whole time. I miss having all the fun,' he said. 'You know?'

I thought of him sewing up my costumes. I knew.

'But.' He shrugged. 'You reach a certain age, you've got to give up "fun". It's like . . . part of the rules.' He whispered it, a secret, but his voice was rough with something else. And my tummy cramped as his eyes came level with mine. 'I just miss it,' he said.

'I didn't mean that was what I thought,' I said quietly. 'I like surprises.'

He just shrugged, though. Like it made no difference. It did make a difference. I was sure of it.

I just couldn't work out why.

I wanted a stereo. Maybe I'd known that right from the beginning, I'm not sure. But by the end of the week I knew it for definite. Matt black with a CD player, double tape deck, AM and FM radio bands, surround-sound speaker system and one of those remote controls that make you feel like you should be reclining on a *chaise-longue* and eating Galaxy chocolate. I had a tape player already but every time you tried to rewind it got stuck in high-gear squeak mode, and the 'twenty-four-hour' clock setting only seemed to have three to choose from. Two of which were half past zero. I wanted a stereo a lot. And three days before my birthday, Dad finally took me to get one.

He hadn't mentioned my birthday at all since I talked to him, which was funny because usually he spends hours trashing out the finer points of our last argument. He didn't even talk about the beach again, and every time I tried to bring it up, say how I couldn't wait to see the sea again, he turned away from me. He changed the subject, and every time I felt a bit like crying. It didn't put me off my stereo though. That was the most shameful thing.

*

Dad met me in his lunchtime on the day we went to buy it, coming all the way to pick me up. His rings had got bigger over the last couple of days, and they made creases down his cheeks. I wondered if he'd slept badly or if he was just hung-over. He was wearing his sunglasses, even though it was cloudy, and he didn't take them off to say hello. I'd put on my long skirt, button-up, with little flowers all over it. And a grey jumper that might have started out white. He liked me in the skirt, or he'd said so once.

He leaned across and unlocked the passenger door for me. He always locked the door when he was driving round town now, ever since he'd seen the television documentary on drive by robberies. Even though it'd been about America, and then only Los Angeles. He smiled at me, but with the sunglasses on I couldn't really be sure if he meant it.

'Want to get some lunch in town after?' he said. It didn't sound much like a question.

'I'd love to!' I wondered if that was overdoing it a bit. 'Whereabouts?'

He shrugged, putting the car into reverse, looking into the mirror. 'Nikki's?'

Nikki's was the only choice really. It wasn't the nicest place in town or anything. The Garlands Tea Rooms was the nicest place, but that wasn't the point. Garlands charged £6.50 for three chips and a sausage, just because they had pine panelling round the walls and put doilies underneath the plates. Not that I'd ever been in there. But Nikki's was cool, none of the girls wore uniforms or anything, and the smoke hung just about eye level, so that if you sat down, you couldn't quite see the ceiling. Dad liked it because it was cheap, and because he said it was 'unpretentious'. I liked it because you could play spot-the-interesting-skin-disorder while you ate. There was The Herb Garden I suppose, but Dad said that a rip-off. I wasn't surprised either, the kind of wages Holly got.

We didn't go to Nikki's first, though. Dad turned the corner when we got into town, right for the High Street, not left for the cafés. I didn't talk much, and Dad talked less, and I didn't say a thing when we turned the other way. I watched the wool shop go past, all the thirty-five-year-old mums who dress like they're sixty, and I wondered if knitting did that to you. They had a special sale on, with a basket out the front full of yellow balls for only 50p. I thought there'd be a lot of kids going round with yellow jumpers, come this Christmas. The gift shop that was full of postcards with the town clock on the front. It always looked nice on the postcards, and I thought people must get pretty disappointed when they actually came here. The man that served behind the counter in the gift shop had cross-eyes, and everybody tried not to look at him while he was giving change. He wore bow-ties not proper ties. Usually in really bright colours or spots or something, and people looked at them instead of his face. I thought he must always be wondering what was wrong with them, the way everybody stared.

We pulled in next to Stead and Simpson, and I could see a girl on the padded bench trying on shoes. Her mum was next to her, reading the paper and waiting to sign the cheque. They were huge shoes, platforms with heels in a kind of see-through glittery plastic. Sandals, and they matched the knickers I could see poking out under the girl's skirt. Tiny little skirt. The girl couldn't have been more than eight. Maybe nine, and she couldn't walk in them. Stead and Simpson was two doors down from Audiovision.

Dad took off his sunglasses and stared at his hands, resting on the steering wheel. Behind, on the dashboard, I could see my Easter thank-you letters. I wondered if I should remind him to post them again. He breathed out, watching his own feet.

'I can't go over a hundred and fifty,' he said. 'I'd like to, but you know how it is.'

'A hundred and fifty pounds? That'll be a big meal.' I wondered why I was bothering.

'You can get one with a CD for that, right?'

' *A hundred and fifty?* But . . .'

'You might not be able to get a double tape deck, but you can always make copies on mine. I'd like to do two hundred, but we've got the electricity coming up . . .'

'I don't want a double tape deck.' One hundred and fifty pounds, I thought. Said like that it sounded like so much to ask. 'Are . . . are you sure? You don't have to do this.'

He didn't answer, thoug h.

All he said was

'Please . . .'

And looking up at me, I knew he meant it.

Audiovision had sliding glass doors, like a supermarket or

something. I remember, when I was a kid, I used to try to sneak up on them from the side, or run in really quick to see if I could catch them out. I didn't do it now though. I thought it might look silly.

Dad went in first, one hand in his pocket. He looked cool. He looked like he knew what he was after. The strip lights were on, even though it was the middle of the day, and they shone off the little bald patch at the back of his head. I don't think he even knew it was there. The collar of his shirt stood up a little bit over his jacket. But that was Ok, that was kind of relaxed, and I wondered why I was worried.

There weren't many people milling about, and I could see the carpet had just been hoovered. A kind of creamy beige, and Michael would have approved. It was a pretty big shop really, big for the High Street. Over on the right was a kind of glass cabinet, full of pocket calculators and that sort of stuff. On top of it was a till, and a girl behind it with a ponytail and a name-tag I couldn't read. Her cravat looked like it was throttling her, but she was smiling anyway.

The TVs were first. Huge things, and every one of them matt black. I didn't care. Ours was matt black too. Some had videos underneath. Some had the box things that pick up satellite, and they were all tuned to different channels. *Neighbours* was on, and *Vanessa*. I thought Vanessa had put on weight but then I hadn't watched it for a while. The stereos went from cheap at the front to expensive at the back. Ones with just tape and radio. *Shiny* black, some even had AM written in neon letters on the front. I went past them pretty quick, just in case Dad saw me looking and got it into his head I wanted one.

There were headphones plugged into a couple of the portable ones, but I didn't put them on. Headphones always looked crap on me, and they messed up your hair for good. I pressed the buttons instead. Not switches, but proper buttons, where you only have to touch them to make them work. Tape CD Radio printed in a little read-out at the top. Playing music would be pretty much irrelevant, I thought, when you could watch it switch from Tape to CD to Radio and see that little light flick.

'Hello.'

The man behind me had nice teeth. I saw them first, they seemed to kind of shine out of his lips. Lots of them, I thought, and every one aimed right at me. His hair was short, cropped around the sides, but a little bit fell over his forehead into his eyes. It wasn't proper black like Joel's but it was pretty close. The name on the tag said Oliver.

'Oliver?' I looked back at the stereo. I wondered if that'd sounded rude.

'That's me.' He was still smiling. It made the skin around his eyes crease up a little bit like Dad's. Quite big eyes, though, bigger than Dad's. 'Nice system, that one,' he said.

'Yes.' So nice I couldn't quite pull my eyes away. 'I'm choosing a birthday present.'

I hoped he'd caught the word *choosing* in that sentence, but I didn't look to check.

'Ah. You're a birthday girl. How old are you going to be? Twenty-one?'

I laughed. 'Not quite.'

'Nineteen?' He had a small nose, and there weren't any blackheads. I wondered if the thing that held his tie together was real gold. Dad wanted to save up for a real gold one. I remember I'd been surprised when he said that. I'd sort of thought he'd think a gold tie thingy was pretentious. Oliver's looked like real gold. None of his buttons were undone either. 'So what sort of thing are you looking for?'

'Well . . . I like this one.' I nodded back to it, and he nodded at me. I wondered if I should nod again, just to make sure. I didn't though, I turned round so he could see it.

'Good taste too.' He laughed, but I didn't get a chance to fit one in as well. 'What sort of price range are you looking at?'

'Well . . . maybe £150?' I looked at him. 'Maybe a bit more though.' I said it quickly.

'Well, *that's* not bad for a birthday present. What sort of features are you looking for?' The smile came out again. It was a nice smile, I thought. I wondered if he smiled at everyone like that. 'CD? Tape deck – double or single? You can have a turn table.'

'Oh . . . no, I haven't got any records.'

'No, but I bet your old man has.'

I thought about Dad's record collection. He kept it in a cardboard box under the kitchen table. Some of them had cases – sleeves, I think he called them, even though they didn't look anything like sleeves. But they usually weren't the right ones. It was a big cardboard box, though. Half the sides were ripped off where they'd

been used to light the fire. The cat slept in there sometimes.

'Oh yeah. Dad's mad about his records. He's got . . .
oh, hundreds.' I smiled, and I thought it looked like a good
smile. A grown-up, kind of just-between-ourselves smile.
'He's got them alphabetically,' I said. 'In a rack.' And I
wondered why I felt nervous.

'Is it going to go in your bedroom?'

'Well, it's not going to go anywhere else.'

Oliver took a breath. He looked like he was deciding,
and glanced back at the counter.

'Ok, this is the one I *should* sell you – it's a brand new
model, right? But the one *I'd* choose,' he pointed over to
the door, 'is this one.' He took a couple of steps and I
followed. 'Can I be honest with you?' he said. 'This model
isn't brand new.'

'Looks it.'

'That's the beauty. It looks it but in fact it's two years
old. When they *released* it, though, it was over £250. Only
reason it's £180 now is so they can sell it and make room
for new ones. More profit that way, but the bottom line
is, you'll get more out of it. Better sound, better
features. Like you said yourself, doesn't look two years
old.'

It didn't either. Maybe a bit bigger than the other one,
but not by much.

'Look,' he said again, 'the best thing for you to do is
listen to it. What sort of music you into? Nirvana right?'
There was a gleam in his eye.

'Oh *definitely*.'

'Thought so,' he said, and he looked past me. '*Tom?* Get us the Nirvana CD, yeah?'

Someone looked up. He wasn't quite scowling, but it was close. He went though. He didn't even say anything. And I watched Oliver's face, a little twitch around the mouth. Maybe it was a smile. He looked good like that, I thought. He looked a bit like Robin.

'Here.' Tom didn't look at me before he walked off. I thought he looked pissed off.

'Right.' Oliver didn't even glance at the CD case while he opened it. 'This is an excellent album,' he said. I nodded. It was funny, he didn't really look like the Nirvana type. 'Ok.' He clicked the button on the front, not quite as smooth as the other, but I guessed that didn't matter. A plate thing slid out. It made a nice sound, soft and kind of satisfying. He placed the disk on it and it slid back in like a good pet. 'If you want to come and stand' – he touched my arm round the elbow and I walked a couple of steps with him – 'over here. You'll get the best sound.' He handed me a remote, and I think I might have sighed. 'Play button's the big red one,' he said. And I pressed it.

Kurt's voice blasted over the background: mumbling Radio 2 and the comforting voice of Vanessa.

'Oh my God!' I fumbled for the Off button. 'Oh, Jesus.' People were looking round. I wondered where Dad was. *'How do I turn it off?'*

He looked around. Everyone was staring now, as guitar came sailing out of the speakers across the room. Their faces were blank, stupid. I wondered vaguely if mine looked the same. He smirked.

'Don't worry about it,' he said. 'Fuck them,' he said, and then he turned back to the stereo. I took one more glance around at all those stupid faces. I smiled to myself. *Fuck 'em*, I thought, and then I turned back too.

'*Hello!*' The voice came from behind me, just before an arm settled on my shoulders. I looked at Oliver, but his arms were by his sides.

'Oh. Hi, Dad.'

'So, have we found anything?'

'Well . . .' I thought about the price tag. 'A couple of things. Maybe.'

'Right,' Oliver said. 'Well, I'll leave you two to discuss it, yeah? Call me if you want anything.' And he moved off to one side, walking kind of backwards. It didn't look funny on him, though. It almost looked right.

'Isn't this one *cool?*'

Dad took his arm away and stuck it in his pocket. Well not the whole arm, obviously. Just the hand. 'Look around before you make a decision, eh? Fair bit of money, £150.'

'I know . . . But have you seen the little read-out thing? And Oliver said he thought this'd be the best one. You know, for my particular needs. And it sounds so cool!'

'Sounds alright. But I mean, it's not brilliant, is it?' He looked at me. He wasn't smiling anymore. 'Alright,' he said, 'hang on.' And I saw Oliver standing to the side now, staring out across the shop and through the window. He'd got that little bit of hair out of his eye. It was tucked behind his ear, but still kind of threatening. Dad flicked his hand, sort of calling to him. But I guess Oliver didn't see, because he didn't move to come over. I heard Dad's breathing get heavier. '*Oliver?*'

Oliver looked across then. 'Can I help?' He didn't walk towards us though.

'Yeah,' Dad said. 'You can tell me what makes this one so special.'

'Sure. Basically, it's a more expensive machine, right? But because it's an older machine it's been reduced. The quality is still that of a more expensive stereo, though.'

'Well, you would say that. You're on commission.'

'Not a lot of difference in £30. I'm just trying to get the best deal for your daughter.'

'For us, you mean.' Dad watched him.

'For both of you. It depends if you want a better machine or if you want something with more knobs. Like I said, take the CD, play it in a couple. See what you think.'

'Thank you,' Dad said. 'We will.'

And we did. But in the end, we bought the one Oliver suggested.

I watched the box on our back seat as Dad pulled out. It was small and square and perfect and I smiled, clicking in my seat belt. 'Thank you,' I said. Dad shrugged, turning the corner. Turning, I saw, in the wrong direction. 'Dad, Nikki's is left . . .'

'We're not going to Nikki's first.' He stared ahead. 'We're going to pick up Dawn.'

I looked up as Dad breathed out. 'I asked her if she wanted to come to lunch, alright.'

'Oh,' I said. 'That's nice.' But looking at his jaw set tight, I wasn't really sure.

Dawn didn't just come to lunch with us, Dad asked her if she'd like to come back and stay the night as well. I guess she didn't have many other pressing engagements because she seemed pretty happy to come. And he smiled at me, stepping over Mum's papers in the porch. I watched Dawn walk through the door before me and I only caught a glimpse. It was a funny kind of smile, though. I didn't really like it.

Mum's jigsaw was still spread on the table, blue bits and red bits in groups, and I had to push them to one side, placing my stereo down. It was beautiful. Even in the box, I thought, as Michael's door swung open. It was smooth and cream with pictures.

'So you bought it.' He only glanced across the table, though, before he looked at me. He had a V-neck jumper on and his trousers looked ironed to me. I wondered how he managed to be so smart, Mum left his clothes in the cat box same as everybody else.

'It's only got one tape deck,' Dawn said. I thought about explaining to her that, one tape deck or two, at least I hadn't been bought it so my dad didn't have to talk to me.

'I'm only going to buy CDs,' I said. 'They're much better listening quality actually.'

I gazed at it. It wasn't dented in a single place, even if it was two years old, I thought.

'Well.' Michael turned away like he was bored already. 'I hope you're happy now.'

I wondered what that was supposed to mean. 'I am thank you, Michael. Very happy.'

He was taking a little look at the picture on the box though. He wasn't so fucking holy.

Perfect, square black diagram, with every button set in symmetry. DIGITAL, it said. I heard Dad come up behind me and his breath was pretty regular, even if it was a bit deep. He stood behind us, me and Dawn, and he stared down at it too. Twelve inches high.

'I'm glad,' he said, and I bit my lip a little bit. I hadn't meant for him to hear as well.

'Yeah,' Michael said. 'Glad *you're* happy.'

'And the remote doesn't activate the tape deck.' Dawn wasn't looking at the stereo now, though. She was staring down at her nails, like they were loads more interesting.

'Doesn't matter,' Michael said. 'Now she's got everything *her* way, doesn't matter.'

I tried to ignore him. 'Thank you Dad,' I said, still looking down at it. 'I really love it.'

Dad just turned away though, walking off towards the kitchen. 'Yeah,' he said quietly. And I felt my head drop down a notch as he closed the door behind him.

Dawn came round a lot those next few days. Which was funny really because I didn't once invite her. I wondered if she was having some problem at home, something going on that I didn't know about, and Dad was taking pity on her. I don't know, though. It didn't really feel like that.

She didn't come round on my birthday, though. I kind of made sure about that. Dad was taking the day off work and we were going to the beach after all. I didn't want Dawn there, I didn't want anyone to see me with her. Not that I told Dad that, of course. I told him I wanted it to be a family day.

I spent a long time sitting on my bed that morning, trying to work out what to wear. It didn't seem to matter what I chose, whenever we went to the beach I looked crap in comparison to all the other girls. Even if I thought really hard, spent ages choosing, adjusting, getting the right shoes, swapping the right shoes, swapping them back. I'd stare in the mirror before I left and I'd look fantastic. Cool, sexy, sophisticated. At least seventeen. Then when I got there I'd suddenly find I was wearing a shell suit.

I picked out my best ripped jeans that morning. The only pair that'd gone naturally, without a razor blade, plus a strappy blouse that I thought would pass for white under a dark enough sky. I plaited my hair. It was fine, I thought, but I kept an eye out. Shell suits can leap out from anywhere. And I was feeling pretty confident till I saw Michael.

He was really dressed up. One of Mum's old shirts that'd gone grey and yellow round the cuffs, buttoned right up to the neck, and he looked like he was choking on it. He'd put his school tie on around it. And gelled his hair back.

'You're going to wear that are you?' I gave him my best look.

'Yes,' he said. 'It's called looking good.'

'You look like you've just been released.'

Mum was wearing culottes, because that was what mums

wore when they went to the beach. It was weird though, considering she was the one who paid attention to the weather forecasts. Dad didn't ever listen to them, not since Michael Fish told everyone that hurricanes were ridiculous. Mum pretty much lived by them though.

'I'm really not so sure about the beach, Philip. Have you seen the clouds out there?'

'You're the one wearing shorts.'

'But it said on the weather last night. Cold front coming westwards. From the sea.'

'We live on an island, Liz. The sea is in every direction.'

'I s'pose we can always go round the shops,' she said.

The weather started getting worse as soon as we got driving. Dad was driving as always, even though I was pretty sure Mum could too. I had to sit in the back, next to Michael, because Mum was my mother, even though it was my birthday. That was what she said: *I'm YOUR MOTHER, so I'll be going in the front if you don't mind.* I did mind, but I knew not to answer, they'd taught us rhetorical questions in English. It was better if she sat in the front anyway. She got to argue with Dad better that way.

'Look,' he said, when she pointed out the clouds for the fourth time, 'if you thought it was going to rain, why didn't you change into a pair of fucking trousers?'

'Well, according to you, I didn't need to.'

'That's not what I said. You know what . . .'

'You said it was going to be fine. If it's going to be fine, I can wear shorts can't I?'

'Wear what the fuck you like, but don't complain when you're freezing your arse off.'

'Oh, so it's *not* going to be fine?'

'Fuck off . . .'

'You've gelled your hair again, haven't you?' I said. Michael gave me one of his sliding glances. 'It looks shit. You do know that, don't you?'

'And I'm s'posed to take advice from a fourteen-year-old who still wears bunches?'

'You fuck off! You're the one who wanted to go to the fucking beach!'

'Oh, so you don't want to go?'

'To be honest with you, Philip, I don't want to go anywhere with you at the moment.'

'Yeah, well the same goes for me. Don't worry about that.'

'I *wasn't* worrying, Philip. I don't *give* a shit!' She leaned over to me and Michael then. 'Please don't bicker,' she said. 'You'll ruin the day.'

We stopped off in town first, so everyone could get some space. Also to buy crisps and Coca-Cola. Dad parked on a double yellow line because Mum asked him not to. I got out of the car so no one saw me sitting next to Michael. I leaned against the side of the shoe shop and watched an old bloke pick out his first pair of slippers.

'Hello, stranger.'

I recognized the voice, but I didn't turn round at first.

'Oh,' I said after a moment. 'Hi.' Oliver had a different shirt on and a different smile as well. 'Are you working?'

'On my break,' he said. 'Happy birthday.'

I smiled my best birthdays-are-for-kids smile. I flicked my eyes up while I did it.

'How's the stereo?' His smile got wider and I saw he had a little crack in the corner of his mouth. I thought it must hurt, little things do. He was smiling through it, though.

'Haven't tried it yet.' I looked at the window, trying to think of something else to say.

'You wanna get the speakers about twelve foot apart. If your bedroom's big enough.'

'My bedroom's big enough for anything.' It wasn't though. It was tiny. 'I'll have to get someone else to do all the plugging in for me, though. I can't even wire a plug.' I smiled at him, tossing a bit of hair behind my ear. Holly would have been impressed.

'So who's doing your plugging in at the moment?' His smile got wider. A nice sort of smile.

'No one special.'

'Could call that a vacancy, I s'pose.'

I laughed. Across the street I saw Dad come huffing out of the newsagents. I didn't really want to go to the beach now, though. I wondered why that made me feel guilty.

'I tell you what, why don't I call you. Check you've got everything wired up right.'

Dad was halfway across the road. 'Yeah . . . Uh, Ok.' I took a step away. 'Have you got a pen?' He reached into his pocket. I was expecting a Bic. He brought out a fountain pen. It looked like a Parker, only with Waterson written down the side. It was gold.

He held out the back of his hand and grinned. I grinned too, but I could see Dad opening the boot. I held his hand underneath to brace myself. Strong hands, he had. Clean nails too.

644 188: See you!

We reached the seaside about an hour later and it was raining when we got there. Dad parked alongside the pier and we ate our picnic in the car, watching the windscreen wipers smudge the view in rhythm. The sea goes a horrible colour in the rain, dirty grey, and I tried not to look at it. I think the sea's kind of depressing anyway, the way it just goes on and on.

Across the street there weren't that many people shopping and I guess I'd got dressed up for nothing after all. I could see a couple arguing underneath an umbrella, huddled outside Miss Selfridge. The woman was staring down at the wet pavement. All the nice shops are on the High Street in beach towns, Dorothy Perkins and Chelsea Girl. Places with nice clean carpets and clean shop assistants to match. But, if you look a little further, you get the shitty shops as well. Just down a side alley between Marks and Spencer and Boots, there'll be this dirt-brown door that doesn't even have a window to go with. They're always called BARGAIN BASEMENT!!! where the T's fallen off, and the only truth in the title is that all the goods are underground because they haven't got a licence. Same with the pubs, where just down the road from Ruddock's Wine Bar – the one with all the neat tiling and fake copper horseshoes – you'll find The Broken Pool Cue. Really quaint, with tarpaulin in the windows instead of glass.

Mum made a cup of tea for everybody, nodding to *The World at One*. She always brings a flask of tea on picnics, even though Dad says it spoils the whole point. I think it's pretty funny really. You could put Mum on the Mir space station and she'd still listen to *The World at One* while she made her cup of tea. I reckon she'll be buried with her yellow tartan flask, just in case there is a God and he only has those polystyrene cups. Dad picked at his chips while she poured and I watched the water dribble down the windows, making shiny see-through worms on the glass. They reflected on Mum's and Dad's faces, shiny and transparent, as she added in the milk. Michael sniffed. His eyes were red from playing on the Megadrive. His lips were pulled in tight, sucking ketchup off his food, and the rain drummed the radio down.

'Nice chips,' I said quietly.

We put all the rubbish in a big pile by Michael's feet when we'd finished. Dad lit a cigarette and opened the window so the rain could clean the upholstery a bit. He blew a funnel of smoke outside, where the wind caught it and pushed it back in. I watched an old woman shuffle past with a mauve rinse in her hair and a stripy umbrella. Her face was all squinted up, even though the water wasn't getting on her. It was funny, I thought, the way women reach sixty-five and suddenly start thinking that blue hair really suits them. Mum folded the newspaper over so it only took up half the car. Dad turned in his seat to look at me. 'Don't s'pose you want a present now,' he said.

'A present? You didn't have to get me anything . . . not after the stereo . . .'

Dad was quiet for a moment. His eyes deflated to the steering wheel before he carried on. 'It's only a little thing. I hope it's not too stupid.' He handed me something in brown paper. It wasn't a little thing at all, it was big. He turned back so he wouldn't have to watch while I opened it. I tore at the corner. Brown wood. Some kind of box.

'Uh . . .' I screwed up my eyes to open the rest, crunching up the paper. I undid the clasp on the top with difficulty, it was done up pretty tight. I flicked the clips.

'COOL!' I saw the corners of his mouth turn up in a smile, even from behind. It was an art box. There were gouaches and charcoal sticks, some *really* flash pencils, chalks, a sponge, a putty rubber, an ink pen, oil pastels and brushes. All set out in neat little rows. Hand-made rows, I saw. He'd made the box himself. And on the top a little note in cardboard with a red heart drawn on. *All my love . . . Dad*, it said. All my love.

'It's . . . beautiful . . .'

'You like it?' He turned back, his mouth twisted, unsure. 'Pretty boring after the stereo I guess.'

'It's *not* boring!' The tubes stared up at me. 'Must . . . must have taken you ages.'

He shrugged. 'Yeah well,' he said. 'It did take me a pretty long time. I just bothered.'

'It's . . . it's beautiful! Gouaches are my favourite.' I

looked at the box, lying open on my lap. It felt very heavy, weighted on my knees. 'It's gorgeous,' I said. 'Really.'

Dad didn't speak for a moment.

He turned away from me and his smile faded in the soft reflections.

'So,' he said, staring through the window. 'I guess not all surprises are boring then.'

The funny thing about going out with Oliver was that I couldn't tell when it started. With Robin it had been clear-cut, and I'd known the exact moment when I stopped being just some girl he couldn't stand and started being his girlfriend instead. Oliver didn't ask me if I'd be his girlfriend, nothing concrete like that. He asked me out to dinner instead.

It was a week before he called. A long dull week after my birthday, and I hadn't thought of him a lot. Sometimes his face had popped up in my head, between the day-to-day. I smiled that evening though, picking up the phone. I flicked my hair behind my shoulder, making room for the receiver, and I took it in the study.

His words were very smooth, like it hadn't been a week at all. No cracks between the sentences, and I could have said *Sorry, I can't. I'm washing my pet candlestick*, and he wouldn't have paused for breath. He would've glossed right over it. It sounded like he had it all worked out.

'I was just wondering if you fancied going for a meal.'

'A meal. That sounds nice . . .' I let my words trail off into a sexy smile. I thought he'd be able to imagine the rest. Which was good because I certainly couldn't.

'Great,' he said, but he didn't really sound overjoyed. 'Shall I pick you up?'

Pick me up. I thought of the alternative: kissing Dad on the cheek as he dropped me by the door. 'That'd be lovely,' I said.

'Right.' He sounded like he had something else to be doing. 'About eight alright?'

'Eight? What . . . tonight?'

He paused, halfway to hanging up it sounded like. 'Well, tomorrow if you'd rather.'

'No no.' Tonight. Dad'd probably put a movie on. Mum would read the paper. I'd go to bed at ten. 'No, tonight's Ok . . .' I wondered what excuse I'd make. 'It's just . . .'

'If it's too soon, just say.' *Just hurry up*, I thought.

'It's not too soon,' I said.

It was funny like that, talking to him didn't seem real, more like something from a movie. And I wasn't nervous, saying yes. I knew he couldn't really see me.

Picking out my clothes, I tried to think of what I'd say to Mum and Dad. *Just off to have dinner with a strange older man I don't really know* didn't seem to have quite the right ring. It was quiet in my room upstairs though: just the blips and blops of *Sonic The Hedgehog*, some annoying tune. I couldn't hear where Mum or Dad were, and maybe I wouldn't have to excuse myself at all. There was the meowing of the cat stuck out in the porch and I could almost hear the clicking of Michael pressing buttons. Quiet felt weird in my house. I didn't like the sound, and I sang

Pearl Jam songs while I put my make-up on so I wouldn't have to hear.

I chose a little black dress, strap-shouldered. High heels and a jacket with a rip on one side to play it down a bit. I looked in the mirror, breathed out, and I was glad I wasn't nervous. Five minutes to go, I thought. Just long enough to brush my teeth again.

The bathroom light was on, though, and the door closed tight as I walked through the study again. Four minutes, I thought. But then I could be four minutes early, and I was turning to go when I heard that little noise.

It came from behind the bathroom door where the light dribbled, very yellow, through the cracks. It stippled shadows on the carpet, slapped a line of dye across my shin. It was a hitched-in breath. It was a gasp, I thought. The gasp before a sob.

I'd never heard Mum cry before, she's just not the crying type. Like Dad said when I'd asked him about the present, she's the nagging type, not soft around the edges. I know because it makes him sad. He tries to hide it by acting pissed off, but underneath he's sad. Every time she has a go. And standing there, caught halfway to leaving, I heard it come again. It wasn't a pretty sound, clean tears like out of *Brief Encounter*. It was dry and out of rhythm and I could hear her suck the snot back in before another sob. No, Mum doesn't ever cry, she's a bitching kind of person. I know that. She's never sad, not even when they fight and they hadn't fought today. They'd hardly even talked.

She never cries.

I nodded in the empty room.

And I made my footsteps very quiet, backing out.

Oliver picked me up by the main road. Not that it was the M1 or anything, but I still remember Dad never let me go down there on my own when I was little. Not even when I knew my Green Cross Code by heart. He worries about me. And I wondered what he'd think now, seeing me going off in a car with a strange man. It was Ok though, I thought. I'd know to get out the minute he offered me sweets.

It was windy by the main road, and my toes were aching from the heels. Not nervous, I thought, and I wondered what the hell I'd say to him. I tried to stop my hair from blowing in my face, thinking about how Mum would say *It'll be autumn soon.* Only she'd usually say it in March, when it was still winter. She's stupid like that. And watching the cars whip past, left in the silence between them, I thought about the bathroom door. I couldn't see the drivers' faces through their windscreens. The light smoothed their reflections into the same blank glass. They hadn't even argued, I thought. I wondered why it mattered.

Oliver's car looked the same as every other one, Sierras and Mondeos. I guess I was surprised by that. I'd sort of expected a sign in the window or something: *the occupant of this car is new, different and exciting.* It was a Citroen Xantia, in maroon, and he'd left the garage stickers on the back window. Dad's always taking those stickers off our car. He says he doesn't see why garages should advertise themselves on our property, only he says fucking garages.

I sort of understood why Oliver had left his on, though. They weren't from the motor pool in town. They were proper Kwik-Fit stickers.

I watched it slow down and I hoped I looked romantic, standing in the breeze by the side of the road. Stupid was equally possible, though. I held down my skirt and smiled across the window. I thought I'd probably catch his face. He opened the door for me.

'Hello there.'

I bent down to climb in. I tried to purr it: 'Hello.' It sounded like I had something stuck in my throat. I coughed.

'Am I late?' He pushed his elbow out a bit to look at his watch. I didn't know a lot about watches, but it wasn't one of the plastic ones from the gift shop. 'Five minutes,' he said. 'Sorry.' He didn't really look it.

'Don't worry about it.' I laughed, trying to get in without rocking the car. 'I don't keep a watch. I think . . . you know, keeping a watch makes you run around, always worried. Makes you live by the clock. Better to enjoy things.' I shifted in the seat, trying to find somewhere to put my hands. 'I reckon anyway.' I coughed.

He looked down, over my jacket, and I watched his eyes hook on the rip. 'Well,' he said, 'I wanted to be on time.'

'Mm.' I kept my eyes on the dashboard instead of his face. I could see my reflection in it, my nose all big and splayed out, olive skin on the black vinyl. 'Well . . .' I tried to find a joke there. I don't think there was one though. 'You are.'

I let my eyes slide over to him, I sort of couldn't keep them back anymore. His hair was flicked back, with something that might have been gel or water. Only a little bit though, nothing like Michael. It was tucked behind his ear, all delicate and pink, slightly frilly on the edge, with tiny lilac veins running through. He didn't seem to have an earwax problem. 'I like your car,' I said. 'Does it have one of those key-ring things that unlocks the car even when you're not standing next to it?'

He grinned. 'Shit,' he said. 'I was going to pretend it was magic.'

'Hm,' I said, but it didn't sound much like a laugh.

He put the car into gear and we started off, leaving his hand on the gear stick, even when he wasn't using it. I looked out of the window for something to point out and talk about. The sound of the engine was quieter than our car and it didn't have that clunk that goes round and round underneath the passenger side of the bonnet. I thought that was probably a good thing, though. Oliver was wearing a different pair of jeans and a kind of checked, hooded top with a zip up the front. I didn't really like it.

'So,' I said. I lifted up my hands, dumped them back down in my lap and breathed. There wasn't really much I could say, though. I watched our lane drag off behind us and I wondered if Mum had come out of the bathroom yet. I wondered if she'd start putting the meal together, if Dad would notice the redness in her eyes. Glancing over at Oliver, I found a weak smile. I tried to think of something else.

*

Garlands wasn't really the way I'd expected it to be. There was a lot of pine panelling, but the people weren't eating in silence or reading the *Financial Times*. They were just a bit cleaner than the people in Nikki's, and they had fewer chins.

We sat in a table by the window too. You could never do that in Nikki's. The draughts made it too cold to eat and you had to watch your clothes for the chewing gum people stuck to the walls. It wasn't like that in Garlands. All the chairs had cushions built in, and the menus didn't leave your hands sticky. I was surprised to find I kind of liked it.

Oliver pulled my chair out so I could sit. I tried to remember if Robin'd ever done that.

'Oh . . . whoops.' I trod on his foot stepping over to the chair. 'Sorry.' But he just smiled. I pulled my chair forward and it made a screech across the floorboards. I wondered why I felt like a fool. The waitress came before I'd even picked up a menu.

'Can I help you?'

'House white, please,' Oliver said. 'We haven't decided yet.'

'Fine.' She smiled, glanced over at me and walked off. I smiled an apology at Oliver.

'What do you fancy then?' He scanned down the list and looked back at me.

'Um . . . I don't know.' I giggled, and it sounded stupid. *Duck à l'orange, Boeuf Bourguignon, Pork in Cider, Pork Stroganoff.* 'Not much vegetarian stuff is there . . .'

'Are you a vegetarian?'

'My parents are.'

'Oh,' he said. 'Well, there's spinach and mushroom pancakes. Or the gnocchi . . .'

'I s'pose I could have meat, though.' Oliver didn't respond. 'Could I have the duck?'

He laughed. 'You can have what you want. I want the steak,' he said, and shut his menu. He was quick, I thought, and I should hurry up. I closed mine, trying to make it bang like his. It just smacked together, though. I thought it sounded kind of pathetic.

'Duck then,' I said.

'Duck and . . .?'

I looked at him. 'Chips?'

'What sauce?' he said, explaining.

'Oh . . . orange.' I played with the fork. '*L'orange* . . .' Clean steel, swivelling around. '*Le orange* . . .' Not like our ones at home. We had to be the only people in the world to get our money back from the stainless steel company. Dad'd sorted that out, even if it was Mum that'd made them so dirty, always leaving them wet on the draining board.

The waitress had a towel round the wine when she came over. I almost said something. I didn't really like the idea of hot wine, but she only poured it into Oliver's glass.

'Er . . . Can I have some too?'

He smiled, held up his hand and I shut up. The waitress had an annoying look on her face that seemed to centre round her nose. He emptied the glass. 'That's fine, thanks.' She nodded and smiled at him. I was glad to see her go. 'It's so I can taste it,' he said.

'Oh . . .' I waited. 'Is it nice, then?'

'It'll do,' he said. He sounded like Dad saying that, I thought. So in control. I wondered if Dad had ever taken Mum out for dinner, when they first got together. I couldn't imagine them smiling over the tablecloth at each other. Mum would have complained about something and spoiled it all. Because she's always the one that spoils stuff, a killjoy Dad says. I wondered if she was being a killjoy when she was sitting in the bathroom crying. Staring at my napkin, I blinked the thought away. 'So do they always put it in the man's glass?' I said, trying to smile.

'Yep,' he said. 'It's sexist really, I suppose.'

I watched him and he was waiting. That was Ok. I could be a feminist if he wanted.

'It is,' I said. 'I mean, women have just as good tastebuds as men.' He nodded, but I didn't feel like I'd got it right. 'Can I have some now?' I said. He poured for me and I almost drank before I saw his glass held out.

'What shall we drink to?' he said.

'Oh . . .' I tried to think of something good. Something grown-up, like you read in Mills and Boon. 'Beginnings,' I said and looked him in the eye.

'Beginnings.' He tipped his glass, smiled at me and I smiled back. I was having a great time, I thought, and I tapped the glass against my lips. I wasn't thinking about Mum and Dad, not at all. About those sounds, so small inside the bathroom.

After a while, the meal came.

I let him kiss me when he dropped me off, I guess he had

paid for dinner. It was only a short kiss, though. No tongues, like we used to say in Primary. The stubble on his cheeks when he bent over to the passenger side kind of surprised me. It didn't feel like kissing Robin, he never had any stubble. More like Dad's cheeks, and the feel of it when he tucked me in at night.

It was dark by the time I walked back up the lane, and I didn't turn to watch his headlights move away. Thinking about it, I didn't know what to make of Oliver, of the way he looked or talked. He didn't act the same as the boys at school, that was pretty obvious, but Garlands wasn't really so much different to the rail outside the community centre. It was me that was different, I thought. In that way it didn't matter what Oliver said.

I smiled, listening to my heels click on the concrete. It reminded me of that poem Dad used to say, when he still read me stuff like that: *When she was good, she was very very good. And when she was bad, she was AWFUL.* I could be awful. I bet he'd never guessed that.

Sneaking off in the evening to have a candlelit dinner with a dark and handsome stranger. Funny that it sounded so much cooler than it felt; trying to cut into a duck breast without it skidding off the plate. I didn't have to remember that, though. I could blur over stepping on his foot. I could make the reality match up.

And I wondered what Oliver had thought of me, he didn't even know my surname. Mysterious and secretive, I thought. Independent. Wild. Anything like that would've done. Anything that wasn't someone else's introduction.

I did like him too. I liked the way the muscles in his jaw

clenched when he grit his teeth. I liked the way he knew so much and I didn't. I thought about those tough dark eyes, I wondered how he'd look above me and my stomach rolled over. I'd let him kiss me, I thought, and my hands felt sweaty, pressing them together. One lingering kiss. It didn't matter that the seatbelt had cut into my tit. I shivered, going up the hill. I smiled.

I should have given him a different name.

And it was Ok, I decided. I didn't need a reason to go out with him.

I knew pretty early on that I'd let Oliver fuck me. It seemed like a natural progression. It wasn't like a decision or anything, I just didn't have a lot of choice. He was a grown-up after all. I would have let him do it straight away only we didn't see much of each other in the first fortnight. He phoned a lot, though, and we talked for a pretty long time. It's funny. Thinking about it, I'm not even sure what we said.

I didn't mind just talking to him. I almost liked it better. It was easier to pretend, I suppose, and I didn't have to wash my hair. We couldn't talk about the usual stuff, though. He wasn't interested in *Star Trek*, and Oliver didn't bother to pretend about stuff he wasn't interested in. No polite hmms? and reallys? He just told me straight off.

'I don't watch *Star Trek*.'

'Oh.'

So I knew right away that particular line of conversation was a dead-end.

I didn't tell anybody about him those first two weeks,

even though I wanted to. Having a secret was kind of cool, but secrets get boring after a while if you've got no one to share them with. There's only so long that smiling to yourself mysteriously can keep you entertained. And somehow, I didn't think Dawn would really understand.

'D'you reckon Axl Rose is better-looking than Sebastian Bach?'

'Hmm? Gazing romantically out of the window.

'Like Sebastian's got nicer hair. More . . . glossy.'

'Mm . . .' My whimsical Mona Lisa smile was starting to make my face ache.

'So how come everyone fancies Axl Rose better, and he's this great big sex symbol?'

'Dawn. It . . . it's not really that important, is it?' I hitched up my smile again: Colgate+.

Still she didn't notice.

'*Sorry* if my conversation's so *boring* for you. God. I can't help being *me* . . .'

And she couldn't.

Yes, I think I knew pretty early on that I'd let Oliver fuck me.

I thought it'd happen the first time that I went to his flat. I even put on my best pants in case. I couldn't think of much else two people could do inside a flat. And I wondered if I'd feel much different with my hymen broken.

I was nervous the first time I walked in there. It was weird, that. I hadn't been nervous in the restaurant. Well, not too nervous anyway. But somehow it seemed different, meeting him on his home ground. Sort of like there wasn't any turning back. I had all my comments set up for when I got there. I'd gone through it in my head. Something tasteful, something grown-up, like: *Oh, I love the way the curtains highlight the grain of the pine.* When I got there, of course, I couldn't think of a bloody thing.

Oliver's flat looked just like Michael's bedroom. There wasn't a single thing out of place, and all those places were hidden away, just like he was embarrassed by them. *Exactly* like Michael's bedroom, only with a stereo and TV and video instead of toys.

'Where's your bed?' I looked around the room, like I was searching for it.

'Oh,' he said. 'It's just a single. In the other room.'

'Just a single?' I smiled. It was a good smile, I thought. Knowledgeable.

'Yep. Guess I'll have to rectify that.' And he smiled back.

'Guess you will,' I said. 'Some chairs too,' I added, and then wished I hadn't. Chairs didn't have anything to do with sex.

There was lots of floor in Oliver's flat. More floor than there was ceiling, I was pretty sure of that. And there were no chairs, so it looked even bigger than it was. There was a light blue carpet, but it wasn't expensive. It was thin and worn away round the edges. Incredibly clean, though. I wondered how anyone could keep their carpet that clean.

'God . . . You could like, start a record shop.'

'I collect them.' He was leaning against the window, hands spread out beside him.

'I can see that,' I said. I flicked my finger along the line of CDs. Hundreds of them. Leonard Cohen ... Elvis Costello ... Bob Dylan ... 'They're all in alphabetical order!' The Palace Brothers ... Liz Phair ... Pulp ... Lou Reed. He didn't say anything. 'I s'pose you've got enough though ... you know, to put them in alphabetical order.' Velvet Underground ... Tom Waits ... 'How much did you *pay* for all of them?'

He shrugged. 'I'm not sure.'

'Fifteen quid a head,' I said. His fingers squeaked, stretching against the sill. 'You must *have* three hundred. . . .'

'Three hundred and twelve.'

'Christ, so three hundred and twelve times fifteen . . .'

'It's not the money that's important,' he said. 'I like them.'

'Right.' I glanced away from the CDs. 'Course.' I sort of wished I hadn't mentioned it. 'Anyway,' I said. 'I'm shit at maths.'

I wandered round for a little while and every so often I looked across at him. It was hard to see his expression against the light coming in, but I knew he was watching me.

'I like your stereo,' I said.

'Thanks,' he said. 'They're NAD separates. BOSE speakers, top of the range.'

'What, like Panasonic? Dad's got Panasonic speakers on his stereo.'

'Not really,' he said. 'BOSE speakers are good.' I turned round a moment, looking at him. Panasonic speakers *were* good. I knew they were good because Dad'd had them for years, and he said they were the best speakers he'd ever heard. Because they didn't have any 'wa and flutter' or something.

I wondered if we should snog now.

'Can I smoke in here?' I said.

'Sure.' Oliver walked across to one of his bookshelves, took an ashtray off the end. He had lots of books. That wasn't a big deal, I had lots of books too. Only his books were all hardbacks, and all pretty, and none of them had the creases down the spine that reading puts in books. I wondered if they were in alphabetical order too. The top shelf was all biographies; the same people as the CDs. Bob Dylan, Leonard Cohen, The Kinks, The Clash, John Lenin. The second shelf was novels, or at least I thought they were novels. No Stephen King. No Ray Bradbury. There were a lot of French names, and one of the shelves was poetry. I could see that, because all the books had matching covers and the titles all started with *The Collected Works of* . . . Weird books. I wondered if he ever read any of them.

'Nice ashtray,' I said. It was a big glass job. It looked like it'd had a recent Pledging, and I wondered vaguely what he'd think of my room. 'It's very . . . clean.'

'Mm,' he said. 'That's probably because it's just been washed.'

'*Really?*' I took a cigarette out of the pocket in my jacket, and tried to make it last a long time so I wouldn't have to say anything for a while. He sat down opposite me on the floor, but he kept the ashtray between us. 'God,' I said.

'You wash your ashtray . . .' Oliver didn't say anything. He didn't cross his legs like Robin did, or sit with one knee across the other leg like Dad. He just left them there, lying apart, and put his hand between them on the floor. His face was very oval and his eyes looked darker now he wasn't standing by the window. They had tiny soft creases around them. I watched him light a cigarette, looking down at the end with his lips pursed. He lit it quick, like he'd done it a lot, and blew the smoke up towards the ceiling.

'I've got an ashtray in my room,' I said. 'It's one of those old Stilton jars. You know, about so high? And it's absolutely completely full of dog ends. I'll have to empty it sometime.' I watched him but I couldn't see any expression. 'I'll have to . . .' I said.

'Your room.' He exhaled. He was staring down at his fingers, pale against the carpet, resting his cigarette between them. I crushed mine out on the bottom of the bowl. A little bit of smoke trailed up, and when I took my hand away he reached out to stub it properly. He seemed like a quiet kind of person, I thought. And I wondered for the first time then just why he'd asked me out.

'Sorry I made your ashtray dirty,' I said.

He looked up. 'What's that s'posed to mean?'

'Nothing. I . . . I meant it.'

'What: apologizing for using my ashtray?' His eyes didn't blink, tepid and brown as they stared at me. Looking at me that way, I couldn't even think why I'd said it. And I backed my eyes away. I tugged at one leg of my jeans, twitching the loose strands of cotton. I pulled a thread from the edge of the hole. It was long and grey and it flopped in my fingers. It fell lifeless to the carpet as he put his hand on mine.

It wasn't a soft touch, and he didn't do it to make me feel better. He did it to stop my fingers from moving. They were annoying him I guess. And looking back into his eyes, I knew I wouldn't let them twitch again.

That was the first time that Oliver kissed me properly. I thought it'd be different to snogging Robin, and in a way I suppose it was, just not as different as I'd expected. I thought his hand would touch my knee and lightning would shoot up into my head making me drunk with luuurve. I thought our lips would meet and violins would rise up in the background to some wonderful crescendo. We'd part for just a moment, we'd gaze at each other and he'd say: *Darling, I don't ever want to be apart from you again.* In fact, he got a bit of my hair caught between his teeth.

It was good snogging though. He didn't try to choke me to death with his tongue. He didn't suck my whole chin off. He didn't make those funny little sucking, slurping noises that Robin'd been so prone to. He was good at it and I was glad, thinking of his eyes, the way he'd asked me what I meant.

We snogged for quite a long time before he stopped. He'd got his hand halfway inside my shirt, and I'd sort of hoped he'd keep going. Once he'd touched my tits, I thought, I'd be pretty much on safe ground. You *can't* dump someone straight after doing that. As it happened, though, he didn't. Maybe he knew it too and he didn't want to feel himself into a corner.

I watched as he leaned back from me, looked away at something else. He breathed out.

'Phew . . .' I said. It felt like I should say something. He didn't turn around though. He looked like he'd just remembered the cooker was on. It was funny, as soon as he turned away from me, like I might as well have not been there. A total blank. 'Well . . .' I said, and I pressed my lips together. Still he didn't look at me.

I straightened my shirt a little bit, tugging at the collar. Oliver didn't move, and I wondered if I'd done something else wrong. I wondered if I should just leave.

'Oliver . . .?'

'What?' His shoulders swung back towards me. Like I'd disturbed him just as he was cracking the theory of relativity or something. His tongue flicked at the split between his lips. I didn't say anything else though, there wasn't a good enough excuse, and he reached a hand up to his nose. He pulled at it, slid the movement out across his chin.

'How old are you?' he said.

'What . . . what's that got to do with anything?'

'How old are you?'

I bit my lip. 'You don't want to know.'

Oliver sat back, leaning even further from me. I watched him reach for another cigarette. He was staring at the window.

'It . . . it doesn't really matter,' I said.

'Course it fucking matters!' He shook his head, looking down at the lighter in his hand. I wondered how many times he could read the word Bic before he got bored.

'Course it matters . . .' And it did. I'd known that all along, I guess, and I felt my head sink down till I was watching the pile in the carpet. I heard the spark and a sharp breath in. 'Just tell me,' he said.

'If I tell you . . . you won't like me anymore.'

'I'll like you.' But he didn't sound as though he liked me now. 'You have to tell me,' he said. 'I've got a right to know.'

A right? I looked up at him. It was a funny way of putting it, I thought.

'Well . . . well how old are you?' I said.

'Twenty-seven.' His eyes levelled at me and I tried to swallow without him seeing it.

'Oh,' I said.

Kiss'n'tell, I thought. Kiss'n'tell, and the words ran round inside me without meaning.

'I'm fourteen,' I said.

And there was silence.

'If you want me to go that's Ok,' I said. 'I mean, I won't be offended or anything . . .'

Oliver was staring at the crotch of his jeans. His cigarette burned away, collecting ash. I wondered if I should laugh or apologize, thinking about birthday presents and little girls in costume. It was hard to look at him like that, and I let my hair hang down on my face instead. Hiding.

'Do you want me to go?'

I heard a pause before his eyes came back to me. He blinked, slow and barely tolerant.

'I don't want you to go,' he said quietly.

*

165

Oliver didn't fuck me that day. It's funny, you hear all about schoolgirls being sexy and everything, but he didn't even snog me again after I told him. I guess the word 'fourteen''s not such an aphrodisiac after all.

I called Dawn when I got home. Not because I had anything to say to her, but I hadn't phoned her that day and she gets worried about me if she doesn't hear. I sat at the kitchen table watching Mum chop the vegetables as Dawn's phone rang out. She did it quickly but then I guess she's had a lot of practice. Michael and Dad were in the other room, and she had her back to me, elbow working up and down. I couldn't see her face. It would be settled though, I thought. Blank and kind of dragging. I couldn't imagine it any other way. I couldn't imagine her crying.

The ring cut off as Jack's breathing muffled into my ear.

'Six double four double one seven, Jack speaking.'

'Hi,' I said. 'Is Dawn about?'

'Hello.' I could hear his voice change as soon as he recognized me, I could hear his smile surfacing. I've never seen Jack smile at anyone the way he smiles at me. I kind of wish he wouldn't do it. 'Haven't seen *you* for a while.'

'No,' I said. 'I've been . . . busy.'

'Oh yeah.' He laughed. Jack's always laughing at things that aren't funny. 'Busy sunbathing, I bet.'

In the other room, Dad turned the volume down on some Tory sleaze. Usually he likes watching stuff like that, I thought he must be in a pretty bad mood. Mum started on another pile of veg and I waited.

'Dad . . .? Can I still have a surprise on *my* birthday . . .? I still think surprises are best.'

'For God's sake, Michael,' Dad said. 'Your birthday's not till March.'

It took a long time for Dawn to get to the phone. I always think the reason that she walks so slowly must be the weight of those big feet. Maybe it's not, though. Maybe she just hasn't got anywhere exciting to go.

'Hello,' she said.

'Hiya. What you been doing?'

'Nothing,' she said. And the funny thing was, I could imagine it too. Dawn just sitting on her bed with the world going on around her. Just staring at nothing. Not thinking. 'There's never anything to do here,' she said.

'Been playing your flute?' I said. Mum scooped up the pile.

'I'm giving up the flute. I haven't got any natural flair, that's what Jack said.' She waited.

Flattening my fingers on the pine though, I couldn't think of anything. 'Yes you have.'

'No I haven't.'

I gave up. It was difficult to talk to her sometimes.

It's funny, I used to have a lot to say to Dawn. When we were in Primary we used to talk for hours. I can never think of much these days though. Every question seems to end with a full stop and she never asks what I've been doing. I wished she would. That day, I wished she would. Who knows, maybe I'd even have told her. She didn't ask, though. She went back to doing nothing.

Hanging up the phone, I heard Dad's footsteps thump off to the bathroom. He spends a lot of time in the bathroom, he always has done, and it makes me wonder what he does in there. He used to say it was because 'That and my office are the only places I can lock your mother out', which used to make me laugh. It gave me pictures of her clawing at the pine, scratching and wailing and drooling uncontrollably. I never saw it happen though. And watching her move around the kitchen, she didn't seem to bother rushing after him, desperate to get in as well. I thought of those small snotty sounds, standing in the study, and I wondered where that fitted in.

Mum doesn't do much really. She grows flowers, and she does the shopping, but I remember when I first started French we had to do sentences about our parents. *Mon père travaille dans Cartwright's. Ma mère* ... and I couldn't think of anything to put after that. She used to do Saturdays in Oxfam too, sorting clothes and stuff like that. But Dad wasn't too keen on her working there. He said there was no need, they had plenty of volunteers, and she was better off helping us at home. I was sort of glad when she stopped. I didn't want to have to write *Ma mère travaille dans l'Oxfam.*

'What are you cooking Mum?'

'Stew.' She didn't turn round.

'Oh,' I said quietly. 'That's nice.' Chopchopchopchop. I glanced down at the table.

'Can I like, help or anything?'

Her face came round. 'Well, if you want to. You can peel some potatoes.' I thought about telling her that there was no need to look so surprised. I don't know though, last time I peeled potatoes I had trouble reaching the sink. Maybe she was right.

I nodded, standing up slowly, and I moved towards the unit. They were lying against the metal plug hole in a cluster. Brown and yellow and they didn't look anything like the roast potatoes in Garlands. I picked up the peeler. 'This one's green,' I said.

'Just cut off the green bit.'

I turned to look at her. 'Mum, green potatoes are *poisonous*. They're a relative of the deadly nightshade family. Absolutely lethal. Dad said . . .' But I stopped then, stared at the brown thing in my hand, and I squeezed my lips together. I didn't tell her what Dad said, I guess she'd heard it before. Thinking about it, she'd heard pretty much everything I said to her before. It made me wonder if there was any point in even talking. And after a moment, I put the peeler down. 'Mum? If I tell you something . . . will you promise me something?'

'Promise what?' she said, scraping the vegetables into a saucepan with one hand.

'It doesn't matter what. You've got to promise.'

'I can't promise if I don't know what I'm promising,' she said. 'Pass me the salt.'

I frowned. 'Mum,' I said. 'This is important.' And she turned around then, leaning the small of her back against the edge of the unit. She was staring at me and smiling with the corner of her mouth. Like she didn't dare smile with the rest of it. I didn't speak, just kept my eyes near hers. After a moment she took her apron off. I watched her hang it on the peg as she brushed a bit of hair from her face, rubbing her cheek while she did it. I watched the flesh pull against her hand, catch on her wedding ring. It had tomato juice on it and left a stain across her skin.

'I think I'll put the kettle on,' she said.

She placed each mug carefully on the table when she'd made it. I hadn't watched her, staring at the grain of the pine, trying to work out how to say it. I looked up as she sat down opposite me though, heavy, like her bum was dragging her there. She smiled, leaning forward and putting her chin in one palm. The folds of it doubled over, not flesh just skin, and her fingernails were dirty. None of it seemed much like a movie anymore and Mum was no Meryl Streep. I wasn't sure I could go through with it. I wasn't even sure why I wanted to.

'God,' I said, and I laughed a little bit. 'I feel like I'm in *Neighbours.*' I didn't, though. I coughed, reached out and tried to take a sip of tea. No noise from Dad yet. I wondered if that was a good thing or a bad one. Three walls away, Michael's Hoover groaned.

'Well . . .?' she said, but now I didn't know how to start. Her T-shirt sagged out as she bent to take her mug. It had a picture of a zebra on it, and I didn't recognize it. Maybe it was new.

'Well,' I said. 'I've met someone.'

'Met someone? I thought you were with Robin.'

'You didn't like him.'

She put her tea back, resting her eyes there for a moment. 'Your father did,' she said.

'You'll like Oliver.'

I took another quick, slurping sip.

'Oliver, *eh?*'

She raised one eyebrow but it only looked silly. It made me think of when I used to play Happy Families with Dawn, brushing out a little patch of garden with a branch, pretending it was home.

I looked away from her.

It was a crap build-up really. I should have planned it better. I should have thought of some really great lead-in. Except there wasn't one. There wasn't any lead-in to what I had to say.

'He's twenty-seven.'

'*Twenty-seven?*' The words came out without enough air to back them up. Her hand twitched the mug, brown liquid wobbling and slopping in a tiny wave. 'Philip didn't say anything!'

'No . . .'

It was funny. I didn't want to make her sad, or angry or upset or any of those things. But watching her jerk her breath back in, I thought again of that single raised eyebrow. However it went, I was kind of glad that look was gone.

'How long have you . . . When did you meet him?' she said.

'About three weeks ago.'

'And he didn't say *anything* . . .' Back to the tea, like there was some tricks-of-the-trade list on motherhood there. 'He could have *told* me,' she said. She blinked like Wile E. Coyote after a particularly nasty brush with Roadrunner.

There should be cartoon stars, I thought, and I wondered vaguely why I felt this way. It wasn't the right way to feel, Oprah wouldn't have approved. I moved my hands against each other under the table, thinking of that light behind the bathroom door.

'He didn't know,' I said.

'What . . .?'

'I . . . I haven't told him yet.'

I didn't say anything for a moment then, watching as she sat there still and blank. We must look odd, I thought, if there'd been anyone to see. Her hands folded slowly over each other, a safe distance from the cup, but she didn't look like she knew she was doing it. I watched her chest rise, breathing. The zebra looked pretty ruffled as well.

'I'm glad . . .' She swallowed, her chin stretching up as she looked at the overhead light. I could see the tendons in her throat. 'I'm glad you felt you could . . . you know, come to me.' Her top lip stuck on her front teeth as she tried to smile. 'That's nice . . .'

'Yes,' I said, but I wasn't really sure what she was talking about.

'Cos you . . . you can trust me.' Her fingers moved, unseen, towards the handle of her cup as she tried to relax her smile. They shook a tiny bit. And with her other hand she flicked a strand of hair back, glossy in the light. 'I am your mother after all,' she said.

Mum agreed to tell Dad for me. She looked surprised when I asked, like she hadn't even thought about it. I thought it was pretty obvious, though. I wasn't exactly sure why I'd decided to tell her about Oliver, but finding a way to tell Dad had to be one of the reasons. The biggest one, I thought. After all, what other reasons were there?

She seemed surprised but it didn't take long to convince her, and she nodded when I said he'd take it better if it came from her. She looked kind of shell-shocked, I thought, hearing Dad's footsteps come out from the bathroom as she cleared away the empty mugs. Information overload, and she turned round just before she put them in the sink. She looked at me and she opened her mouth. She didn't say anything though, like her brain was still busy putting all the bits together. And after a moment of staring at me, she turned away again.

She said she'd find just the right moment. 'After all, I've lived with him for twenty years.' But I didn't really feel safe in her hands, remembering each time Dad had told me how unsubtle she could be. They were the only hands around though; I thought she'd do a better job than Michael.

I watched a whole load of changes move across her face as she carried on with dinner. Frowns and nods and she looked like she was listening to the radio.

It had been easier than I'd thought it would be. No piece of piss but at least she hadn't shouted or anything, and she'd only told me twice that she was worried. Almost like she wanted to get it over with so she could get on to the interesting stuff: asking what he looked like, what he did and things like that. And it was funny, giving her the answers. When I said it out loud, it didn't sound that exciting. Maybe nothing ever does. But, telling her he had brown hair and owned a Citroen Xantia, I wondered if those things were really worth the hassle. They didn't send a shiver through my stomach, like the thought of telling Dad.

I tapped my fingers on the table as the volume of the TV rose again. No, she hadn't really freaked at me, not like I'd thought she would. I watched her wash the mugs up, bending down above the sink. And in between the problems catching up across her face, I saw her lips twitch upwards. It might have been a smile.

I went to see Oliver the next day. It was a Saturday and Dad didn't look like he was setting up to go out anywhere. They'd be around each other all day, I thought. Long enough for her to tell him and I reckoned it would be best to get out of the house. I took a long breath, walking out of the front door that morning, and I wondered why I felt so nervous. Dad wasn't going to hit the roof. Dad was going to be cool about it. I knew he was going to be cool. I mean, I was fourteen now. I was an adult.

The walk went pretty quickly, thinking about what might be going on at home. It was pretty sunny and I walked with my head up, my legs stretched out. I went past Kwik Save, with the rubbish bins overflowing on to the tarmac, and the cars that had to steer round the ripped-up card-board boxes. I watched the drivers' faces, pulling out of the car park, looking in the rear-view mirror as they went. I wondered how I seemed to them. Not a kid, I thought. Not a schoolgirl, no way. Liberated. Independent. The kind of woman who has somewhere to go, someone to see. And smiling to myself a little bit, I brushed a strand of hair from my face. I couldn't wait to show myself to Oliver.

He was still working when I got there and I stood outside the window, watching him before I went in. Maybe lunch break was later in a job. Maybe he was doing *overtime*. I could see through the glass pretty well, what with the sky being grey behind me. No reflections or anything. He was standing near the back with one hand on his hip and the other pointing to a television/video set. There was a couple watching him, listening to him, but I didn't look at them much. They were pretty young; maybe just married or something. He was wearing the jacket to go with the trousers today. Matching. Standing back from the shelf he moved to let them forward. I watched the bloke kneel down, and he smiled at the woman over her husband's head. At least, I think he smiled. I waited about five minutes, standing there. The two people bought their TV/video.

I wasn't surprised.

And, when they'd finished, I chose my entrance perfectly.

'Hello there.'

He turned round quick to look at me, but his eyes were only there a minute. I watched him flash a glance round the whole shop before he was back to me again. There was no smile.

'What the *hell* are you doing here?' Biting at me, through his teeth.

'What? I . . . I came to see if . . . uh . . . lunch?'

'Jesus Christ, you can't just come walking into the fucking shop!'

'Why . . . why not?'

'Why the fuck do you *think?*' He looked round again, wiping one hand across his mouth. It made a dry, scratchy sound. 'Go outside, alright? I'll meet you there.'

I bit my lip and I looked up at him. I think I was trying to stop myself smiling. And I wondered why I'd want to smile. Why I'd want to, when I wasn't even happy. I did go, though. And a few minutes later, he followed me.

'I'm sorry,' I said quietly. I didn't look up to his face. I thought maybe he'd like that.

'Don't be sorry, alright.'

'I didn't know.'

'No,' he said. 'Obviously.' He gritted his teeth. 'It was my fault. I should've told you.'

'I'm sorry . . . Do you want me to go?'

'For fuck's sake! No I don't want you to go. Just . . . just right in the middle of the fucking shop. You can see how it looks.'

I stared down at myself. 'Well . . . do you want to go get some chips or something . . .?'

'Look, I'm not really hungry right now.' He looked away.

'What . . . what about a walk then?'

'A walk?' He sighed and his hair flopped forward. 'Alright.'

He turned in between Boots and the Red Cross Shop and I followed just a step behind. I remember Dad told me once that Muslim women have to walk three steps behind their husbands. It was a nice kind of image, I thought.

'Do I embarrass you?' I said.

'No,' he said, staring straight ahead. I wondered if he was lying. He had a right to be embarrassed. I'd acted like an idiot.

We walked for five minutes before Oliver saw a bench. He sat down heavily, eyes hitting the opposite wall of the alley, and I ran my finger along the arm of the bench. I wished someone would walk past so we'd have an excuse not to talk. I wished we could just get on and snog. I tried to remember how I'd felt walking through the town fifteen minutes before. It was no good. I couldn't feel that way again.

'I really am sorry about . . . about coming in like that. I won't do it again.' I paused, not looking at him. 'Do you hate me?'

'What?' Oliver stared down at me, and I could feel my head want to sink back. Back and down and away, with that cold look in his eyes. 'Of course I don't *hate* you,' he said. But he didn't tell me that he liked me either. He didn't say anything at all. He just snogged me instead.

He wasn't a deep kisser. More of a shallow kisser, and he went for the lips as well as the tongue. He smelled of aftershave, which was nice, and an underneath, sour kind of smell that wasn't. After a minute I moved closer to him so my back would stop aching.

Oliver was taller than me, even sitting down. And I had to stretch up to get to his mouth. Well, I s'pose he had to stretch down too. He leaned on to me and I could feel his tie-pin sticking in between my boobs. Just to go along with the wooden slats under my bum. I tried biting his lip just to make a change. I was surprised when he bit back.

'Oohmmp.'

I wondered if mine had hurt as much as his did. I thought I'd make a note of that for next time. Maybe he was only doing it to get back at me. He put one hand on my neck, behind my head. But he didn't stroke the tiny little hairs or anything. He gripped it. Hard, and I felt one of his fingernails that had grown a bit too long. His thumb slipped over one of the tendons and I felt it snap back into place. It set off a tingle in that bit that goes in, just above my bum. He bit again, so I guess it wasn't just a pay-back thing. I slid further towards him. I thought maybe it'd release a bit of the pressure on my neck. It didn't, though. It made him squeeze me tighter.

I think that was the first time I enjoyed someone's kisses.

Sitting there and remembering how sorry I was.

I felt stronger, going back that afternoon. Ready to face the music like just before a shoot-out. There were a lot of phrases like that going round in my head as I wiped my shoes on the mat in the porch. Movie phrases like *illicit meeting* and *older man*. I thought of Oliver with his hand around my neck and I wasn't really scared. In some ways, I thought as I opened the porch door, the whole thing was really kind of cool.

But Mum hadn't told Dad that day.

I knew as soon as I walked in because everything was

normal, and in the kitchen I could hear them shouting. It sounded like Mum had left the mousetrap by the bread bin again. For a moment, then, I didn't move, standing on my own in the living room. Their voices tangled, breaking over each other till the words didn't make any sense. I looked down at my fingernails and I wondered why I felt disappointed.

The kitchen door rattled as Dad slammed it behind him, stalking out into the room.

'Your fucking mother! Maybe you can tell her you don't want fucking germs all over our eating equipment. Maybe you can get it through her pigshit stupid head, Christ!'

He wiped a hand across his mouth but I didn't say anything.

I watched him walk off to the bathroom.

Mum was sitting at the kitchen table. She looked like she should have a cigarette in her hand even though she gave up smoking years ago. She looked up at me as I walked in and a smile flickered, on then off like some faulty kind of lightbulb. It made the skin underneath her throat twitch, and I kind of wished she wouldn't do it. It was off-putting just before dinner.

'Hi,' she said. It sounded like some kind of punch-line. Which was good I guess, because it gave me an excuse to dive right in.

I laughed a little bit. 'So you haven't told him yet then.'

'What?' The bags underneath her eyes cast yellow shadows as her chin came up again. 'Well no. Not yet.'

'I was only asking.'

Mum didn't say anything though. From the other end

of the house, very quiet, I heard the toilet flush. I glanced at the door.

'Look,' she said. 'You know . . .' Her hands went up, limp, towards the sound of the cistern. 'He hasn't exactly been in a receptive mood.'

'No.' I smiled but I didn't really agree, and I couldn't look at her as I did it. Mum breathed out a long sigh. She sounded a bit better, I thought.

'It's got to be the right moment,' she said finally. 'No good rushing these things.'

'Maybe I should be there.'

Her breath cut off. 'There's no need for that. It's fine how we planned it.' But we hadn't planned it, not really. And I didn't want to wait. 'I'll know the right moment when it comes. I think I've had a little more experience at these things than you.'

'Mm,' I said. I wondered why that didn't make me feel any better.

Mum's shoulders sagged a little bit with the sound of his footsteps through the study. Her eyes fixed somewhere on the wall. There wasn't really much to say now, though. I wondered why she couldn't see that.

'I'm sorry it had to happen this way,' she said. She didn't move. 'You know, us . . . getting closer.' I rubbed my feet against the stone-slab floor as her face turned back to me. I didn't ask her what she meant. And I didn't know quite what to do as her hand slid out across the pine.

Palm down, it rested there.

I didn't have much choice but to pat it with my own.

*

So she hadn't told him that day. It's funny, how things always go like that. Nothing ever happens when you're ready for it. When you aren't, that's when the shit leaps out.

Oliver called me two days later. Two days of not seeing him, and the memory of his hand behind my head had kind of faded out by then. I'd just started to get used to normality. Mum hadn't found her moment I guess, because she still hadn't told Dad. I'd stopped hassling her though. And I wasn't even thinking about it when the phone rang.

We were sitting in the kitchen again, me and Dad, doing some of my art homework: 'Depict one of your hobbies'. Brushes from the box he'd given me were soaking in a jam jar and Mum's books were stacked one on top of the other. Plato's *Republic* and *The Reprieve* by Jean-Paul Sartre. Looking at them made me smirk a little bit, I'd made sure the titles were written big enough to read.

Dad reached upwards to the phone, still watching the cigarette in his other hand. 'Six double four one double eight. Philip speaking?'

It's funny, his expression didn't change that much, not even his tone of voice, but something in the way he paused made me look up. His eyes were level with my own.

'Right,' he said. He didn't blink. And when he took the phone down from his ear, I saw him cover the mouthpiece with his fingers. 'Some man wants to talk to you,' he said. His words were just as even as his look and, pressing my knees together underneath the tabletop, I felt my stomach

sink. Sink and flutter, like the sound of bad speakers.
'Some man from the stereo shop.'

'Really?' I got up, stretching my eyebrows into arches.
Dad didn't speak. 'Well . . . I'll take it in the study.' I
watched him rest the receiver on his shoulder, and balance
in there as I walked towards the door. I could see the tiny
hairs, dark and fluffy, round his bald patch. I could see the
stubble round his mouth.

Still, he didn't answer as I opened the kitchen door. I
wondered if he'd seen me twitch.

'Customer services eh?' I shook my head, edging away.
'Bloody good these days.'

'I called to say sorry.' Oliver's voice sounded tight as I
picked the phone up in the study. 'About getting angry
with you. It wasn't your fault. I should have told you not
to come into the shop. You didn't know, I'm sorry.' He
paused. It sounded like dictation.

Sinking slowly to the phone bench, I frowned a little
bit. 'Oh,' I said quietly. 'Cheers.'

'I had no right to shout at you and . . . Oh fuck, I don't
know. I shouldn't have rung.'

'No. No, I'm glad you did.' I leaned forward, trying to
catch up. 'I appreciate it.'

'Really?' he said, and hearing it I smiled to myself. *I
appreciate it*. It was a grown-up-sounding phrase. *Bing!*
I thought, correct answer Number One. 'Well,' he said.
'Good.'

I let myself lean back on the wall, tapping one hand on
the table. Small nails, neat as they dropped in a line. They

made a clicking noise. And sitting on my own there, quiet in the empty study, I watched them tap again. My fingers. I liked the sound they made.

Dad was still in the kitchen when I got back and from the doorway I could see him bent over at the table. It felt a little like those cowboy movies they show in the afternoon. The kind of thing you always seem to end up watching when you've got the flu. The Ranger'll say to Billy: *Quiet, tonight*, and then The Kid'll say back: *Yeah, just a little too quiet*. The kind of quiet that hangs just outside Dad's mouth and you know there's something wrong.

I walked over to the sink but I didn't turn the tap on for a drink.

'What did he want?' Dad said.

'Wanted to ask if we had any, you know, problems setting it up.' I didn't turn round.

'Oh,' he said. 'And what did you tell him?'

'Just that we hadn't set it up yet and . . . if we have any problems I'll call them.'

'I won't have any problem setting it up.'

'I know that . . .'

I glanced round to where he was sitting. Just above his collar, three little folds of skin curved up against each other. They looked very soft in the shadow, underneath his hair. I wondered just what I should feel.

I had to look away from him after a second, down at my own hands. It was easier I guess, remembering the way they could tap. Dad breathed out but it wasn't a sigh. It sounded like he was thinking.

'Well,' he said quietly. 'Let's go and set it up then.'

'What?' But he was already getting up, picking up his beer. 'But . . . there's no rush.'

He didn't turn to look at me. 'You said the other day you wanted it done.' I bit my lip.

'Yeah, but . . .'

'So let's go and do it then.'

His voice was quick and distant and it didn't leave me any room.

'Ok . . .' I said. 'Thank you.'

He nodded a little, walking out of the kitchen.

And after a moment, I followed.

Dad already had the box open by the time I got upstairs. He was sitting in the middle of the carpet, legs crossed, in between the pile of dirty laundry and my school books. He wasn't doing anything though, just sitting there and staring into the box. His shirt was runkled, baggy around his stomach. His fingers were playing with the cardboard flap, and I didn't move from the doorway. Sitting there, he looked too much like a kid with a broken toy. I had to look away.

I stared out of the window instead for a while. The paint was peeling a little round the frame, and the glass was pretty dirty. I could see the hills and the hedges, and just beyond that a little stretch of the main road where the cars went past. I wondered where they were all going.

'Do you need anything?' I said.

He just shrugged, didn't even bother pulling out the cables. I could feel my stomach flow slowly over and on to itself. Still, he didn't say anything. Maybe he was waiting for me.

I coughed.

'So . . .' I said, nodding, even though it didn't sound quite right. 'Dawn told you I split up with Robin . . .'

'I was pretty sure it wouldn't last.'

'It wasn't like that.' I paused. 'You know . . . we just weren't right for each other. And . . . and you didn't like him anyway, did you?'

'He was alright.' Dad carried on staring at the box. His chin doubled over when he spoke. 'Just a bit young.'

'Mmm,' I said. 'It's funny you should say that actually . . .' *Hands*, I thought. *Look at your hands*. I tried to picture them tip-tapping. Just like a grown up's hands. The thought made me want to laugh. Laugh and shut my eyes. 'Cos you know, you saying Robin's a bit young. Well . . . recently I met someone who . . . who's not.'

'Not.' The word fell short, kind of clearing his throat. His fingers lay still on the cardboard.

'You've met him already actually,' I said. I tried to make my voice sound light but it only came out too high-pitched, too fast and false. '*Actually*,' I said, 'he's the one that showed us this stereo.'

'What?'

'And it was a good choice, don't you think? I mean, I'm pretty happy with it.'

'The salesman,' Dad said, like he couldn't get a handle on it. I guess I couldn't really blame him for that though. 'The salesman in that shop.'

'Audiovision yes.'

I wanted to add other things, just run and run with all the little sentences I'd worked out about how much we had in common. I stopped though. I didn't say another thing. Somehow it felt best.

'So you're . . . you're what?' Dad said. His forehead creased, watching my carpet. He looked like he couldn't find the right word. Like he wasn't even bothered. I wondered why that made me so nervous. 'You're asking to go on a date with him?' I breathed, knotting my hands together in front of me. And I was glad when he carried on, not waiting for my answer. I didn't want to lie. 'You're asking to go on a date with that slimy fucking salesman from the hi-fi shop, am I right?' He looked at me. 'Or did I miss something?'

A date. I thought of drive-in movies and petticoats. Tuxedos that don't fit and cars with pull-down roofs. Quiffs. 'I'm not asking to go on a date with him,' I said quietly. 'I . . . I already kind of . . . did.'

'You already did?'

'Yes.'

'Without . . . without asking me?'

He looked at me but I didn't answer. Through the window, I could hear the sound of one car passing. It blended with the wind. Dad's eyes were soft as his hands fell down from the box into his lap. They looked too light, lying there, floating on the thighs of his jeans. I saw his thumb was resting on a long, stiff dent. I saw it twitch. His breath caught a little bit and he held it there, maybe he was trying to think of what to say. After a moment, I watched his eyes fall down. He tried to frown.

'You went off without telling anyone,' he said. 'What . . . just what was the fucking point in trying to teach . . .?' He trailed off. 'How many times have I told you not to . . . to just go off with someone you don't know.' His breath came out in a gush, like he couldn't hold it in anymore. And when he looked back up to me, his face seemed very plain. 'How many times have I told you that's a stupid . . . dangerous fucking thing to do! I mean . . . Jesus!' He shrugged, a hard kind of jerk as his hands came up and out.

'What was the fucking *point?*'

'I didn't think you'd let me go.'

'No! No, fucking right I wouldn't let you go. What father in their right mind *would?*'

'Nothing happened!' It came out too loud and I had to look away then. 'Nothing happened . . .' It was a funny little word, I thought. Happen. Funny, when it said so much. 'I . . . I wanted to go. I knew you wouldn't let me . . .' I said slowly. 'That's all.'

'Wouldn't let you? Course I wouldn't've fucking let you. What'd you want me to say? *Yeah!* Go on a date with some . . . *man* I've never met! Go and get yourself *raped!* GO FOR IT!'

'I wanted you to be *reasonable!* I wanted . . . *I don't know!*' I bit the inside of my lip. Dad shut his mouth then. I almost heard the snap. I wished he hadn't stopped, though, I wished that he'd just gone on screaming. I watched his shoulders sag, his neck give out, my eyes all hot and stinging. I could see the tiny dented scar across his chin, a clean line through the stubble. I tried not to watch him as he shut his eyes, and I wondered how it had got to this.

'How old his he?' he said. 'Do you . . .' His face rose up again. 'Do you even *know?*'

Inside my stomach, I felt something sink again. There was none of the flutter that'd come before, though. Staring at my bedroom floor, I wondered just what I'd expected.

'Twenty-seven,' I said.

'I . . .' He just looked at me. 'I don't know what to say.'

'Please don't be angry with me.'

Dad's face twisted round the mouth, looking at me. Don't be angry, I thought. Don't be angry. Like if I repeated it over and over, maybe it would come true.

'I'm not angry at you! It's just so fucking *stupid!*' He stopped, trying to find some normal tone of voice. Like there's a special one spare for these occasions: the dealing-with-your-fourteen-year-old-daughter-fucking-a-twenty-seven-year-old voice. 'I know that . . . that when you reach a certain age, you want to start . . . experimenting. Finding out about stuff. But he's *not* your age. He's already *been* through what . . . what you're going through. I mean . . . Have you even *thought* about that? *Have you?* This man . . . this man is dating a child, for fuck's sake!'

'*That's not fair . . .*'

'Oh really. You think he just *happened* to really like you? That it just *happened* not to matter to him that you were *fourteen years old!*'

'*It wasn't like that!*'

'So just what the *fuck* was it like?'

Dad stared at me and I swallowed. I could see the whites around his pupils, the top of his teeth through his open mouth. He was looking for an answer, I guess. Some reason that would make it all perfectly natural, perfectly understandable. In the quiet I heard denim move against my carpet. The small wet sounds of his mouth. Just one little sentence. Thinking about it, it wasn't a lot to ask.

Still, I had to look away.

'I'm sorry,' I said.

And Dad breathed out.

'I know . . .' Dad moved one hand up, slowly to his face. 'Oh Christ,' he said. I watched him rub a knuckle across his eyes. He looked so tired, I thought. So very tired, and I wondered why I hadn't noticed that before. 'I know I'm . . . I'm probably not a very good role model for you. Maybe it's *my* fault. I . . . I don't know.'

'It . . . it's not your fault,' I said. I looked at the window. I was going to cry.

'Maybe I just did something wrong. I mean . . . I thought I'd taught you not to . . . not to do *stupid* things. So . . . so maybe it's my own fault.' Gradually, his face came round to me. His eyes locked there, they caught me very still. 'Who else's fault could it be?' I didn't answer him. He was right, it had to be somebody's fault. Not his fault, though. Not his, when he was almost crying. When he'd done so much for me. Never ever his.

I dropped my eyes away from him.

It had to be my own.

It was a couple of days before I got up the courage to ask Oliver round. Not that I didn't want him to come over, to meet Dad and Mum. I knew he'd make a good impression.

But I think it was the good impression I was worried about. I'd seen him in the shop that time, selling the TV and video. He was different when he did it, pretty charming, but I didn't want him to come round and do his smiling charming thing on Dad. It wouldn't have been real. Thinking about all the time I'd spent getting to know him, I didn't want him to come round just so as he could make a good impression. And sitting by the phone, just two or three days after Dad and me had talked, I wondered why it mattered so much that Oliver be real.

I touched the receiver lightly, running my finger over cold plastic. I wanted everything to go smoothly when he met them. I wanted everyone to like each other. I just didn't want to see that false face on him, that charming little smile.

It's funny, I don't remember worrying that Robin would put on an act when he'd first come round. He just hadn't seemed like the charming type. He had been though, with Dad he had been. And the smile he'd used had made his face look uglier than ever. I stopped my hand from moving, clicked my nails down on the plastic, and I picked the receiver up.

It was a while before he answered, and I was almost going to put it down again when I heard the ringing cut off. Oliver's voice was quick in my ear, but he didn't sound unfriendly. I shifted my bum on the bench.

'How are you?' he said.

'Alright.' I gave a little laugh, made sure it wasn't too jolly. 'Recovering,' I said. I leaned forward a little bit, glanced towards the door. 'I . . . I told Dad about us.'

'Oh,' Oliver said. His voice didn't change one bit. 'Was that bad then?'

'Well . . .' I frowned. I'd expected something. Some nerves or a little bit of excitement. He sounded like he was asking about my cold, and it almost made me want to say yes. 'He was Ok,' I said. 'You know, Dad's pretty cool . . . It was alright. Not *too* bad.'

'Good,' he said, like now we could move on from the small talk. I didn't want to move on though, and I wondered why his tone annoyed me. 'Good,' he said again.

'He wants to meet you.'

There was a pause. It was something, at least.

'Really?' I heard his voice move away slightly. Maybe he was looking at the clock.

'He wanted me to ask you round. You know, for dinner or something.'

'Your Dad always asks your friends round for you then, does he?'

'What?'

'Well, you know.' His laugh sounded more like a snort. 'You could ask me yourself.'

'Oh,' I said. Funny, the conversation wasn't quite going the way I had planned. I sat up straight, my back away from the wall. There was nothing wrong with Dad wanting to meet him. It was a perfectly bloody normal thing to want, I thought. Considering the thirteen-year factor, it was pretty surprising he didn't want an internal inspection as well. 'He just said he wanted to meet you.' It came out sounding lame, like he'd attacked me. 'He's allowed to ask you round for dinner. He asks lots of my friends round.'

Well, one of them anyway. One didn't sound quite as good though.

'Mm,' he said. 'And that's Ok with you is it? Your father asking your friends round?'

'What? Of course it's Ok. He . . . Look, I just phoned to ask you if you'd come, Ok?'

'I'll come,' he said.

'Well I'm sorry if it's such a hassle for you. Strangely enough, you know . . . I thought you'd want to meet him. I thought you might want to meet both of them.' I trailed off. Thinking about it, I wasn't really sure that was true. I couldn't even remember him asking about them.

'I'm going out with you,' Oliver said quietly. I thought that was pretty obvious, though. 'Not your entire family. I'd like to come round,' he said. 'To see *you*.'

'Well . . . yeah,' I said. 'I will be here.'

And that was pretty much the end of it, I hung up not long after. And sitting in the study for a moment before leaving, I thought of what he'd said again. *Your father always asks your friends round to dinner does he?*

Not *always*, no, I thought.

Just every now and then.

There was no one in the living room when I wandered out, no sounds from the rest of the house. I looked through the hall, up the stairs, but I didn't see Dad anywhere. It was cloudy and the place looked grey without any of the lights on. Through the french windows, I saw Mum bending over, halfway through the vegetable patch. Her coat hung down in two long flaps, each side of her waist. Her hair was getting in her eyes. And I looked around the house once more before I went outside.

She looked up as I slid the window shut, smiling as she dropped a handful of pulled-up grass into her bucket. It looked torn and muddy and it hit the pile with a thud.

'Guess what,' I said.

'Ooh . . .' She made a face like she was trying to think. It wasn't very funny though. And I didn't bother to wait for her to answer.

'I've invited him,' I said.

Mum stopped, her back half bent to tear up another unsuspecting patch. Her neck was stretched at an angle, staring at my face. I watched her reaching hand drop shut.

'*Oliver?*' she said.

'Yep. Next Saturday. Dad isn't working that day or anything is he?'

'But . . .' I watched her glance behind me through the glass, turn and look around. Like Dad was really going to be lurking in the bushes behind her, eavesdropping on the weeding. 'But I haven't told him yet!' she said. She stood up straight and I saw her arms fall to her sides like they were too heavy for her shoulders. She was wearing sandals even though it wasn't that warm, jeans and a sweatshirt that had Joe Bloggs written on it. I've always hated those sweatshirts, and the jeans they make too. You can't tell mums about stuff like that, though. I watched her big toe move against the rubber, making a tiny creaking noise. The varnish had chipped off, yellow, and it looked like it needed repainting. She pushed the hair from her face. 'Saturday!' she said. 'It hardly gives me much time, does it? I thought we were s'posed to be doing this together. How am I supposed to break it to him gently when you've . . . you've put me in a rush?'

'Oh,' I said. 'No you don't need to worry about that.' I sat down on the concrete step, picking up a piece of gravel while she watched me, dropping it back down with all the other bits. 'I've already told him,' I said.

'Told him?' Her face changed as she straightened further. Behind her, the traffic made a low, whispering kind of noise. I watched her eyebrows fold. 'Told him? Why . . .?'

'Well . . . it was like you said . . . I don't know, just seemed like the right moment.'

'Oh,' she said, but I don't know what she'd been expecting. 'But I thought . . .' She didn't finish, but her eyebrows still made her face into a question. Hairy eyebrows, she had. I was kind of glad that I'd got Dad's.

'Thought what?' I looked at her.

'I thought we were going to do it together.'

Over the lip of the bucket, I watched a strand of grass pick up and flap over in the breeze. It made a ticking noise.

'Yeah . . .' I said. 'Well . . . I don't know. It just seemed like the right thing to do.'

'But . . .' Her voice was soft, looking at me. 'You said he'd take it better coming from me.' She glanced away for a moment, off at the main road. 'That's what we said . . . I thought we had an agreement.' I shrugged, reaching down for another piece of gravel. Looking at her though, I wondered why it mattered. 'Well . . .' she said. 'I guess it doesn't matter now.' She turned back to me but only for a moment. I watched her reach down for the watering can.

'Well anyway,' I said. 'Saturday.'

She moved away and started in on the potatoes, one hand on her hip to balance her up. She didn't look at me. The water splashed over the paving slabs too and I shivered. I was just about to get up when I saw her stop watering. She turned round to face me again.

'Well . . . well was he alright about it?' she said. 'I mean . . . how did he take it?'

'I don't know . . .' I said. I thought of his face, sitting there on my carpet. The way his back had sagged. 'I don't know.'

'Was he angry? I mean, you shouldn't worry if he was. He . . . he just gets like that sometimes. You mustn't worry about it. Ok? Please don't.' She smiled. A very small smile. 'He'll get over it,' she said. I shrugged. 'He just . . . doesn't know how hurtful he can be sometimes. I know what he's like. Really.' She took a step towards me, the watering can pulling down one shoulder. And with the other hand she reached out to touch me. It curled around my elbow. 'Ok?'

'He . . .' I looked away from her a moment. 'He was alright, Mum,' I said. I tangled my hands in a knot on my lap as that frown kind of hit me again. 'You know, he was fine.'

'Fine?' she said. The hand dropped from my elbow. 'Oh.' And then she looked away too. I heard a little sigh. 'You don't . . . you don't have to pretend, you know,' she said. 'I'm on your side. You know that.' I didn't say anything, there didn't seem to be much I could answer.

After a second, she put the watering can down, smoothing the front of her sweatshirt. She looked like she was going to sit down, and I didn't like it. 'I wasn't going to say this, but . . . but maybe it's a good idea after all.' She took the concrete step next to me, crossed her legs, and stared out towards the road. You couldn't quite see the cars, just flashes of light that might have been windows. The sound of engines was very far away. 'I understand what you're going through,' she said.

'I'm alright, Mum . . .'

'I know you're *alright* . . . I just wanted to tell you that I know what you're feeling.'

I saw her tongue move round her teeth underneath her lips. She breathed out, and she didn't look at me. 'I know because . . . because I had a boyfriend who was twenty-six when I was pretty young.' Staring out away from me, I saw her eyes swivel back for one moment. 'Fifteen,' she said.

'*What?*'

'When I was fifteen,' she said. 'But I mean . . . I was a year older than you are now.'

'How *come?*' I stared at her. 'How come you never *told me?*'

'Well . . .' She looked round and into my eyes. 'You never seemed all that interested.'

'You went out with a twenty-six-year-old and you never even *told* me? Who *was* he?'

'Oh.' Her eyes faded back to the road, watching something that I couldn't see. 'He was a . . . musician.'

'And he was twenty-*six?* 'What did your *parents* say?'

'I never told them,' she said. 'We weren't very close.' She smiled at me, a little wider than before. 'Not like you and me.'

'Wow,' I said quietly. I looked out towards the road again. I watched the flashes go past, and I tried to picture Mum going out with a musician. A *secret* musician. *Mum!* I wondered what she'd been like then. She'd have had one of those ugly biker jackets on, I thought, but then I guess they'd been fashionable in her day. I tried to picture them, sitting together at a table in some really cool club. You know, low lights and drinks and everything: *I'm Elizabeth*. I wondered if her hair had been long then. I wondered if they'd smiled at each other over a rum and Coke. It was funny, though, trying to picture it. The only face I saw was Dad's. 'Wow,' I said again. 'So . . . so why didn't you go out with someone your own age?'

She shrugged. 'Girls mature faster than boys I think.'

'*Definitely.*'

'Fifteen-year-old boys . . .' She looked at me. 'They can be very immature sometimes.'

'God yes! They're like . . . they're like ten-year-olds or something. I mean, I can't relate to that at all. I've got nothing in common with boys that age. You can't have really, *can* you?' I looked at her to see her response, but she'd drifted into a frown. 'Mum?'

'No,' she said. 'No, that's probably true . . .'

'Mum?' I said again. 'Are you Ok?'

'Yes . . .'

I saw her try to shake the frown, cover it with a smile. Something had gone, though. I could see it in her face. 'I

197

s'pose you must have been ... quite a different person then.'

'Different?' she said. For a moment she seemed surprised by the question, hands hanging low between her knees, her face just close to mine. Just a moment, though. Not very long at all. 'Yes,' she said quietly. 'I suppose so . . .' And then she took her eyes off me.

I think Mum was the only person who looked forward to Oliver's first visit. Dad didn't seem to care one way or the other, which was weird after the way he'd made it sound so important. Michael didn't give a fuck, and I wasn't surprised. I think he knew that I'd done something bad, he just couldn't see how to turn it to his advantage so he decided he just wouldn't be interested instead. As for me, the closer Saturday got the more often I needed to go to the toilet. I just hoped it would tail off when the day finally came round. Bladder problems never sound that romantic.

I kept mentioning it to Dad, every now and then just slipping it into the conversation. He never really answered me though, like he wasn't even bothered. And every time he shrugged or turned away it made me think of Oliver. It made me think of what he'd said. *You think that's Ok do you?* Like he didn't think it was Ok, like he thought, in fact, that it was pretty fucking weird. Remembering it made me wonder what other things he'd think were weird, and every time I wondered I had to head back to the loo.

By the time Saturday actually got there I could hardly stop thinking about it, smiling and feeling sick. Every time

I walked past our cat or a picture on the wall I wondered what Oliver would think. And when the phone rang that morning I almost felt relieved. It'd be Oliver making some excuse, I thought. Ill in bed or having to work, and I bit my lip as I picked up the phone.

It wasn't Oliver though. It was Dawn. And she didn't even bother saying hello.

'I've been waiting for you to call.' I could hear the slurping noise crackle down the phone line as she sucked her cheeks back in behind the words, stifling. It sounded like the noise of suffocating goldfish, and I wondered vaguely if I should sit down for this.

'Sorry,' I said. 'I didn't know I was s'posed to.'

'Three days,' she said, 'I haven't even talked to you.' She stopped speaking, waiting for me to answer, I guess. I looked out through the doorway, trying to see the clock in the living room. No good. 'I thought . . .' She coughed. 'I thought you'd at least call before he came round.' I stopped looking out. Turning back and staring at nothing, I heard the last sentence again. I licked my lips.

'Oh,' I said.

'I've been waiting. You know, thinking you'd call. Thinking you'd tell me . . . But no.'

'I . . .'

'I thought best friends were meant to tell each other everything. I guess we're not best friends.' There was silence for a moment, even louder down the phone. I listened to it and I wondered vaguely how long this might take. I hadn't even got changed yet.

'I was going to tell you,' I said.

'When? After the honeymoon?'

I couldn't think of much to say to that. Usually I'm pretty good with snappy comebacks. This didn't really feel like a snappy comeback situation, though. I wanted to ask her how she knew, how long she'd known for. I figured that wasn't the right thing to do, though, too much like pleading guilty.

'I was just, like . . . waiting for the right moment.'

'No you weren't,' she said. 'You weren't going to tell me at all. And I don't know why because . . . because I'm a *good* friend. I've always been a *good* friend. Look how much I helped with Robin!'

'I . . . I know . . .'

'So why didn't you *tell* me then?'

I didn't answer for a moment, staring at the study carpet. The fact was, I didn't really know why I hadn't told her. It hadn't been any big decision not to. I just sort of hadn't got round to it. It hadn't really seemed very important. Listening to her crackling, snotty, down the line, I took a deep breath. 'I was scared you'd be hurt,' I said. 'You know . . . I didn't want you to feel . . . hurt.' I tried to think of some other, better word. Nothing sprang to mind. 'But I was *going* to. I was just . . . waiting for the right time.'

Her voice was quiet, deciding. 'Why did you think I'd be hurt?' she said.

'Cos . . . with Robin, you were worried all the time that I didn't want to be with you. I didn't want you to feel like that about Oliver, that's all,' I said. 'I worry about your feelings.' It wasn't a *huge* lie. It wasn't even a very *big* lie, but still I felt a little twinge. I had to say something, I guess, something to make her feel better. And the main thing was that she believed it.

Oliver arrived at five minutes to six, and I was still changing when I heard the car. My jeans and a checked shirt. I wanted to look pretty, not sexy. Not anywhere near sexy.

Dad was reading the newspaper when I got downstairs, sitting in the big armchair and smoking a cigarette. I couldn't see his T-shirt, but I prayed it wasn't Tony Hancock. I stood there, looking at the living room. It was a mess, I thought. But maybe it was a comfortable mess. Maybe it was homely. Dad didn't even glance up, he looked pretty absorbed in the sports section. I took a breath. A long breath. And that was when Mum came trotting out. 'Is that him?' she said. 'I thought I heard a car.'

She had a dress on, which was nice, even if the hem had gone a little bit at the side. It was flowery and to her ankles with buttons down the front. One of them didn't match.

'I guess . . .' I said. 'Shall I . . . um . . . shall I go and ask him in? Or something . . .'

But Dad was already getting up. I watched him as he put the paper down, frowning.

Tony Hancock stared me straight in the face, frowning just as well as Dad.

'What are you doing?' I looked at him. 'I mean, I can ask him in. There's no need . . .'

The engine sound got louder, mud squishing off the wheels, splashing in the puddles.

'I want to say something to him.' He looked around at all of us, as if to say *Ok?*

'What? What do you want to say to him?' The sound of the car grew louder.

'What does it matter to you?'

'Can I come?' Michael said. His face was poking out of his bedroom door, grinning.

'No!'

'Let him come, for God's sake.' Dad shook his head. 'Don't be so precious about it.'

'Yeah,' Michael said. 'Don't be so precious about it!'

Dad walked out to the door. He had one hand in his pocket, but he wasn't smiling. I watched with my mouth open as Michael went after him. He'd gelled his hair as well.

'Well . . .' Mum said quietly, wiping her hands. 'I s'pose I'd better go out too now.'

And that was how Oliver first met them: standing in a line outside the door. Waiting. Staring. He drove into the yard, one hand on the wheel, and I saw his head turn slowly as he passed us by.

'Christ!'

I watched Dad walk towards the car, his face all tightened up. I saw Michael skipping to keep up with him. Oliver opened his door.

'Took that one a bit fast didn't you?' Dad slung his thumb back towards the gate, he was staring down at Oliver, fixing him through the glass of the car window. Already I could feel my stomach knotting.

'What?' Oliver's leg swung slowly off the seat. He put his boot down, trying to avoid the mud, and I wondered vaguely if Michael might tell him that it's rude to say 'what'. That would just top off the whole introduction business.

'Took it a bit fast, I said.' And Dad didn't take his hand out of his pocket. 'Could have been little kids around.' Oliver brought his other leg out, and I tried not to look at his face. He pushed the sleeve of his jumper up slightly. Nice, big, baggy jumper. It made him look a little younger.

'Nice car,' Mum said from beside me.

I watched Oliver stand up, putting his feet in all the right places. He had sunglasses on, and I wondered why. It looked like it might even rain. They levelled at Dad, the house behind me all dark and rounded in reflection. I watched him pause, not moving, before he said 'What little kids?'

'Any kids.' Dad crossed his arms over his chest, breathed in. 'The speed you took that corner, you could have run me over.' His voice was slow, not loud, but he was standing very still. And waiting there, watching them both, I could feel my stomach clenching up, kind of tingling below my chest. A smile was trying to break through my teeth. Not a nice smile, not a proper smile, but the kind of smile you can't get rid of when you watch your little brother getting bollocked. I didn't like the feeling of it in my mouth.

Oliver didn't speak for a moment and he didn't look across at me, but I felt his hand fall, heavy on my arm. It rested there, his fingers round my elbow like a ring.

'I'm a very careful driver,' he said. I felt those fingers move. 'Aren't I.' Oliver looked down at me, not smiling, not asking, and for a moment I wished he wasn't wearing those glasses. I wished that I could see his eyes.

'Yes,' I said.

And as Oliver looked away from me, satisfied I guess, I saw his other hand reach out.

For a moment, Dad only stared.

'Oliver,' Oliver said, and he held his hand there.

Dad nodded. 'Philip,' he said back, and he shook the hand. 'There could have been little kids around . . .' he said again, letting go of Oliver's hand.

I watched as Oliver turned towards Michael, said his name again. And then he did the weirdest thing: he put his hand back out. He had to hold it down a bit, and for a minute Michael only stared as well, his mouth hanging halfway open. This is Michael, I thought. Usually we don't bring him down from the attic, but you know . . .

'Michael,' my brother said loudly, and as Oliver shook his hand, I heard Dad cough a little.

'I'm going in,' he said.

'You'll have to excuse the mess,' Mum said as we walked through into the porch. 'I haven't been here all day.' I looked back to see Michael still staring at the car, and I wondered why I felt like telling Oliver she was lying.

'Don't worry about it,' he said, and I watched his back disappear through the doorway. I just hoped that Mum had cleared out behind the ironing board. And after a minute I followed them.

'Did you find us alright?' She waited for me to come through before she shut the door. Dad was sitting in the armchair again, but he hadn't picked up the paper. He'd lit another cigarette instead.

'I think I went the wrong way once,' he said. He stood by the wall and stretched a little bit. 'I would have been on time otherwise.'

'Wouldn't worry about it.' Dad stretched too. 'Better to get here in one piece than rush.'

Oliver didn't say anything.

'Well . . .' Mum smiled all round. 'Dinner'll be ready in a minute. I'll just go check.' From the porch I heard Michael's footsteps. 'Cool car,' he said, pulling the door open. Dad and Oliver faced each other, both sitting straight in their chairs. I watched Oliver reach for a cigarette.

'This is a nice house,' he said. He wasn't really looking at it, though.

'It was a wreck when I found it. Had it all renovated. All the walls, windows, built an extension. They had to put a roof on too.' Dad looked at him, waiting. 'But what we got, effectively, was a very cheap house. Not that it shows.'

'Mm,' Oliver said, and I wondered what he was thinking. It made me kind of nervous, not knowing; I didn't know what I should say.

'Well,' I looked around. 'Does anyone want a cup of tea? I'm going to have one.'

'You could get me one of my beers.' Dad flicked his hand out. 'Want a beer, Oliver?'

'Or wine,' I said quickly. 'We've got wine too.'

'No thanks. I'm fine.'

'No need to be polite,' Dad said.

'Really. I'm fine.'

'Suit yourself,' Dad said, glancing away.

Mum was dishing up the spaghetti, smiling at me as I walked through the door.

'He seems nice,' she said, nodding. But moving to the fridge, I thought of Dad and Oliver sitting, staring at each other through the room. He didn't seem nice. He didn't seem nice at all. Opening the fridge, I let my smile spread. It was tight and twitching, and I didn't answer her.

Oliver knew how to eat spaghetti. He didn't even use the knife that Mum had put out for him. He didn't need it; just the spoon and the fork and he wound it up on there like he'd been weaned on it. I, however, had to cut it up into Heinz-sized pieces.

He'd been sat next to Michael instead of me, and I wondered if that was on purpose. If Dad had asked for it specially or something, trying to put him off with Michael's slurping and dribbling.

'This is delicious,' Oliver said, winding up another mouthful. 'Really delicious.'

'What's for afters?' Michael's chin had gone a delicate shade of bright orange.

'Oh,' Mum said. 'I . . . I didn't make any pudding. Should I have?'

'I don't want any,' Oliver said. 'This is fine.'

'There's fruit,' she said. 'And salad . . .'

'It looks lovely.' He glanced up at the salad bowl. It didn't look lovely at all. Lots of home-grown stuff, all dark and cabbagey. No tomatoes. No iceberg lettuce. I thought I'd probably skip the salad.

'It's all home-grown,' Mum said. 'This is pretty much the last of the crop.'

'Must be great having your own fresh vegetables. The stuff in Somerfield's awful.'

'Yes,' Dad said. 'Well, that's one of the disadvantages of living in town, isn't it.'

Oliver nodded at the salad bowl. 'You're very lucky.'

'It's not luck,' Dad said. 'Just having the good sense to buy somewhere with land.'

Oliver didn't answer him.

It was funny, all week I'd worried over this visit, over how he'd act with Mum and Dad. He didn't seem so different to the way he acted with me, though. I still couldn't tell what he was thinking. Staring down at the spaghetti in my bowl, I just hoped that he wasn't pissed off.

'Is there orange juice in this sauce?' I heard him say it but I didn't look up. I'd tried to tell Mum not to make spaghetti, tried to tell her in a nice way but she didn't seem to get the point. I pushed my fork across the china.

'Yes,' Mum looked up, a frown creasing just above her eyes. 'Does it taste funny?'

'Not at all.' Oliver smiled, but at the plate not Mum. 'I put it in mine. Sweetens the tomatoes, right?'

'Well yes.' Mum looked back to the cooker, just a quick glance. I saw her mouth twitch round the corner. 'I think so anyway . . .'

'Did you use the last orange then?' Dad said.

'What?' She looked over to him. 'Probably. Did you want it?'

'I was going to have it for breakfast,' he said quietly. 'Doesn't matter.'

Everyone pushed their plates away after they'd finished. I watched Oliver place his knife and fork next to each other, very neat, and I wondered if I should do the same with mine. He'd finished the spaghetti anyway, and had a portion of salad. Maybe he'd even enjoyed it.

Looking at him, reaching into one pocket for his cigarettes, I thought again about what he'd said. I wondered if he still thought it was weird, Dad inviting him round. He hadn't mentioned it since that time.

'Is it alright to smoke?' Oliver looked at Mum. She always was the slowest. 'Do you want me to wait?'

'Course it's alright,' Dad said. He smiled. 'You don't mind, do you Liz.'

She shook her head as Michael pushed his knife around his empty plate. I wanted to tell him to wash his face before he put everyone off their cigarettes.

'Your whole face is covered in spaghetti sauce, Michael. It's disgusting,' I said. Mum made a face at me like she was trying to tell me to shut up without actually speaking. 'Well it is! You want to see that while you're still eating?'

'You've got some on your chin too,' Dad said. I almost smiled for a moment then, nodding towards Michael. I almost smiled, before I saw he was pointing at me. 'Under your bottom lip,' he said. 'Being as you're so eager to point it out.'

There was silence for a moment as I looked round the

table. Oliver had taken a sudden interest in the grain of the wood. 'Fine,' I said, but no one answered. 'Well . . . At least I'll go and wash *mine*.' Still, no one said anything. 'Alright . . .' I squeezed out from behind Mum's chair. And I hadn't even started on my pear yet.

The bathroom was too far away to hear them talking, even when I left the door open. They knew that too, probably. Perfect opportunity to talk about how I couldn't eat spaghetti properly. Not even when I cut it up into little pieces. I went to the mirror. Big and dark over the sink, I stared back at myself.

'Fuck.'

'Fuck,' I said in the mirror.

It was huge and orange and it glared at me from under my lower lip.

'You could have told me.'

'You could have told *me* too.'

I ran the tap till it went cold. Really cold, and I splashed a handful against my face. It didn't matter. It was just sauce. Christ, most people get sauce on their chins eating pasta. Everybody, in fact. Well, everybody except Oliver. I scrubbed at it and my finger left a little red mark. I watched it bloom as the water dripped in trickles off my chin. It was hard and bright and pretty. I pressed again. I took my finger away. It was like a little stain against my skin.

I used my nail the next time, and I wished I'd never mentioned Michael's face.

*

They were talking about vegetarianism when I got back to the kitchen, and Dad was halfway through his cigarette. I'd thought Michael would be gone, excused, but he was still sitting there. Waiting. He hadn't washed his face either.

'I think it's barbaric. In one hundred . . . two hundred years' time, people are going to look back and wonder how it was possible. I mean, *the consumption of flesh*. That's how they'll see it.' He took a drag. 'It's not good for you either. Doctors have proved that it's not good for people to eat red meat. Christ knows why they still do it.'

'Probably because they enjoy it,' Oliver said.

I walked around his back to get to my place at the table. He was leaning, very comfortable, against the chair and I could see a couple of his hairs had fallen, dark, on to the wool of his jumper.

'We're supposed to be a civilized people. I mean, people enjoy beating each other up in the pub. Doesn't mean to say they're just allowed to go and do it.'

'Hi.' I smiled all round, sitting back down at the table. I picked up my pear. 'God,' I said. 'I'm stuffed.'

'I think it should be against the law. Simple as that. Make it illegal.' Dad nodded to himself, like that proved his point.

'Some people like eating meat, though,' Oliver said.

I took the first bite, trying to make sure the juice didn't run away.

'So did I.' Dad put his cigarette out. 'But then I realized what I was doing.'

'I used to like venison,' Mum said. 'And beef. Steak

Tartare, but I couldn't eat that now. I mean, not after the whole BSE thing. Not even if I wasn't a vegetarian.'

'Just another example of the meat industry,' Dad said, 'putting people's health at risk for their own profit. I mean, do you think they give a fuck if people get BSE? I bet they only wish it hadn't come out. That's *their* only regret, I bet.'

'It's CJD in humans,' Mum said. 'BSE's in cattle. And in sheep they call it scrapie.'

'When did you give up eating meat then?' Oliver looked at her. I took another bite.

'Was it before I met you?' She looked at Dad. 'Maybe after. About twenty years ago.'

'Do you miss it?'

'Oh no, not anymore. Can hardly remember what it tasted like,' she said.

'Did you when you first stopped?' Oliver crushed his cigarette into the ashtray, blew out a little plume of smoke. I wished he'd look at me. Just once. Just for a minute.

'I missed sausages,' she said, and she laughed. 'And I didn't even *like* sausages that much. Missed them when I stopped, though. And I missed bacon sandwiches too.'

'Mmm,' I said. I took another bite of pear and wondered how to change the subject.

'Did you miss it?' Oliver looked at Dad. 'When you gave it up, I mean.'

'Yes,' Dad said. 'Yes, I did miss it. But that wasn't the point. I wanted to stop.'

'What did you miss the most?'

'I can't remember now,' Dad said. And he tipped his beer can up to finish it.

'Oh God, and I missed *pork scratchings!*' Mum said suddenly. 'I used to *love* them!'

She looked around at us. 'I . . . I probably wouldn't like them now, though,' she said.

'What are pork scratchings?' I looked at Oliver.

'They're like pieces of pork fat,' he said, and finally he smiled at me. 'Deep fried.'

'Mmmm,' Dad said. 'Sounds *lovely.*'

'I don't know . . .' I smiled back at Oliver. 'I think they sound pretty nice, actually.'

'Come off it! *Deep-fried fucking pork fat?*'

I looked back to Oliver but he wasn't smiling anymore. Or looking at me either. He was staring down at the table like he was sick of the whole subject. He only had himself to blame for that though, I thought. I'd been sick of it ages ago.

'Pork fucking scratchings,' Dad said. He breathed out, heavy and loose, but no one bothered to answer him. Mum twitched the salad spoon against the edge of the bowl and I heard the tiny clicking noise it made. I pressed my hands together.

'Does anybody want a game on my Sega Megadrive?' Michael said. 'I've got *Sonic.*'

Oliver went home at nine o'clock, which was good because everyone had pretty much run out of things to say by then. I said I'd walk him out to the car and I was glad when no one volunteered to help me. He followed me out and I held the torch beam on his car. I listened to him fumbling for the locking thing. 'Are you Ok there?'

'I'm fine. I . . . *Shit!* I just trod in a *fucking* puddle.'

'Oh,' I said. 'Sorry . . .' I heard him walk a few more steps. 'Are you Ok?'

'Why wouldn't I be Ok?'

'I . . . I didn't mean that. I just . . . wondered.'

'I'm fine.'

'Ok,' I said. 'Good.' There was a breath behind me, then. Short and hard, and I felt his hand on my shoulder. He let it rest there for a moment, the blind leading the blind.

'I'm sorry,' he said slowly.

'That's Ok.'

But I smiled in the darkness. And I knew he couldn't see me.

Dad didn't mention Oliver at all through the couple of days after they met, and I wondered if that was a good thing or a bad one. I left a fair amount of pauses in the right places so that he could say something. It wasn't any good though, he just paused with me, and I couldn't quite work out how to bring it up myself. Oliver wouldn't talk about it either, he wouldn't tell me what he thought. And all in all it made me wonder why I'd bothered to invite him.

I asked him quite a few times if he thought I looked like them, it seemed important for some reason. I was glad when he said he couldn't see the resemblance, though. Not that I think that Dad's ugly or anything, actually I reckon he's pretty handsome. It was just that I didn't want to look like anyone. Anyone at all.

I asked Oliver a lot of questions over the last week or so of the holidays but he didn't answer many. He seemed kind of pissed off that I asked. Oliver got pissed off quite a lot, though, so it was difficult to tell what caused it.

The only person who really seemed to want to talk about Oliver was Mum. She said he reminded her of the guy that she'd gone out with. She said that they had the same eyes.

Michael didn't mention him on purpose, but I could tell by the way he looked at me sometimes that he wanted to. I didn't care what Michael thought, though. I didn't give a fuck. Which was maybe why I didn't pay too much attention when he finally spoke up. We were playing on the Megadrive and he'd been looking at me from the corner of his eye for ages before he asked.

'So when is *Oliver* coming round again then?'

I shrugged. 'When I ask him to.'

Michael looked away, off at the screen. Maybe it hadn't been what he was hoping for. I hadn't thought of inviting Oliver round again though. Dad hadn't even asked about it.

'D'you like Oliver then?' Michael said, smirking. 'D'you like him better than Dawn?'

'Fuck's sake, Michael. I'm trying to *play*.' He was silent for a moment then, thinking.

'I bet he thinks you're sexxx*yyyy*!' He laughed, retching at the carpet underneath him. I didn't answer him, though, looking at the screen above me. I wondered if it was true.

I didn't get to find out how Dawn knew about Oliver

until the first day back in school. It was a sunny day but pretty cold for September, which had given Dawn a good excuse to revert to 300-denier tights. She stared at me as I walked into registration. She stared, and then she turned away.

'Hiya,' I said. I looked around the room for Holly but she hadn't got there yet. 'Ok?'

'Ok . . .' Dawn tapped her fingers against the grey plastic table. She couldn't do it as good as I could though. Hers was just childish. 'No I'm not "Ok" actually. I'm not "Ok" at all.'

'Oh,' I said. I sat down next to her, staring out in front of me at the teacher's empty desk. I knew what was up. Maybe I'd known it before I'd even got into the classroom. Dawn sends out pissed-off waves like a radar. Still, she didn't turn to look at me, her back looked like it was in a brace. 'Have you got a summer cold or something?' I said.

'No I haven't got a summer cold!'

'Oh,' I said. 'Right.' I folded my hands together. 'So what's up then exactly?'

'*Worried about my feelings*, you said. *Worried about my feelings!* If you're so *worried about my feelings*, how come you haven't rung since last Saturday?' Her head swung round, *Exorcist*-style, like it wasn't joined on to her body. 'Busy with *Oliver?*'

Looking at her, I felt my neck trying to sink slowly into my shoulders, to help my head escape maybe. I knew I should have called though, really. If only to save me this hassle.

'I thought I'd be seeing you today,' I said. 'I didn't think I'd need to phone.'

'No, right, but I bet you called him.' She didn't leave me room to answer. Obviously she'd been working on the speech all morning. Three minutes into registration, I thought, and I'm already bored. 'I bet you spent all *week* on the phone to *Oliver.*'

'I'm sorry Dawn,' I said. It didn't come out sorry though, it just came out exhausted.

'You're *always* sorry. You don't give a . . . a *crap* about me and then you're *so* sorry.'

I watched her turn her whole body. 'I think it's *disgusting*,' she said. 'Absolutely *DISGUSTING!* Twenty-seven! He must be a *PERVERT!*'

I stared at her, legs crossed like an insect, her eyes squinted, neck twisted towards me. I stared at her and I couldn't quite believe it.

The little voice in my head just said *bitch*.

'Is that what you think?' I said quietly. 'Well maybe that's why I didn't tell you.'

Her mouth fell open just a little way, hair dangling in verticals by her cheeks. I could see a line of spit, quite shiny, dragged across her teeth, and her tongue looked very lax.

It took her a second to come back, I think. I saw the flesh by her nose twitch in spasm.

'Your dad said you'd *change*,' she said slowly. The spittle was gone from her voice. She just looked so surprised. 'He said you'd change but I didn't think it'd be so soon.'

She sucked her bottom lip back in. I even heard the

tiny wet smacking sound it made. And after a moment I looked away.

'When did he say that?'

'He said it as soon as he knew. As soon as he knew about . . . about you and *Oliver*. He said it right away but I said no. I said you'd stay the same. I *defended* you! I defended you and you just . . . you just treat me like dirt!'

'I haven't changed,' I said. I stared down at stippled plastic stained with Tippex all over the desk. 'It's not . . . it's not disgusting. And he's not a pervert.' I looked at her, shoulders pulled right up. 'He just likes me,' I said. 'That's all.'

Dawn glanced away, over at the doorway as the tutor came in. Her lips curled together, first downwards then up.

'Everyone'll think it's disgusting,' she said. 'You just wait and see.'

It took me ages to calm her down after that, to convince her we were still friends. I smiled and I said sorry and I did all the stuff that I'd always done. But every time I said something I was thinking about what she had said. That Dad'd said I would change. I wondered just how long they'd spent talking, a nice cosy little chat, and Oliver's voice went around in my head. *And that's alright with you is it? Your Dad asking your friends round?*

I don't know. Maybe I was just overtired or something, not used to seeing Dawn. But as the bell rang for Assembly and I watched her thumping out, she looked taller than before, more bulky.

And I wondered for the first time if it really was alright.

I lost my virginity the second time that Oliver came round. I never really thought of it as losing my virginity, though. Virginity just didn't seem like a particularly cool thing to own, like owning a TV or a dress from French Connection. And when Holly said I've got an ounce and a half of top fuckin skunk, I never thought to answer back yes, but I've got a virginity.

I didn't think I'd be a virgin after me and Oliver spent the night together for the first time. It wasn't a romantic kind of thought, more a question of logic: spending the night with someone meant having sex with them, I'd never had sex before therefore I'd be losing my virginity. It was just the next step, like marriage is the step after engagement. Like snogging a bloke is the next step after meeting him. Thinking about it, it sounded like one long slope. Once you were on there, it was just too much effort to stop.

So yes, I knew I'd lose my virginity that night. I even got out my morning-after pills, pills I'd got for Robin, and I wondered vaguely if that was a betrayal. I wasn't nervous. I knew it was something that had to be done.

It was a Tuesday, I think, not long into the school term, and it was Mum that asked if he'd be staying the night. Not in my room obviously, she got the spare room ready when I said yes. Still it was a start, I thought. And she'd smiled, going upstairs to do it.

He got there at a quarter past five, and he parked in

exactly the same place. No one wanted to come out and meet him that second time. Dad said he was too busy, even though he didn't look busy at all. Mum just smiled at me and said 'You go on out and meet him on your own.' Michael explained to me that he was also too busy. That he had 'a lot of important things to do'. That was Ok, though. I figured maybe he'd started wanking. So I was the only one standing in the yard to watch the car crawl in at three miles an hour. I was the only one he smiled at.

I watched him open the car door and bend out, searching in the shadow of the house for me. He was wearing his sunglasses again, still dressed in his suit from work. And when he did smile at me, his face a TV-orange colour in the afternoon sun, I felt my stomach go all loose inside, like having gastric flu. I smiled back anyway.

'Hello,' he said. And he shut the car door with his foot. 'You look nice.' He looked over my shoulder as I walked towards him. 'Where's the welcoming committee?'

'Inside,' I said. I kept my smile up, just. 'They . . . they were only trying to be friendly.'

He shrugged, still looking around. 'Yeah . . . well I brought a present for them anyway.'

'A present?' I looked at him and I guess there was something wrong with my face when I said it. My face or my tone of voice. Looking down at me, his smile went cold.

'What,' he said but it wasn't a question. And wiping his nose fast, he said 'Forget it.'

Dad was putting his coat on when I walked through into the living room, Oliver behind me. He nodded at the space above my shoulder, and I heard Michael's door swing open.

'Alright?' he said.

'Uh-huh,' Oliver said. 'How are you?'

'Just off out.' He looked at me, and I saw Mum come in from the kitchen.

'Hiya,' she said, and I wondered who she was talking to. 'How are you?'

'Fine.' Oliver pushed out from behind me. I moved a bit to one side.

'I'm going to get an Indian.' Dad checked the car keys in his jeans. 'Alright for you?'

'Yeah . . .' I said. 'Sure.'

'I brought some wine.' Oliver held the bottle out and I watched him put a four-pack of lager down on to the table. 'Oh, and some beer.' He brushed his hair back behind his ear, but Mum wasn't looking at him.

'I'm making lasagne,' she said.

'What?' Dad turned to her.

'Lasagne,' she said. 'I've already started.'

'Well, this is white anyway.' Oliver smiled, but then he didn't really understand. I watched Dad glance round at him. 'It'll go with anything.' He waited.

'I fancy an Indian,' Dad said.

'But I've . . . I've already started.'

'Well you can save it can't you? Put it in the fridge or something. Have it tomorrow.'

Oliver was looking at them, still holding out the bottle.

'Not really, no. It'll go off. Anyway I . . . well, I fancied lasagne.'

'Yes, and I fancy a curry.'

'But I thought . . . I've made the tomato sauce and everything.'

'Uh-huh? Well we're going to have an Indian.'

'Mmm,' Oliver said, and he put the wine down.

'I . . .' Mum looked around. I watched her eyes go from person to person. I watched them hit the floor. 'Nevermind,' she said.

'Ok then. Who wants rice – who wants chips?'

Nobody said anything.

'Well come on . . . rice or chips?'

I looked at Mum. Mum looked back, and for one stupid moment I tried to smile. In the gap between so many people's words, I thought I could hear Oliver breathing. Maybe not. Maybe it was only Dad. I bit my lower lip and I took my eyes away from Mum.

'Come *on.*' Dad tried to laugh. 'Rice? Chips? I'll get both if you want . . .'

But there was silence. Just silence, and the sound of Oliver clearing his throat.

'Well, I . . . I'll just . . . get a selection then. Right?'

And no one looked at him when he turned to walk out.

Mum sat down on the sofa as we listened to the engine fade away. Oliver still hadn't moved. He was look-ing at the label of the wine bottle. I think he was waiting.

'Well . . .' Mum said slowly. 'Guess I'll go and put the

cooking things away.' But she didn't get up. Instead, she said 'How are you anyway?'

Oliver took his hand off the bottle. 'I'm Ok . . . tired. I just finished work.'

'Right,' she said. And then he picked it up again.

'I brought this for you. It was white, wasn't it? When I was here on Sunday?'

'I like both.' She tried a smile but it didn't fit too well. I hoped he hadn't noticed.

'Good,' he said. 'Good.' And he held it out for her.

'Thanks. For the wine, I mean . . .' She laughed a little bit. 'I hope you like curry.'

He shrugged. 'It's alright.' And I tried to think of something I could say. He put his hands in his pockets and sat down in the armchair. He rubbed his temple with one hand.

'I'll open it then, shall I?' she said, and she sighed as she got up.

'Sorry. It'd probably be better chilled.'

She turned back to look at Oliver, halfway to the kitchen door.

'To tell you the truth,' she said, 'I don't really give a fuck.'

I think that was the first time we all laughed.

We didn't get up to my room till about ten-thirty, what with TV and talking and dinner. Mum'd made a bed up for Oliver in the spare room. Not only that, but she'd cleared a path so he could get to it. Past the cardboard boxes, all pushed to one side. Next to the rabbit hutch that Dad'd made for my seventh birthday. And I had to wonder if it still stank the same as before. My She-Ra dolls were in there, and the Sindy horse that only had three legs. That was Ok, though. I don't think Sindy minded. She didn't have a head so I guess she never noticed. Sindy at the amputee hospital. It was really touching.

I wasn't really worried about any of that stuff, though. The toys or the rubbish or anything like that. *Really*, I was worried about the orange peel in the corner. Mum had put it there last year when she heard on *The Home Front* that it took away the smell of cat piss. It wasn't orange peel anymore, though. And the smell of cat piss had become pretty much irrelevant. Because upstairs, laughing in the face of EU regulations, we were now cultivating our very own strain of biological warfare.

I didn't say anything to Mum about it though. Maybe because she'd done it specially. Maybe just because it didn't matter.

And it was funny, I hadn't thought about it all that evening. Not once. Not at all. But walking up the stairs with Oliver following, I was kind of surprised to realize that everything had been alright.

Oliver sat down on my bed and he looked around without a word. It sort of made me wish I'd tidied up. But then I guess it was like Dad said really, when Robin first came round. That you can't change the way you are just to impress someone else. I just wished I'd taken out the dirty teacups.

'You Ok?' I stayed standing. Somehow it didn't seem right to sit down next to him. And I didn't want to move the laundry on my chair.

'Fine, yeah.' He didn't smile, though. 'Full.'

'Mmm,' I said. 'Me too.' But I wasn't. I thought I could probably just fit in some Nutella on toast, actually.

'So this is your room.'

'Yes,' I said, because there wasn't really any way to wriggle out of it now. He didn't answer, though, and I wondered if I should take that as a bad sign. 'Well . . . that was nice, wasn't it. You know, having dinner. You and me and Mum and Dad and everything. It was . . . well, nice.'

'Mmm,' he said. 'I see you got the stereo set up.'

'Yeah . . .' I wondered for a moment if I should push the nice thing. Looking at his expression, though, it didn't seem like such a good idea. 'Curry was great wasn't it?'

'It was alright,' he said. 'It wasn't that good.'

His words made me stop. I wondered how anyone could say that. 'Yes it *was.*'

Oliver didn't bother to reply. He sighed, sitting back on the bed, and I watched him do that temple-rubbing thing again. I wondered why I was annoyed. He closed his eyes and just breathed for a little while. Maybe I was supposed to say something. He moved his hand down in a sweep over his face.

'This is *stupid,*' he said. 'This is so fucking stupid.'

'No it isn't,' I said, because I couldn't think of anything else. He didn't look at me.

'I don't know what the *fuck* I'm doing here.'

'It was . . . it was *nice.*'

'No it wasn't. It wasn't fucking *nice* at all. It was argument after fucking argument. I mean, why should I have to listen to it? It's got fucking nothing to do with me!'

224

'I'm sorry . . .'

'Christ!' He breathed out again. Heavy and loaded and I wished that I'd just kept my mouth shut.

'I didn't . . . I didn't realize you were . . . unhappy.' But watching his face, I thought back. And I had realized. I'd realized from the beginning.

'*Unhappy?*' He looked at me and I watched a nasty little smile pick up around his lips. 'Doesn't it get on your nerves? Bicker bicker *fucking BICKER . . .*'

'No. They weren't bickering.' I turned away, picking up the clothes on the chair. I had to handle them carefully, the jumpers and the skirts and that, so as not to let him see the dirty underwear that was lying underneath. 'They just . . . I don't know, they're just talking.' I stood in the middle of the room, no clothes left to move, but I just didn't want to sit down.

'Why the fuck are they still together? They obviously fucking hate each other.'

'No they don't!' I took a breath, trying to find some sentence that would make it true. My mouth didn't say anything. 'They weren't arguing,' I said finally. 'They just . . . disagree sometimes.'

Oliver didn't speak, only looked at me.

'They're happy,' I said.

'*Right,*' he said. He raised his eyebrows in a swing, and he turned his face from me as his breath came out. 'Fuck's sake,' he said. 'Didn't even say thank you for the fucking wine! How much effort does it *take?*'

'They *did* say thank you. Don't you remember? They did . . .'

'*She* said thank you.'

'Yeah?' I said. 'Well? They'll buy you a bottle back! I'm sure they'll buy you a bottle back.'

'I don't want a "bottle back". I wanted a thank you.' He paused for a moment, just sitting there. And his voice was quiet, almost soft, when he spoke again. 'Come here,' he said.

I looked at him on my bed. He didn't pat it or smile, he just held one still hand towards me. And I walked over to him. What else was there to do?

'Your father,' he said, looking up at me, not touching me, 'is possibly one of the rudest fucking men I've ever met.'

'No he's . . .' I started to speak. It came out too quickly though, like not having total bowel control. And Oliver's eyes didn't move on mine as his fingers flicked out. They tapped against my arm in one light, sharp snap. My mouth closed.

Nothing moved.

For one long moment we just stayed that way. I could hear my own dumb breathing. It was a relief when he touched me.

Oliver reached for my hand first. Which was weird really, because my leg was loads nearer to him. He patted it, like Dad sometimes pats it when he thinks I'm feeling depressed. Then he just let his lie on top of mine. It was hot and I could feel a little bit of sticky sweat. But then, I had said he could take his jacket off. I felt his fingers move into the gaps between mine, till he was holding my hand.

Laced in. I wanted to look at our hands sitting there together. I wanted to see what our fingers looked like mixed in with each other. I didn't look, though. I didn't turn. I guess I was scared he might take it away.

He squeezed and my skin caught a little bit on his. I tried to squeeze back, and I could feel his thumbnail lying against my palm. It was softer than I would have thought, and I wondered if his toenails felt the same.

His nose got close to mine, till I had to look at him. Full in the face. I tried not to search for blackheads. I tried to concentrate on his eyes. Big dark brown eyes, with lines of green like broken blood vessels. And if I looked really hard, really deep, without blinking. If I looked in just exactly the right way, I could find my own reflection.

My face was shades of grey and black. Shiny like an oil slick. Dilated.

And when he snogged me I was glad to close my eyes.

His mouth was dry and not like I remembered it. His tongue felt harder and there were tiny lumps on the inside of his cheeks. He turned round to face me more, so he didn't have to stretch his back. I leaned away from his, slowly, so as not to bump my head on the wall. And after a moment we were lying down.

He didn't touch me, though. Not for ages. And I had to reach out for his bum before he reached for mine. I wondered if maybe he didn't like to touch people. Only to kiss them. He grunted while he snogged me, with our noses side by side.

His suit didn't feel smooth, even if it looked it. It was rough and I could feel the grain of the material with my palm. Tiny little squares, it felt like. But maybe they were only circles. And I wondered if it rubbed at the skin of his arse the same way it rubbed against my hand. I wondered if it hurt him and I squeezed to find out. He moved his hip towards me, though, and he didn't seem to mind. I thought of Robin and bony pelvises and I wondered if he had as many pubes. I wondered if he'd tell me to wank it.

I felt his hand come round and touch my side. Not my tits. Not yet. Maybe he just didn't like them. He squeezed around my ribs. I followed with his bum, and his hip bone pressed into my bladder. I tried to remember where I'd put my morning-after pills.

The flesh of his nose was bent against my cheek and his hair was trapped between. That was when I felt it, I think. Just next to his hip bone, just missing my bladder. And I smiled when I thought that it felt bigger than Robin's. It was rounded and long, and if that suit itched him as much as it itched my hand then he must have been in hell every moment it was on him. He pushed again, deeper in, and I wondered if I should go piss. He grunted once more, but I didn't push back.

I tried to work out how long it took him to get a hand inside my top. But it's funny, you can't really count time when you're snogging. It was ages, anyway. And when he did, he only got it as far as my stomach. I had to slide my way lower down, just to get him anywhere near.

He touched the bottom of them first. The bit where they start bulging out from your ribcage. I wondered if he could feel the stretch marks there. Maybe that was what he was looking for. But slowly his fingers went up. All the way round the outside of the first. Up to my collarbone. I could feel him massaging the muscles underneath my skin. Then he touched them. Properly. Both of them. And the skin of his palms was clammy against my nipples. His palms stuck to me, and when he pulled his hands away slightly, my nipples followed.

The black behind my eyelids turned red as he pressed his face on to mine. And he gripped. I felt his fingertips press into them. Into the gland that's in the middle. Maybe he could feel it too. I wondered if he knew how big my nipples were. I wondered if he knew that Robin had laughed. And perhaps he could sense the old fingerprints there. I wished that he'd squeeze harder. I wished he'd make them hurt.

He didn't say wank it when I put my hand inside his trousers. He didn't say anything that I could hear, but I felt his back tense as his neck stretched away from me. I felt his spit on my lips and I had to look up. The tendons in his neck were standing out. I could see the veins underneath his chin and the way that the bone tightened the skin. His teeth biting down. Gripping. And I thought I'd like to know how that bite felt. On my shoulder maybe. On my neck. I'd like to know if it left tooth marks. Or maybe if it broke the skin.

I squeezed with my left hand. I felt my elbow slip a little on the duvet, and I watched him strain further from me. I hoped he wouldn't bump his head.

'Uuuuggghh . . .' he said.

The skin was funny. Smooth. More like nipple skin than

any other kind. And I wondered why I hadn't noticed that with Robin. I moved it upwards, where one piece of skin will end and another one will start. From underneath. Or from inside, I suppose. And that skin was different. Rounded and not half as smooth. It caught underneath my fingers, and I rubbed. I guess I didn't know what else to do. And I wondered if Oliver would want to gob me off. I wondered if I'd just let him.

I rubbed again, up and down, up and down, and I felt the pins and needles in my wrist start up. That was when the slime came. I thought for a minute that it was over. Finished maybe, and I guessed that Robin hadn't missed much.

But it wasn't over. I guess it wasn't really even started.

And after a moment, I closed my eyes again.

I pushed Oliver's trousers down to round his hips. I didn't look at what I was doing. I just didn't want to see. I felt his hands move from my chest. Down, over skin. My stomach and further. I felt him push my trousers down as well. The elastic of my pants was stretching. And then I felt him touch me.

It wasn't nice. Not really. But when I thought about it, it wasn't quite as bad as Robin. At least I didn't hate him. And I didn't think he'd laugh. His fingers moved in. Not gentle. Not roundabout like he had been with my tits. I guess it was do or die by now, though. I guessed he might as well.

He put his finger inside. Burning and stretching but he didn't seem about to stop. It hurt. It hurt a lot. But it didn't matter. I suppose that nothing ever matters, not really. I tried to think of biting and it got a little easier.

I felt his hips shift downwards and my eyelids ached from shutting them so hard. Two fingers, and the nails caught. Down further with his chest pressing hard, squashing my tits. I tried to breathe easy, I tried to breathe slow. Suck it. The feel of a handkerchief scratching on my lips. Teeth, I thought. Teeth.

But when he fucked me, there was nothing in my mind.

The pain was worse than anything. Worse than I'd ever thought it could be. Hot and heavy and grinding in my stomach. Like being stabbed. Like being punched from the inside out. Like a twisting, pulling fist. Like getting fucked. And I wanted to scream.

He pushed further.

Fast and sharp and nasty. I could feel the hairs on his thighs, scratching at mine.

And I wanted so much to pull away. Just make him get off. Just make him stop everything. To push him out. I'd hide, I thought. I'd close my legs. I'd run.

But I didn't pull away from him. I didn't move. Every muscle tight against him, I lay there as he hurt me and hurt me and I didn't pull away. I lay strained. Rigid. And I waited for it to be over.

Further and further inside. More pain and more, and my teeth made a hole in my cheek. Harder. Digging. I felt his hip bones knock against mine. I felt a cramp somewhere down in my shin. My nails biting into my palms. And as he banged, I wondered if they'd made half-moons. If they were purple, red or white. I hoped he wouldn't look down. I hoped he wouldn't see my face. He rocked in.

Another grunt.

A curse.

Hating.

I saw him come. His face was ugly and hurting. I saw him through the squints of my eyes, piercing the gaps where I couldn't shut him out. Everything around his face was grey, collapsing in towards him, in towards me.

Like drowning, I thought.

Like drowning as I clawed my way up.

He rested his head down on the side of my face when it was over. His heart was beating in his cheek and I felt a little drop of sweat fall on to my nose.

I listened to his breathing in my ear and I put a hand on the small of his back. There was a tiny puddle there, warm, and dribbling down into the crack in his bum. It made his skin shiny and it made me smile. I'd never really figured sex would be that sweaty.

His legs were collapsed between mine, his ribcage really heavy on my boobs. And if I stretched my big toe I could feel the arch of his foot, the wrinkly skin. His hair was flattened out, tickling my face. The little black strand across my eye. Funny, though, close up it didn't look that small. It looked huge and fat and blurred round the edges. It was wet.

Our necks were touching, his skin all rough and red. Tiny black dots that needed shaving, and a scar I'd never seen before. Just a little white line, slightly puckered at one end. The murmuring noise of a car on the road that took a long time to pass by.

The flap of my curtain.

He shivered once. And I could feel the movement when he blinked.

'I think I'm in love with you.'

It was easy to say really. Whispering, like I had my fingers crossed behind my back. And it made me think of Mills and Boons. Lush jungles and deserted beaches and a woman in a bikini who knows just where she's going. Men with perfect noses, and slick-back hair like Ken. Nipples that don't ever poke through bras. It made me think of passion flowers and daiquiris. *Alabaster skin* and *perfect, swelling bosoms*. Ones that heave and quiver, never sag. *Daahling! Don't leave me, daahling!*

I felt his hips shift a little bit on mine. They made a squelching noise.

I don't know, it made me think of stupid things. A whole load of bullshit. I could feel the come sort of dribbling out. Like period blood when you run out of tampons. I wished I'd never heard of Romance. Stupid nasty shit. And I would be in love with him, wouldn't I. Of course I would. He'd just fucked me.

'I think I'm in love with you too.'

'No you're not,' I said.

*

I looked away from him, waiting, lying in his sweat. Oliver didn't say anything else, though. He was silent.

I think I said it so that he'd tell me again. Stupid, really. Like fishing for compliments. I thought he'd touch me and lean over, I thought he'd stare into my eyes, pull us closer to a Mills and Boon. I thought he'd make it true. But Oliver just lay there.

With one arm touching mine, his elbow I think, I could feel it building up beside me. It felt like electricity, bunching and cramping and tightening. I felt it getting louder as the pause for his answer stretched out. Still he didn't speak.

With my head turned away from him, I chewed my lower lip. And I wished I'd kept my mouth shut.

I had to look at him then, I had to see what was going on. Oliver was staring at the ceiling, his jaw clamped too shut. I could see his eyes were moving, though. A little to the left, to the right, like they were tracking out his thoughts. He was gone. And in the living room below, I heard the volume of the television rising up. There was nothing I could do.

After a minute I got up and I walked over to the cupboard. I turned back once but his expression hadn't changed, and I felt something sinking inside. I watched the floor.

My pills were on the top shelf, in a little cardboard packet at the back. It made a popping noise as I squeezed one out of the foil. A tiny pink pill, Barbie Contraception, and I could feel the sperm was halfway to my knee.

I picked up a shirt from the floor and wiped it up the inside of my leg. Egg white, I thought. It stretched out in dribbles. I would have shown it to him. I would have made some joke, and smiled or something stupid like that. But I didn't show it to him. My mouth wouldn't have made any sound worth his hearing. I dropped the shirt on the floor beside me.

I thought the pill would be bitter. Or sweet with one of those children's coatings. It was just tasteless, though. And I swallowed it as quickly as I could.

'Do you want a drink?' I said. 'Like . . . a cup of tea or anything?'

'No,' he said.

'What's wrong?' I tried to smile at him. Smile, like everything inside me was normal.

'Nothing.' His voice didn't change. Tight, like he was scared that something else might come out. 'Nothing's wrong,' he said.

I watched him rub his forehead with one hand. He'd turned on his side a little bit. I couldn't see his dick now, just his hip, and the sweat had dried away. I wanted to sit down. Quickly, before the time got between us again. But he wasn't looking at me, and I couldn't do it on my own.

His hand reached round, behind his back, and when he threw something at me, I sort of caught it without thinking.

'Put your pants on,' he said.

I stood there, three feet away from him, and I stared down at the fake silk and stretched elastic in my hand. It had been black once, but now it had faded to a shiny kind of brown. *Put your pants on.* But I only stared at them. I stared, and then I closed my eyes.

There was rustling and the spring in the middle of my

bed creaked as he got up. My head fell lower, and halfway down my throat I could feel the pill still caught. I heard his breathing. And in the blacks and the colours I could see the tiny scar underneath his chin. I could see the way it crinkled at one end. I heard his feet land on the carpet. He sighed as he got up. Somewhere just above my stomach I could feel a shining knot. I pressed my lips together as I heard him pull his trousers up.

He sniffed, quickly, changing.

And I wanted so hard just to have the right line in my head. The words that'd make him turn round and stop. The words that would put his smile back on and make him say he loved me. I didn't have those words.

I guess it didn't matter anyway. How fucking stupid it would be to hear them come from my mouth. I don't think my mouth was meant for words. My mouth was meant for other things.

So I just stood there with my knickers in my hand, and I waited for him to leave me. The door didn't slam. It just swung closed with a tiny click as the latch fell. The knicker elastic had frayed round the hip. The gusset had a little hole in the middle that showed polyester through cotton. I didn't move. I stared at the hole and I listened to his footsteps creak away on the landing. I wondered if he'd put his shoes on.

I couldn't look up to see the place he'd been sitting on the bed. The way the duvet had creased into his shape. I couldn't, so I just looked at my knickers instead. I thought about his stubble and the wrinkly bit of skin in the arch of his foot, while that little shiny web played in and out on my chest. Tight and loose, like shock waves on a graph we'd do in maths.

I didn't start crying till I heard the spare room door shut. The first ones came quietly. Big and wet while I thought about the expression on his face, sitting in the spare room, surrounded by shit. He'd hate it in there, and I suppose he must have hated my room too, really. He must have, what with all the crap. Must have hated it, and his eyes would be cold, they wouldn't touch that stuff spread out around him. The way they sort of didn't touch me. And I laughed, watching wet circles drop on to the gusset of my pants. Just a little laugh. It could have been Oliver's, except it turned into a sob.

Christ. I pressed my teeth down, hard, against each other. I must have made him sick. Dirty teacups and paintbrushes, underwear and collapsed candles, paper and books and a teddy bear whose ear I hadn't sewn back on. So much shit. With food and old make-up and magazines that left ink stains against the walls where they'd been lying. My shit, it was. All that stuff. Mine. And I hated every filthy piece of it. Hats and dolls, my pencil case, and a music box that only ever fucking worked when you held it upside-down. It was useless, and it crowded in on me when he kept himself apart. Put your pants on.

I bent over while I cried, and I hugged my underwear against my chest.

I couldn't even remember where I'd got that music box. Or why. The spunk slipped down my leg, and I tried to think what tune it played. It had a little plastic ballerina stuck to the top. and she wobbled when you pulled at her.

She just fell from side to side. And I sat down on the dirty carpet.

My tin pencil case, with the top all painted in Tippex. *Holly Is A Mong* was straggled over it in black marker. Next to *Andy Wanks Over Gail*. I pushed the corner of it as a tear dribbled over my top lip. I listened to the pencils inside, all rattling. And that was when I saw the compass.

It was red plastic with a blue arm, and there was a stub of pencil in there. It didn't draw full circles anymore, because the arm had got all loose. They always wobbled near the bottom. It lay there, and I couldn't see the metal point. It was hidden in the carpet.

I wanted to see the way the light looked on that metal. I wanted to see if I could find my reflection there. Like I'd found it, all black and shiny, in Oliver's eyes. I just wanted to look while I cried. So I picked the compass up.

The plastic felt very still in my hand, and I watched the flesh shake round it. Funny, jittery little fingers. I aimed it, point downwards, and I rolled it between my fingers. I watched the bits of white reflection circle after the bits of black reflection, and after a moment I stopped sobbing. The ridges in the plastic blurred when I twisted it fast. But when I stopped, you could still see them there. Thin shadows, all lined up. Is there blood round my mouth?

I don't know. I think I might have smiled, just twisting it back and forwards like that. It looked very pretty, I thought, for a little piece of coloured plastic. And MADE IN SPAIN was stamped on to the side. I wondered if Oliver was asleep yet. I wondered what he was looking at.

I'd lost my tan from the summer, and the hairs on my

arm weren't as white and soft as Holly's. I couldn't see my elbow pimples on myself. I couldn't twist my arm round far enough. I saw the three little moles on my skin though, all huddled together. And I saw the way the flesh was netted into little diamond shapes when you looked close up. It looked very plump, my arm. It looked like it had lots of padding. And the compass made me still as well.

It didn't break the skin, first time I pressed it in. It left a little ripped scratch, and I was kind of disappointed. The skin went white and torn around the edges, but there wasn't any blood. That was Ok, I thought. I'd just have to press harder.

I dragged it through the scratch again, and it hurt a little bit the second time. Horizontal, across my forearm, and I watched just a few little spots of red come up. They showed through against the bits of skin that hung on round it. Little transparent bits. Just the first layer or so. Miss said in biology that there are a lot of different layers in the human epidermis. Maybe that was why it took so long to break through. And when the first line had shown up red all the way along, I started on the cross bar. The skin all round it going pinky now, and it stung more about half an inch away from the cut than it did right inside. It wasn't big. Just small enough to cover with a plaster.

The compass point wasn't really very sharp, and it didn't slice the way that I imagined it would slice. It tore and bounced, and caught on the bits that it couldn't cut through. I had to run it through the cross bar three times before the blood came. And a whole patch of my arm was stinging now. It made the pores stand out bigger than they had before. It made the freckles sink.

I was harder with the third line, and it came in only one stroke. More diagonal than I would have liked it, but I saw that my hand wasn't shaking anymore. The second letter was easier, and the cross bar caught just once. It made a hole. Tiny and circular like the hole in the gusset of my knickers. That one filled up pretty quick, with the hairs around it flattened or loose.

And it was only when I finished that I heard I'd stopped crying. I watched the pink and porous swollen skin and I think I might have smiled. The word on my arm said

HATE

I didn't see Oliver the next morning. By the time I got up his car was gone from the yard, and you could only see the ditches that his tyres had left in the mud. I didn't look at them for long. I didn't want to think about it.

Dad was eating cornflakes when I sat down at the table. Mum was huddled in the corner with a dressing gown and a cup of tea.

'Morning.' I went to put some bread in the toaster.

'Hi,' Mum said, and then she buried her head back in her teacup. Her hair was tied back and falling out of a ponytail. The bags under her eyes were bigger, and I sort of wished she'd put some make-up on.

'Good morning,' Dad said, and spooned some cornflakes. I had to be kind of careful moving around, getting the bread out of the bin and everything. When I bent my arm too quickly I could feel the plaster pulling underneath the shirt. It was tender, and the plaster gripped at the hairs. Still, it made me smile when I felt it. 'So where's Oliver then?' Dad looked round at me. 'I saw his car's gone outside.'

'Oh,' I said. And I pushed the toaster down. 'Yeah . . . he had to get to work early.'

'And he couldn't have waited ten minutes?'

'He . . . he really had to be there.' I didn't look at Dad. I stared at the unit underneath my hands. 'He didn't want to leave.'

'That's Ok.' Mum nodded at me. 'I understand: he has to get to work.'

'It wasn't like that . . .'

'Uh-huh?' Dad said. 'Just wondered why he didn't bother to say goodbye, that's all.'

I tapped my fingers in a pattern on the surface. My nails made tiny clicking sounds.

'He asked me to say goodbye for him . . . And . . . to say sorry. That he had to go.'

'Well,' Dad said. 'Must be an *awfully* important job he's got.'

'Look.' I turned round to face him properly. 'He said he was sorry, alright?'

'I'm sure he did. It's just a bit fucking rude. He didn't even say thanks for the curry.'

'He did say thank you.'

'If he did, then I certainly don't remember it.'

'Well . . .' Mum looked around, pulled her dressing gown tighter. 'It doesn't matter.'

She turned back to her tea. And I would have waited then. I would have let the whole thing blow over. Except I didn't really want it to blow over. Thinking about it, I didn't want it to blow over at all.

'He *did* say thank you, actually Dad.' I watched him glance round at me. 'And if you want to talk about thank yous, why don't you try all that beer and wine he brought?'

'What?' His eyes moved between me and Mum. 'All the beer and wine he brought?'

'That bottle of wine? Remember? Four cans of beer? I didn't hear *you* say thanks.'

'Thanks? What the fuck're you talking about? He didn't bring all that beer and wine, as you put it. He brought a bottle. So *what?*'

'So you shouldn't go on about thank yous when *you* didn't even say it! That's *what!*'

Mum didn't look at either of us. She picked her tea up slowly, and she blew inside.

'I don't know what the fuck you're going on about,' he said. 'So what if he brought one poxy bottle of wine? What did it cost him: *three quid?* For fuck's sake . . .'

'Well so what if you bought a curry, then!'

'Listen to me! I spent a lot of money on that meal last night. I went all the way down to town to get it for you! I don't need *you* shouting at me over my breakfast. *Alright?*'

'*I* said thank you.' I looked at Mum, staring at me over the rim of her cup. Her eyebrows were up, I saw. '*I* said thank you to him just before I opened it.' She smiled at me.

'Yeah,' Dad said. He turned on her, nodding. 'After I left. I meant to say thanks for that.'

'*Sorry?*' She gave a small, nervous smile. 'I opened it when he *gave* it to me, Philip, it happened to be when you were off getting your curry. I *offered* to make lasagne . . .'

'What's that s'posed to mean, you *offered* to make lasagne? All I know is by the time I got back, the wine was already half fucking gone! I notice *he* wasn't drinking!'

'What do you care anyway? It's just a poxy bottle of wine, isn't it?'

Dad stared at me. He stared at Mum, mouth open, like he was just about to speak.

And behind my back, some toast popped up.

It's funny. I remember thinking, when I first started going out with Oliver, that secrets weren't any fun unless you had someone to share them with. I didn't feel that way, walking into school at nine o'clock, though. I kept one hand free, the bag over my shoulder, and I felt the plaster through the cloth of my sleeve. Soft and lumpy. He fucked me, I thought. The word had a hurting sort of sound and the pain from my arm made me wince a little bit. Pretty skin. I smiled to myself.

He fucked me.

I don't know. Maybe I was a secretive kind of person after all.

I didn't mind seeing Dawn so much that morning. It was funny, hearing her talk. She said a lot of stuff, stuff she'd said before, stuff about Oliver. But every so often I could reach to touch that plaster. She didn't know that I was armed.

'I just want you to think,' she said. 'We all do.' She

reached a hand out gently, laid it on my arm. Still, it made me jump. Her fingers were resting three inches from it. I looked up into her face but she didn't move her hand. 'He's twenty-seven. You just have to think – what's a twenty-seven-year-old going out with *you* for? I mean, why doesn't he get a girlfriend his own age?'

She stared at me, her face serious like she really did want me to think. I couldn't though, not with her hand so close to my secret. All I could do was try and keep myself from smiling.

'He's only after you for . . . You know.' She nodded but I guess I didn't look as though I understood. 'For the *sex*,' she said finally. 'What other reason could there be?'

'I . . .'

Her fingers shifted but she didn't seem to know.

'I'm only telling you because . . . because you have to know sometime.' She smiled but it wasn't really sweet, more like Canderel, I thought. 'He . . . he's not a nice man,' she said. 'He *can't* be.'

I nodded, looking at her.

But she didn't seem to realize that I didn't really care.

I didn't expect Oliver to apologize. I don't know, it didn't really feel like he had anything to apologize for. It felt like the whole thing was important in some way I didn't understand, and it didn't hurt my chest anymore when I thought about his face. It was strange, thinking about all the stuff that had happened last night. I felt very close to Oliver, close to his distance even though that sounds stupid. I felt like he must know about my arm. He'd know all about the way I felt and he would understand. Looking at it logically, of course, it couldn't be that way. He couldn't know. Still, I guess that it was kind of nice to dream.

I would have apologized myself really. I would have phoned him after school and said that I was sorry. I *was* sorry in a way. Not sorry that it had happened, just sorry because it felt as though I should be. It felt right to be sorry. More than right, it felt perfect. Yes, I would have phoned him, I think. I was almost looking forward to it. Except that he was already there when I got home.

His car was the first thing I saw, walking through the gate. The passenger door was open but there was no one inside. I smiled. Really smiled, for the first time all day, I think. And I lifted my bag up higher on my shoulder. Moving my arm was still hurting. But then, it wasn't getting better as fast as it should have. I had to keep taking the plaster off and looking at it when no one was around.

I jogged the last few steps to the front door, with my bag banging against my hip the whole time. Robin'd said that I looked like a headless chicken when I ran. He'd been watching me do athletics on the football pitch. My excuse had sort of run out with the games teacher after cross country the week before. She told me if I had my period once more that month she'd have to take me to casualty for a transfusion. I had to do the 400 metres. And if I thought about it, it was hardly surprising that I looked like a headless chicken. I hadn't run anywhere since Deborah stole my favourite Care Bear and took it to the dinner lady because we weren't allowed to bring teddies into school. Not like Holly, of course. Holly, who ran for the sheer *joy* of running – *knowing life*. Feeling the wind in her bosoms, or something like that. But Robin wasn't there that day to tell me what I looked like. No one was there. So I ran.

Oliver was sitting in the living room, drinking a can of Coca-Cola. He was talking to Mum, so I figured Dad must still be at work. Not only that. He was smiling.

'Hiya!' I dumped my bag down and tried to rub the stitch out of my stomach.

'Are you alright?'

'Yeah. Fine . . .'

'Oh,' he said. 'You looked . . . looked like you'd just been *running* or something.'

'So what you doing here? I mean . . . did you get off work early or something?'

'Yeah,' he said. 'Sort of.'

Mum got up off the sofa. I watched her smooth her skirt down.

'That's . . . nice.'

She rubbed her hands together in front of her.

'*Well* . . .' she said slowly. 'I think I'll go and make a cup of tea.'

'I'll have one.'

She looked up at me, and there was a strange little smile on her face. I wondered what she meant by it. Still, I couldn't quite help but smile back.

'Ok then,' she said. And I watched her disappear into the kitchen.

'Do you . . . do you want a cup of tea or anything?' The words made me think of last night, and I glanced to see if Mum was gone. I wondered if he remembered it too.

'I'm fine thanks.' He tilted the Coca-Cola can at me. I smiled at him. I nodded, and I wondered what the hell to do next.

'Did you have a good day at work?'

'Not really,' he said, and smiled back.

'Right . . .' I watched the floor.

'I . . . I got you something.' But when I looked back up, he was staring out of the french windows. 'I just wanted to . . . bring it over,' he said. 'I can't stay long.' He got up from the armchair and I watched him stretch his back, put his hands on his hips. 'It's out in the car if you want to see,' he said. But he didn't seem very bothered.

'Thank you.'

He glanced over at me, like he hadn't been expecting me to say anything. He nodded.

'Right . . .' he said. 'Right.' And he walked past me towards the front door.

'How are you?' I said, and I followed him through the porch. I wondered why I couldn't just ask the question I wanted to. I wondered why it wouldn't come out of my mouth.

'Alright . . .' he said.

And for a minute I didn't bother with anything else. I watched the way the hairs on his neck caught in the wind. They'd been right next to my face, those hairs. It was funny. I couldn't quite believe it now. His boots had dust covering the soles of them I could see each time he lifted his foot. One turn-up was snagged over the top, and I saw his hand go up to rub the bridge of his nose.

'I came to apologize,' he said. And he turned round

247

when he got to the car. The passenger door had blown half shut. I couldn't see any present inside.

'Apologize?'

'Yeah, I wanted . . . I wanted to say sorry.'

'You don't have to say sorry for anything.' I smiled at him. The wind pushed my hair in my face, and I had to hold it back, behind my ears. 'Really,' I said.

'I shouldn't have . . . I don't know. I shouldn't have just gone like that. This morning, I mean . . .' He rested his hand on the top of the door, and I tried not to think about where those hands had been. I tried to think about my arm instead. He sighed, and I watched his head drop a little bit. He rubbed his nose again. I waited.

'It's Ok,' I said after a moment.

But all he did was pull the door open wide. I watched him sag down into the seat, and his shirt puffed out over the waistband of his trousers. He stared at the dirt.

'I just get . . . I just get really grumpy sometimes. I don't mean to. It's not you I'm grumpy at. Or . . . or, I mean, anyone else. I'm just . . . grumpy.' He stopped a moment, looked up at me. 'I don't mean to be,' he said.

I smiled, because I couldn't think of anything else. I felt the wind pull my skirt a little.

'I shouldn't take it out on other people. On . . . on you. I don't want to,' he said. 'I shouldn't . . . because it's not you I'm angry at.' He stared at the ground again, like he was cross with it. I wished he'd bring his head back up then. I wished he'd look at me like that. 'It's me,' he said. 'I'm angry with myself.'

'It's Ok now though,' I said. Put your pants on, I thought. 'I mean . . . it's gone.'

'I . . . I missed you today,' he said. 'I sort of hoped you'd come over at lunchtime.'

'I thought you said I shouldn't. You know . . . because it gives the wrong impression.' And I wondered just what the wrong impression might be. That he was fucking a fourteen-year-old, perhaps.

'Fuck them,' he said quickly. 'I mean, what's it got to do with them anyway? It's my . . . our personal life,' he said. 'They're just fucking nosy anyway. All of them whispering over the latest piece of gossip. Just because *their* lives are so fucking dull.' He nodded. 'Fuck them.' I wondered if he had anyone specifically in mind. 'Small-town snobs,' he said. Which was weird really. I'd never thought of it as a *small* town before. 'So I think . . . I think you should just come over.'

'Ok,' I said, and I nodded too. It was the only thing left for me to do.

'Well . . . anyway. Here's what I go you.'

I watched him reach his arm up over the back seat. I tried to look through the window but the reflections cut everything out. He was smiling properly – *really* smiling – when he pulled his arm back out. It was a coat hanger, with something under a long sheet of black plastic. He held it, folding it halfway down so it didn't drag in the dust.

'I saw it in this shop . . . and it just made me think of you. So I bought it. Don't look at it yet,' he said. 'You've got to take it upstairs . . . so you can try it on.' He grinned.

'Ok . . .' I said, but he didn't hand it over.

'I don't know if it'll fit or not. I just . . . I don't know. I've got a feeling it will.'

And he stood up, with the plastic still draped over his arm, he pushed the door shut with a foot. It looked heavy, whatever was inside, and it dragged against his arm. Like a coat, maybe. Something like that. My stomach fluttered, but not like before. It was different. Happy, maybe that was all. Because when I looked at him he had a smile on his face.

A smile for me.

I followed Oliver up to my room. His boots were heavy on the stairs, like Dad in a bad mood, and I tried to make mine quiet. I didn't want to set him off. Just thinking of him staring at me, looking down along his nose, made my stomach start to drop. I didn't want to make him angry, not after that small smile. Still, watching him turn the corner and pull the handle on my door, it felt nice to know his rules. To know them and stick by them. It felt like being good.

He stopped inside the door and I had to walk past him to sit down.

'I hope it fits,' he said. 'After all this.'

I sat on the bed, holding the duvet either side of me, soft clumps inside my fists. My feet tapped on the carpet as I watched him look around. 'It'll fit.'

'Alright then,' he said. And he handed it to me. I was careful not to let it drag along the floor. The plastic sort of rustled as I laid it out on my lap, and the material underneath felt weighty, kind of stiff. It was very long. Ankle length at least. I smiled. 'Go on,' he said. His smile slipped back on to his face. Like an infection, I thought vaguely. But that was a stupid thing to think. Stupid, when it was such a lovely smile.

I took the coat hanger out first. A flash kind of coat hanger, not one of those cheap wire ones. It had padding all around the shoulder bits, embroidered. Must have cost a bit in itself. I put it down next to me on the bed. And then I started on the plastic. It slid over my tights as I pulled it off. It snagged under my nails and stretched into pale brown. It made a hissing kind of noise, and I tried to keep my feet still.

The dress was white. Long and round-necked and scattered with huge red roses. Stiff cotton, old-fashioned, with a scarlet bow. It had short sleeves. And it was beautiful. 'Do you like it?' he said. He was nodding even before I answered.

'It's beautiful . . .'

'It's old. I mean, it's from the nineteen-forties. I just saw it there . . . hanging in the window. And it made me think of you. Do you like it?'

'I love it.' There was nothing else to say. 'It must have cost you . . . loads.'

'The price doesn't matter,' he said slowly. 'Try it on. I . . . I want to see how it looks.'

'Ok.' I looked up at him and nodded. I felt small, sitting there, as he watched. 'Ok.'

I remember wondering once what sort of clothes Robin would have liked to dress me in. I remember wishing that he'd tell me, give me some clue, so that I could look exactly how he'd like. He'd never told me though. Maybe he hadn't really cared. And looking at the dress across my knees, creasing into pleats from the sash on down, I heard Oliver shifting his feet. A rustle on the carpet. I smiled.

'Go on,' he said.

It was what he wanted me in. His dress, I thought, not mine. His perfect picture.

I reached up and undid my tie. Hideous blue polyester, and you could always tell the people from my school. Even out of uniform we all had matching neck rashes. I pulled out the loop and I didn't glance up at Oliver's face. I wanted to. I wanted to see his expression. It wasn't my place to look though, I thought. I was the one here on show.

I pulled off my tights, trying to do it without getting up, without lifting my skirt. I felt the nylon peel away where four straight hours on a plastic chair had stuck it. I pushed them off my feet. From the other side of the room I could hear him breathing softly. Small sounds inside his mouth.

My feet looked very white above the dirty carpet as I kept my eyes down, as I unzipped my skirt. I let it flop on to the floor. His dress, I thought again, and something in my windpipe tightened. I wondered how I looked to him, unbuttoning my shirt.

The dress was difficult to get into, without a zip up the side or anything. I heard the scratching of Oliver's jeans as he moved his leg a bit. I heard him sniff. And biting my lip, I wondered how I could make it look elegant. I wanted it to be right for him.

I had to hoist it over my head like a tent, shifting round to find the arm holes, one elbow pinned hard to my side by the sash thing round the middle. The light was grey and blank through cotton and I swallowed. I pulled and pushed and wriggled, feeling my stomach sink lower every moment I was struggling. Feeling my mouth drying out. He's watching me, I thought, and cotton smacked against my shins.

And as I pushed my head through, hair flattened round my neck, I smiled at him. I settled the bow against my stomach. 'Do . . . do you like it?' I looked up at him.

'You've got it on backwards,' he said.

'Huh?' I looked down at myself, flapping the skirt at him with my hands. It made a heavy sound, like sheets on a windy washing line. 'But . . . but the bow's at the front . . .'

I flicked at it to show him but I guess I knew already that he was right. He would be. It was just the sort of stupid fucking thing that I'd do. Just the sort of thing to ruin everything. I stared at the floor, something big moving inside me. Just the sort of thing.

I breathed out, pulled my arms back in. I turned the dress from inside and I didn't look at him.

And when I had it on the right way, standing with my head down so that he could see me, I held my hands out either side. I turned in one slow circle and I squeezed my eyes shut tight.

'God,' he said. 'It fits you . . . perfectly. Could have . . . could have been made for you.'

I smiled but that didn't make it better. Nothing would, I thought. Because I'd ruined it.

'You look like a model out of the forties.' He shook his head. 'It fits perfectly.'

'Thank you,' I said.

'Goes beautifully with your hair,' he said. He raised his hand and waved it at my head.

'Do you think so? It needs washing really. My hair, I mean . . . not the dress.' I sat down on the bed. I tried to do it delicately, so the material would flow around me as I sank into the feathers. So my hair would just float down and I could cross my hands, all demure, in my lap. It didn't work very well. I made a plopping noise. Even in his dress, I thought, I still acted like me.

'What's that?' he said quietly. And I saw his head was all tipped to one side.

'What's what?' I said, but I couldn't find a smile. 'Oh that.' I saw where he was looking. 'Nothing. I burned myself this morning. On the toaster, that's all,' I said.

'On the *toaster?* What did you do: stick your arm in it or something?'

'No, I . . . I just wasn't watching what I was doing. It's not that bad or anything.'

His frown didn't go away, though, staring at my arm. And seeing that stare, I wanted to hide it behind my back, hide it away. Maybe then he'd step towards me. Maybe he'd make me pull the plaster off.

'Shouldn't keep plasters on burns,' he said. 'It's best to let them breathe.'

'It's fine,' I said. 'My shirt . . . it was rubbing.'

Still his expression didn't change. His forehead folded over, and he wasn't looking at my arm now. He was looking into my face. I guess I knew then what was wrong, or what he thought was wrong. Sitting there and talking about a burn on my forearm, I'd been looking straight at him. And I hadn't glanced down at that arm. Not once.

I couldn't bring myself to look. Not even now, when he was waiting for it. A casual glance or maybe lift it up and show it to him. I couldn't do it. I was scared to. Because I'd lifted my sleeve up already that day. Standing in the cloakrooms, hearing Dawn's piss spattering in the toilet, I'd waited. And I'd had time for just a little look. The plaster had been cleaner then, as I'd unbuttoned my cuff and rolled it to my elbow.

'He'll dump you,' Dawn had said, over the clanking of the bog roll thing and the whisper of the paper as she pulled it out. 'I've heard stories about men like him. You'll reach a certain age and then he'll dump you.' There was the soft purring noise as she ripped the paper free. The plaster stared up at me, blank pink among the hairs. 'He'll dump you for someone else who's fourteen. Or maybe even younger.' It looked very calm, between the moles and skin and downy fluff. 'I'm your *friend*,' she said, and biting my lip, I couldn't help but pull the plaster up a little way. 'I *do understand*.'

There was a clunk, a groan, as the cistern tried to flush. And the light was blue-grey, dim through the little frosted window. Dirty glass and dark, stained paint, and the sticking, burning pain of pulling a plaster from unhealed flesh. The cistern crashed, roared as I leaned back against the cold sink. 'But you *can't* take it out on me. I'm . . .' There was a giggle in the distance, muffled, and the sound

255

of the end of break bell. I heard the latch open, metal grating over unpainted metal. And I tore the plaster off.

Wet and sore and beautiful, it was still there.

And as Dawn's footsteps clapped back towards the cloakroom, I stared without hearing. And I hardly got my sleeve back down in time.

Yes, I'd looked at it before that day. In a different light, cold and grey and echoing. I'd looked at it, and it had been so pretty that I didn't want to stop. It had been so *mine*. So I didn't even glance at it now, with Oliver's face so heavy on my own. I didn't dare glance. I only tried to smile.

'It's *nothing*, Ok?'

But he didn't answer. I saw his mouth drop. I saw his forehead wrinkle.

'How can you burn yourself on a toaster?' he said, and it didn't even sound like he was talking to me. 'All the elements are on the inside.'

'For God's sake, Oliver. It's just a *burn* . . .'

I felt lumpy, though, sat on my bed in his dress. Small and ugly and out of place, and I didn't like the feeling that was going around in my stomach. It was an excited kind of feeling. It matched the way his eyes were staring.

'It's not a burn.' He looked down at the carpet. 'Is it?' he said.

And there was a moment then when I guess I could still have answered him. I could have shrugged it off and laughed, and there was something in his face that would have agreed. Even if he didn't believe me. There was something in his face that would have shrugged as well, just so he didn't have to see. A moment, and I could have changed the way things went.

Instead, I didn't speak.

Finally, he sniffed.

He rubbed one hand across his mouth, and he rested his forearms on his knees, gazing at the carpet.

'Show me,' he said.

I sat on the bed, I listened to him waiting, and I stared at the spot on the carpet where I'd stood last night. I remembered how he'd stared at me, with that one cold sentence spitting out. I hadn't been wearing his dress then. I was wearing it now, though. Maybe it was right that he should see.

I took the plaster off with my right hand.

It pinched and sucked at the skin when I pulled it.

'Fucking hell . . .' he said quietly. And I didn't look at him.

The flesh was bright, still wet-looking, and it puckered up towards the scab. The E was too small, and the stroke of the H too diagonal. I supposed it didn't matter, though. I supposed he wouldn't notice.

Some of the hairs were torn out, and the whole patch of skin was swollen into a rise. I thought about the way my English teacher always used to tell me not to write on my hand in Biro. It gives you ink poisoning, she said. And I wondered if I might have metal poisoning.

'Fucking hell.'

'It doesn't hurt anymore,' I said. 'Like a bramble scratch . . .'

I waited for him to say something, but he was just

looking. There was a fleck of dirt on the T, I saw, and I moved my hand to wipe it off. The skin felt damp just like it looked.

'Why . . .' He stopped, coughed. 'Why did you do it?'

'I don't know. It just . . . it doesn't matter. It's like I said: doesn't even hurt anymore.'

'It's horrible,' he said. 'Horrible. It . . . it ruins the dress.'

I stared up at him. I could see him biting on the inside of his lip, and my eyebrows ached from pushing them down. I thought he'd look angry. I thought he'd look cold. He didn't look like that, though. Just sad. Just very sad.

'Ruins it . . .' he said again. And he turned his head away from me. 'It's ugly,' he said, and his head snapped back much quicker. '*Ugly. Pathetic.* You expect me to *fancy* you with *that* on your arm? You expect me to find that *attractive?*'

He shook his head, hard back and forwards, but I didn't answer him. I only gazed down at the carpet, and I kept my mouth tight shut. Because thinking about it, about fucking and the grunt that came out of his mouth – *put your pants on*, I thought – the answer was yes.

'Is it sympathy?' he said, his mouth pulled down. 'Is it sympathy you want? I'm not going to give you any fucking sympathy.'

'I don't want your sympathy,' I said.

And it was true. I wanted something else.

'Well, obviously you do. Obviously that's exactly what you want. Or you wouldn't fucking well do it, would you?'

'I didn't even want you to see it!'

I felt my face scrunch up, and the snot in my temples,

building. It came out too quickly for me to wonder over truth.

'Bollocks,' he said. 'You thought I wouldn't notice an ugly fucking thing like that?'

I was silent. I thought about telling him that long-sleeved shirts had been invented a long time ago. But it was bullshit, all of it bullshit. Maybe that was why I didn't speak.

After a moment he turned to look at me again.

'You're not . . . you won't do it again,' he said. 'Just tell me that.'

So I did.

And it wasn't difficult. Thinking about it, it wasn't difficult at all. Just another lie. Oliver touched my hand before he got up off the bed. My other hand, and he didn't look down at the arm. I watched him turn towards the door.

'You look . . . you look very beautiful in that dress,' he said. 'You *are* very beautiful.'

His face twisted, looking somewhere past my shoulder.

'Very beautiful . . .' he said again. 'When you're not trying to make yourself uglier.' But it was funny.

I listened to his footsteps creaking on the landing, down the stairs. I listened to him cough a little bit, and looking at my arm, I couldn't quite agree with him. That sore pinky wetness, and the way the letters sprawled. The see-through scab, a little bit torn off along with the plaster, and the way the hairs got matted. I could have looked at it for quite a long time, I think. Just staring. Just taking it all in. The mottled look of the skin where the plaster hadn't let it breathe. The tiny rise that I could trace with my left finger. Like a platform, raising it up.

No. I couldn't agree.

It was beautiful.

And sitting alone in my bedroom, crowded with my shit, I wondered how he couldn't see that. In some strange way, I thought, some way that I couldn't work out, it didn't spoil the dress at all.

It matched.

I hadn't heard the car come in. Maybe I was talking when he drove past, maybe I was in the bathroom. I don't know, maybe I was only thinking. Not sensible thoughts, not sentences all in a row. Just a jumble, each next thing falling over the last as I put on a new plaster. Maybe it was that. Either way, I didn't hear. And it was kind of surprising when I walked into the living room and saw Dad. So surprising that I couldn't really think of much to say.

I just stood there.

He didn't look at me when I walked in. He was staring at Oliver instead. Oliver, standing in the middle of the room. He looked like he was halfway out and Dad was staring hard. I looked at them, arms hanging heavy each side of me.

Neither of them moved.

'Oh!' Mum said. I turned too quickly, felt the cotton swish around. I hadn't even noticed her till then, and the smile on my face felt empty. An idiot's smile. I was sure she'd notice it. 'Oh! It looks *beautiful!*' She took three quick steps towards me, picked up the hem round my shin. 'It's old isn't it?' she said. But I could only nod.

'You left in a hurry this morning,' Dad said slowly. A hand was on his hip, his jacket slung through the crook of his elbow, watching Oliver stay still. 'What happened?'

'Yeah,' Oliver said. 'Sorry about that. I had to get to work pretty early. I had to go.'

'Oh,' Dad said. 'And why's that?'

'Moving some stock in. We all had to get there early. Carry it up to the store room.'

'Oh, doesn't Audiovision employ people to do that then?'

'No.' He didn't move towards the door, with Dad in front of it. 'It's part of the job.'

'Doesn't matter.' Mum looked up from my hem, and still I couldn't think of anything to say. I felt two steps behind them all. She smiled over at Oliver. 'I know what it's like. Need to rush off and everything, I know.'

'How do you know?' Dad laughed. 'You haven't got up for work in eighteen years.'

'I still have to get up, Philip. You might have noticed by the way I'm always *there* in the morning.' She turned back to look at me. 'It's super. Really. Fits you very well.'

Dad's eyes followed down her arm. 'New dress?' he said.

'Yes . . . Oliver bought it for me.'

'Well. That's nice. Looks quite expensive.' He nodded over at Oliver. 'Cost much?'

'It's not the price that's important,' I said, and he glanced back to me. I blinked, trying to clear my head a bit. Trying to stop thinking of the plaster halfway down my arm. 'You know . . .' I said. 'It's a present.'

'Right,' Dad said. 'Well . . . it looks . . . very nice on you. Very pretty.'

'Thanks.'

'Is that a bow it's got at the back there?' He took a step towards me and I almost wanted to back off. Everyone crowding around me, everyone closing in. He reached forward. 'It's hanging down on one side there. Let's just adjust it.'

'No,' I said. I didn't move, but I did give him a smile. 'It's meant to hang like that.'

'What: all crooked? Course it's not meant to hang like that.' He looked around their faces with a smile. Like a magician, I thought. It was a stupid thought with no reason behind it. 'Just turn round,' he said. 'Only needs pulling up a little bit. Just take a sec.'

'I like it like that, Dad.' I coughed a little bit. 'That's how it's meant to be,' I said. I could feel Mum standing straight beside me. She was looking at Dad, I think, but I didn't glance round to find out. Oliver looked at his watch. I bit my lip, seeing that. I didn't want him to be cross.

'Come on . . .' Dad still had his smile on. 'It won't take a minute. You can't just leave it hanging crooked for God's sake. Looks like someone's pulled the end or something. Come here. I'll be quick.'

His smile twitched, looking in my eyes.

Behind him, Oliver sniffed.

'I don't want it adjusted, Dad. I like it how it is.' I kept my eyes there while I said it. I had to I suppose. But as soon as it was out of my mouth I could feel my head dropping down. I wanted to reach across and touch my plaster. I couldn't do that, though.

Dad's smile faded out. I heard his breath catch in that pissed-off way, from way down in his lungs. His eyebrows moved closer to each other and he almost looked confused. One finger twitched. I felt it. And my stomach tilted hard.

'Well,' Oliver said. 'I better get going really. I haven't eaten or anything.'

'There's no need to go yet is there?' I looked from him to Mum.

'You can eat here, Oliver,' she said. 'I haven't done you my quiche yet.'

He smiled.

'We won't be eating for a while, though,' Dad said. 'I only had lunch an hour ago.'

'It's nearly five o'clock, Philip.' Mum's hand was still hanging by my dress. I heard her fingers brush against the cotton but I didn't feel it. She was staring at Dad, all the way across the room, and I saw that she had lipstick on. It was smeared a little above her lip from all the talking, greasy on her skin. And I wondered vaguely, standing between them all, why Mum would be wearing lipstick. Usually, she only puts it on for Somerfield.

'Doesn't matter,' Oliver said. His hands were in his pockets, moving. 'I ought to go.'

Mum didn't hear him, though, still staring at Dad. 'It's nearly dinner time,' she said. A strand of hair was stuck in the corner of her mouth, twitching as she spoke. Her words came out slow and careful, every one of them on purpose, I thought. 'If you want to eat later you can have it cold, Philip. The world doesn't revolve around you.'

'Look,' Oliver said. 'I'd really better go.' I don't think anyone heard him, though.

Across the room, Dad's eyes came into sharper focus. I could see my own reflection there: very small, bent out of shape and darkened. The colour of old photographs.

'I don't expect the world to revolve around me. Why should I have to eat cold quiche for dinner? I've been working all day. I mean' – he laughed – 'what've *you* been doing?'

'I've been doing *loads*, thank you. Not that you'd notice. Not that you *ever* notice.'

'I'll see you all soon,' Oliver said. His voice was taut, moving to the door. It made me think of physics lessons, tensile strength and how much pressure things could stand.

'There's no need for you to go, Oliver.' Mum's hands were folded together. 'Just because *he's* in such a bad mood.'

'I'm not in a bad mood!'

Mum's jaw stuck up, chin out. 'Couldn't even say she looked nice in her new dress.'

Oliver stopped moving. He turned around. And there was silence.

Outside and over their breathing, I heard the gutter rattle. Wind's picking up, I thought. I reached across to touch my plaster.

'That's not true. I told her she looked nice.' Dad looked at me. 'Didn't I say that?'

'I . . . Yes. I don't know. It doesn't *matter*. I mean, it's just a dress.' Oliver stared at me. 'It's a beautiful dress, I mean. I love it. And you did say that. I . . .'

'It's not just a dress.' Oliver said quietly. The gutter smacked again as I looked at him. I could feel my face crumpling up, snot threatening as it moved up behind my eyelids. It made me wonder how we'd got to this. 'And if you want to know how much it cost, it cost me seventy-five pounds,' he said. 'Actually.'

'I . . . I *love* this dress.' In my head I heard his voice again, so soft. *It looks beautiful on you.* Only I'd put it on backwards. Fucking backwards. So like me to fuck it up.

'Seventy-five pounds,' Mum said. She whistled. 'I hope you appreciate it,' she said.

'Of course I appreciate it! Why *wouldn't* I appreciate it!' But Oliver's eyes still rested on me, one step from the door. It wasn't meant to be this way, I thought. Wasn't meant to be this way at all. Looking at him made me want to cry, say something small and desperate, anything that might help. I couldn't speak, though. My mouth was dry.

'Seventy-five pounds . . .' Mum shook her head, but I couldn't look away from Oliver, from his eyes. 'That's a lot of money. I'm not sure I've got *anything* worth that much.'

'Don't be so stupid.' Dad's voice was harsh, but it passed in front of me. Between us. 'Course you've got something worth seventy-five quid. It's not that fucking much. TV cost a hundred and fifty.' Seventy-five pounds, I thought. I wondered how long it had taken him to earn it. How long, when it had taken me one second to fuck it up.

'The television's hardly mine, is it Philip? I'm talking

about something that's *mine*. Really mine. And you know something? I haven't got anything worth that much.'

My stomach was turning again, twisting as Oliver was chewing his lip. I wished that I could make it better, tell him how sorry I was. I touched the plaster gently. There was nothing I could tell him. Fucking nothing. But maybe actions speak louder than words.

'Yeah?' Dad was talking still. Talking, but I hardly heard. 'Well, you'd probably have a lot more money to spend if you went out and got a fucking job. Wouldn't you, Liz?'

'I don't have *time* for a job! I don't have a moment to spare! Not that you'd notice!'

Actions, I thought. I traced the outline of the plaster, new and pink and soft. Actions.

'Don't talk to *me* about noticing! When was the last time I got home and you said thank you? When was the last time you offered to make me a cup of *tea*, for Christ's sake? When was the last time you asked me how my day was? Don't talk to me about fucking *noticing*, woman! Not when I'm getting up at seven every morning to try and keep our *heads* above water!'

'I appreciate what you do! I *know* what you do. All I'd ask is for you to do the same!'

'*You don't DO anything!*'

Dad's voice cut through.

His head stretched back. I could see the skin of his throat pull taut, his arms out. He looked like he was praying, I thought, with his hands palms up that way. Laughing.

Everyone else was silent. Mum looked across at me, Oliver still staring.

And in the quiet, with one nail against my cut, I pressed.

'She . . . she does, Dad,' I said quietly.

And Oliver snorted as he turned away.

'You see?' Mum smiled, but I couldn't work out who it was aimed at. 'You *see?*' Dad's eyes turned slowly over both of us. I bit my lip. And Oliver shut the door behind him. 'You don't know anything about it,' Dad said, but I wasn't looking at him anymore. Oliver was gone, I thought. It was my fault, and now Oliver was gone. 'You don't know. Neither of you knows how hard it is. I struggle every day to buy you stuff. You don't know anything,' Dad said. 'Nothing at all . . .' And I didn't answer him.

'Oh come off it Philip! I know when you go to work in the morning. I know when you come home! So don't try and make out you're some slaving fucking martyr, because it's bullshit.' She turned away. 'You don't work any harder than the rest of us do.'

'You don't know what I do,' Dad said softly. 'You just . . . you just have no idea.' He looked at me then. He looked at me, and maybe he was waiting for something. I don't know. Whatever he was waiting for, I couldn't give it to him. All I could do was look down at the ground. All I could do was listen to his footsteps as he left.

Mum's face was set and funny and she stared around the room. With the front door open, I heard Oliver cough, walking towards his car. She blinked at me, breathed in.

'Well . . .' she said quietly, and she flicked one eyebrow like it was all a kind of joke.

'Look.' My stomach was churning. Oliver was leaving. 'Mum . . . I should go . . .'

She glanced over at me. The front door flapped a little, banged back against the wall.

'Go? Go where?'

'I'm gonna go . . . you know, back with Oliver . . .'

For a minute she just stared at me. I tried not to think about where Dad was. I tried not to think about what he was doing. Oliver's car door slammed shut.

'But . . . I mean, don't go now. I thought . . .'

'What?'

'I thought . . .' She looked at me and her forehead was all wrinkled. 'Nevermind . . .'

'Michael'll be back soon.'

'Yes . . .'

I listened to the engine start up.

'I . . . um . . . I'll see you tomorrow, yeah? After school.'

'You're going to stay then.'

'Well . . .' I trailed off. 'We could get a movie or something. Tomorrow, I mean.'

'Yeah . . .' She looked away and her hand rose up to her head. I watched her fingers rubbing through her hair. 'Tomorrow,' she said. And then she laughed a little bit.

I should have stayed maybe, tried to make everything alright. But outside, I heard Oliver reversing, and I took a step towards the door. 'See you tomorrow,' I said. She tried to smile. 'Take . . . you know, take care.'

'Yeah.' But I was already halfway out. 'Yeah . . . I will.'

'I love you,' she said, and I glanced back. Her hand was still moving, fuzzing up her hair. She was waiting for me to say something. And looking at me like that, I had to.

'Mmm. Love you too.'

She nodded slowly to herself as I picked up my school stuff off the floor. I didn't look at her again. And I shut the front door as quietly as I could.

The wind had picked up outside, scattering the leaves in circles and sending the grass into Mexican waves. I tried to keep my hair off my face, waving to Oliver. He'd turned the car around, ready to move out, and I had to walk carefully, trying to keep the hem of his dress out of the September mud. The tails of the bow kept flipping round my middle. I watched the ground.

'What're you doing?'

He'd wound his window down, but he was looking up at the sky. I thought it might rain soon, seeing those clouds, and I hadn't thought to get a coat. I shivered.

'Well . . .' I tried to smile at him through the turning in my gut. 'Coming . . . If it's Ok.'

He stared out of the windscreen and I tried to hold my skirt down. After a moment, he shrugged.

'If you want.' he said.

Nothing in Oliver's flat had changed. I stopped inside the doorway as he took his coat off and I looked from space to space. Nothing. One CD was lying on the carpet next to the stereo. His clothes all folded like Benetton on the shelves. Reds together, and blues and greens. His ties were laid flat along the top. There must have been thirty of them.

'It's very tidy in here,' I said. I made my voice as small as it would go.

'I like it tidy.' He hung his jacket on a peg on the front door. 'Do you want a beer?' he said, but he didn't seem very interested in whether I did or not. I watched him walk through to the kitchen, and I wondered if I'd done the right thing by coming here. I reached with my right hand and stroked the plaster.

It would be Ok, I thought. I would make it Ok.

'There's Budweiser or Beck's,' he said. 'Whichever.' He looked at me. 'And the garage down the road stays open till eleven.' He disappeared behind the door. 'In case we want some more. Or anything.'

I listened to the fridge door open, and I waited. I picked up my beer bottle, sipped a little bit, but it had gone warm. Slightly flat, and I just picked round the label instead. Sticky white paper came off in wisps, and I rolled them round in my fingers. Tubes and balls, and playing with them made me wonder how this flat would look untidied. I could almost imagine it that way, even through the spaces and the alphabetized CDs.

His whole room seemed empty, and I had a funny feeling that nothing had been touched since I'd been there last, that dust was beginning to settle there because of it. Empty, I thought, but I looked down at the mess of paper rolling round in my palm and suddenly I knew how it would look when it was full. Full with beer bottles and cigarette butts. Wrapped in the night before.

I smiled to myself as the stereo played, and I scattered them over the carpet.

Oliver picked up my portfolio when he walked back into the room. He looked across at me. 'What d'you bring this for?'

'I thought . . . if you were busy . . . I'd have something to do.'

'Oh, what? In case you got bored?'

'No . . . no, not at all.' Oliver just looked away. It was funny, he had a way of managing to look pissed off without even changing his face.

I bit my lip. 'Do . . . do you want to help me?' I looked up at him. 'I mean . . . would you?'

Oliver didn't answer my question. All he said was 'What's the assignment?'

And I smiled a little to myself.

The pastels had come out of their places in the car and I stacked them back in slowly. They made me think of Dad, of that beautiful day at the beach. And I wondered what he'd think of this, at home and lonely after what I'd said. I wondered and I closed my eyes. There was nothing for it now, I guess. Breathing out, I reached for the pencil sharpener. I scraped the pencil shavings into the ashtray pretty carefully. From the corner of my eye I saw Oliver shifting, but I didn't look up. I concentrated and I wondered why I felt so nervous. Another scrape, it hit the side and bounced in among the cigarette butts. And each time I moved my arm, stretching and slackening, I felt the skin pull into lines. Scar lines, tight and kind of full-feeling. It made it easier, to think of them not Dad. Much easier.

'What are you doing?' He looked over at me.

'Just . . . just sharpening the pencils.'

'Why?'

'Well . . . cos they need to be. You can't produce good work if you use bad tools. And they should be sharp. Or the lines won't be . . . sharp . . .' I watched him.

'And you want the lines to be sharp, do you?'

'Well . . . yes. Why?'

'Well, you know . . . it's not exactly *usual* to want great sharp lines across the paper.'

I stopped sharpening. I stared down at the lead in my pencil. It was blunt still, I saw.

'But . . .'

'But what?' His eyes were heavy, looking at me. He leaned back and he stared.

'Look. Just leave the pencil blunt, alright? You use this *big sharp* pencil, you're staring down at the paper *so carefully*, and that's why these ones look the way they do.'

'The way . . . they do?' I looked up at him.

'They're just a bit . . . childish,' he said. And he pointed at them. He pointed, like I couldn't help but see it. I stared down with him. Plato's *Republic* and Sartre's *Reprieve, and* you could read the lettering on them. 'You haven't *seen* them,' he said. 'It looks like you just did it so the teacher could read the titles.' I didn't speak. Oliver's breath came again. Still, I couldn't look up at his face. 'Look,' he said.

'Start with . . . Oh *fucking* hell! *Forget it!*' He turned away. 'I shouldn't have got involved.' Oliver shut the portfolio as he moved away from me. And we didn't draw a picture.

We talked for a while, but Oliver's talk was slow, like he was fitting it around his thoughts and wished he didn't have to. It made me wonder if he was still angry at me, for my arm, or my parents' arguing. I wondered if he wanted me to go.

Sitting on his carpet and drinking his beer, I only glanced down at that arm when I knew he wasn't looking. I thought about the feeling of the compass as it grated on my skin, and his words flowed over and past me while I nodded. I could do it again. I could sit up in my room and listen to my parents' silence and I could do it again.

Oliver drained the last of the bubbly bits out of his bottle with a sniff. He put it down and reached for a cigarette. And looking at him then, I realized something. I didn't have to be here. I could have stayed at home, I thought. I could have sat with only myself, and I was kind of surprised I hadn't thought about it before.

I'd had a choice, I guess, to go or stay. Only I hadn't taken it. I'd followed where Oliver had led. I'd forfeited my right to choose.

And it felt good.

Oliver crushed out his cigarette with most of it still there.

'Shall I . . . shall I put some music on?' I said.

He shrugged a yes and tipped a new bottle up to his mouth. He looked good, I thought, in that position. His hair was falling down across his face and his stubble was half-grown. I watched his tongue flick out around his lips as he put the bottle down, but there wasn't much choice really. I had to get up now.

I stood up, heavy, and walked towards the CD rack. My legs looked stupid, thick and gawky, coming out of that pretty cotton hem. I wondered if he'd noticed. I wouldn't mind, though, I thought. I wouldn't even mind if he told me how awful it looked.

'Do you like it on, then?' I said. I kept my eyes on the CDs but none of them meant anything to me. I just picked one at random, opened the case.

'Be careful,' he said.

But when I turned round to face him the words were gone. I looked down at the CD in my hand. Dumb, I thought for no reason at all. And after a moment, I took it out. I would be careful.

'The dress, I mean.' I pressed Open on the stereo, slid the CD in. 'Does it look Ok?' He didn't look round at me when he answered, so I guess he was going by memory alone. And I took a moment before pressing Play. His shoulder blades were very big underneath the cotton shirt. Very strong, I thought, and in my head I knew just what they'd look like, holding something down. 'I think it suits you,' he said slowly. The words were slow and the spaces in between seemed too long, like there was a catch hidden somewhere in the gap. And he paused before he carried on. 'Your Dad didn't.'

I listened to him say it but I didn't answer. There wasn't any answer there. He'd put all the strength on 'Dad', I thought. Like it was the punch-line of some joke. That was Ok, though. I wasn't going to disagree. And I listened to the voice come flat, from the speakers.

'He was jealous,' Oliver said quietly.

'Jealous?' I said. It sounded sluggish, coming out of my mouth. It sounded wrong and horrible and I wished he hadn't said it. 'Why would he be jealous . . .?' He only shrugged at me, though. Shrugged like it didn't really matter what I thought. He was probably right.

'I . . . I don't think he was jealous.'

I shook my head, but disagreeing didn't make it any better. Standing, lumpish, by his stereo, I was still four miles from home. And I wondered why that made me feel so guilty.

Oliver put his bottle down. He didn't even answer me.

'I'm going to get another beer,' he said.

'Another one?'

Oliver paused, a step away from standing still.

'Yes,' he said. 'Another one.'

The way he looked at me then made my stomach churn. A fly-on-dog-shit kind of look, Dad would have said. I remember Dad saying something else once too, that in Victorian times children were Seen And Not Heard. Speak when you're spoken to, I thought. And I wondered if that was from Victorian times too. Letting my chin sink downwards, I stared at the floor. Looking at me now, I thought, Oliver'd only see the top of my head. Exposed. In a way, I thought, that was only right. And I closed my eyes softly.

There was silence then. I didn't look up to see Oliver's face. And I heard his voice much clearer with no sight.

275

'Have you ever . . . have you ever taken speed?' he said.

Dawn had asked me about drugs once, when I'd still been going out with Robin. She disapproved, she'd told me, and she knew that I was *doing* them. Still, I think she'd been kind of curious. Which, I guess, is why I'd lied.

'Sometimes . . .' I'd said, and I tried not to smirk at the way she was still looking down at the pages of her book. Like she hadn't even asked me. Like she wasn't really interested.

'Do they make you sick then?' she said. She ran her bookmark across the lines, kept her eyes away. 'They're bad for your body, you know.'

I shrugged. 'They don't make you feel sick. Well . . .' I crossed my legs on the splintered wood of the cloakroom bench. 'I guess it depends which ones you're talking about.'

I risked a glance and Dawn was staring at me. Her hand nearly dropped the bookmark.

'I wasn't *talking* about any of them . . .' She fumbled around. 'Cannabis?' she said.

'No, it doesn't make you feel sick.' I smiled, and it wasn't a nasty smile. Sometimes she made me feel that way. Soft, I guess. 'Magic mushrooms do,' I said. Robin had told me about magic mushrooms. He'd said they'd made a brew so thick it was like snot. I hated mushrooms anyway. The thought of making a soup out of them so thick it looked like snot was enough to make pretty much anyone nauseous. 'They make you sick,' I said. She nodded, face back in her book.

'Have you done any others?'

She didn't look up.

'What others do you mean?'

'LSD. Amphetamines . . .' I watched her turn the page and shifted my bum on the seat.

'I've done speed,' I said. 'Doesn't make you feel sick either. Makes you . . . speedy.'

I didn't think she'd know any better.

'Speedy?' she said. 'Why would anyone want to feel speedy?'

'Dunno . . .' I said, and I looked away as some First Years shuffled past.

It hadn't been a big lie. Not big at all.

And I didn't think it'd be any bigger if I gave it to Oliver too.

'Yes,' I said. I looked up at him slowly. His tongue was poking his cheek out, a tiny rounded bump. His hands were moving. 'Yes,' I said again. I could have cracked a joke, I guess. But seeing him so far up, I didn't feel too in the mood for jokes. And I liked the sound of one-word answers.

He tapped his fingers against his leg and glanced towards the stereo as another song ended.

'Alright then,' he said, like he'd made a decision. I didn't speak. It wasn't up to me.

I watched his hand reach up to the top pocket of his shirt. It was funny, I hadn't seen any bulge there before, but now I was looking for it: small and saggy, it hung in the cloth.

His fingers had to walk around in there till he could get a hold of it. Eventually, he pulled it out between his first finger and his second. I tried to watch without staring. It was small. Loads smaller than I'd have thought, in a little plastic bag like Midland gives their pound coins out of. It was just powder really, and it creased up and clung to the plastic.

Oliver walked across to the wall and took down a face mirror hanging there. It didn't have any frame, I saw, but he didn't seem to care. He didn't come to sit back down next to me either. Instead, he went to stand by the television, with his legs splayed out in front of the dark grey screen.

He put the mirror down, and I didn't interrupt him.

On the stereo, another song started up.

He opened the bag really carefully. Gently, so he didn't spill any of it, and I watched him tip a tiny bit on to the glass. I would have asked him to tip out more, but I thought maybe that would seem rude. He didn't turn round at me or smile or anything. That was Ok, though. I didn't really want him to.

He sealed the bag again, and shook it slightly so all the stuff would go back down to the bottom. He put it back in his pocket. Watching him take his wallet out of his trousers, I thought about Holly and what she might say. Oliver might not smoke dope, but dope wasn't such a big deal anyway. And she'd understand when I told her about this. If I told her. I smiled to myself as he flipped through the cards and stuff. After a minute he chose one, took it out, and reached into the other section. I tapped my feet up and down on the floor. I tried to think of something I could say.

He scraped the stuff into a pile in the centre with the edge of the card. I couldn't see it very well, but I thought it might have been Barclays Bank. Or maybe Visa. It was that dark blue colour anyway. I sort of hoped it was Visa. I sort of hoped it wasn't his video club card. He pushed it around for quite a while, and I thought about telling him that I didn't really care what pattern he put it in – it didn't make any difference to me. I thought about it, but in the end I didn't say that either.

'It's pretty good actually,' he said. But he didn't turn around to look at me. 'Not too harsh.'

'Yes,' I said. It sounded reasonable enough, I thought. 'Good.'

'Nice . . . and . . . smooth.' He kept on pushing and tapping and clicking his card up and down on the mirror. I just watched him. I thought he probably knew what he was doing. He looked back over his shoulder then and grinned at me. I tried to smile back, but after not being looked at for a while, it felt funny to have his eyes on me again. I waited till he turned away. 'Pretty pure.' He scraped a line down the middle of the little pile, and I listened to the sound of plastic on glass. After a minute, he turned around completely.

He held his arm towards the TV when he'd finished, like he was holding a door open for me, offering me a chair or something. And I wondered why he didn't just pass it to me – the mirror looked kind of portable. I got up, though. It seemed like the right thing to do.

I thought he'd stand with me. I thought he'd watch or something, I don't know. All he did was walk away and crouch down by the stereo. He didn't look at me. He didn't speak. He looked like he was being busy.

I stared down at the glass, because I didn't really have much choice. I could see my own face, leaning over, kind of bright and double-chinned. I could see the way the flesh hung down, sagged towards the mirror. I could see a whitehead forming on the spot I'd been picking at.

I stared down at the powder, and I was kind of surprised by how thin those lines were. When Holly talked about lines, I'd always sort of pictured great fat worms, all heaped up on a table. They weren't like worms, though. They were scraped and beautiful and delicate. And I wasn't disappointed.

The top of the television set was layered with dust, and I could see lines in that too, where the mirror had scratched it clean as it moved. A bit of mascara had come loose from my eyelashes and landed on my cheek. I wiped it away, and I thought about the bathroom mirror. About pinching and redness. I thought about my compass, and I think I might have smiled.

Everything was perfect.

I wondered if I should just bend down close enough to get at it or what. I wondered if the tip of my nose would push his lines into messy piles. I looked across at Oliver. But Oliver was still busy.

I was just about to bend down, get my nostril as close to the glass as I could, when I saw the ten-pound note. It was rolled into a thin and perfect tube, secured with a plain silver ring. It couldn't have been Oliver's, that ring. He never would have fitted it on his finger. And I wondered why he'd bother keeping a ring that didn't even fit him. I didn't wonder for long though. I picked up the cash instead.

I love the feel of money. Pound coins are nice, they've got a good weight to them. But notes are best, even if they're lighter. There's no other paper like money paper in the world. It crinkles and crackles, and when Dad gets it fresh from the cash point it isn't even creased. Yes, I've always loved the feel of money. But I don't think I've ever loved it quite as much as I did then, rolled into a perfect tube.

It fitted right into place. With my arm, and his beer, with those pretty little lines. With me.

I stuck it in my nostril, and I felt his eyes rest heavy on my back. Like watching me undress, I thought. Watching every single move for a mistake. I smiled.

The second line was fatter at one end. But then the other one was thicker in the middle. I tried to gauge it out. The second one went much too thin, but it was deeper on the glass. I stood there staring at my own reflection. Too much lipstick and a ten-pound note stuck up my nose. I was disgusting in that mirror. Somehow that fitted too.

I went for the one nearest to me. It seemed like less hassle than to turn the mirror round. A speck or two got blown away by my breath. I held my left nostril shut, and I leaned down against the glass.

Watching myself, bisected by the tiny line of powder, I could see the concentration on my face, like I was working on a quadratic equation. My eyebrows pulled down over my nose, my teeth took a grip on my lip. I sniffed.

It was numb at first, and I didn't really feel anything. I wondered if it was going up the tube at all. I moved myself along, and the glass was clean behind me. I went on sniffing, with the squeaking noise coming out behind me. Then it started to sting.

It didn't hurt in my nose. In my nostril, where I thought it would have done. It hurt at the back of my mouth instead. Not that it mattered. I went all the way along, and I had to weave my way from side to side a bit, so as to get it all. The hurt in my mouth got worse, like the feeling of bronchitis starting. I ignored it.

And after a moment, it was done.

He was smiling when I turned round, his beer bottle back in his hand. 'Well?'

I nodded to him, so I wouldn't have to speak. I swallowed. The back of my mouth was all coated in bitter stuff, like snot or something. And I guess I must have winced because he shrugged a little bit and laughed. He handed me the bottle but I only stared.

I wouldn't have taken it, except that the taste in my mouth was so bad. I could feel the snot trickling down inside of my nostril as I nodded. And I guess then it was his turn.

I watched him as he walked towards the TV set and bent over. I watched his foot tap on the carpet. I didn't feel that different. I grabbed a cigarette and lit it. I chewed at the corner of my mouth. No, I didn't really feel that different at all.

He moved his face along the mirror. I watched him sniff, tip back his head. I watched.

And I think I really loved him in that moment.

Oliver got more beers, but after a while I stopped drinking them. I wasn't getting pissed, and there seemed like more interesting things to do. I drank water instead, and half listened to the CD go round.

My nose was running, and every so often I had to sniff the slime back in. The taste at the back of my mouth went, though. Along with my cigarettes. Every so often he threw one of his over to me, and I wondered why I felt so grateful.

It was funny. I've always thought of drugs a bit like the spinach on *Popeye*. Not that they made your arms bulge out and gave you a stupid accent, but like an injection of cool. Like you'd go up to the mirror with knocking knees saying things like 'fab' and 'brill', you'd snort, stand back against the wall while it sunk in, and suddenly become James Dean.

Strangely enough, though, it didn't quite happen that way.

I wasn't stoned or falling over. I wasn't bouncing round the room. It just made me want to chew my lips, smoke a lot of cigarettes. And it made me want to pick at my arm.

It started with the plaster, I think. Just talking and listening and nodding too often, I felt my hand wander down somewhere, and then I started pulling. It came off in ripping tugs, so small he didn't notice. They hurt, I think, each time I pulled but it didn't seem to stop me. I felt the hairs being plucked out, a little by a little, and I felt the cuts get worse. No matter, I thought. Pick and bite and smoke and chew. No matter. And my jaws ached from pushing them together.

And staring at the carpet, it was weird to think that so much had happened today. It didn't really feel like one day at all, but like loads of days, all crammed together without the nights to keep them normal. I wondered if Dad was asleep yet. I wondered if Mum was lying next to him, but I couldn't really picture it. I sniffed. And I thought about the mirror.

I moved my legs, getting stiff in the knees. The street lights made zebra patterns through the blinds on the opposite wall. They criss-crossed the carpet in bright stripes of yellow.

'Can I . . . um. Can I have a cigarette?'

'Huh?' He looked up at me. 'Yeah . . .' he said, but he didn't smile. That was Ok. I didn't want him to. 'Just take one,' he said.

'Thank you.' I reached for the packet. 'Oh. Your card's lying on the floor. Here . . .'

'I don't want it,' he said. And after a moment I watched him walk out of the room.

I thought his hands were empty when he came back in. I couldn't see anything there. But when he walked to the television set and turned his back to me again, I heard that little chopping noise. He hadn't picked his card up off the floor.

I listened to the last scratching noises and then he

moved away. He didn't hold his arm out this time, but then he didn't really need to. I stood up fast.

'I'm gonna get a beer,' he said.

I didn't answer. I was busy.

I walked to the TV set, and I didn't watch him as he left the room. I didn't hesitate either. The ten-pound note was in the same place, and I saw that the ring had slipped a little. I picked it up, adjusted it, and then I saw what it was that Oliver had gone to the bathroom for. Lying on the corner of the mirror, well away from my line and from his, a razor blade was resting on the glass. I didn't give it much of a second look, though. Instead I bent my head down.

My heart was going a bit when I turned around to step away. I could feel it jumping. Oliver was standing by the door, more beers in his hands. And I wondered how he could fit that much beer in his fridge. I wondered if he kept any food at all. He was watching me carefully, and his face was kind of still. The blind shadows fell over his neck and the bottom of his chin, like something out of an old detective movie. It made his skin look yellow and his stubble darker. I think he might have been smiling – with the corner of his mouth.

I went to press Play on the CD again, turning so I could see him do his line. He pulled back, stamped his foot on the carpet, and I felt my stomach roll. He looked so angry.

And it was only turning back to me that I saw the expression change, looking at me crouched by his stereo. I followed his eyes. Down past my shoulder, and over my hips. Round and curving and dark, through my waist, his eyes were stopping. Stopping, where my left arm lay.

And I guess it was like the cigarettes in a way. Lighting and smoking them, and suddenly they were gone. Another and another and I'd hardly noticed I was doing it.

My arm was bleeding.

The plaster hung by a tiny sticky bit on the corner. It was dirty and yellow underneath. It was sagging. And I could feel Oliver's eyes as he stood there. I could feel them on me.

It was the E that'd gone, and I wasn't surprised. I guess I'd just got more confident as I'd gone along, and it was so much deeper than the H. The trickle had worked its way around and down. And it was dripping on the carpet. It had made a tiny stain.

That stain made my stomach roll again, dirty on his carpet. His carpet that he kept so lovely, so hoovered, and I felt the sting of some weird kind of guilt. A good sting. And I guess I was smiling when I looked back up at him.

I guess that's what made him angry.

'You're *smiling*,' he said.

'I . . .' But I couldn't get rid of it, it felt so right. It fitted with that expression on his face.

'What . . . have you just been sitting there picking at it?'

'I got it on your carpet,' I said. 'I'm sorry.' And still, the smile was there.

'On the . . .? Jesus *Christ!* You're *bleeding* for fuck's sake. What am I s'posed to *say?* What do you want? You want my *sympathy?* You want me to feel *guilty?*'

'I . . . I don't want you to feel guilty.' I looked down at

the stain for a moment. 'It's just . . . it's a nice kind of colour,' I said. 'Pretty.'

'Pretty.' Oliver stared at me, but I didn't understand.

'Just . . . just under the lamp, like that. Don't you think . . .?' I looked at him.

I could see the muscles bunch on the sides of his face. 'I told you what I think,' he said quietly. And I frowned at him, confused. 'I think it's ugly,' he said. 'Horrible.' I kept looking. His face gave me nothing, though. Nothing, and I didn't understand.

'Fuck,' he said. And the floor creaked as he stood. His footsteps were heavy on the floor towards me, and I just stayed there. Crouching down.

I wondered if his hands were clenching. Or if his little finger twitched inside his palm. I could feel him coming forward, I could feel how tight he was, and I could feel my crouch reducing. I wondered how far his boots were from me. And I breathed.

I thought about the ten-pound note. I thought about white lines of powder and that lovely lovely taste. About his eyes and the feeling of redness creeping over my cheek.

I could feel the muscle in my calf twitch. I could feel the plaster sticking to my arm. I wished I could look at it, what was under that plaster. I wished I could show it to him.

I wished he would look. Because if he looked right, I thought, then he'd see it in the same way I did. I knew he would. I knew.

I wondered if he'd hit me then. I wanted him to.

*

I looked up when nothing happened, and Oliver's face was still. He hadn't hit me, and I guess he didn't understand after all. Not even after everything we'd done.

'I don't want anything to do with . . .' He shook his hand in my direction, but he didn't look at my arm. 'That,' he said. 'It's got nothing to do with me. Understand?'

But I didn't. I didn't understand at all. I only felt like crying.

'I'm going to bed.'

I nodded dumbly, staring at the floor. He stood up, picked up the bottles next to him. I didn't pick my head up as he left the room. I couldn't watch him go.

And I'd sort of had to wonder how everything had got to this. How weird this day had been. I listened to his footsteps as he walked away. I listened to the door shut and the sound of him switching on the bedroom light.

I didn't even know which room the bedroom was.

Funny that.

I looked down at the cigarette case but I didn't pick one out. I tapped my fingers on the floor. They made soft thumping noises as a new song started up. I watched the way they moved, perfectly in rhythm, and I thought about how far my finger-tapping had come.

The light went off, and I wondered if he was lying in the dark there.

Like me.

And sitting alone in someone else's room, I wondered just how I'd expected it all to turn out. I don't know. Maybe this had been the only way. Maybe this had been the way I wanted it.

I got up then. I walked to the other side of the room, to the TV set and the mirror he'd left there. Specks of white were traced across it. Scattered, like I'd thrown those little rips of bottle label.

They made a mist on the face of the glass.

And after a moment, I picked up the razor blade.

I slept in Oliver's living room that night, wrapped up in my new dress.

And when I woke up next morning, I didn't go in to see him. I picked my head up, tried to breathe slowly to stop my heart from skipping, and I went straight to the phone.

I caught Dawn just before the bus.

'Can you bring in an extra shirt and skirt?' I said. 'And a tie if you've got one?' I tried not to think of what I'd look like in Dawn's clothes. Her lovely laddered tights and knee-length polyester skirt. Spots and rings under my eyes, greasy skin and lipstick that had bled. Ahh, the joys of fresh-faced youth. There was snot at the back of my mouth.

'Why?' Dawn made the word sound too long, like there was too much behind it, I thought. I don't know, maybe it was just my head. I had to keep refocusing my eyes on the wall in front of me to stop myself from falling over. Holly wouldn't feel this way, I thought. Holly would jog to school.

'I . . . I haven't got my uniform with me,' I said. I tried to make it quiet, I didn't want to wake him. He'd be cross with me again if I did that, and it was a nice kind of image,

I thought, sneaking out, trying not to disturb him. The sleeping dragon sort of thing.

'Really?' Dawn said, but she didn't ask me why not. She didn't ask me where I was. Instead, she said yes. And she told me we'd meet in the cloakrooms.

It felt weird, walking through the corridors at school, out of place, like I shouldn't be there. The battleship blue on the walls made everything look dim, and everyone stared at my clothes. I'd changed the dress for a pair of Oliver's jeans and one of his Benetton jumpers. I didn't want to wear that dress in school. Still, I didn't feel natural, turning the corner into the cloakroom.

'Oh my God,' Dawn said. She was sitting on one of the benches, the old brown wooden kind with a million obscenities carved in. She had to sit forward on it, I saw, to keep her head from bashing the metal coat hooks that ran in a row above. It was even darker in the cloakroom and the dirty frosted glass made blank, straight-line shadows on the plastic carrier bag by her feet. Dawn's head moved up and down as she stood up, picked up the bag from the floor. She looked like a chicken with mental problems, I thought. Mental problems and acne. 'You look *terrible*.'

I thought about telling her that she'd looked terrible for years and she hadn't even had an excuse. Instead, I glanced back down the corridor, reached for the carrier bag. She gave it up, her hand flopping open like she wasn't even thinking about it. And she didn't take her eyes off me. After a moment, I looked down at the ground.

'You stayed at his house, didn't you.'

I opened the bag, picked at the stuff inside so I wouldn't have to look at her. There was a faded shirt and the skirt was worse than knee-length. Mid-calf. I shuddered. She shifted her feet, tights sagging out around her ankles. She had big ankles, I thought, like she was suffering from water retention.

'You know we've got a French test today,' she said. I could hear her voice tighten up a note, she must have been raising her chin. 'I revised all last night . . . I didn't bother to ask if you wanted to revise with me.' She paused. 'You're so busy these days.' I didn't say anything. It felt like I didn't have enough breath to keep my heart going. I didn't want to waste it on Dawn. 'I hardly understood it,' she said. 'And I'll fail, but I s'pose you don't care about that anymore. You only talk to me when you want something.'

Behind me, I heard a bunch of boys bouncing through the corridor, shouting and laughing and swearing. I heard the thud of a bag being thrown. It echoed, and their noises sounded loud and thin. I looked up at Dawn. I had to sometime, I guess, or she'd think that I needed a neck brace. 'Your dad says I'm too giving.' She stared me in the face and I wished I could turn away again. I didn't want her seeing me. 'But that's just the sort of person I am. I can't stop being nice.'

Dawn flicked her hair back with a twist of her neck. She had a new flush of blackheads, I saw, just underneath her jaw. 'You don't even say thank you anymore.'

'Thank you.' My voice sounded croaky and I coughed. I must have smoked a whole B&H plantation last night.

'Your breath smells of tobacco,' she said. 'And all your clothes. I s'pose he smokes.'

I shrugged. All I could smell were the toilets, damp and cold and kind of mouldy.

'Oh, so you don't even talk to me anymore. You ask me to get you a whole uniform together, almost make me miss my bus, and you can't even be bothered to talk to me.'

'I'm just tired,' I said. I rubbed my eye with one hand, red balloons expanding behind my eyelid. And when I opened it again, I saw one had escaped, was floating against the grey-blue wall.

'Yeah,' she said. 'Yeah I just bet you're tired, going off with a twenty-seven-year-old, smoking, not revising, not bothering to call your friends. I bet he takes *drugs*.' She looked away from me as I opened my mouth. I could see the old purple scars, healing dots across her cheeks. I could see the pock marks.

I don't know what I would have said, looking at her standing there. Her shirt was ironed into creases, her buttons all done up. My mouth hung there a moment, waiting for me to tell it what to do. And in my head, one line ran through. *Your dad says I'm too giving.* And on the heels of that: *That's Ok with you is it?* I watched Dawn, her jaw all bony and tightened in profile, and I knew that it wasn't Ok. It wasn't Ok at all.

I couldn't tell her about last night, not even about the cool stuff. I couldn't tell her I'd done speed. Because Dawn and Dad were close these days. Obviously. And it wasn't fucking Ok in the slightest.

I saw Dawn blink.

I swallowed.

'It's none of your business,' I said.

'*What?*' Her head shot back, catching on that starched collar of hers as she stared.

'It's none of your business what Oliver does and . . . And if you can't think of anything nice to say about him then why don't you just *shut up!*'

Dawn's eyes got wider in the dimness.

Wider, as her mouth fell down.

I could see the white stuff on her tongue.

'You . . . bitch,' she said.

And behind my back, the bell rang.

Dad was already home when I got back from school at four-thirty. He was sitting at the kitchen table, his tie lying next to him and a can of Löwenbräu in his hand. His bald patch was pink underneath the kitchen light, and I could hear the blips and roars of FIFA from Michael's bedroom door.

He looked tired, I thought, walking in. But then I was tired too. Everyone was tired.

'Hi, Dad.'

'What? . . . Oh. Hi.' But he only looked round at me for a moment.

'Are you Ok?'

'Yeah . . .' he said. 'Well, you know. Usual stuff.'

'Mmm,' I said, but I couldn't really be bothered to ask what the usual stuff was. My back ached from sleeping on the floor all night, and the skin on my face felt like it was suddenly discovering the fun of gravity. I felt like I needed to puke. 'Where's Mum?'

'Not sure,' he said.

'Oh . . . I know. Isn't she having her hair done today?' He didn't speak. 'She usually gets it done . . . you know. Middle of the month.'

'She's not having her hair done. I don't know where she is.' There was a pause as he stared at the beer can. 'She might be in the garden,' he said.

'Oh,' I said. 'Right.' I dumped my bag on the floor, trying not to stretch my arm, and I let my hair fall down across my forehead so he couldn't see my face. Dad looked up at me when I sat down at the table. He smiled, but it just seemed to fall into the wrinkles round his mouth.

'So . . . how are you finding that stereo of yours?'

'It's great. It . . .' I looked away. 'It's got such a cool sound. No . . . no wa or flutter.'

He nodded slowly and his smile improved a little bit. He didn't say anything though, just sagged back into silence.

For a moment I only sat there, trying to think what to say. The rain was starting up again outside. I heard it swish and clatter on the living-room french windows. Dad shifted his can side to side, but still he didn't speak.

I arranged my arms on the surface of the table, stretched my jaw and yawned. It felt false though, looking at him.

'So,' he said. His voice was flat, more like an end than a beginning. 'Where's your dress?'

I looked at him. 'It . . . it's in my school bag.' I wondered exactly what I'd been meant to say to that, but when I took a breath Dad just stared down at the table. Like he'd asked me for no reason. 'I ought to go and hang it up,' I said.

'Hang Dawn's uniform up too,' he said, but he wasn't looking at my clothes. He was leaning, face forward, all the weight on his forearms. 'Don't want it to get creased.'

'I . . .' I said, but there was nothing to put after it. They're very close, I thought again.

'She says you stayed up late all last night, didn't get any revision done for some . . . test.' His tone didn't even alter as he said it, not grumpy or waiting for me to answer. I rubbed one hand across my eyes, wondering what I should say.

'I passed.'

Dad only shrugged.

'It wasn't an exam. It . . .' My voice wound down to nothing. 'I got a B-plus,' I said. I ran my fingers along the wood. 'Well . . . I must go. Unpack my stuff, I think. Don't want my dress getting . . . messed up.' I pushed myself up from the table.

Dad's cigarette was burning away in his hand, and I saw the tie lying next to him had a little stain down the front. He looked up at me as I stood, and I tried for a small smile.

'Yes,' he said, but he paused a minute, looking at me. 'Tell me . . . that stereo I bought you . . . You've only got two discs to play on it, haven't you?'

I nodded.

'I . . .' But Dad didn't finish his sentence either. He blinked it away as I watched him reach into his shirt pocket.

His fingers came out, big and round, pinching a twenty-pound note. It was rolled up, I saw. Rolled up like a straw, and I felt guilt turn over in my tummy. Dad didn't hand it to me for a moment, staring at the table as he breathed. 'I s'pose three isn't much better than two,' he said quietly. 'But . . .' His eyes dragged slowly up to me, they rested on my own. 'But I'd still like to buy you things,' he said.

The phone rang when I was halfway up the stairs and I turned as soon as I heard it. In the kitchen I could hear the fridge door shutting, Dad's footsteps on the floor. And I had to run to get to the study. To pick the phone up first.

Oliver was quiet, I thought, on the edge of being pissed off, and I tried to speak softly.

'I . . . I missed you this morning,' I said. 'I . . . wanted to say sorry. About last night . . .'

Oliver was silent for a moment. 'I missed you too,' he said finally, 'this morning.' He paused. 'I wish you'd left a note or something . . . I didn't know where you were.'

'I didn't want to wake you. I'm sorry if you were worried.'

'Doesn't matter. Some woman . . . Miss Anderson . . . said you'd got there alright.'

'Miss *Anderson?*' I said. 'When did you see her?'

'She answered the phone when I rang up . . . Annoying fucking woman she was too.'

'You rang up *school?*' I took a breath, trying to get my heart back to normal. 'Why?'

'I was worried about you . . . I didn't know where you were or anything.'

'But . . . but you know I had to go to school . . .'

'Look, you weren't there!' His voice was sudden, loud, and I had to pull the phone away. I had to bite my lip. 'I didn't know how long you'd been gone, did I? You should have left a fucking note! What the fuck did you expect me to do?'

I heard the echo of the line as Oliver stopped speaking. It sounded very loud.

'I was worried,' he said again, breathing deep. 'I didn't know where you were.'

'You're right,' I said. 'You're right. I'm just not used to it . . . People being worried.'

'Well I worry,' Oliver said quietly. His breath was very shaky. 'I care.'

Oliver hung up soon after that. I stared at some jigsaw-puzzle pieces scattered over our dirty carpet, and the phone hung limp, in my left hand. All of us on our own. Dad in the kitchen, Mum in the garden. Michael with his Megadrive, me with my telephone. It was funny I suppose.

The plastic clicked softly as I laid the receiver down. I rubbed a hand across my face. I didn't know whose fault it was. I couldn't even guess. But, sitting the study, I closed my eyes. And I was sure it never used to be this way.

It was a couple of weeks before I went to Oliver's flat again. We saw each other a lot in the lunchtimes. Dawn had stopped talking to me, she wouldn't even look me in the eye, so there wasn't much for me to do in school. Holly seemed to have kind of lost interest since the holidays, since I split up with Robin, I guess. It was funny, though, that didn't seem to bother me as much as I'd have thought it would. It didn't even make me sad.

Oliver'd left the keys in the lock for me that evening. It was a Friday, I think. I watched them swinging back and forth as I tapped them, stretching my legs out after the walk. It was quite a way from the school to Oliver's flat and my hair had gone straggly from the rain. It was in a pretty nice bit of town, his flat, well away from all the estates. Next to the golf course and the pavilion, but it hadn't looked so nice that day, hunching under the weather. The lake by the golf course had looked a dirty kind of grey and it rippled in the wind. It's not a natural lake. You can tell by the way the ducks always look like they don't know what they're doing there. It's in a kind of natural shape, though. Or at least it looks like that when you stand next to it. It curves away in a teardrop, with a little island at the fat end where the swans hang out. It's funny though. If you look at an aerial map of the lake, it doesn't look natural at all. It looks like a great big tit with a nipple in the centre.

I shook my hair behind my shoulders, hearing it smacking against my coat, but I didn't go straight in. I felt my right hand go up, reach across and touch my arm. The rest of the house was silent, kind of creepy in the twilight. I tapped the keys again with my left hand, hearing them clatter on the plywood door, and I sighed. I listened to myself, and I wondered how I'd got here. It all seemed very fast. There was nothing I could do about it, though. I could only keep running and hope that things wouldn't catch up. I could only go forward. I could only open the door, I guess.

Oliver's hall was all steamy on the ceiling. Warm and wet, and the sound of his clunking and splashing came from the bathroom. I looked round. I wondered if he'd heard me come in.

'Hello?'

'What the fuck . . .?' His voice sounded different, I thought, surprised out of its accent. I didn't move in the hallway. I heard his splashing stop, and I didn't even put my bag down. 'What are you doing here? I'm in the bath! I thought . . . I thought you were coming at half four for fuck's sake! It's only quarter past!' I heard him pause. '*Shit!*'

'I . . .' I raised my voice so he could hear me. 'Well, I got here a bit early. Is that Ok?'

There was a long silence, like he was just sitting still, in the water. I stared at the wall in front of me, at the phone. Last time I was here, I thought, I was sneaking away. I glanced towards the bathroom. I almost wished that I could do the same thing now.

'If it was Ok,' he said, 'I would have asked you to come earlier.' There was a thud.

'It's . . . it's only fifteen minutes,' I said. 'I didn't think you'd mind.' That wasn't true, though. I heard a second thud, stepped back from the bathroom door. I hadn't thought about it at all. It hadn't even crossed my mind. 'It doesn't matter does it?' I said.

I heard the lock grate back behind the wood. I heard it give as Oliver opened the door.

The light behind him was very yellow and I could see

the mirror on the wall was clouded, wet. Oliver's hair hung down into his face. Like mine, I thought, but not from the rain. He had a towel wrapped around him, his whole body not just his waist, and it swamped him. It made him seem skinnier than he was.

'Don't worry.' I smiled. It made my top lip flicker. 'You look sweet like that.'

It was meant to be a compliment, I guess. I don't even know why I said it. Except I didn't want him to be cross, not again, not when I wasn't ready. I wanted to make him happy. Oliver wasn't smiling though. His mouth was twitching round the corner, but it wasn't a smile. He was staring straight at me. I could feel the expression drag down off my face. I could feel my mouth go loose. He looked the way he had on that first night, *put your pants on*, only it wasn't anger anymore. It was clear and caustic and I couldn't look away. I didn't want to look away. And the silence seemed very big.

'Half four, I said.' His fingers squeaked as they shifted on the door handle, pinching the corner of the towel there too. His eyes were muddy, tiny, bloodshot feathers running through the white. Like lines, I thought. Like little rough lines. Like the wrinkles that formed round the skin of his lids. Like white powder on a mirror. Like my arm.

'I . . . I'm sorry.' The towel quivered a little by his wrist. A huge blue fluffy towel, baggy over his body. It didn't seem to fit with his face.

'Half fucking four, did you think there was no reason for that or something? I don't *want* you barging in when I'm still in the bath!' His other hand flicked out, gesturing

300

at something but I couldn't tell what. I couldn't take my eyes off his face. His gritted teeth. 'It's just rude! Just plain fucking *rude!* Learn that one off your father did you!' His head swung away from me, jagged and fast. '*Fuck!*'

'I'm sorry . . .'

He snapped back.

'I . . . I didn't realize you'd be in the bath,' I said. He took a step towards me, just two feet away. 'You know, I thought you'd just get back from work. But it doesn't matter does it?' Another step. My hand went back up to my arm. I hardly noticed it. 'Really, you look very cute. You look like a little kid or something.'

Oliver's hand clapped down across my mouth.

It wasn't a hit. Not quite.

He held it there, staring at me, as I felt warmth like a bruise on my chin. The corner of the towel tickled on my nose, still clamped between his fingers. I wasn't really thinking about that, though. The hand was wet, covering my mouth. Warm and I smelled soap on his fingertips. I felt a trickle of water run down my neck. And I wasn't thinking about any of those things.

I just watched his face get closer.

The pores on his cheeks were clean and pink and a burst blood vessel had put a tiny spiral underneath his eye. His eyelashes didn't look like Robin's. They were dark, like his hair, not watery yellow. Still, it reminded me of Robin. Maybe it was on his lips.

I felt his little finger move, up and underneath my nostrils. It made my breath whisper, hot and spread across my face, and I felt a muscle in my stomach twinge. His eyes got closer and the tips of his fingers got harder in the hollow of my cheek. I wondered if he could feel my teeth through there.

And I'd never seen him look so angry.

Oliver pressed harder, downwards, and I felt my knees give out a little. He pushed me down, very slowly, very hard. He pushed till I was kneeling on the carpet. The hall floor, I thought for no reason at all. And Oliver followed me down.

He didn't kiss me, though his face was close enough.

Every muscle in his face clenched, he leaned past and bit my ear.

It wasn't like you see in movies, quick and kind of playful. His teeth gripped slowly and harder, clamping down. Clenching. It hurt. It hurt a lot. But I didn't make a sound.

Oliver's breath was very loud and his mouth was dry, like mine felt dry. Wrinkly, like skin that'd been in hot water too long. His front teeth were bumpy on the bottom. I hadn't seen that, looking at him, but I could feel it now.

I felt my bum slide down across the carpet. The tights made crackling static noises. My skirt hitched a little bit higher. I watched him kneel from his crouching position. Kneel, and then lean closer. And his eyes were still on mine.

I wondered then how I must look to him.

Just two eyes above his heavy hand.

He put a hand inside my pants, dry and sharp, and it felt like it was cutting me. He didn't play, though, not this time. His stared into my open eyes, and I couldn't look away. He rubbed hard, round and round in sore and biting circles. And he stared. I felt his thumb touch my thigh and take a grip there, balancing. I felt it make an indent, blue bruises as he pressed. His breath was very hot, and I could feel it stirring at the baby hairs around my head. I lay back as he held, as he rubbed. I lay limp. I let him do it.

I don't know what it was that made it happen. I don't know what made the change. But looking up at his face, his cheeks hanging down and the way he pressed his teeth together over me, I felt myself get wet. It came from inside, and I could feel the muscles flowing, giving out that liquid. It was horrible.

I remember Holly telling me about some guy she'd seen in a club once, about the first time she saw him. *Just creamed my pants*, she'd said. And I'd thought then it was disgusting. The most disgusting thing I'd ever heard, and I thought so now as well. Now, even though I couldn't stop.

And Oliver smiled down at me, so I guess that he could feel it too. He turned me over and I heard the towel fall, crumple on the floor. I heard it, even with my face crushed into the carpet. Even with his hand there, holding me down.

Hard and steady on the back of my head, I could feel his fingers tangle in my hair. His palm print on my neck. It was a good feeling. And I got wetter.

The sweat was kind of oily when he lay down on top of me, and between my back, his chest, and the elastic of my tights pressed my legs together. I held my eyes shut on the rough of cheap carpet. I listened to his breathing and I felt the weight rub burns into my legs. I felt it as he stuck his dick in.

It didn't hurt so much that second time, not in between my legs at least. But he squeezed my arm once, fingertips scratching over swollen, numb flesh. That hurt. Still I didn't cry out, instead I opened my eyes to see.

Purple. Blood on blue cotton.

It was a beautiful colour. I thought of Robin's hand, of that lovely welt across my face.

And as he pushed his arse down faster, hurting and deeper, and hearing some noise go squelch, I thought about that welt again. I felt something heat up, deep in my stomach.

Oliver was gasping and grunting. Shallow, bruising sounds. Harder and faster, and they sounded like a fist. A fist on someone's face, I thought, and he dug in again. The ball in my stomach felt like metal, like hot heavy metal, like the mercury they talk about in chemistry. It felt like it was leaking.

And my forehead scraped across the carpet, burned there for no reason as I whispered, hit me.

Oliver heard my words. There was a pause as he was halfway out, free air between our skin. A pause as he heard. As he listened. A pause, before he did it.

It made a cracking sound across my cheek. A violent whipping smack. A welt before he rushed back in to fuck me. And the heat on my face was like blood. Rushing up to fill the gap. Scalding. Like the thing that leaked in my stomach.

Hit me, I thought.

And I felt that thing give way.

It took a long time to pick my head up off the floor. I listened to Oliver walk off, to the bathroom light click on, and I rubbed my cheeks back and forward against the carpet. They were sore and warm like sunburn, but I didn't mind. Lying there felt good. And when Oliver walked back in, I wanted him to see that I hadn't moved. I thought about my arms, about speed and beer and Oliver, and I didn't want to move. I didn't ever want to move again. My face was right, slammed against his floor.

Oliver's footsteps came up behind me, and I felt something soft fall against my thigh.

'Tissue there,' he said.

'Oh.' I turned my body just enough to look up at him. He had the towel wrapped round him again, sagging over his whole body. I could feel the breeze on my back, where he'd pushed my shirt up and I smiled. 'Thank you,' I said.

But Oliver walked past me.

'Oliver . . .?'

He didn't answer, though, as the towel and his back disappeared into the living room.

I sat there for a moment on my own. I couldn't think of what to do. There was the grip and the spark of a lighter, Oliver's sharp breath as he inhaled.

I pulled my tights up slowly, staring out and into nothing. The bathroom light was still on, steam clearing in the cold. I could feel the rash, hot and bumpy, where my skin had been pressed too long on to the floor. It ran over the front of my legs in a regular pattern, but I didn't look at it long.

There were other things to look at. More interesting things.

I don't know which scab had burst, which line. I wanted to take my shirt off, I wanted to find out but I didn't quite dare. Not with Oliver so close, so angry. The blood was small really, spreading down in a blot on my shirt. It was dark and it made the cloth stick to my arm.

I'd only wanted to make him happy. All this time, that was the only thing I'd wanted. And I'd failed. You're just fucking rude, I thought. I watched the patch grow softly. I didn't smile.

But I reached to touch that stain.

Oliver was facing away from me when I walked into the doorway. I could see his back, the towel, and the hand that held the cigarette. It was warmer in the living room.

'Oliver,' I said.

'What?' He didn't turn, like he'd known I was there all along. Like he didn't care. I couldn't think of any answer, though, and I wondered why I'd opened my mouth.

'Oliver, I'm sorry.'

He shrugged. His shoulders rose and fell in one smooth movement. The towel flopped. The blinds were drawn, making everything look like twilight, the gas fire made burbling sounds. Hissing. There were no lights on. It made his skin go grey.

'If I'd known . . . that you were in the bath, I would've waited or something. I . . .'

'Just forget it! It doesn't matter alright? Forget it!'

I shut my mouth as Oliver inhaled again. Still, he hadn't looked at me. His hair hung limp on his neck, in tiny points. His shoulders were hunched, his knees drawn up.

And he seemed smaller like that, I thought. Younger somehow.

I glanced back behind me. Through the open door I could see the way out.

'Are . . .' His words caught. He flicked his cigarette hard at the ashtray. 'Are you Ok? Your face.'

'Yes.'

He didn't respond. Not even a nod.

'Are you?' I said.

Oliver's shoulder twitched, smoke drifting up around him. His voice gave me nothing.

'I'm fine.'

I felt my forehead crunch. It wasn't supposed to be this way, I thought. It wasn't supposed to be this way at all. He was meant to look at me, look down with some cold and faraway expression. Put your pants on. He was meant to smile and walk away, let me hunch somewhere in a corner where he couldn't see. It wasn't meant to be like this.

'I wanted to be ready.'

His hand was very still, holding the cigarette there.

'I just wanted to be ready when you arrived. That's all,' he said. 'That's all.'

I nodded in the silence, even though he couldn't see it. I smoothed my skirt down on my legs. But Oliver didn't speak again, like that was all he had to say. And after a moment, I sort of had to walk across to him.

My feet were quiet on the carpet as he took another drag. I could see damp patches on the towel between his shoulder blades, sticking to his skin. It made me think of my arm again. It made me wonder what was going on. Wonder if it was my fault.

Close to his back, I could just make out his breathing. It was soft and low like he was trying to hide it. It didn't make his shoulders rise. And standing above and behind him, I saw his feet coming out from the towel. It was wrapped all the way to his knees, like a blanket, I thought vaguely. His feet were very white in the dimness, against the shadow of the carpet, the tendons very clear.

I put my left hand on Oliver's shoulder.

'GET THE *FUCK* OFF ME!'

I almost screamed.

I stumbled back, but Oliver's hand was quicker. Twisting, he slammed it down on my own, crunching my fingers in his. His face was red, lips live, teeth out. I felt the skin on my arm breaking, lines peeling as his eyes bulged out at me. Dimly, somewhere else, the sound of the towel falling. Drops of spit on my cheek as I felt my face collapse. I could still feel the damp on his hand.

Oliver's breath hitched in. My eyes squeezed shut against him.

And I was crying.

I didn't even notice when his hand relaxed on mine, I didn't feel it as his fingers went loose. I didn't hear the stuttering, no words just sounds, falling from his mouth for no reason. My tears were very hot. They hurt me. 'I'm sorry . . . I'm so sorry . . . so sorry . . .' They stung on my cheeks and I felt my make-up running. Uglier and uglier. Disgusting.

Oliver's hand moved on mine.

Not hard but soft, and slowly.

He was stroking it.

'You're . . . you're bleeding,' he said quietly.

I didn't open my eyes. I couldn't look at the expression on his face, seeing me. Seeing my little piggy eyes, black-rimmed, revolting. This is me, I thought, and the words cut through my head. This has always been me.

'Please,' he said. 'Look . . . don't cry Ok? I'll . . . I'll get you a tissue. A tissue? Yes?'

I nodded. I wanted him to go. Just leave me be. Just leave me alone where he couldn't see my face. Where I could sit with myself. Where I could find some kind of blade.

I heard him get up slowly, not leaving my hand on its own. He squeezed it gently before he let it go, nervous, but I didn't look at him. I didn't look at anything. I watched the red behind my eyes.

Oliver was only gone a moment. It seemed like nothing. I listened to him in the hall and I wiped the knuckles of one hand across my face. Black smears there'd be now, I thought. From my eyes to my chin. And my fingers came away wet.

His footsteps were quick and he pressed the tissue into my other hand. I just held it for a moment, though. I couldn't think what I should use it for. 'I'm sorry,' I said again.

I felt him touch my chin.

'Look at me,' he said quietly.

My eyes were burning when I opened them.

'There . . . there's blood,' he said. 'Down your shirt. How did that happen? When . . .?'

I shrugged. I squeezed the tissue in my hand, brought it up and dabbed my face.

'Look . . . take your shirt off. I'll wash it for you. How about that? Yeah? I'll wash it.'

He nodded at me, but I just stared down at myself. Stupid, moon-faced. Dumb.

The stain across my sleeve was dark and drying sticky. It spread in a blotted line below my shoulder. It wasn't huge or bright. Just a shadow. A wet kind of shadow.

I watched him touch a fingertip to it, and he didn't press my skin. He stroked the cotton gently, holding my hand with his. He didn't look me in the eye. And when he brought his hand away, when he turned so he could see it, I watched his mouth draw tight around its edges. The stain on the tip of his finger was red.

'Take it off,' he said quietly. And I did what he said.

'Fucking hell,' he said.

I didn't answer him. I didn't tell him that they weren't as bad as they looked, that they hardly hurt at all. I didn't say anything. I just stood there as he looked.

The lines had hardened, some of them still intact, and the goosebumps made my skin seem whiter than it was. They stretched in stripes down my left arm, covering it. From the shoulder to the elbow. And then, below the elbow, that small word was healing. I hadn't gone back to the word. It seemed pointless when I could start all over. On new skin, like virgin snow. Like putting your footsteps where no one else's have gone. They cut, horizontal, across my flesh.

Some of them were close together, some half an inch apart. And I could see where they'd got deeper, easier towards my shoulder. Where I'd had to find more room. More space. The broken ones were drying now, brown smeary trickles where the cloth of my shirt had rubbed away their perfect shape. There were tiny ones, all close and friendly. Long ones, far apart. One crossed through a mole on my biceps.

They were cleaner than the word had been, a sharper tool, I think. The skin wasn't torn but neatly sliced. Symmetrical. So pretty. Tiny pieces of the scabs had crumbled free.

I don't know how many there were. More than fifty probably, less than a hundred, I'd think. Lots. Lots, for such a short time's work.

'Fucking hell,' he said again.

I glanced up.

My face felt swollen from the tears now but at least they weren't coming again. My heart had slowed and my stomach wasn't tipping. They're very calm, those lines. They made me calm as well.

'You said . . .' He coughed. 'You said you wouldn't do it again.'

I shrugged. There didn't seem any point in speaking.

'Why?' he said.

He looked at me.

So I gave him the only answer I knew.

'I just want to make you happy.'

'And you think . . .' Oliver turned away from me, his mouth curling downwards. 'You think that makes me happy do you?' I watched him get up, move away from me. 'You think it makes me happy to see *that*?' He took a step away, turned. 'Happy?' he said. And I looked at the floor. I was too far above it, my face should have been down there.

Oliver stopped walking, standing still in the centre of the room.

He looked at the opposite wall, above the television, to where the mirror was. His hand moved by his side. It closed and opened. I wondered if it was the hand that'd hit me.

'I'm . . . I'm not taking fucking responsibility for that,' he said. 'It's nothing to do with me.' But he wasn't even looking at me, my bare body in his room. He was looking at the mirror instead. 'I could have . . . *Fuck.*' His head swung away and back, still staring. 'I could have had any fucking person I wanted! Any . . . woman. Fucking anyone!'

'*Well why didn't you then!*'

Oliver turned.

'Why didn't you have anyone! Why didn't you just . . . find someone better!' I twisted away from him, looked down at my own tits. 'Why didn't you?'

He didn't answer my question though. He only looked at me.

'I lied about my age,' he said. 'My age is thirty-one.'

'What . . .?'

'Thirty-one. I lied. There, you see! I lied to you!'

He stared, like he was waiting, but I didn't understand. 'Yes,' I said.

'Well *don't you care?* Don't you care that I lied to you? A thirty-one-year-old man!

I lied to you and I fucked you and . . . and I hit you! You've got scars down your *fucking* arms?' He stretched this own out. Like a crucifixion, open wide. 'DON'T YOU CARE?'

'No,' I said quietly. And Oliver looked away.

Behind my back, I heard the rain begin again. It tapped a pattern on the window, clean.

'You should care,' he said softly, but his head had fallen low. And as he took a step away from me, he looked at my face. 'Give me your shirt,' he said.

Oliver washed my shirt. He took it through to the kitchen and I watched him leave without speaking again. Thirty-one, I thought, but the words had no real meaning. And I just sat there on my own.

The phone rang as he closed the washing-machine door. I know because I heard it slam. He wasn't angry though. Not anymore. And it was funny, that brought no feeling either.

'You'd better get that,' he said. I looked up to the sound of is voice, but there was no emotion in the words. They sounded drained, I thought. And after a moment I walked back to the hall. I picked up the receiver.

'Hello?' I said.

But no one answered me.

'Hello?'

Still there was no sound.

The phone line crackled. Silent.

'Who is this?' I said. I closed my eyes, so very tired. 'Is there anybody there?'

And then it was dead.

'Oh,' I said as Oliver came through.

'Who was it?'

I stood up slowly. 'I don't know . . . They didn't say anything.'

'Oh,' he said, but his eyes didn't hold any question. After a moment, he sat down.

'I could hear them breathing,' I said. Shallow, caught-up breaths. Like hurting breaths, they'd been. And I wondered why the sound of them should bother me.

I stood there, listening to the humming of the machine. I felt a little like my head was swimming. Swimming away, and I couldn't quite catch up with it. Thirty-one, I thought again. And I knew there should be some emotion there. I knew there should be something. But standing in his hallway with the empty phone still buzzing in my ear, I felt a little like I'd lost the race. There wasn't any feeling. There was nothing. And all I could do was follow him through.

Dad and Michael were talking in the living room when I got home next evening. I only said hello as I walked past, though. I made straight for the kitchen. And I heard Dad pause, mid conversation, as I passed. I felt him look at me.

I'd heard Mum clunking from a distance, splashing

water as she did the washing-up. I'd heard the clink of dishes on the drainer and the mumbling of Radio 4. I shut the kitchen door behind me, and I dropped my bag down on the floor.

Mum had her back to me, and I could see her hair was coming undone, all straggly around her ponytail, and her apron strings had got caught in the waistband of her jeans. I stood for a moment on the doorstep, silent, only looking at her. I watched her wince away every time the water splashed. I watched the way she bore down on the roast-potato pan, really going for it. I wondered who she was thinking about.

'Mum . . .?'

'Oh. Hi.' She smiled, but her hands didn't stop scrubbing. She turned round, squinting for a moment under the overhead light. She looked a little like a mole, I thought. Coming up for air. Her eyes had lightbulbs shining in them, and her skin was too shiny. I smiled back at her, though. Maybe it was sweat. 'Have a good day at school?'

'Uh-huh,' I said. But it hadn't been a good day, not really. I had sat by Holly in art but she'd hardly spoken to me. She'd brought her Walkman in. Then there was Dawn. I sat down at the table, Mum still busy with the washing-up. She looked up at me and smiled again. Maybe she just couldn't think of much to say.

No, it hadn't been a good day. I guess it was my own fault really, I knew how to make Dawn better. But I couldn't quite bring myself to say sorry. Not yet, I thought, maybe soon. She'd started sitting at a different desk in registration, and every time I looked across at her she only turned away. She'd had a book with her today, and I'd watched her stare down at the pages but she hadn't turned them over. I don't think she'd really been reading. I wasn't angry at her anymore though. I felt too tired to be angry. And with her chin up, paper bookmark getting soggy in the corner of her mouth, I'd watched the way the clouded daylight made her spots fade down. I'd wondered just what she was thinking.

'Dawn . . .?' I'd said quietly. I leaned across my desk to her, glancing up at the teacher.

She'd ignored me.

'Dawn? I . . .' I'd stopped, though, looked down at the table. 'What are you reading?' Her face came slowly up to me and she put one finger on a line. Any line, I thought. She probably didn't even know what book it was. Her hair flopped down on her cheeks, but it was clean, I saw.

'Is it good . . .?' I said.

Dawn looked at me like she was staring at a wall. Apologize, I thought. Apologize was all I had to do. Still, I couldn't quite get it out of my mouth. And I wondered why now was so different. I'd never had any problem before.

'Did you get your biology homework done?' I said.

Dawn didn't answer me, though. And I would have said something else then, offered to help her with her maths. I would have said pretty much anything, I think. Anything except sorry, perhaps. I didn't get the chance to speak at all though.

When I opened my mouth again, I heard the teacher say my name.

And I'd only looked at Dawn.

Looked, as she'd turned back to the page.

Mum flicked the soap off her fingers and she wiped them on her apron. I watched her reach behind her back, undo the strings with one smooth pull. And she turned to face me again.

'Is that a new shirt?'

'Huh?' Mum was still holding the apron in one hand. 'Oh,' I said. I smiled but it only felt sad. 'Oliver washed it for me.'

'Hmm.' She nodded, lacing her hands together on her legs. 'Looks nice,' she said.

'Thanks.'

She came across to me, sagged down into the chair opposite. One of Dad's ashtrays still sat in the middle of the table. It was full of cigarette butts, but she didn't move to empty it. I pushed it with the end of my finger.

'How long since you gave up, now?' I said.

'Two years.'

'Christ,' I said. I pushed it again, and it slid easily. Glass against wood. It reminded me of Oliver's with all its screwed-up bits of paper, chewing-gum wrappers and stuff. I thought of going upstairs, unpacking my bag, maybe listening to my two CDs. Still two. The twenty pounds that Dad had given me was tucked under my bed. I hadn't spent it yet. I'd hardly even thought of it. But I didn't want to go upstairs. I didn't want to be in my room. 'It's a long time,' I said slowly. 'Two years. Don't you think?'

She shrugged. 'Doesn't seem that long.'

'I was finishing the First Year.'

'Yes.'

In the other room I heard Dad's voice rise just above a mutter, Michael laughing. But Michael was always laughing, I thought. Always, when Dad was laughing too. ' . . . I had to take it to Alan's anyway . . .' he said. 'Fucking colour control's gone haywire . . . I knew it was going when Bruce Forsythe started looking good . . .' Giggle giggle giggle.

Mum looked down at the surface of the table, her smile fading slowly away.

'Feels like a long time,' I said. I heard Dad's groan as he got out of his chair. I heard his footsteps cross the room and pass us, up the stairs. I pulled the ashtray back towards me, and it swivelled on my finger. There were matches in there too, I saw, and dust, flicks of ash across the pine. I lifted my arm, careful not to get any on my shirt. 'Mum . . .?' I said. I spoke a bit quieter. 'What was . . . you know, the age gap between you and your boyfriend again?' I scratched at the wood under my fingernails. I didn't catch her eye. Out of the corner of my own, though, I saw her face come up.

'Well, um . . . I was sixteen and he was twenty-six. So ten years.' She laughed. 'Ten years.' She shook her head, pushed the cuticles around one nail. Her hands were pink and pruny from the water. They looked weird, I thought, when I was used to seeing them all grimy from the garden.

'Right,' I said. But it wasn't really what I'd hoped for. I felt a chip of wood peel off under my fingernail. It made a splintering sound, and she looked down. 'Whoops,' I said quietly. And I coughed as I scraped it into the ashtray.

There was a pause, and no sound in the house to distract

us. I wished that I could leave now. I wished Dad would come into the kitchen. He didn't though. I heard him shut the study door, and I guess I sort of had to carry it through.

'I suppose it depends on the people, though, doesn't it?' I was glad when she didn't answer. 'I mean . . . ten years could be a lot between . . . two other people. But between you and him it was . . . nothing.' I watched her but she only nodded. 'Like, between me and Oliver, it's nothing. I mean, the gap could be *bigger* and it wouldn't make any difference.' I watched her. Her eyes were focused and clear, looking back.

'Yes,' she said. 'I s'pose so.'

'Could be loads bigger,' I said. 'Without making any difference. Don't you think . . .?'

'That depends on how much bigger,' she said. 'Doesn't it.'

I didn't look at her. 'Well . . . Could be *loads* bigger, couldn't it? Could be *anything*, really . . .' I paused. 'Could be seventeen years,' I said.

And with that, Mum was quiet for a moment.

I picked at my nail with one finger and it was sore where the splinter had gone in. I kept my head down low. And in the background, our old gutter was banging.

'Christ,' Mum said, and I watched her laugh. Her hand was pulling at the lines around her mouth, and she wouldn't look at me. 'Seventeen?' She raised her eyes up to my level and I could see sleep there in the corners. 'What do you mean . . .?'

'I . . .' My nail was picking again. Picking, and I couldn't seem to stop it now. There was dirt in them, I saw. And it looked brown against the skin. 'He ... he told me last night. He ... he said he was sorry and everything, for lying to me. And if I'd known ... I would have told you.' I looked at her, and she didn't break away. 'I would have.'

She nodded.

'It doesn't make any difference, though, does it? I mean ... you've met him. You know how nice he is. The number doesn't change anything ... Not when we're happy.'

'*Are* you happy?' she said slowly.

Her eyes felt weighted on my skin.

But I didn't hesitate before I said yes.

'That ... that is the most important thing.'

'Because when two people are happy together ... when ... when they love each other, it doesn't matter how old they are, does it? Nothing matters,' I said. '*You* know that.'

'Yes,' she said. She nodded hard, but her gaze slid away from me.

'Like you and your boyfriend,' I said quietly, and that was when she looked up. 'You were in love with each other ... and it didn't make any difference how old you were, but you didn't tell your parents, right? Because you couldn't ... you couldn't trust them or whatever.' I held her eyes. 'But I can trust you, you know? Because you ... you understand and everything. I can trust you,' I said. 'Can't I?'

'There ... there's a big difference between ten years and seventeen,' she said. She shook her head and I watched her eyes skid easily away. 'And I was sixteen, I was two years older than you. I mean, seventeen years . . . God, that makes him thirty-one.'

'Yes,' I said. She was still shaking her head, swishing back and forth as she spoke. I looked away from her.

'Nevermind,' I said quietly. I drew my hand slowly from the tabletop. 'Nevermind.' But my hand didn't get quite to the edge of the wood. She stopped it halfway there, when she put her own on top.

'Don't . . . don't go,' she said.

I looked up.

Her hand was hot, still wrinkly from the washing-up, and I didn't like the feel of it on mine. She was smiling. It dragged her mouth up at the corners and made her forehead sag.

'You can . . .' She glanced away, over the draining board. 'You can trust me.'

'Are you sure?' I didn't move my hand. 'He'd just worry.'

'Yes,' she said. She nodded at me and I felt her fingers flex on top of mine. 'It . . . it doesn't make that much difference, I s'pose.'

'Thank you,' I said.

Mum shrugged away from me. And looking at her face then, her hair skew-whiff across it, I thought about my school bag. I thought about it, lying in the corner. And I smiled.

'Hang on a sec,' I said. But even though she hadn't moved, Mum was busy already. Her eyes were moving out across the units, for things to make and clean and do. She took her hand away from mine, and I reached behind me for my bag.

The sandwich box was sitting on top of all my books, next to my D&T folder. It was Tupperware, like one of those things that women sell at parties. It was Oliver's. Which sort of made me wonder where he'd got it from. I couldn't imagine him sitting round with all those wives.

I picked it off of the top of my bag. I put it on the table as she turned back towards me.

'What's that?' she said. Her voice was light, small talk, I thought. But she didn't look at me.

'Oliver made me some sandwiches this morning. They were gorgeous, loads of them.'

'I thought you didn't like sandwiches,' she said. 'I'll always make you sandwiches . . .'

'Well, I didn't have any dinner money today.' I took the lid off. 'I just wondered if you'd like one,' I said. I smiled up at her. I pushed the box forward.

'I can have a fresh sandwich . . .'

'Mmm. Well, I just wondered. They're so nice. Seems like a shame to waste them.' They were nice too. Sitting in their kitchen foil. We never had kitchen foil in our house. I'd have to remind Mum to get some.

'Oh.' She peered into the box. That was Ok, though, she couldn't see inside. 'What's in them?'

'Oh loads of stuff. They're just . . . really nice sandwiches. Like . . . um, lettuce and tomato and onion. Mayonnaise . . . lettuce . . .' I thought about him standing there, bent over his little kitchen unit and fitting them together. He'd smiled at me when I'd walked in. Smiled, and said they were for me. 'Bacon . . .' I said. And I watched her.

'*Bacon?* I don't eat meat anymore. I haven't touched

bacon for . . . twenty years.' She didn't take her eyes off the box, though. 'Fried or grilled?' She didn't sound bothered.

'Grilled.'

'I always liked it grilled . . . God,' she said again. 'I haven't had bacon for years . . .'

I smiled. 'It was your favourite, you said.'

I heard Dad's footsteps from upstairs, then. Coming, heavy, just like they had before. I glanced at Mum, but I guess she hadn't heard them. She was still looking at the box. And that was when she laughed.

'Well God. It can't hurt, can it.'

I could hear Dad coming down the stairs. And I wondered vaguely why it mattered. But Mum reached into the box, then.

The bread was soft and white. Proper bread, from a baker's, not just Sunblest from the shop on the corner. The lettuce still looked fresh and it poked out round the edges.

It poked out while she took a bite.

She smiled around the crust. Smiled at me, and it was good to see her smiling. A piece of tomato fell out of the opposite side. I watched it fall. I watched her put a hand out to save it. But she didn't pick it up when she missed.

'Oh yes,' she said. She laughed again. A little bit of bacon was dangling from her mouth and I watched her as she sucked it in. 'Really nice,' she said. And she nodded at me.

'Is it?' I looked at her face. 'I'm glad,' I said.

Mum took another bite.

'Well,' I said. 'There's another one in the box if you'd like it.'

She nodded, sandwich bouncing up and down. And that was when the door opened. Her hand froze in front of her mouth, teeth halfway through. I turned around too quickly. Dad had to duck a bit, coming through the kitchen door. He was breathing, deep and heavy. Staring at the floor.

He saw her, though.

He saw her, looking up.

'What's that?' he said.

'Cheese sandwich,' she said back.

And she didn't look away.

Still, I had to wonder why she'd lied to him.

After all, it wasn't like we had anything to hide.

I stood in the doorway to my bedroom for quite a long time. I held my bag on my right shoulder and I looked into the room. I still hadn't unpacked it, my bag. It seemed that I never got a chance to take the crap out of it these days. It made me think back to First Year, for ages there'd been this funny smell hanging around that I couldn't quite work out. Everyone seemed to talk to me from a distance. It was only when the PE teacher finally decided to rifle it for tampons that I understood. Her hand came out coated in slimy yellow sludge and she had to vomit in the showers. Personally, I didn't think it was that gross. The banana had only been there three weeks or so, and at least it explained why all my books looked like someone with sinus trouble had sneezed in their direction. It had an upside too: the PE teacher never mentioned my period again.

It seemed funny, thinking back to it, but it hadn't been so hysterical at the time. No one really likes to have friends that smell of rotting fruit.

I shifted the bag against my collarbone. There just didn't seem much point in moving. Until Dad shouted 'PHONE!'

I dropped my bag on the floor, hearing the crack as my pencil tin fell open. It used to mean a lot to me, that tin, with the names of my friends written over it. The names were still there now of course, but it wasn't quite the same. Oliver'd told me it was childish, writing names across your things. And walking down the stairs again, I didn't glance back. It used to be important, I thought. I wondered what was important now.

'Hello?' I said in the receiver. Standing with my back to the wall, I felt my breath mist back up at me. Cold condensation on the plastic. I didn't sit down to talk to Oliver, I hardly ever did these days. We never talked for long enough.

'Hi.' His voice came out flat from the phone line. Leaning back, I watched the ceiling.

'How are you?' I said.

'I was Ok till your fucking father picked up the phone. What *is* his bloody *problem?*'

'What? He . . . he's fine. He's just tired. Did he sound a bit grumpy or something?'

'*Christ!*' His voice echoed away from my ear, and I

wondered if he'd turned his head away. 'It's *rude*. There's no excuse! All I am is fucking *polite* to the guy!'

'I'm . . . sure he didn't like *mean* to do anything.'

'Come off it! *Oh*, he goes. *It's you*. I don't need that kind of shit! It fucks me off! Screaming at the top of his voice. Can you really blame me?'

'I was up in my room.'

'Don't make fucking *excuses* for him! There's no excuse for being rude! I don't give a *fuck* if he's tired. I shouldn't have to deal with *his* shit.' I heard his anger fade to silence. For a while, he just breathed. 'Look, I phoned to ask if you'd called me.'

'Called you? How'd you mean?'

'For fuck's sake, *called me*. On the *telephone?* Thing you're holding to your ear?'

I bit my lip. I'm sorry, I thought. But I tried not to say it. 'No . . . I didn't call.' There was silence. I wondered if I should have apologized after all. My hand wanted to reach up, touch the opposite arm. I couldn't do it, though, not with the phone by my ear.

'You didn't just ring me then,' he said.

'No.' A radio went on in the kitchen. A babble of voices, and I tried to think. 'Why?'

'Someone keeps calling me. I thought it might be you. Some kind of fucking joke.'

'Like . . .' I cleared my throat. 'Like last night?' I said. 'When I answered it?'

'Oh.' I heard him sigh. 'Yeah . . . I thought it was a wrong number the first time. They don't say anything, so I thought . . .' He trailed off. 'I don't know. Forget it,' he said. But I wasn't going to forget it. I opened my mouth to say something. And I saw Dad.

'Can you hurry up,' he said. He leaned through the door. 'I need to use the phone.'

'What?' I looked at him. Oliver's breathing rattled in one ear.

'*The phone.*' Dad stared at me. 'Can you hurry *up*. I need to use it. It's important.'

'But . . .' I watched his face. 'So's this.'

'Come off it,' he said. He turned his head from me. 'You can talk to him any time.'

'But . . .'

'Look, I'm not going to have a fucking *discussion* about it. Just get off it. Alright?'

I didn't say anything else. I just watched him turn his back as he walked out.

'*God . . .*' I said softly as I turned back to the phone. There wasn't any answer, though.

Oliver was gone.

The trek back up the stairs seemed to take a very long time, and my legs didn't want to lift up. Back to my room, I thought vaguely. But I didn't really want to get there. I guess it was just another place. *Can you really blame me*, I thought, and I felt a smile curl up my lip. Because I couldn't. Funny that.

I sniffed. The sheet on my bed had come untucked. It was hanging, grey, over the mattress. There was a stain on one corner, but I didn't know what it was. I didn't care. Exercise books scattered out across the floor. Lying with their pages bent beneath them, and far too many gaps that should be copied up. Tippex on every cover. Some stupid word, I thought, and sniffed again. A plate. A cup. A spoon, and I wondered why that was, I couldn't remember using a spoon up here. But then I couldn't think what I had eaten off that plate. I couldn't think of anything. The carpet was dirty. The clothes weren't washed. I could see the head of a Barbie doll in the corner. Her hair had been cut off with a pair of scissors. Close-cropped over her plastic skull. I always was the jealous type, though. Not that I could think of when I'd done it. It might have been years ago. The paint on her blue eyes was rubbing off. Either that or corroding. I'd used to squeeze that head between my thumb and finger just to watch her forehead bulge, I think. Just to watch her nose double back into those high cheekbones, and her eyes would squish together in the middle of her face. And when you did it really fast, when you popped her in and out as quick as possible, her head would make a sucking noise. Like gobbing someone off, I thought. I guess it didn't really matter who.

My portfolio was leaned against the wall, but none of the stuff in there mattered either. It was stupid, childish shit with too-sharp lines across the paper. A hair-dryer and a towel, a cigarette lighter, and a copy of *More!* Must have been from a while ago, though. Must have been a long while. There were hats, and I could see the screwdrivers I'd got Dad to do my stereo with. And I wondered if the stereo was something that mattered. Because there had to be something. In this whole room full of useless stupid childish shit there had to be a single thing that mattered. One thing, I thought. Just one was all.

I stared for a long time, though, standing by the doorway. I stared for ages and I didn't find that thing.

Maybe that was why I started cleaning.

I was standing with my back to the door when Dad's cough came from behind me. Holding a toy car in my hand, I was trying to work out where it might have come from. And I'd known it was him before he coughed. I'd known by the way his feet worked slowly on the floor.

I didn't turn around.

'I . . . uh . . . I was just looking for something to wash with this tie. It's got toothpaste on the front, looks like. God knows how it got there.' His voice faded out. 'Have you got anything?'

I stared down at the car. Red, a Ford Capri maybe, I wasn't sure. And all the paint had peeled off round the wheel arches. It wasn't mine.

I snorted quietly, and I knew that he could hear it.

I turned round to look at him.

He was leaning back against the wall, his shoulder ruffling the corner of my Nirvana poster. He had a beer can in one hand, his tie in the other, and I could see a little bit of chest hair coming up through the collar of his shirt. Kurt Cobain smirked at me over Dad's head, sitting on the top of his skip, and I could see the tights he was wearing through the holes in his jeans. Dad was frowning at the floor.

'I thought you needed to use the phone.'

'I'm expecting a call.'

'That's not what you said before.'

I stared at him.

'Didn't I?' He raised his eyebrows at me lightly, but his gaze still skirted the floor.

'No.'

'Well . . .' he said. 'That's . . . that's what I meant.' He looked up. 'It is important.' He watched me for a moment, but I didn't move. 'Well,' he said, and he shrugged at me. 'Have you got anything?'

'No.'

'What about . . .' I watched him shake his hand in my direction. 'About all that stuff?'

I looked away. 'Oliver said he'd do my washing for me.'

'*Oliver?*'

'Yes,' I said. 'Oliver.'

'Why? We've got a washing machine here, in case you didn't . . .' He stopped.

'He did this shirt for me. Last night.' I looked at him. 'It's good, don't you think?'

'Looks exactly the same as normal.'

'I think it looks cleaner,' I said. I watched his eyes fall back, away from me. 'And Mum did.'

He shrugged. 'So . . . Oliver's going to be doing your washing from now on then.'

He snorted. 'Is that s'posed to be some kind of dig?'

'No.' I didn't take my eyes off him.

'Right . . .'

He laughed again, but the sound was weak. In my hand, I turned the toy car round. I didn't say anything.

'Oh come *on* . . .' He looked up. He was smirking too, now. Just like Kurt. But I didn't think it looked so real. 'For fuck's sake, I needed to use the *phone*.'

'I know,' I said.

He opened his mouth to speak again. Nothing came out. And after a minute, he sighed.

'Christ,' he said. He shook his head. 'I think you're being pretty fucking childish, I have to say.'

I watched.

'It's just the *phone*, for God's sake. You can call him later.' He threw his eyes up to the ceiling. 'You can call him *any time*. What's the big deal? Look . . .' He nodded his head at the clothes in the corner. Shitty dirty clothes. 'Let me take that stuff down and wash it. Ok?'

'It doesn't need washing, Dad.' I looked away. 'Just leave it there.'

'Of course it needs washing.' He took a step towards me, then. I don't know what he expected me to do. I didn't move, though. And I guess he sort of had to stop. He breathed out. He took a swig of beer, and I thought of Oliver's voice on the crackly phone line. I thought of him hanging up, and I felt my stomach roll.

Dad took the can from his mouth, and his hand moved up to his forehead. I watched him rub his eyes, the tie dangling from his fist.

'It's just the phone,' he said again. He stared into the eye hole of his can.

'I'm not having a dig,' I said quietly.

I turned the car again, looked down at it. There was a dent in the bumper, I saw. Head-on collision with pebble. I breathed.

'Really,' I said.

'Well why the hell can't I wash my tie then?'

'You can wash your tie,' I said. 'It's . . . it's got nothing to do with me.'

He was quiet then, and all I could do was listen to it. I couldn't think of anything to say. Maybe there wasn't anything. I don't know. But standing there, I kind of wished there'd been a lock on my door.

'I'm . . . I didn't mean to . . . you know, to piss you off telling you to hurry up.' There was a whistling sound as he blew the air from his cheeks. 'It really was important. *Is*,' he said quickly. 'It *is* important . . . But . . . look, I didn't mean to piss you off, alright?'

I nodded.

'So will you let me wash that stuff?'

'I . . . Oliver's going to wash it for me, Dad.' I raised my head. 'I'm not being funny.'

'*Look*, I *told* you I didn't mean to piss you off! *Jesus Christ!* What do you want? A written *fucking* apology? It was *important!* It's a lot of fucking *hassle* keeping things together here!'

'THAT'S NOT MY PROBLEM!'

Dad stopped.

He stared at me.

And there was a clunk as the little red Capri fell on to my carpet.

'I . . .'

It had fallen on its side, one wheel spinning like the dead kid's bicycle in a Green Cross Code video.

'I . . .'

My mouth felt very dry, looking down at it. The plastic windscreen dirty grey from dust. I didn't move, though. It was better than seeing Dad's face.

'Shit,' I said softly.

And I bent down to pick it up.

The metal was still warm from my hand, and my fingers scraped grit in the carpet when I reached. I could hear Dad's breathing, and after a few long seconds, the sound of him drinking his beer. I didn't stand up, just crouched on the carpet. I held the toy car in my hand, and I closed my eyes.

'Ford Capri,' Dad said. There was a croak in his voice. Low, almost whispering. I didn't look at him, though. I didn't look at anything. And behind my eyelids, I watched red slide into black. 'It's . . . uh . . .' He coughed. 'It's Michael's isn't it? I think I gave it to him . . . a couple of birthdays ago.' He trailed back into silence.

I didn't make a sound.

'Eighth maybe,' he said. 'Or seventh . . .'

'I . . .' I held it out, palm open. 'Give it back to him if you want. I . . . I don't want it.'

He didn't reach out and take it, though. I opened my eyes a little at a time, and Dad hadn't moved at all. Still, he stood against the wall, his shirt ruffled out around his stomach, beer can just as it had been before. Veins lined the back of that hand, a purple kind of colour, and the skin was faded. Transparent.

Kurt's expression hadn't changed. I wondered if my own had. And after a moment, I closed my hand again.

'I don't think he'd want it anymore,' Dad said.

'No . . .' I glanced away. 'No. You're probably right.'

My knees popped as I stood up, and I could see the curtains shifting slightly in the wind. Shifting, I thought, like they had on that first night Oliver had stayed. I kept my eyes there anyway.

'Shouldn't you go and use the phone?' I said. My voice sounded too hard. 'If . . . if they haven't called you, I mean.'

'They . . . oh, it doesn't matter. They won't be there now,' he said.

'I'm sorry.'

He shrugged. 'Like you said, it's not your problem.'

I had to look away then. I watched a moth flutter in, head straight for the lightbulb. It looked brown and dusty and the wings made clicking noises on the lampshade. I listened to the crackle of my poster as Dad leaned his head back against the wall.

'Well . . .' he said. 'I guess I'll go and wash this in the sink. If you change your mind or anything . . .'

I didn't answer.

He sniffed.

I listened to him take a final swig.

'I'll . . . I'll see you later,' he said. I only nodded. 'I'll help you with your art if you want.' He turned away. 'You know I'll always help you. With anything,' he said. He breathed out as he reached for the handle.

'Dad . . .'

He paused.

Dad. I'm sorry.

The words almost formed, I opened up to say them.

I'm sorry.

Knees numb from the carpet, I wanted to say them. I wanted it very much.

I'm sorry for everything.

I guess the truth was that I couldn't. Not now. Things had gone too far for that, and wanting something didn't make it any different. Dad didn't wait for long. And as I listened to his feet trail down the stairs, I shut my mouth. Unspoken.

I counted my possessions out in black plastic bags. Fifteen in all, and it took me hours to fill them. I started with the little things, toys and stuff. Pens, books and the posters off my wall. I took Kurt down. I was sick of him smirking at me anyway. Hats and old clothes and underwear that'd been ripped for years. Old make-up, tubes of face cream, ruined tapes. Madonna and Prince and stuff like that. Folders full of things I'd drawn when I was little. I found the body to my Barbie head as well. I guess I'd known it'd be there somewhere. I didn't try to fit them back together, though, just dumped them in with everything else. I didn't watch them fall.

The bags got heavy pretty quickly, nothing fitted too well. My things made awkward shapes, sticking at the plastic. They made stretch marks across the shiny black. And they broke against each other when I carried them down for the dustbins. Seven trips. I managed to carry three on the last one.

I stood them up against the garden wall. Fifteen, in a funny little row. They reminded me of Tweedledum and Tweedledee. A whole class of them. Fat kids waiting to be punished. It was raining that day but very cold as well. The cold got down into my chest, breathing too hard. It misted the air up in front of me as I stared at them. I cracked my back, stretched my arms behind my head and I breathed. Staring at them. The drizzle hung in the air around me, sort of sweating on my cheeks. I watched the plastic catch it, just like my skin. Dribbles on the lumps and bumps of black. Pricks of moisture, gathering themselves up till they got strong enough to fall.

One of Barbie's legs was sticking out, I think, had punctured through. But that's what you get for having stupid pointy toes. The cold stung my nostrils when I sniffed. Her tan didn't look so great in the December rain. It didn't look so great at all. Not tearing through black polythene. It looked, I thought, a little like a body bag.

It was funny, I suppose. Standing in the cold and staring at them. Funny, I thought. But maybe sad as well. Because looking at them there, I hadn't even known which things were in which bags. I couldn't even guess, the way I'd thrown them in together. Collecting puddles in the winter air, it might not have even been my stuff, I thought. It might have been a stranger's.

And I was kind of glad to hear Mum's voice behind me.

'You alright there?'

She said it softly, standing in the doorway, but I thought her smile looked put on anyway.

'Huh? Yeah . . .'

'Lots of stuff,' she said.

'Yeah . . .'

'Dustmen'll probably wonder what the hell's going on.'

'Hm,' I said. But it didn't sound much like a laugh. Not even to me.

'So what's next, then?'

'Hmm? Oh. Painting probably. I don't really know.'

'What colour you painting it?'

I shrugged. 'White. Same as before. Just . . . just a new coat, you know?' I listened to her sniff, and shivered in my jumper. I didn't want to stand here anymore.

'I should repaint the kitchen at some point, actually,' she said.

'Well it doesn't need it yet.'

She didn't answer, shrugged back at me instead. And I followed her through as she turned to go inside.

'So,' she said. 'When d'you think you'll have it finished?'

'Dunno, really.' I glanced back out through the door, but I couldn't see them from this angle. I was glad. Which made me wonder why I'd bothered to look back in the first place.

'Oh,' she said. 'Right.'

I shut the door behind me, watched her stop by the sofa. She stared out through the french windows, her back turned to me. Her shoulders slumped down in a funny way.

'Christmas maybe . . .?' I waited for her to answer. I sort of hoped she would.

'Right,' she said again. 'God. Christmas. I ought to dig the tree up soon as well.'

'Mm,' I said, but it wasn't much of an answer. 'Do you . . . d'you want to come up and see my room? Looks bizarre with all the stuff taken out. Do you want to see it?'

'Huh?'

She twisted round, one hand on the arm of the sofa, to look at me.

Her face looked funny, I thought. Slack and kind of blank, and the hand on the sofa seemed too light. She smiled at me, though. Even if it was only her lips that moved.

'Yeah . . .' she said. 'Yeah, Ok.'

'Good,' I said. I nodded. But she missed the smile I gave her back, walking already into the hallway.

'Gosh,' she said quietly, when she reached the top of the stairs.

It did look bizarre, my room. And with the clutter taken out, it was easier to see the work that had to be done. The walls were covered in peels and scratches, places where my posters had come down. The carpet was filthy with dust. In the corner, I'd sat two cardboard boxes: the only stuff I was going to keep. School books mostly, a few bits of clothing. And my stereo, of course. My bed was stripped down to bare wood, the mattress in the spare room, airing. Not that there was much air in the spare room, what with the stink of cat piss and mouldy orange peel. Not airing maybe, then. Gasping, perhaps.

'Yeah . . .' I said. 'Yeah, it does look weird, doesn't it.' I wanted to add something else, something that might make it a little less harsh. There was nothing I could think of though.

Mum didn't answer me, she only looked around. 'Have you looked through all that stuff? I mean . . . so much of it. There's bound to be some things worth keeping. Could put them in the spare room, maybe.'

'Yes . . .' I watched her, trying to think how to say it. 'It's just that . . . I don't really want to keep them, Mum. That's why I've put them out by the dustbins.'

'But there must be loads of stuff in there.' She looked at me.

'Well there is. Loads of stuff. And . . . and it's all stuff I don't really want to keep.'

'But . . . but other people might want it.'

'Mmm,' I said. I couldn't really picture them though: the kind of person with a gap in their life that could be filled by a beheaded Barbie doll. *Just what I've always wanted!*

'I . . . I don't want them kept, Mum. I don't want anyone to keep them.' In the tiny pause, I bit my lip. 'Do you understand?'

Mum frowned a little as she stared at me, a soft, dumb frown. There were too many lines around her mouth.

'Yes,' she said quietly. I watched her mouth close as she looked away. 'Yes. I suppose so.'

I smiled at her, then. I thought about her thin little

mouth, the way she'd grinned around that sandwich. And I smiled because I wanted to.

'So!' She clapped her hands together, hard, and it sounded very loud in my empty room. Loud, and she gave up, rubbing them together in front of her like she didn't know what else to do. 'All your stuff's in those boxes, is it? Your stereo . . .' she said. 'And your CDs?'

'Well I've only got two.' Still only two, I thought. I hadn't bought the third. And my smile faded slowly away.

'Yes,' she said. 'Yes . . . of course.' She nodded again. 'Oh! What about your dress? The one Oliver gave you.' She didn't stop to hear me answer, though. And I didn't interrupt. 'It is gorgeous, that dress. Really . . . really *special.*'

'Yes . . .' I said. 'It's, uh . . . it's folded in the little box.' I tried to think of something else to say about it, but there wasn't anything. I shrugged, looked away from her.

'You'll never find another one like it, you know. And it fits you so well too. Could have been made for you.'

There was quiet for a moment.

'You know,' I said. 'You could try it on if you want.'

'Try it on?' She looked at me, and laughed. 'No. I don't think so.'

'Well why not? It's in the box there.' She glanced over at it, sitting in the corner.

'No . . .' Her gaze didn't move, though. 'No,' she said. 'It's yours.'

'Well, I know . . . but you can still try it on. I don't . . . I don't wear it much.'

But she turned her head, then, away from the boxes. I

watched her clap her hands for the second time, but she didn't seem to have anything to say that might go with it.

'No,' she said again. 'No, wouldn't suit me. Mutton dressed as lamb.' She laughed.

'Mutton dressed as lamb?' I snorted. Still, I had to look away.

'Well . . .' She flexed her fingers on the edge of the wood.

'Mum . . . you're not *mutton* dressed as *lamb.*' My laugh came again, but it sounded tinny without any clutter to soak up the noise. I looked at her, folding her hands in the front, resting against one trouser leg. The Sta-Prest slack type, I saw. 'That's . . . that's a stupid thing to say . . . I bet it'd look good on you.' My voice faded out. Pathetic. Mum didn't speak.

'You're *not* . . .' I said again. I picked at one nail with another. They were pretty clean, though. She smiled at me. It was a good effort, I thought.

'I didn't mean anything by it,' she said. 'Anyway, you've got it all packed up.'

'It's right on top. It's no hassle . . . please . . . I'd . . . I'd like to see you in it.'

Mum turned to me again, but this time the smile was gone from her face. She rubbed one hand down the side of her leg. 'No,' she said quietly. 'That's fine.'

I had to look away from her, staring like that. And I wondered why I was embarrassed. The chips in the paint showed through mint green, I saw. But I couldn't remember the room ever being mint green. There were tiny shadows cast from overhead by the peels that had sprung up, away from dry plasterboard. The boards underneath my bed had warped as well.

Mum sighed. I listened to her footsteps as she moved away from me, towards the bed. I listened to creaking as she sat down. Funny, I thought. It'd never creaked like that with me lying on it.

'Mum . . .' I said.

'Uh-huh?'

But there was no way I could put it, really. No way that didn't sound stupid. I looked at her. Her hands were flat on the wood either side of her legs, and her head hung down, symmetrical. She was wearing loafers, I saw. Old ones, and they looked baggy round her feet.

'Nothing,' I said.

'I'm not doing some big thing,' she said. 'It's Ok.'

'I know,' I said. There was a *but* in there somewhere, though. I just couldn't find it.

'It probably wouldn't fit me anyway.' She shrugged. 'It's no big deal . . . I mean, you reach a certain age . . . you have to accept that. Like I see them in the street,' she said. 'These women. And they're my age, you know, and still wearing miniskirts and high heels.' She shook her head. 'They all look very old.'

'You don't look old,' I said.

She didn't answer.

'You don't look like mutton dressed as lamb either.' I laughed. 'That's Dad in his Tony Hancock T-shirt.'

I watched Mum's mouth pick up into a giggle. It fell out, and the hand that shot to cover it missed by half a second.

'That's not true,' she said.

Her eyes were crinkled over the knuckles hiding her lips.

I smiled again, though. And I felt a little bad when she looked away.

'I . . . I ought to go and do the washing-up.'

I nodded. 'Ok.'

Mum got up slowly. She was quiet as she stood in the doorway.

'Your . . . your room looks good, anyway,' she said.

'Thanks . . .'

She nodded, didn't move.

'You . . . you will put *some* stuff back, won't you?'

'Course,' I said. 'Yeah, course I will.'

But even then I knew I wouldn't. There was no point in clearing if things were going to stay the same. Standing in my empty room, I turned in a slow full circle. It seemed to stretch out too far on either side of me. It seemed to be too big. And there was nothing left of those little reminders, things with memories stained on. I sniffed, with my arms hugged around me. I'll be finished by Christmas, I thought.

You can always tell when Christmas starts creeping up in our house, because Mum starts making me wear my winter coat; one of the polyester ones that make a sound like nails being dragged down a blackboard every time you move. Every year she makes me wear it, just in case I get struck down with hypothermia between the school gates and the bus. Every December she takes it out and always just before the end of school term. Presumably so that the lasting image in all my fellow pupils' minds will be me, waving Merry Christmas, wrapped in a three-foot-long, neon-pink hot-water-bottle cover.

It doesn't seem to matter where I hide it either. Behind the fridge, underneath the sofa – I'd chosen the newspaper pile in the porch this year – Mum could always find it. She had a nose for it, I think, like a sniffer-dog. And every year she'd hold it out, all squeaky and nylon and pink. She'd smile at me and say

'Funny, I found your winter coat wrapped in inch-thick steel chains, buried under the floorboards in the living room. I wonder how it could have got there.'

Every year.

It's kind of like a Christmas ritual. One of the many Christmas rituals really, because Christmas has always been important in our house. More important than birthdays, even. It's a family thing; just the four of us. Well, the four of us and the cat, anyway. But then the cat's never been much into Christmas. He doesn't like nut roast. I don't like nut roast either. But I don't make a big deal out of it by spraying diarrhoea round the base of the tree.

We don't have a proper Christmas tree in our house, and I suppose that's one of the rituals too. Mum refuses to buy a proper tree because it's cruel to waste a tree's life over frivolous, disposable convention. A tree is for life, not just for decorating with small shiny objects. So, instead, we have the same tree every year: dug out of the garden and replaced on New Year's Day. It's about eight feet tall now, and it's not even Christmas-tree-shaped. It's normal-tree-shaped, which makes it kind of difficult to walk past, what with all the limbs sticking out and branches getting in your face. We have to water it to stop it dying. It wouldn't be so bad, I guess, except that the tree doesn't even appreciate it. It has razor-sharp needles, all of them pointing outwards, and they puncture the skin at every single opportunity. We have to put on protective gloves to decorate it.

Sometimes it draws blood though, even through the gloves. Sitting there, all innocent and full of seasonal good wishes, it's easy to think that that Christmas tree means no harm. Then it stabs you when you turn your back. Everyone spends Christmas Day opening their presents with plasters on each finger. And I sort of have to laugh, seeing it covered in our cat's diarrhoeic shit.

Mum makes a pudding every year. I guess it's the only time she has an excuse. She puts half a bottle of sherry in it, and every time Dad finds the pound coin in his bowl they have a huge great row. Even if she's washed it first. Even if she's disinfected it.

We're each allowed one present on Christmas Eve, but it has to be a boring present. From an aunt or an uncle or one of those other people who want to make absolutely sure that you never run out of talcum powder. Never ever a good present, never a big one.

On Christmas Day we watch whatever's on opposite the Queen. Out of protest, I think. Like it's going to make a difference. But I guess that's part of the ritual too. Part of it maybe, but not the biggest part. Because the biggest part of Christmas is just being together.

The four of us. A family.

It's always been that way.

And I knew it always would be. I knew that it would be the same this year as it had in every other. The tree and the nut roast, getting back on the last day of term and wrapping up the presents. They were definite things, things that you could run your clock by. Things that would never change. No matter what else had happened, Christmas would stay the same.

I knew it would. And I wondered why that brought no smile.

I went to Oliver's on the last day of term, and I didn't phone Dad to tell him. Our phone at home hadn't worked for a good three or four days. Dad said it was something to do with the line but I had a feeling it was just sulking. It had looked kind of bored for weeks.

He hadn't left the keys in the lock for me. No reason why he should have, I guess, he hadn't known I was coming. Still, though, standing and staring at the blank white paint across his door, it made me feel weird, as though I shouldn't be there. The house was very quiet underneath and I sniffed. I watched my silhouette, still in school uniform, move in grey across the door. Raised brushstrokes, they caught the darker side of twilight. I didn't even know why I'd come.

Taking a deep breath, I gave one little knock. They'd be missing me at home by now, I thought. And I knocked again, just harder this time.

It was funny, thinking about him as I listened to his

footsteps. They were shuffling, kind of messy behind the door. Funny, because I should have felt something, waiting to see his face for the first time in a while. There should have been some movement in my stomach. That's the way it always is in books. There should have been some feeling. There wasn't any feeling, though, just a single, quiet thump. Just a click as he pulled back the latch.

I got my smile on.

Oliver was drunk. I knew it from the moment that the door cracked open. Maybe I knew it before. He opened it two inches, his fingers bent around the frame. His eyes were in the gap.

For a moment, then, he saw me grinning for him. I watched my face hit his retina, I watched it travel down the optic nerve. It took him ten seconds to process.

'Hi,' he said finally. His voice was very thick.

'Hi!' I bent towards him, into the smell round his face. 'I thought you didn't recognize me or something.' My kiss caught the side of his jaw. I heard him make some wet sound, his lips three inches from my face. 'God, I've missed you,' I said.

'I've missed you too.' I watched him turn away, back towards the living room. His skin looked very red, and I could see the blemishes that never seemed to be there in the day. It had lines, creases, and it sagged in the places where it shouldn't. His shoulders lifted in a shrug, his head rocking like it wasn't bolted to them well enough. And when he walked away from me, I sort of had no choice but to follow.

CDs were lying everywhere on the carpet, lyrics sheets pulled out. The cable from a set of headphones snaked out where he'd let it fall. There was the ashtray and a tall glass tumbler half full of something fizzy. I watched his weight shift too quickly to one side. Vodka, I thought. Vodka and something else that didn't matter. He had the lamps on in the corners, slicking little circles of yellow on the carpet. The rest of the room was too dim. The mirror was gone from the wall, but I couldn't see it on the television either.

Oliver sat with a thump, picked up a burning cigarette, and he didn't say a thing.

'How are you then?' I said. I didn't move from my place by the doorway. I didn't take my gloves off. 'Are you Ok?' I wished I could reach over and kiss him again, not have to think of anything to say. He was too far away to kiss, though, and I couldn't walk to him.

He shrugged.

'What've you been doing?'

'Oh . . . loads. You know. I've been really really busy.' His head dragged a little to one side. Really busy, I thought. I looked at the glass by his hand. I wondered if the refills had hit double figures yet. Busy.

'Uh-huh?' I said. 'What, like work and stuff?'

'Yeah . . . work.' His sigh sounded like a cartoon and he kept staring a second too long, like he'd forgotten he was looking at me at all. I coughed a little, listening to the ticking of music from his headphones. I rubbed my gloves together.

'Well,' I said.

348

He didn't answer, though.

'I really have missed you, you know.'

His grin stretched out, too many teeth and not enough flesh. He was aiming it at my face, I think. He missed.

I opened my mouth to say something else, something pointless and empty and quick. I didn't say it. Instead I only looked at him. He didn't seem to notice.

I suppose there was a reason why I'd come, even if it was small and not enough on its own for a twenty-minute walk. Half a reason, maybe, but at least it was something to say.

'I was wondering if you wanted to come and stay for Christmas.'

'Christmas,' he said, no meaning in the word.

Just like there was no real meaning in the invitation. I didn't feel any overwhelming urge to celebrate the festive season with him. I hadn't felt any urge for that, even when I'd first had the idea. But then I hadn't really been thinking of Oliver when I'd had the idea. It was rituals that I'd been thinking of. Presents and sprouts and how Dad would remind us we were having a good time. Looking at Oliver, I bit my lip. I didn't want to think that.

'Will you come?' I said.

'Why?'

'Well, I . . . I just thought it would be nice.' My voice died out but Oliver's eyes kept on at me. I don't know, maybe it was just the vodka.

'Nice,' he said. 'Oh yeah. I just can't wait to sit around watching your parents tear chunks out of each other, listening to your father be a rude fucking arsehole and . . . and . . .'

I was glad when he didn't finish.

I stared at the carpet, his words churning round. But I didn't answer back. Rituals, I thought. I wanted to leave.

'You know what your father's fucking problem is?' Oliver's hand flicked up and down at the carpet as he squinted at me. 'He's *fucking* selfish, that's what his problem is. He's a fucking self-obsessed bitter old man. I watch the way he looks at me, just fucking jealous cos he's never done anything with his small-town fucking life!'

His arm snapped up, pointing in my face. 'Out of his head every fucking night and hung-over every fucking morning!' It shot to the left, fingers twitching. 'Just another bitter old *cunt* drinking himself into fucking liver . . .'

Oliver's glass fell over.

It hit the carpet with a smack. And the vodka flushed away.

'Stop,' I said.

Oliver swallowed softly. I heard a fizzing, lemonade or tonic as it soaked in round his feet. A dark wet puddle of carpet. He stared at it like he didn't understand.

'Stop.'

Oliver was silent. Around his feet, the drink seeped in some more. I saw his hair had fallen forward across his face, trying to get his breath back in. And standing still against the wall, too hot in my coat and gloves, I heard the phone ring out.

I glanced at the door as Oliver looked up.

'Don't answer it,' he said. His voice was a little better.

It caught, jagged, and I was glad to hear it. He stared out at the hall.

'Why not . . .?' I said. 'Who is it?'

'I don't know,' he said. His laugh was cutting in between the rings. 'Some *cunt.*'

He looked away and I watched him grab the cigarettes. I watched one slip through his fingers as he took it. Oliver stared down at it, lying on the carpet as its paper soaked through, grey.

'They never fucking speak,' he said.

'*They?*' I tried to count up how many days since I'd last seen him. A wrong number, he'd said. A joke. 'Still? How many times have they *rung?* It's probably just some idiot, you know . . . like a ten-year-old or something. Why don't you just tell them to fuck off?'

'*I have told them!*'

The phone rang out again. Oliver turned away.

I watched his face fall in, teeth gripped together, and I could see the red had darkened, spread across his face. Ridges stood out just below his hair. I could see his hands, fists by his sides, with veins across their backs. It seemed that in that moment, I could see a lot of things. Like the way his eyes were red beneath the lids. The way those fists were only gripped to stop his hands from shaking.

'I'll go and talk to them,' I said.

There was a thump as he shambled to stand up behind me. One step, and I reached for it. I heard him call my name as I lifted the receiver, as I put it to my ear.

'Hello?' I said, and I gave a glance behind me.

Oliver stood with his shoulder up against the frame. It

made me think of James Dean, or one of those other old-time stars. Leaning there, smoking a cigarette, watching the babes go past. Except Oliver didn't look so casual as that. And he was leaned against the wall to stop himself from falling. I watched him breathe. I watched him close his eyes, and I wondered again just how much he'd drunk.

'Hello?' I said again.

There was no answer.

'*Hello?* Is anyone *there?*'

I stopped for a moment. Oliver's hand moved from his neck to his face, he rubbed his mouth. He looked very tired, I thought. Stripped. And I closed my eyes as well.

'Look . . .' I spoke loud in the phone. 'Look, if you're there, why don't you just say something?'

There was a crackle. No words.

'This is stupid.' I breathed out. 'Listen,' I said quietly. 'Can I give you a piece of advice? I don't want to be rude . . . but it's usually best for mutes not to use the telephone.'

Oliver reached out, he banged me on the shoulder.

'Tell them they're a *cunt*.' I turned. My foot was tapping much too quickly. His teeth snapped over the words. 'Tell them they're a cunt and I'm going to hurt them.' I looked away from him, facing the wall.

'How many times have you called now?' I said. 'Can you still not think of anything to say? You should brush up your nuisance calls a bit. I mean . . . at least think of something to *say*.' I heard a breath, harsh. I heard it crackle down the line.

And that was when the voice spoke.

'I've told your Dad,' it said.

'*Dawn?*'

Behind my back I heard Oliver shift, reach for me maybe but I didn't turn.

'*Dawn?* . . . Is that *you?*'

'Oh,' she said quietly. 'You still recognize my voice then.'

'What . . .? Fuck, Dawn! Why didn't you say anything? Jesus, I thought we had some kind of psycho phoning us up!'

'Oh,' she said again. 'It's *we* is it? *Us.*'

'What? What the fuck are you on about . . .?'

' *We us we us.* You sound like you're married to him or something.'

'Dawn.' I closed my eyes, head weighing down towards the carpet. I felt Oliver grab me but I didn't move. 'Dawn,' I said. 'What the fuck *is* this?'

'You swear too much,' she said. 'Nice little habit you've picked up from him that is. Yeah, nice little habit. I bet you're picking up all his habits aren't you?' I listened to her pause. Long and studied, before she said 'You know he's got a drink problem.'

I didn't speak then. I heard the silence feather out between us.

'Everyone knows,' she said. 'He goes to AA. He can't help it.' She was quiet. 'He's an alcoholic.' Her words left gaps. Blank and buzzing gaps. I heard Oliver sniff behind me. 'I'm only telling you because you need to know!' she said. 'Someone's got to tell you! I'm trying to be your friend! He's an alcoholic and . . . and a *paedophile!* Everyone

353

says he goes out with schoolgirls all the time! Loads of them! *Everybody knows!'*

'Everybody knows?' My mouth was working, full and clumsy as I stared down at my hand. It was sweaty, gripping there, the fingers tight round the receiver. 'Everybody knows?' Oliver was moving again, waving. I could see him from the corner of my eye. And turning round, he mouthed something. Big and stupid like a fish in a glass bowl.

'Yes!' Her voice was loud, excited. 'He's a *cradle snatcher!* I told you! You *see?* I *told* you! *He does it all the time!'*

I watched Oliver's face twitch, his red eyes dry and viscous. And I didn't hear Dawn's last words. Just a huge and breaking silence, with an echo running through.

Everybody knows.

'You . . . you haven't even spoken to me for a month,' I said.

Dawn's breath caught up. I heard her pause.

'I mean . . .' I felt my other hand go up, rub a place on my forehead somewhere. 'I mean, you haven't said a word to me for a month and now . . . now you phone up with this *shit?'*

'*You were horrible to me!'* It came out all in a rush, jolted from her mouth. There was a break as she sniffed. '*Someone* had to make you see sense. Someone had to . . . to stop it in its tracks!'

'Like with Robin,' I said.

'Yes! I'm trying to *help* you! I'm trying to be your friend!'

'My friend?' I listened to those words for a moment. My friend, I thought. I could see her, stumbling to her bed in the darkness as I climbed up to her top bunk. I heard her small and quiet words as I lay there with closed eyes. Don't go away again.

Dawn's breath was quick and gasping in my ear now. And I could almost see that too. Her face scrunched up and pink, no make-up and no spots. In and out, that breath, in and out with her face an inch above me. A Care Bear ridged in the small of my back. Up and down. Those tiny bruises forming.

'You're not trying to be my friend,' I said.

She garbled something else then but I wasn't hearing. Only that breath. Panting, as she pretended to fuck me.

'You're not trying to be my friend, you just don't want me to go out with anyone! You don't . . . don't want me to be with anyone but you! You don't want me to have sex!'

Dawn stopped. 'Don't be ridiculous.'

'It's true! You don't want me to be happy! Just because *you're* miserable! Trying to help me . . . You're not trying to help me! And if everybody knows it's just because you tell them! You . . . you don't want to be a *friend*,' I said. 'You never wanted to be my friend! So tell me, Dawn. Just fucking tell me, what is it exactly that you *do* want? HUH?'

'I don't want anything! I'm trying to help you! I'm just trying to make you see he's not right for you! He's never been right for you! He . . .'

'Not right for me,' I said. 'You didn't think Robin was *right for me* either.'

I heard the click in my own throat as I swallowed.

'Just who is right for me, Dawn?'

My breath was very quick.

'You?'

And I dropped the phone.

The receiver rocked, it tumbled. It fell on to the carpet.

And I heard the silence rush in.

I looked up at Oliver, trying to focus my eyes. He was hitched against the doorway, his breath all fast and hiccupy as he stared.

'She . . .' I said. But my mouth wouldn't form the rest of the sentence. 'She . . .'

'What?' he said. 'She *what?*'

'I don't think . . .' I took a long, low breath. 'I don't think she'll phone here anymore.'

'You *know* that *bitch?*' he said.

I glanced down at the phone, useless on the floor. I thought again of lying in her top bunk as she spoke in that small voice. Don't go away again. I thought of her standing on the concrete outside the community centre. Trying to flirt with Craig, trying hard, with the flush of Hooch in her cheeks. Her make-up drying thickly in the twilight. I'd made her happy once or twice, I thought. I'd tried.

Oliver reached out again. I felt him touch my arm and almost flinched, his fingers an inch from my cuts.

'Yes,' I said quietly, still looking at the phone. 'I know her.'

I walked past him slowly, back into the living room.

It was like a different night in there, all soft and dim and pretty. My eyes moved slowly from place to place. None of it seemed to make any real sense.

'So . . . so why the fuck is she phoning me up?' His words fell over each other, too many in one sentence.

'What . . .?'

I sat down on the floor as he came around beside me. I watched him bend his knees, hit the carpet with a thump. He was sitting in the vodka, I saw, not even noticing. I looked away.

'Why is she phoning *me*?' he said.

I laughed. Even hearing it myself, the sound was wrong.

'She doesn't think you're right for me,' I said.

Oliver shifted, reached for a cigarette and flicked the lighter. He took one drag and blew it up towards the ceiling.

'What do you think?' he said.

'I think . . .' My tongue came out, licked my top lip as I glanced down at the carpet. Wet carpet, I thought. And then I couldn't look at it anymore. 'I don't know,' I said.

'You don't *know*?' Oliver's eyes opened up too wide. They looked stupid that way, the whites shot through with vodka. 'Oh well that's just fucking great. What the fuck do you mean *you don't know*? If you don't *know* then why the fuck did you say yes? Why the fuck did you *stay*?'

I looked at him, feeling my forehead crumple into a frown. All the stress was there in his voice, all the moves in all the right places. But it was funny, staring into his eyes, I didn't see anything that looked like feeling.

And I tried to think back, remember that first date as I'd walked on up the hill on my own. I tried to think what had gone through my head.

Oliver was silent. Maybe waiting for an answer. Maybe

357

he'd forgotten to wait. His hand was moving to the glass again.

And in the silence, I heard his old voice echo. Just before he'd fucked me, I thought. Just before he'd fucked me. *Bicker bicker fucking bicker. Why do they stay together?* They're happy, I thought. I pressed my hands, still hidden in my gloves, together. They're happy.

'I never . . .'

Oliver's head bounced up to me again, hearing my voice start. The flesh under his eyes sagged into bags. His shoulders were just lumps underneath cloth. He was ugly.

'I don't know,' I said again. In the breath between my sentences I let my eyes drop shut.

'You chose me,' he said. I heard him through the red of my eyelids. I heard him cough bile through the words. 'You chose me.'

There was no sound then. Blind, I reached to touch my arm. Lumps, like his shoulders, underneath cotton. Long, slim lines of shelter.

'I've never chosen anything,' I said.

And even with my eyes shut I knew he was watching me. Watching me touching my arm.

'Is that right?' Thin and tight, stretched speech.

I heard Oliver shift as he stood up. I listened to the door crank open, bang shut, and I pressed my lips together. It was right.

It only took him a moment, out of the room, too short a time for me to think. I opened up my eyes in his empty room. I'd spent a lot of time here, hours talking to him. Funny, though. There wasn't much I could remember.

I didn't look at him at first, coming back into the room. I listened to his footsteps as he sat down. Happy, I thought. Three feet from me, his legs came into view.

Oliver's hand stretched gently out, and he let a razor blade fall through.

It was silent as it hit the carpet, midway between our eyes.

Oliver looked at me. The skin on his arm was very pale, but maybe that was just against his face. There were a lot of tiny moles there, brown dots against the flesh. The cuff of his shirt was stained light grey, dark hairs all running in the same direction. Like a wave, I thought.

The blade lay gently on its side, and the pile of the carpet swarmed round. A proper blade, no thin shaving thing. For a Stanley knife maybe, like Dad had at home. And in its holding edge, a tiny notch picked a semicircle through the line. It wasn't very sharp. A speck of white powder showed up against the grey. Not very sharp, I thought. Not very shiny either. And still he didn't speak.

Oliver reached for it at about the same time as I opened my mouth. I don't even know what I was going to say. Nothing I guess, and I watched his hand move out. He tilted to one side as he got it.

'Oliver, don't . . .'

He stared into my eyes. Holding the blade by the notch, his fingers were pinched tightly on the edge. It's too thin,

I thought vaguely. Too thin to hold. But it wasn't of course. He only had to grip.

'*Don't . . .*'

Oliver's face fixed mine.

'Why not?' he said. 'Why not?'

There was a single solid movement as he brought it down. Sharp and cold and with more hatred in his eyes than I had ever seen. Not for me, though. Only for himself. And I cried out as I stumbled for him, kneeling through the space between us.

I cried out.

Because it hurts. That's why. Because it hurts.

It sleeted on Christmas Eve. The kind of sleet that makes you understand why Nat King Cole was so keen on white Christmases. You would be, I suppose, when your only other option's grey. It started at about four o'clock, when I went outside for the wood. The sky looked like it was about two feet above my head, a dark, solid grey. I did it quick, the wood. Looking at that sky didn't make me feel too Christmassy.

I dumped the basket by the porch door, watched the sawdust flush out of the holes in the bottom. The tree was done, standing in the corner and making an attractive sort of canopy over the sofa, six feet away. The lights were on too, blinking prettily between the razor-sharp needles, and there were mini-Mars Bars hanging from the branches. It reminded me a little bit of Venus fly-traps: enticing some small hand in with chewy caramel and then causing severe lacerations, just for the joy of knowing they'd have to open their presents one-handed. Closing the door behind me, I dusted my hands down.

The cat was locked safely away in the porch, given free reign on the space behind the ironing board for four or five days. He wasn't stupid. He knew exactly what was going on. And every so often, you'd see his head poke through a crack in the door, eyeing that tree in the corner. His eyes would be squeezed low, with a hiss for good measure, and the expression on his face was obvious: *you may have the living room now, but just wait till they get drunk and forget to lock my flap* . . .

From the kitchen there was the sound of Mum banging pans together, running water. I had the feeling that she wasn't really cooking at all – just ordering from Somerfield and making a lot of noise to fool us. Like the Red Mountain coffee adverts, I thought. And I sat down on the sofa. Michael's Megadrive made plastic exploding noises, blips and beeps and not much else. I folded my hands in my lap, and I watched the space where the TV should have been.

Mum had strung our Christmas cards, on cotton, from the window to the door. Six of them, I saw. And they were sagging in the middle. Dad was somewhere. I didn't know where. But all in all, it didn't feel much like Christmas Eve. Dad's footsteps thumped across the landing, and I tapped my fingers on the leather seat. I breathed out, I watched the clock, and I tried to think if there was something I could do.

I got up. The light from the kitchen cast a line, bisecting the cork. It glowed on shadowy brown, and I moved my feet to watch it cut across the toes. Mum coughed, with the click of wood against a saucepan. Like the light from the bathroom, I thought, when I'd been standing in the study. Listening.

After a moment, I turned away. I went to Michael's door.

We played on the Megadrive for an hour or so but it wasn't really much fun. I wasn't paying much attention to the game, I think, too busy listening.

The sound cut through just after five o'clock. I heard it through Michael's window, I dropped the joypad on his floor. I cocked my head. It was the sound of a car engine.

'Ha!' he said. '*Told* you you couldn't beat my score!'

'I've got better things to do than *beat your score*. I've got to go and meet Oliver.'

'Oliver?' Michael stared at me.

'*Yes* . . . Amazing how your ears work when your brain's been out of action so long.'

Michael picked up the joypad. He didn't look at me, and I reached for the doorknob.

'Why is Oliver here?' he said. And I stopped.

'It's nothing to do with you. You shouldn't stick your nose in other people's business.'

'It is my business,' Michael said quietly. He didn't take his eyes off the screen.

'Really?' I laughed. 'Mmm, and how'd you work that one out?'

I watched him glance round at me, and I tried to hold

my stare. He had a funny way of looking, though. And after a moment, I had to turn away.

'Cos it's Christmas,' he said.

'*So?*'

But Michael turned back to the screen then. I watched the lights make dots and dashes like Morse code across his face. And the fluorescent green grass was kind of sickly on his skin. There were bags under his eyes, creases that skewed diagonally over his cheeks, and his hair was lank on his forehead. He jumped a wasp-type thing, and he didn't say anything else. He shrugged, instead. And looking at him, there wasn't much I could say to that.

Mum had turned on a radio in the living room as well, only it didn't seem the same with no one there to listen. Some man's voice was going on about the value of New Wave Indian cinema, but I wasn't very interested. It seemed kind of sad, just talking on and on like that, not knowing he was on his own.

I walked through, tried not to think of Michael's face, and I shut the door too quickly.

It was dark now. Completely dark, and the Xantia's headlights flickered off, just as I opened the porch door. I got a flash of rose beds, dyed white and grey against the wall, kind of frozen in the glare. But they were gone as well after only a moment. And I listened to the clunk as Oliver got out. I listened to his boots squelch through the mud.

'Fuck,' he said. There was a tiny thump, and I shivered in the porch doorway. Wind's picking up, I thought. But there didn't seem a lot of point in it. 'Shit,' he added.

I didn't speak, tucked my hands in my armpits, and watched for his silhouette to come.

Oliver was wearing jeans and a shirt under his jacket that looked a bit like a pyjama top. He didn't look relaxed, though. He looked like he'd ironed them before he'd come out. His boots were wet and thick with mud and I watched, the radio babbling behind me, as he bent to take them off. There were tiny bits of ice, soggy in his hair, and a couple on his shoulders. Across the flesh of his forearm, a small pink plaster was neatly stuck down.

'Sorry. It gets . . . it gets a bit like a swamp out there.'

He looked up and smiled, flicking his hair back with a twist. His face seemed pulled though, I thought. Too tight across the cheeks as he kept on smiling. He'd brought a carrier bag, I saw. Heavy and clinking, with those purple grapes on the side and a vine leaf. A Wine Cellar bag, but I didn't mention it. I looked across at the tree instead.

There was tinsel strung up in loops around the room, breaking for a gap at Michael's door. Michael wouldn't let anyone hang tinsel on his door. He said it looked messy. I didn't really blame him anymore. It was green, mostly, with bits of silver where we'd run out. It shed sparkly little hairs on to the floorboards, and got bald in the places it had hung from the year before.

He glanced up, around the room. I saw him take in the tree, the presents, the tinsel. I saw him look away again.

'Where is everyone, then?'

'Dad's busy. Mum's cooking and Michael's playing on his Megadrive. *Sonic*, I think.'

'Right,' he said. He was prepared, I thought. Prepared, and now he only wanted to get on with it.

'I'm glad you came,' I said. I wanted to reach across and touch him, but I was scared I might feel the slide of a plaster underneath my fingers. 'I thought you might not . . .'

'I said I would.' He looked at me. And standing for a moment, hearing the radio babble on, I felt something clumsy pass between us before he bent and kissed my face.

Oliver turned around towards the kitchen. He looked funny, I thought, standing there without his boots. His socks were thick and itchy, sort of beige, and he seemed smaller in them. I wasn't quite sure how.

He knocked three times, quick and kind of definite, and he waited for Mum's voice before he opened the door. I didn't bother to tell him it was silly. I didn't bother to say that it was only Mum.

'Hello?' Her voice wasn't nervy, like it had been before. Just curious, I thought. And I wasn't surprised. Oliver opened the door.

'Hi,' he said. And following him through, I heard my Mum say

'Oh.'

'How are you?' He walked down off the step, pushed his hair again, and pulled out a chair from the table. Mum was sitting there. She'd redone her ponytail, I saw. She was leaning back in the chair, stomach high and arms hanging down to the legs of the chair. I watched her sit up, sharp. I saw her rub a hand underneath her lips.

'I . . . I'm fine.' She looked at me. I don't think he
saw it. The chair squeaked as he pulled it further. He
settled down and pulled one leg, knee bent, across the
other. I just stood in the doorway. There didn't seem
to be quite enough room for three. 'Well . . .' she said.
'Nice to *see* you. Yes,' she said. 'What . . . what a *nice*
surprise.'

'Sorry?'

He looked round at me, and I caught a glimpse of
something angry there. My eyes went wide, I think, and I
opened my mouth to say something. But that expression
was already gone, burrowed into a frown. Oliver turned
away from me.

'Well . . .' Mum was saying. 'Well, I meant . . . just . . .
just nice to see you. Makes a nice change. Good thing I
made more than . . . enough for everybody, hey?' Her
smile was pathetic. I could have done better than that. I
sniffed, tucked one hand into my pocket, and tried to find
a place that I could lean. There was the sound of Michael's
door swinging open. No tinsel in *that* door's way, I thought,
but I wasn't really cross at him.

His footsteps on the floorboards were slow, not jumping
and ten-year-old like usual. I sort of wished he'd run,
knock something over, and I listened to Mum's coughing
as she covered her mouth with a hand.

'I like the decorations,' Oliver said.

'Oh . . . Philip does most of that.'

Behind me, Michael pushed the door open. I glanced
round at him, and I didn't smile. His eyes were kind of red
and starey. The bags stood out more under kitchen

lighting, and I could see the way his lips were crunched together.

Michael's elbow touched my side as he pushed past. A little quiet fell. He went to the fridge, crouching down and brushing the hair from his face as he opened the door. It reminded me of Dad, the way he stared into the light like there was something wrong, the way his feet weighed up on the toes, holding his balance. Only Michael brought out squash, I saw. Kia-Ora. 'So,' he said quietly, the plastic bottle dangling from one hand as he shut the door. 'How come you're not with your family?'

He didn't look at Oliver when he spoke. He walked to the unit instead, took down a tumbler from the cupboard. I think I felt myself wince.

'They're on holiday,' Oliver said. There wasn't even a pause. 'The Algarve. They go there every year at Christmas.'

'Why don't you go with them?' he said. I watched him handling the plastic thing carefully, holding it with both hands as he tipped a little into the glass. Sickly orange stuff, not liquid enough to be a drink. I watched him put it down again. And still he didn't turn.

'Maybe Oliver . . .' I said, but his voice cut in too quickly for me.

'They left a week ago,' he said. 'I had to work till yesterday.' He paused, looking at my brother from across the room. 'Pile of shite, working,' he said. And he watched.

Michael did smile a little bit, I guess he couldn't help it. He didn't let Oliver see it, though. He was busy, putting the cap back on the Kia Ora. And when he turned to put it back in the fridge, that little accidental smile was gone.

'You could go now,' he said. 'The planes still fly.' He stopped, halfway across. He gave Oliver a look. A very definite look. 'Pilots don't have holidays,' he said.

Oliver only shrugged. 'They'll be back in a few days. Doesn't seem a lot of point.'

I watched Mum staring down at the table. She rubbed the tips of her fingers, slowly back and forward across the wood. She had an expression on her face like she was alone, just passing the time. I wondered if she'd heard what Michael had said.

'So . . .' Oliver tapped his hands together. 'What are you getting for Christmas, Michael?'

Michael turned round, took a small sip of his drink.

'I don't know,' he said slowly. 'We have surprise presents in this house.'

'Uh-huh?' Oliver nodded. 'That's nice,' he said. 'Traditional . . .'

Michael didn't speak again, leaning the small of his back against the sink, he drank his squash and watched us. Oliver tapped his fingers on the table and I watched as Mum folded her arms.

'Have you . . . uh . . . have you shown Oliver your room yet?'

'No! No, I haven't! Do you want to see it? I mean . . . it's different. *Really* different.'

'Yes,' Mum said. She put a hand behind her, tightened the ponytail. 'It certainly is.'

Oliver got up, pushed his chair under the table. 'I'd like to see,' he said. 'Show me.'

I watched Mum turn away from the table, searching for something to stir. And opening the door, I let Oliver go through.

Michael said nothing as we left.

The door was exactly the same. There's not much you can do with a door really. The handle was the same, it was the same colour and everything. Shit brown, which isn't one you see advertised in the Dulux samplers much.

Oliver stopped before he opened the door, though. He didn't even look interested in going in. 'You should have told them I was coming,' he said. 'Or fucking told me that they didn't know.' He looked away and shifted, glancing down at the stairs. There was no movement from the kitchen. 'Jesus Christ, you don't half put me in some awkward *fucking* situations.' He took his hand off the door handle, put it up to his forehead and he rubbed there with his fingers. 'What a nice surprise: *bullshit*. They didn't want me here!'

'That's . . . that's not true,' I said. 'They do.' I tried to smile. 'I . . . I want you here.'

He didn't sound much like he'd heard me, though.

'They *didn't* fucking want me here. And I don't blame them, you know? It's a family thing. I shouldn't be here. It's got nothing to do with me.' He sighed. 'I thought they were expecting me,' he said. 'Fuck, you could have told me!'

And I had to close my eyes then. I guess his anger was mine to take. He was right. But I couldn't have told them. I couldn't have, I thought, because then he couldn't have come. I waited for him to say something else at me.

Oliver had stopped, though. He took a long breath out.

'Christ . . .' he said. His eyes flopped downwards to the floor.

'I'm sorry.'

He didn't answer me, though, thinking his own thoughts. And when he raised his head again, his eyes were slightly clearer. 'You didn't say you'd changed your room.' His voice was quiet as he pointed to the door.

'I didn't think you'd be interested,' I said. 'But' – I tried to smile at him – 'you can see it now.'

Oliver nodded. I waited to see what would happen, nerves flicking up in my stomach. He turned towards the door, though. And I watched him nod again as he opened it. He took a step inside.

'God . . .' He looked around, that tense expression gone as he stared. 'Bloody hell . . .'

'Do . . . do you like it?' I said.

'Like it? Fuck, it's so different . . .' His voice trailed into silence. And it was. It was so different. And I hadn't done what Mum'd asked me.

It wasn't a room anymore. Not really. Not like the rooms downstairs were: the living room or the kitchen. It was a space, I thought. A space, and that was why I liked it. The furniture was gone. The chair, the cupboard, the shelves. The bed was still there, but no teddies or pillows or anything. Just a bed. With a duvet. The carpet was clean. Completely clean, and it had nothing on it. No books, no clothes, no ornaments. My school stuff was under the bed, a single neat stack. There wasn't anything in my room.

And on the walls, new white paint, still smelling, made

it seem even emptier. Nothing. Four walls. A bed, and the lamp by its side. Everything else was gone. It looked, I thought, just like it was for sale.

I'd thrown away all my tapes in the end. There were only two CDs, tucked neatly, symmetrically in the corner of my carpet. The windows were closed. No pictures, and the curtains hung limp. I looked at Oliver to see his face.

'Where's all your . . . stuff?'

'I threw it away.' I waited for something, but he didn't speak. 'Pretty much all of it . . . I didn't want it anymore.' From below I heard Dad's voice. Oliver turned to it too.

'I better go and open that bottle of wine,' he said. I nodded. 'I really like it.' He looked at me, direct, and I think I might have shrugged. 'Really,' he said again. And I said thank you as he turned to go.

I watched him walk back down the stairs. He hadn't been that angry. The thought made me feel vaguely empty, like something had gone missing. Like I'd lost something, I thought.

And it was only when I turned to switch the light off that I saw my stereo was gone. Laid out on the window sill, wide and tiled, there were three blank spaces. Square spaces, darker than the dust on the rest of the ledge. Three clean square spots where the deck had been, the speakers. And the plug point by my skirting board was empty.

'Dad?'

I shouted it, jumping down the stairs. I hit the hall floor, two steps to the living room.

'Dad have you seen my . . .?'

But Dad wasn't looking at me. Standing by the fireplace,

he didn't even glance my way. I felt the words give up inside my mouth because Dad was looking at Oliver.

His face seemed very soft, I thought. Surprised, and his hair looked kind of fluffy over the top of his head. His mouth was open slightly, as he stared.

Halfway across the room, and caught mid stride, Oliver was looking back.

'Oliver . . .' Dad licked his lips, like he didn't know he was doing it. I watched him glance down at the shopping bag, loose and flapping in his hand.

'Hi,' Oliver said. He nodded.

'I . . . I wasn't expecting to see you.' Dad trailed off but I couldn't make out any thought on his face. I watched them, trying to think of something else to say. Behind my back the sleet made a clatter against the french windows. I heard the radio announce the time.

Oliver didn't answer him.

'Well,' I said. I clapped my hands. 'It's Christmas. Let's . . . let's have some fun.'

'Yes . . .' Dad said. He looked around, but he still seemed lost. I watched him fix on the tree behind me. The lights caught spots of colour in his hair. 'Yes,' he said again.

I heard the shipping forecast start, and the click of the kitchen latch opening. I watched the beam that cut across the floor get wider, and Mum's face smiled through. Her eyes stayed on Dad for just a moment too long. And I saw her pick up her smile again, as she turned into Oliver's sight.

'Well . . .' she said. Michael followed her, stepping through. 'Dinner'll be ready soon.'

I coughed. I watched her rub her hands together like she had flour on them or something. There wasn't any flour, though. And she stopped, just a foot into the room.

'How 'bout that wine, then?' I said.

Oliver opened up one of the bottles as everyone sat down. I saw Dad look at him every now and then, but with his back turned, Oliver didn't see. Sitting on the sofa, I could see back through the hall. Back to my bedroom door, to where the stereo was gone. I didn't say anything, though. Not yet. I watched them try to settle in.

'D'you want a glass?' Oliver looked round at Mum.

'Well,' she said. 'If you've got enough . . .'

'Enough?' Dad's face came up from his breast pocket, he was taking out some cigarettes, I saw. 'He's got three bottles, Liz.'

Oliver bit his lip. I watched him glance down at the one in his hand, smooth a corner of the label. I could see through the hair falling down across his profile that his jaw was clenched.

'Do you want one?' he said.

'Well.' Dad laughed. 'If you can *spare* it.' He lit the cigarette that was stuck between his lips, squinting at the flame. It made his face look puffy, I thought, tired and stressed out. The flame died, though. He seemed fine again when he looked up.

'You're not driving, then,' he said, inhaling.

'No.' Oliver wiped a smear of cork from the bottle. 'Have you got any glasses around?'

'Liz? Have we got some glasses?'

Mum smiled, walking off to the kitchen.

She came back with five, balanced in her hands. And she put them on the table next to Oliver. She watched him pour.

Four glasses and an inch in a tumbler for Michael. I watched him hand them out, took mine in my turn. I watched him take his straight up to his mouth, and he flicked his hair free as he lifted.

'Well, hang on.' Dad was staring at him.

Oliver paused.

'Toast?' Dad said. I watched Oliver move his hand away. 'To Christmas Eve?' Dad looked around. 'Let's have a good time and . . . and not let anything spoil it.'

Dad stared down into the glass for a moment, and drank. I watched half of it disappear in one, and I took a sip of my own. In the background, I listened to the presenter's voice change: *And now for a little-known Czecho-slovakian tambourine ballad* . . . Mum was doing a lot of smiling, but it didn't seem to be directed anywhere.

I took another sip.

'Mmm-mm!' Michael said. 'Kia Ora and wine!'

'Dad . . .?'

He tapped the ash from his cigarette into the fireplace. His face was light and easy-looking, but I could still see the wrinkles underneath. It looked like he was trying to hide them, I thought. But I guess that was stupid.

'Dad . . . I was just wondering if you'd moved my stereo. It . . . uh . . . it sounds stupid, but I was listening to it this morning and now it's . . . it's not there.' I laughed.

Dad didn't laugh with me, though. Looking at him, he didn't even smile.

'I had to take the plug off it,' he said. He lifted his wine glass and I watched him peer inside. With the tip of one index finger, cigarette jutting out, he wiped something from the inside of the glass. He glanced at Oliver. 'I needed the fuse for something,' he said.

'Oh,' I said. 'Right. And there . . . there wasn't anything else you could take it off.'

'No,' he said quietly. 'There wasn't.'

'Right. No . . . no, that's fine. I just wondered.' I coughed, looked down at my hands. In the background, I heard Mum say 'So . . . what part of the Algarve . . .?' and below that, on Radio 4, the obituary of a Mexican bongo virtuoso. A true loss to the world of obscure Latin American percussion. I wondered if anyone would notice if I turned it off.

Dad was still looking into his wine glass, frowning. His finger dipped in again.

'Michael?' he said. 'Get us a beer from the fridge. The wine's got cork floating in it.' Michael jumped up. He left his Kia Ora and wine on the table and Dad leaned back in his seat. He closed his eyes, his neck against the headrest.

'So . . . so can I get it then?' I said.

Dad made no answer, didn't even look like he'd heard me. And, sagging between his fingers, I saw a tiny spark float down from his cigarette. It landed on his trouser leg.

'Dad . . .? If you tell me where it is I'll go get it, you don't have to get up or anything.'

'Can't you just leave it till later?' He stretched his back, didn't open his eyes. 'I've only just sat down.'

'But *you* don't have to do it. I can do it. I don't mind.' I paused. 'It's just . . . I'd like to get it back in my room and stuff. In its place.'

'In its place? Christ, I'm sure it's not panicking or anything. Its "place" isn't going to disappear. I said it can wait till later. It's not that important. I'll do it tomorrow, Ok?'

'I know that. But now my room's finished. I just . . . I like having stuff where it's meant to go.'

'Jesus Christ. I'm sorry, but you having everything in the right place in your room is not exactly the most important thing in my head at the moment. I'm trying to relax. *I'll do it tomorrow.* I'm not going to run around like a blue-arsed fly pandering to you and your bloody room, alright? I want to enjoy my Christmas Eve, and I don't want to think about your fucking room, alright?' He looked at me. '*Alright?*'

And then I had to look away. The floorboards, warm and dark, creaked as I shifted my feet. 'Yes,' I said quietly. From across the room, I heard Oliver muttering, and I looked up, kind of glad to have something else to focus on. Mum was gripping her wine glass round the stem, her fingers tapping up and down on the bowl. I could see where she'd left prints, smeared in the condensation of the glass. Oliver had one hand on the pocket of his pyjama top. 'Shit,' he said softly.

'What's up?' I tried a smile but he only glanced at me and said 'Left my cigarettes in the car . . .'

He got up. Dad sniffed, and there was a cracking noise as the kitchen door opened. Michael came through, his head bent down over a glass, holding it with both hands. And still, I saw, it was slopping up the sides. He'd put a cocktail stick in it, but there was nothing on the stick. Dad leaned back as he put it down. 'What's the cocktail stick for?' he said.

'Nothing.' Michael wiped a hand across his mouth. He looked like Dad, doing that, I thought. 'Just. . . just thought it would make it nice for you.'

Oliver pulled his boots on. I heard Mum tap her glass. And standing by the door, I could see them all in the french windows. The back of Dad's head, and Mum's profile. I could see the way the beer held the lamp light's yellow glow. All of them. Shadowed, warm, and orange-looking on the darkness of the glass. The room seemed better in reflection. Much better, I thought, and then I had to look away.

'I . . . I'll come with you,' I said quietly as Oliver walked out.

There wasn't any argument.

The porch was loud, rattling on top of our heads, and I glanced at Oliver before picking my coat off the floor and a torch off the shelf. His face looked very white against the rest of the space, smeared. He didn't see. Didn't even look round, putting on his own. I sniffed against the cold, but I couldn't hear a conversation starting up, on the other side of the door.

'Are you alright?' I leaned against the ironing board, pressed the button on the torch. A wide, bright circle of gingham, and I could see the stains of damp creeping up from the concrete. The light made the shadows on Oliver's face go in the wrong direction.

'I'm . . .' He looked around, away again. 'I'm fine.' He pressed the front door latch, looked back at me and smiled, walking out into the sleet.

I followed him out, with the torch on the ground ahead of me. Sleet hit my ears and my nose in little cold bunches. Dad's car was parked up near the house, Oliver's on the other side of the yard, and I hunched my shoulders up, the ice making ticking sounds against the nylon.

I shone the torch across the Rover, picking up the dashboard and the steering wheel. It looked very cold in there, I thought. Empty, with shadows underneath the pedals, with the lines of light across fake leather. It didn't look like our car at all.

There was a penny coin tucked down in the crack of the driver's side seat. I moved the beam a little. Across grey-velour seat covers, and a petrol receipt. They all looked crackly in the beam. Over dust, and a letter, and the small cardboard box of my stereo.

Dad was smiling when I went back in. I hadn't waited for Oliver. The beer in his glass had reached halfway down, and the top of the cocktail stick showed through, still wet from being covered. There was a cigarette burning in one of his hands, and Michael was watching the presents. I shut the door behind me, popped the poppers on my coat, and I dumped it on the sofa where Mum had sat. Dad was smiling.

'I was just saying to Michael, we could maybe have some presents soon.'

'I'm having mine first,' Michael said quickly. 'Dad said I could.'

I kicked my shoes back into the corner, and I didn't answer him.

'Are you alright?' Dad's voice was light. I pressed my lips down. 'You look . . . you look funny or something. You fancy a couple of presents don't you? It is Christmas Eve. Do you want another glass of wine or something? Cheer up . . .'

'*You're* the one who's been grumpy all evening.' I didn't look at him, though.

'I . . . I haven't been grumpy.' There was a pause. 'Well, I'm sorry,' he said. 'I didn't mean to be. Look, let's have some presents.' He waited. 'Be fun . . .?'

'Yeah,' I said. I stared down at my hands and I wondered why that made me feel bad. I felt my mouth pull down at the corners as I spoke. 'Why is my stereo in the car, Dad?'

'What?'

'It's in the car,' I said. Dad blinked. I watched his smile hold on by the edges, sinking fast, I thought. I squeezed my fingers in a knot. 'On the front seat. I saw it with the torch . . .' I trailed off.

'It's . . .' Dad looked down. He shut his mouth, staring into his own lap. He reached for his beer. 'I thought . . . I thought we were gonna leave it,' he said. 'Can't we just have some presents . . .?' He looked at me. 'And leave it?'

'You said you needed the fuse . . .'

'I . . . I did.' He drank, quickly, and I saw the cocktail stick tap against his nose.

'This hasn't got anything to do with Christmas. Let's . . . let's just enjoy it,' he said. 'Only lasts two days . . .' He put the beer glass down and stared at it. He pulled his bottom lip with two fingers. From behind, I heard the porch door open. Oliver didn't look up, shaking off the sleet.

'Well?' I said.

Oliver didn't sit down, he crossed the room, headed for the toilet. I listened to him go.

'I . . .' Dad's head sank down again, weighted by the nose. 'Please . . .' he said quietly. His face was crumpled, like one of Mum's old newspapers. Like he'd just drunk some of Michael's Kia Ora and wine, and his eyes seemed very deep-set, in between all those wrinkles. 'Please . . .' he said. He looked at me, hand gripped a little on the arm of the chair. 'Please leave it. Let's . . . let's just enjoy our Christmas.'

Our Christmas, I thought. And I glanced at the tree in the corner of the room. The tinsel had melted in places, too hot against the lights. It left little spidery curls, all black on the gold of the rest of it. Same Christmas tree as last year. Same tinsel, probably the same odd bits of wrapping paper, crinkly on our presents. Same lights, and the same knots in the cords. Same bucket, with the cat shit dried and disinfected. Our Christmas, I thought. I didn't even like that fucking tree.

'Just tell me, Dad. I want to know.'

'You have to push it, don't you,' he said slowly. He

picked up his glass again, just a few inches in the bottom now. He stared down into it. 'You have to . . . just push and push and push till everything's ruined. Just so you can have it in the right place in your stupid bloody hospital room.' He swished the beer round with his hand. 'Do you want to ruin it? Is that it? Won't even let me enjoy my Christmas fucking *Eve* . . .?'

'I just . . .' I looked down at my hands. 'I just want to know.'

'You want to know?' he said. 'I thought it wasn't your problem.'

'What?'

'Anything. Nothing seems to be your problem anymore. One of these days . . .' He smiled a little bit, with one corner of his mouth. 'One of these days I might just decide it's not my problem either.'

'What are you talking about? I want to know why my stereo's in the car! That's all!'

'You want to know?' He swished the beer round one final time. I watched him swallow it in a single, large gulp. Like it was Kentucky rye or something, I thought. It wasn't Kentucky fucking rye. It was Spar lager. 'I'll tell you why your stereo's in the front of the car. It's in the car because I took it back to your boyfriend's fucking shop. That's why it's in the car.' He put the glass down, but his smile was gone. 'That's why it's in the car . . .'

'Why . . . why back to Audiovision? There's nothing wrong with it . . . it's . . . it's *fine*.'

'*Because I can't pay for it! That's why!* Alright? *Because I can't pay for it!* Are you happy now?' I watched him put a hand up to his forehead. He rubbed there with his thumb. He closed his eyes. 'Jesus . . .' he said. 'It's s'posed to be Christmas Eve.'

'But you've already paid.' I looked at Dad. 'You paid in the shop . . . *Months* ago.'

'I know it was months ago!' He bit his lip. 'I know it was months ago, alright . . .?'

'Well . . . well you *paid* then, didn't you?' I stared. '*Didn't* you?'

'By cheque.' He laughed. 'Unfortunately . . . seems you have to have the money too.'

'But we've *got* the money. I mean . . .' I shook my head. 'We must have the money.'

'No we haven't,' he said. 'And I don't see why *you're* so fucking interested all of a sudden. I thought it wasn't your problem.' Dad moved his hand from his forehead downwards, and I watched him cover his eyes, like a character in some Shakespeare play. He rubbed them gently with his fingers, and he shook his head.

'Why . . . why not?'

'*I don't know!* Ask the fucking bank! Ask them!' I watched him, leaning back in his chair, with his cigarette burned down to nothing in his hand. In the silence of the room, I heard the sleet take over. Banging on the windows like it was trying to make up for something. It couldn't, though. And I watched Dad squeeze his face closed.

'I . . . I'm asking you,' I said.

'You're asking me.' He laughed. 'Well, I guess the answer is: you have to have a job.' His eyes sank away as he stared out at nothing. I watched him shake his head. 'Yep,' he said. 'That's probably the reason.' He threw his cigarette butt towards the fire. I saw it bounce, hit the tiles by his feet. He rubbed a hand across his mouth.

'What do you mean, a job? You've got a job. You're . . . you're a personnel manager.'

'Apparently . . .' Dad breathed. 'Apparently, I'm not.'

'What are you *talking* about, Dad? What do you mean, *you're not?*'

'I'm not! *Alright?* I'm not a manager! I am not a fucking manager *I'm not anything!*'

'But . . .' I stared at him. 'But you've been working . . .'

'No.' Dad breathed out. His hands played over each other in his lap. 'I haven't,' he said.

'So . . . so where have you *been?*' My voice seemed too quiet. Too quiet through the sleet, and I heard Oliver's footsteps walking into the room. 'Where have you *been* every day . . .?'

'*I'VE BEEN LOOKING! I've been trying!*' His voice sank into nothing. 'I've been doing my best . . .'

'For . . . for how long? Does *Mum* know?'

'For about a month. I . . .' But Dad didn't finish his sentence. I don't know, maybe it didn't have an end.

'About a month? You've been . . . been going out *nowhere* for a month? What about redundancy money? What about . . .'

'*What do you think we've been living on? THIN FUCKING AIR?*' Dad's laugh was horrible in my ears. 'Anyway, why should I give a fuck? It's not my problem, right? It's not *your* problem, why should it be mine? In fact . . .' Dad held a single finger up: eureka. 'In fact, it's *Oliver's* problem!'

Oliver looked up, but Dad's smile had faded quick. He looked back at his hands.

'You're the one who won't be getting your bloody commission,' he said.

'I don't . . .' But obviously Oliver didn't anything, because he just picked up his glass again. Just picked it up and drank.

'And mine . . .' I said quietly. 'I . . . I'm the one who hasn't got a stereo.'

'I don't think that's going to be a problem.' Dad smiled. 'They won't take it back,' he said. 'Will they?'

Oliver sank lower into his wine. 'I don't . . .' He swallowed. He reached for another cigarette. 'I don't think they give . . . refunds.'

Dad laughed. '*Refunds?* No. They *don't*. They *don't* give "refunds".' His face crumpled down, staring into his own lap. 'So you can keep it,' he said. 'I suppose.'

'And they won't . . .' I glanced at Oliver. 'They won't . . . ask for their money . . .?'

'It's not them asking for the money,' Dad said. 'It's . . . oh for *fuck's sake!* None of this matters! I don't know why I'm fucking telling you this.' He breathed out, long and shaky. 'It's got nothing to do with you.'

I watched him lean out for his glass again, pick it up before seeing it was empty. He stared at it for a moment, closed his eyes. And I saw his jaw clench. 'Would you . . . would you get us another beer, Michael?' Michael looked up, jumped off his chair. 'And . . . and I can probably do without the cocktail stick this time.'

I didn't look at Dad anymore then, his face made my

384

stomach roll over. I stared out, not really looking, round the room. The tree and the presents, and Mum's half-finished paper in the corner. The radio. Turned off, I thought. And I wondered why I hadn't noticed that before. Mum probably, I thought. The cotton, our six Christmas cards, the tinsel, the gap by Michael's door, and the space where the TV should have been.

There was no clean square there now, dust had filled it like it'd never been there in the first place. But there would have been a square, I thought. There would have been a square, just after it was moved. Clean and clear and shiny. Just like the spaces on my window sill.

'The TV . . .' I said. There was a funny kind of crack in my voice. I had to cough to clear it. 'The TV, then . . . That's . . . that's gone as well.'

Dad's shoulders relaxed, slumped forwards a tiny bit. The wrinkles on his face smoothed over. 'We've talked enough now,' he said. 'Haven't we talked about it enough? Can we just . . . just please try and enjoy what's left of our bloody Christmas?'

'You . . . you lied, then,' I said. 'About the TV and . . . and about the phone! *The phone too?*' He didn't answer. 'You lied,' I said quietly. 'You lied.'

'Lied?' Dad looked at me. '*Lied?*' His laughter seemed to fall from his mouth, tepid.

'I . . . I didn't think you'd do that.' I watched the floorboards carefully. I tried to get the words straight, in a line inside my mouth. 'I didn't think you'd do that. Lie.'

'*Oh for Christ's sake! Is that all you're worried about? Me lying?*

Jesus! I wish that was the only thing *I* was fucking worried about.'

Oliver's head was low, his wine glass pretty close to his hand. Upstairs, I heard Mum's bedroom door open. Her footsteps on the stairs. There was no noise from the kitchen though. No fridge door, no pop of a beer can. I guess Michael was waiting till it was safe. Stupid that, I thought. Stupid.

'I didn't think you'd *lie*,' I said. 'You ... you *hate* lies.'

'Right . . .' Dad said. 'Right, I lied. What a *bastard*, eh? What a *fucking* criminal. I tell you, you're so worried about fucking lying, it's your *boyfriend* you should talk to! Not me! Not fucking *me!*'

'What?' I looked between them. 'What are you talking about?'

Behind me, Mum's feet clicked on the floor. I heard her stop.

'I'm talking about your *boyfriend*,' Dad said. '*Oliver? I'm talking about his age!*'

'What about his age?' Mum's voice came stiff and too high-pitched. 'What about it?'

'Well he's the fucking liar!' Dad's voice rolled and jumped in the quiet. '*He's the fucking liar!*'

Oliver's face was pale underneath his hair. I watched him run a hand through it. His tongue flicked out across his lips and he took the last drag of his cigarette. I watched him crush it in the ashtray slowly as he turned to look at Dad.

'Well?' he said.

'Well what?' Mum walked a few steps, looked at them both. 'What's going on?'

'He's the liar,' Dad said again.

'Go on,' said Oliver. He took his hand from the stem of the wine glass. 'Tell me.'

'Well he's not twenty-seven for a fucking start!' Dad stared at us. '*He's not twenty-seven that's what!*'

No one spoke. Dad's face drew down at us.

'He's thirty-one,' he said. His voice got lower. 'Thirty-one, not twenty-seven at all . . .'

Oliver's breath was deep. Deep, but Mum spoke before him.

'How did you find out?'

And even then, I was kind of surprised by how calm she sounded.

'I . . . I got a call from . . . what's her fucking name . . . your friend. Dawn . . . Some call.' He shook his head. The smile on his face was nasty. 'Some fucking call . . .' He stopped. I don't know what made him realize, maybe the sound of her voice. But he looked slowly into Mum's face, and his expression fell away. 'You *knew* . . .' he said. And for a moment, there was silence. I heard the sleet begin again.

'I told her,' I said quietly.

It smashed and clattered on the darkened window. On each of our reflections. Dad stared at us. From me to Mum and back again. No one spoke, though. I guess there was nothing to say. Nothing, until Oliver opened his mouth.

'You're a hypocrite,' he said quietly.

'What?' Dad turned to him

'*No!*' I said. 'No, Oliver . . . *please* . . .'

I watched them, both of them. I watched Dad's eyes flick between us in the silence of the room. And Oliver licked his lips. He turned away.

'What did you say?' Dad kept looking.

'Forget it.'

'Just tell me . . . just tell me what the fuck you just said.'

'*I said forget it!*'

Oliver picked up his glass. Picked it up quick. And he drank the remainder in one long go.

'Please don't, Philip,' Mum said. Her voice was very soft. Like Barbie skin I thought.

And after a moment, Dad looked down at the nothing in his lap.

Michael held the door with his shoulder, carrying the tray through. His shoulders were hunched like he expected someone to kick him, and the expression on his face was more concentrated than before. I listened to the tiny swishing noises as he carried it across to the table. I tried to smile at him, when he looked up, but his eyes were somewhere else, as he handed Dad his beer. Dad didn't even look up.

I squeezed my mouth shut, staring down towards the floor. I wished I could close my eyes. And in the silence, the sleet scattered noise through the room.

I watched Mum move across the room, sit down on the sofa. She put her hands down carefully, one on each knee, and I saw her flex her fingers over them. Her hair was loose, and kinky on her neck from having it up for too long.

'Weather's getting worse,' she said softly.

Michael took something off the tray. It was a plate. A long plate, and I watched him push something on it with his finger, adjusting. Mum pressed her lips together. Oliver stared at the ashtray. The clay one, I saw, the one that I'd made. Not that it mattered. Oliver wouldn't recognize it. He swallowed, and I thought I could almost hear the click.

Then Michael picked the plate up.

Oliver was nearest, sitting a foot from him, head down, but Michael didn't carry it to him. Instead, I watched him walk across the room, balancing it over two flat hands. And he held it out for Dad. Dad looked at it.

Reaching down with his thumb and his index, he looked like a crab, I thought. He picked something off the edge of the plate, looked up into Michael's face, and he smiled. A small smile. It looked like it only just caught on his lips. I felt my stomach twinge. He wouldn't smile at me like that, not tonight. Maybe not tomorrow either. Not anymore.

Michael smiled back.

There was a glugging as Oliver poured another glass. Mum coughed a little bit, but I think it was an accident. And she smiled too when Michael moved on, standing next to her.

They were crackers, I saw. A whole plateful of them, and I guess that's what he'd have been doing in the kitchen all that time. Some of them had Cheddar on, and a little spread of pickle. Some of them had Stilton, some just margarine. Mum picked out a margarine. I wasn't really surprised. She took a very small bite, sort of nibbling the edge and for a moment I couldn't work out why. Then a crumb spilled, down into her lap, and I saw what she was wearing. Funny really, that I hadn't noticed it before.

She brushed the crumb away on to the floorboards, and held a hand out when she bit again. It was an old dress, I think, but not ripped or stained or anything. It was velvety stuff, in dark brown, with a V-neck that didn't quite meet her cleavage. Ankle-length, full-skirted. It looked like the sort of thing you'd have worn to a seventies wedding: big sleeves, tight around the wrists, then long and baggy round her hands. Tight around the waist too, I saw. She had a nice waist. And I suppose that was something I'd never noticed either.

Michael held the plate out for me. I took a Stilton one. 'Thanks, Michael . . .' I said.

I bit in. It sounded very loud, I thought. Even over the sleet.

'That . . . that's a nice dress, Mum,' I said. 'It suits you.'

Mum looked round. I watched her glance down at herself with a smile, a small smile. She looked embarrassed, I thought. But kind of glad as well.

'Do you like it?'

'Uh-huh . . .' I said. Dad coughed. I felt my words trail off.

'Probably stupid dressing up just for . . . the evening . . .' She looked down into her lap.

'I don't think it's stupid. It looks nice. Around the waist, it looks nice.' I smiled back.

'Well, thanks,' she said, but she was already looking down again.

'Don't . . .' I raised my voice a little bit. 'Don't you think it looks nice, Dad?'

He looked up at me, beer glass resting on his thigh, but his stare only said shut up.

'Well don't you?' I said, and I didn't look away.

'It doesn't matter . . .' Mum finished her cracker quickly, stuffing it in her mouth like she wished she hadn't said anything. Michael was offering Oliver one, I saw. But I didn't bother to watch.

'Yes it does matter. *Dad*, doesn't it look nice?'

'Oh for God's sake,' Dad turned away.

'Well I like it,' I said quietly. I looked at Mum, but she was hiding now, behind her hair. 'I think it's really gorgeous.' I sniffed a little bit. 'Your boyfriend would've liked it,' I said.

'*Please*.' Mum looked up at me. 'He doesn't . . . It . . . it doesn't matter,' she said again.

Dad snorted into his beer, but it sounded stupid, so late in coming. I didn't even look at him.

'Come on then,' he said. He waved his hand at me. 'Come on then: what boyfriend? It's obviously meant to be some kind of dig, so who is he?' He stared at me, though, not Mum.

'He's no one,' Mum said. 'Can we just . . . just talk about something else. How about another cracker, Michael?' Michael looked down at the plate. He didn't move, though.

'Come on!' Dad said. 'You're gonna have a fucking go at me, at least tell me what it's about! Or am I going to have to work it out for myself, hey? You could do a charade! Sounds like . . .'

'*Please*, Philip. It doesn't *matter*, it . . .'

'Well why not? Isn't that what people do at Christmas. Isn't it . . .?' He looked away.

I listened to the crunch as Oliver bit down on a cracker. He was staring at the unit.

'All you had to do was notice,' I said. 'Just notice that she made an effort. All you have to do is make the effort back.'

'I haven't made an effort!' Mum said. 'I just . . . I had to change. It doesn't *matter* . . .'

'Yes it does,' I said. 'It does matter. All he had to do was *mention* it!'

'Come on then!' Dad said. 'Mention it like who? You're going to criticize me, at least tell me who I'm being compared to.' He picked up his drink. He was ready, I thought. But that was Ok. I was ready too. Sitting there, I thought maybe I'd been ready for quite a long time.

'Her boyfriend!' I said. 'When she was sixteen!'

'What?' Mum looked up. Her neck stiff, taut, as she stared at me. 'Don't . . .' she said.

I didn't listen to her, though. Mum would never say anything. Not if it was left to her.

'When she was in school like me.' I stared at him. 'He was twenty-six and they were in love. And he would've made the effort.'

'Her boyfriend,' Dad said.

And then he burst out laughing.

'What?' I stared at him '*What?*'

'Her boyfriend . . .' Dad's giggles trailed away, lifting his glass to his mouth. 'Jesus Christ . . .'

'What? What are you laughing about?'

Mum didn't move, hunched. On the other side of the room, Michael was laughing too. His eyes looked empty as he watched Dad put his beer glass down.

'Your mother went to convent school,' he said. A smile flicked up between his words. 'A boarding school . . .'

'*So?*'

'A *girls'* school. They weren't even allowed *out . . . Boys?*' The laugh fell through again. 'I met her in university,' he said. 'Two months after she'd left.'

'That . . . that doesn't . . . *SO?*' I said.

'Oh come off it.' He looked away, reached for his beer glass again. 'Tell her, Liz.'

Mum's head came up slowly, almost like she'd been sleeping. Strands of hair were dragged across her nose, and I could see the tip of her ear peeping through. She rubbed her hand across her mouth.

'I went to convent school,' she said.

But she didn't look at me. She stared out to nowhere, somewhere past Oliver's thigh.

'So . . . so what?' I said. 'So you weren't allowed out?'

'It was . . . like Philip said: it was a boarding school.'

'And you didn't . . .' My words dried up.

I watched Mum shrug. Shrug, like that made some kind of difference.

'You didn't . . .' I said again. And then I had to look away. I saw Mum's eyes come round to me, I saw her try to get my gaze. I didn't let her, though. I didn't want to see her face.

There was the sliding of a wine glass, dragged up to someone's mouth.

A breath, too long and tired-sounding. It might even have been mine.

The ticking of a moth, banging back against the lampshade.

The floorboards looked very dark. Staring down at them, I could see the shadows, puddles round my feet. Against the french windows, the sleet made a fresh rattling gust. Like too many voices, all speaking together. Like a wave, I thought. Like some huge wave on a rainy beach, catching up, tumbling over and taking you with it. Because in the end, it doesn't matter how fast you can run. And behind me, from the kitchen, came the sound of a buzzer.

'That . . . that'll be the dinner,' Mum said. I heard the sofa creak as she got up.

Liar, I thought. The word flashed on and off in my head like a dumb broken fairground. In the sound of no one talking, I reached to touch my arm. Heavy and corrugated, I ran my finger there.

And when Mum's voice came from the kitchen, it sounded very strange. It jumped a little, starting off like she didn't want to break the silence. 'D . . . dinner's ready here.'

Dad's breath squeezed out as he got up, and he took his beer glass with him. I looked up for some sign from Oliver, some smile or nod. I don't know. Anything. Oliver was halfway to the kitchen, Michael gone already. And I suppose I had to get up too.

I rubbed a hand across my face, stepped down through the door after Oliver. The light seemed too bright in the kitchen, not warm as it had done before. Dad sat down slowly, and he put his beer down. He stared out, over knives and forks, a dish of salad, roast potatoes in a plate, sitting on a piece of kitchen roll. Salt and mint sauce and jelly and pepper. Mum had put a candle in the middle of the table, already lit, and flicking back with people's breath.

Michael swung his legs, slow and weighted as I sat, as Mum brought the last dish over.

She put it in the centre, and the clock struck half past six.

Mum lifted the lid without any flourish. She lifted it on a leg of roast lamb.

'Merry Christmas,' she said quietly.

I looked at their faces then. The four of them and me, all seated round the table. I looked at them, hard and tight and shocked. They didn't understand. I understood. Seeing them now, I couldn't help but understand, and I knew the real reason that I'd invited Oliver for Christmas.

It did hurt to look at them. The same way that it hurts to look into the sun, to stare and stare until your eyes are burned clean. It did hurt. But underneath the hurting, I felt something give. Underneath my stomach I could feel the first cracks forming. It felt like my orgasm when Oliver fucked me, like bright, creeping red on my cheek. I kept looking at them and I hoped they felt it too. It felt like release.

Dad's voice was clear and airy, and I felt Mum take a step away from the table.

'What . . . what's this?'

'That's . . . that's roast leg of lamb with rosemary,' she said. 'And redcurrant sauce.'

'A roast leg of lamb . . .' Dad said. I saw him nod slowly, understanding.

'With roast potatoes and parsnips and salad and some sprouts. Because you like it . . .'

'Roast leg of lamb . . .' Dad said again.

Mum stopped speaking. Looking up, I watched her brush her hair behind her ear. She bit her lip, I saw, but she didn't look away from him. Oliver picked up his wine glass.

'I can see it's a roast leg of lamb . . .' He paused for a moment. His breath sounded like a sigh. 'And that . . . that's my Christmas dinner is it? That's what I've got to eat.'

'I . . . I cooked a lot of vegetables, sprouts . . . Philip, I want to say that I've decided . . .'

'Sprouts?' He looked at her, and then away.

'I . . .' She stopped, hearing him. 'You *like* sprouts.'

'Sprouts. That's it. So . . . so everyone else gets to eat a nice Christmas dinner, and I get . . . some sprouts . . .' His forehead was crumpled, and I felt my stomach turn. I met his gaze, though. I kept my face up as that thing in my guts released another notch. 'I thought we were all supposed to enjoy Christmas . . .'

He dropped his head, and his sentence didn't end. He stared, a moment, into his beer.

'*Dad . . .*' Michael said. 'Dad, *please*. It's Ok . . .'

'Is it?' Dad said quietly. 'It's Ok for *you*. I . . .' He shut his eyes and clenched his jaws together. 'What a great Christmas . . .' he said. His eyes were red, too many wrinkles.

'Thanks,' he said. 'Thanks. All of you.'

He looked around the table. In turn, his eyes hit everyone of us.

'Philip.'

Mum breathed out, tight and long, and she pressed her hands together.

'Philip. The reason I've . . .'

But Dad was getting up already.

'Philip, the reason I've cooked . . .' she said.

He turned away, heading for the door, and that was when Oliver's voice came, clear.

'Fuck's sake.' he said. 'Why don't you just stop trying to make everyone feel guilty?'

Dad stopped mid stride.

'Guilty . . .?' he said. He looked down at Oliver and his forehead pulled down further.

Oliver didn't flinch. He didn't turn away. His hair was glossy, brushed back in a wave to his ears, and I could see the skin, delicate, through the V of his shirt. He held his wine glass with a steady hand, and the stubble round his chin was obvious under the kitchen lamp. Dad looked crumpled, standing next to him. Crumpled all over, I thought. 'I'm not trying to make anyone feel *guilty* . . .'

'Yes you are.' Oliver shook his head, took a sip of wine. 'Jesus . . .' he said quietly.

'*Guilty* . . . ? I . . . I've spent the last two hours trying to keep this Christmas *going*.'

Oliver only made a sound, not quite a snort, and glanced away to somewhere else.

'What?' Dad said. 'What? Don't . . . don't fucking make that expression at *me*. I've been doing everything I *can* to keep Christmas together. I . . . *Look*,' he said. He waved a hand at the table. '*Just look* . . .'

'I am looking,' Oliver said. 'So what? You've got to eat some vegetables. I thought you liked vegetables . . . You're the fucking vegetarian . . .'

Oliver's eyes were squinting, bitter. I didn't speak to stop him, though, not even when I saw Dad's mouth buckle, flinching. Not even then.

He didn't even look round at me.

'You're . . . you're not the one with no Christmas dinner! You . . . look, you've got a *lovely* Christmas dinner! You don't even *live* here! No one even *invited* you! You . . .'

'No right. No one even invited me, so I should shut up and listen to your fucking guilt trips, right? Well I'm sorry.' Oliver looked up. 'I'm not a member of your family. I don't have to put with this shit.'

'*Put up with* . . . ? You're damn right you're not a member of this family! You think I *wanted* you here for Christmas? *I* fucking *put up with it!* So don't tell me about what you've

398

got to put up with . . . Fuck *me!* No one *asked* you to come here! You can fucking well *leave* if you don't like it!'

'I know I can leave,' Oliver said. 'I didn't even want to come. I came because she asked me. No other reason. Believe me, now I wish I'd stayed away . . .'

'*Not as much as I do.*' Dad spat it at him. Saliva made tiny silver balls through the air.

'Philip!'

Mum's hand was up. A stupid kind of position, like she'd forgotten to put it down, I thought.

'Philip *don't!*'

'*Why?*' Dad stared at her. '*Why shouldn't I?* I know perfectly well *you* don't give a shit about my feelings!' Dad's face was changing to a horrible, ill purple.

'That's not . . . that's not fair Philip. I . . .'

'No course it's not. But it's perfectly fair that you don't even fucking *tell me he lied!* It's *perfectly* fair that you make Christmas dinner and I'm not even *included! That's fair!*'

'For Christ's sake!' Oliver's voice made my stomach flip. 'Is that what it's all about then? *All* this? – fucking sulking over not being included?'

'*Shut up!*' Dad stared at him.

His eyes were tight, his teeth shown through his lips.

'Yeah,' Oliver said. 'Shut up. Listen to you spout your bullshit and then shut up. I'm not your wife or your fucking kid, *Philip.* I don't have to shut up when you tell me.'

Oliver's expression was clear and empty as he looked up into Dad's eyes. A smile was ticking round the corner of his mouth. But not a nasty smile, I thought: the kind of smile you can't wipe off your face when the headmaster asks why you swore at Mrs Midwinter. His eyes seemed very open as he sat there. Maybe he just wasn't scared.

'Don't you swear at me,' Dad said. 'Don't fucking swear at me, Oliver. What the *fuck* has this got to do with you anyway? *Hey? What the fuck has it got to do with you? NO ONE EVEN WANTS YOU HERE!*'

'I want him here,' I said quietly.

I felt Dad round on me. He stared.

'I want him here,' I said. The words felt like puke in my mouth.

Dad's mouth fell and closed, small and weak, and it hurt me to watch him. No sound came out. And I was so glad when he turned away.

'I think you should leave,' he said.

'Leave?' Oliver nodded. 'Yeah, I bet you do.'

'Yes,' Dad said. 'Please leave. If you're still capable of driving, that is . . .'

He looked away from Oliver and there was a pause.

A very light pause.

And Oliver's face smoothed out before he said

'What?'

'If you're still capable of driving a car I want you out of my house!'

'What do you mean, "if you're still capable"?'

Oliver got up slowly. His chair creaked across the tiles as he stood.

'What do you think I mean? You've just put away half a bottle of your fucking *wine!*'

'So?' Oliver pushed the chair back further.

'So take the rest of it and *fuck off!* Go and drink yourself stupid somewhere *fucking* else!'

Oliver's head tilted slowly back.

He looked at Dad, focusing, his mouth a tight set line.

'You've no right to criticize me.' He shook his head, slow. 'You've got no right at all,' he said.

'*Right? Don't talk to me about fucking rights! You're a liar! You're a liar and a fucking alcoholic! NOW GET OUT OF MY HOUSE!*'

'Who told you that?' Oliver said. 'Who told you that?'

'No one has to tell me! It's plain to fucking *see! Jesus Christ! EVERYBODY KNOWS!*'

Dad laughed.

Six inches from Oliver's face.

And that was when Oliver hit him.

Dad's head rocked back as the tiny hoarse sound of Oliver grunting fell into the room. And I wanted so much just to close my eyes then, just to hurt and be alone. I didn't close my eyes.

'Oh my God . . .' And then I could see the stubble underneath Dad's chin. I watched him stumble. A step. I watched him lean against the wall. 'Oh my God!'

He stared out. He stared at Oliver. And they blinked very slowly.

They blinked at the same time.

That was when Oliver turned away. Spinning, he strode past me, towards the other side of the kitchen. He shook his hand, limp and floppy at the wrist, and pressed his lips together. Three paces, and he was at the opposite wall. He turned, walked back, another three, and he stared at the four of us standing there. 'Fuck,' I heard him say.

There was silence.

Dad's chin came slowly down, his eyes levelling across the room. There was blood in his nose. Blood, I saw, and it was bright on his white skin. I thought for a moment that he might hit back, the way his face came gradually down. I thought so, until I saw his eyes. They were different, I saw. Too different, and the light in them had stuttered off. It had let go, just like the knot in my stomach was letting go.

'You're the one with the drink problem.' Oliver's voice, still walking, still moving was hard and low and there was a catch there somewhere. 'You're the one with the fucking drink problem. You're the one who can't even keep their fucking money together, till you've got to take your own daughter's fucking stereo back to the shop it came from.' His head came up. He glanced, first at me then Dad, and his eyes were still as hard. 'Well?' he said. 'You're the one who comes home every night and needs a beer! A beer to relax and a beer for the telly and a beer for dinner and a beer for fucking after dinner!'

'*Stop . . . Please* stop . . .' Mum's voice was far too small, though. Too small, too late to make a difference. '*Please. This . . . this is a very difficult time* for him . . .'

'*Difficult time?*' Oliver shook his head, jagged on top of his shoulders. I watched him point a finger. '*You're the one with the one with the fucking drink problem! You're the alcoholic!* YOU'RE THE ONE WITH THE DAUGHTER SLASHING HER OWN FUCKING WRISTS!'

I stared at him.

No one spoke. Not Dad. Not Mum. Not me.

In the silence, Oliver was the only one left.

He stopped walking. I saw him hold his wrist loose in the other hand. He looked back.

'Well it's *fucking* true . . .'

Dad didn't move as he watched him. As Oliver sat down. He didn't speak again, though. His shoulders were hunched against something. He was still, inside the room.

'THERE'S NOTHING WRONG WITH DAD!'

Michael was crunched against the table, his face a heap. He stared at Oliver. Stared, and I could see him quiver with the way his hair moved on his head. His mouth was pulled down. Ugly. And I saw a tear leak out.

'There's nothing wrong with Dad . . .' he said.

But Dad didn't even turn to see him, still looking at Oliver's face. He shifted his back against the wall, flipped his neck to get the hair from his eyes. He didn't straighten up, though. I saw the blood trickle slowly on to his lip. 'What . . . what do you mean?'

Oliver moved his hand to his wine glass.

'Show him,' he said quietly.

So I did.

It was a tight kind of top, a lot of Lycra in the material. Not a body, though, I thought. Because that would have been hard to take off. That would have been hard, what with the poppers underneath. I pulled at my right sleeve first, and my arm came out easily. Then the left, still under my top, with both sleeves flapping loose around me, arms trapped underneath.

I pulled it over my head in one go.

And I handed it to Oliver.

'Jesus Christ . . .' Dad said quietly.

Mum didn't look up. One hand over her face, her head was weighted to the floor. In a funny way, it was perfect. Perfect, that I had started and I should be the one to have to finish it. Perfect that it should end here.

Dad's face was level with mine, a patch of purple spreading, his eyes dug into me. They ground into my stomach. Edged in puffy white, the bruise was raised on his cheek. And his eyes didn't stop. They bit like my scars as we held each other there. Motionless.

'I'm sorry,' I said.

It squeezed from my mouth. It hurt like being fucked hurt. Inside me.

Mum's shoulders shook, a single silent sweep.

I felt my own breath as Dad started to cry.

But I didn't look away.